Bibliography of New York Colonial History

Charles Allcott Flagg, Judson Toll Jennings

University of the State of New York

Subject no.
016.9747

New York State Library

Bulletin 56   February 1901

BIBLIOGRAPHY 24

BIBLIOGRAPHY

OF

NEW YORK COLONIAL HISTORY

SUBMITTED FOR GRADUATION

by

Charles A. Flagg B.A. (Bowdoin) B.L.S. (N. Y.)

AND

Judson T. Jennings

New York State Library School

Class of 1897

ALBANY

UNIVERSITY OF THE STATE OF NEW YORK

1901

L149m-D0-2500

Price 35 cents

University of the State of New York

REGENTS

With years of election

1874 ANSON JUDD UPSON L.H.D. D.D. LL.D.

Chancellor, Glens Falls

1892 WILLIAM CROSWELL DOANE D.D. LL.D.

Vice-Chancellor, Albany

1873 MARTIN I. TOWNSEND M.A. LL.D.	– –	Troy
1877 CHAUNCEY M. DEPEW LL.D.	– – – –	New York
1877 CHARLES E. FITCH LL.B. M.A. L.H.D.	–	Rochester
1877 ORRIS H. WARREN D.D.	– – – –	Syracuse
1878 WHITELAW REID LL.D.	– – – –	New York
1881 WILLIAM H. WATSON M.A. M.D.	– –	Utica
1881 HENRY E. TURNER	– – – –	Lowville
1883 ST CLAIR McKELWAY M.A. LL.D. L.H.D. D.C.L.		Brooklyn
1885 DANIEL BEACH Ph.D. LL.D.	– – – –	Watkins
1888 CARROLL E. SMITH LL.D.	– – – –	Syracuse
1890 PLINY T. SEXTON LL.D.	– – – –	Palmyra
1890 T. GUILFORD SMITH M.A. C.E. LL.D.	– –	Buffalo
1893 LEWIS A. STIMSON B.A. LL.D. M.D.	– –	New York
1895 ALBERT VANDER VEER Ph.D. M.D.	– –	Albany

1895 CHARLES R. SKINNER M.A. LL.D.

Superintendent of Public Instruction, ex officio

1897 CHESTER S. LORD M.A. LL.D.	– –	Brooklyn
1897 TIMOTHY L. WOODRUFF M.A. Lieutenant-Governor, ex officio		
1899 JOHN T. McDONOUGH LL.B. LL.D. Secretary of State, ex officio		
1900 THOMAS A. HENDRICK M.A. LL.D.	– –	Rochester
1901 BENJAMIN B. ODELL JR Governor, ex officio		
1901 ROBERT C. PRUYN M.A.	– – – –	Albany

SECRETARY

Elected by regents

1900 JAMES RUSSELL PARSONS JR M.A.

DIRECTORS OF DEPARTMENTS

1888 MELVIL DEWEY M.A. *State library and Home education*

1890 JAMES RUSSELL PARSONS JR M.A.

Administrative, College and High school dep'ts

1890 FREDERICK J. H. MERRILL Ph.D. *State museum*

CONTENTS

New York State Library

Bulletin 56   February 1901

BIBLIOGRAPHY 24

NEW YORK COLONIAL HISTORY

PREFACE

This bibliography covers the history of New Netherland, or New York as colony and province, from its discovery to 1776. Though New York's sway extended at times over lands now included in New Jersey, Pennsylvania, Delaware and Maine, the list includes only the territory within the present limits of the state.

The first settlement in New Jersey was made in 1623 by the Dutch; the first permanent settlement in 1664, when New Jersey was granted by the duke of York to Berkeley and Carteret. In 1702 the provinces of East and West Jersey were united and surrendered to Queen Anne, and from 1703 to 1738 New York and New Jersey were under the same governors. Pennsylvania was settled by the Swedes in 1643, the Dutch settlement of 1623 having been abandoned. In 1655 the Dutch under Stuyvesant took possession of both Pennsylvania and Delaware, and they were claimed by the governors of New York till 1682, when Penn obtained a quit claim from the duke of York. That part of Maine known first as Pemaquid and its dependencies, and in 1683 organized as the county of Cornwall, was under the governors of New York from 1673 to 1686, when it was annexed to New England. For relations with other colonies, their histories and colonial records should be consulted.

Southold, Southampton, Easthampton and other towns in eastern Long Island formed part of Connecticut previous to 1664. For their history during that period the student is referred to the histories and colonial records of the Connecticut and New Haven colonies.

Different editions of a work have been noted when at hand, but no attempt has been made at bibliographic completeness for editions or full titles. Those wishing this information should consult the works under " Bibliographies consulted." Printed indexes and calendars of manuscript are included, but not the manuscripts themselves. Many histories of special churches are included for the large amount of local history which they contain. Of city charters and legislative journals only the best reprints are given. Newspaper articles, historical fiction, legends, Indians and Indian missions, boundary disputes, genealogies of single families, French settlements in western New York, and material relating to Columbia university, formerly Kings college, are omitted.

Maps are also omitted, but information may be found in the following :

Asher, G; M. *comp.* List of the maps and charts of New Netherland and of the views of New Amsterdam. 22+23p. N. Y. 1855. (*in his* Bibliographical and historical essay. 1854–67) 016.97 As3

Davis, W: T. Staten Island names. p. 20–76. New Brighton N. Y. 1896. 917.4726 D29

Special no. 21 of the proceedings of the Staten Island natural science association. List of maps used in collecting names, p. 21–23.

Grolier club of the city of New York. Catalogue of plans and views of New York city from 1851 to 1860 exhibited at the Grolier club Dec. 10–25, 1897. 38p. N. Y. 1897. 016.9127471 G89

Index to the maps and engravings in Valentine's manual. (see Old New York, Aug.–Oct. 1889, 1:24–37, 105–16, 165–76) 974.71 qO71 v.1

Based on the list in *Manual of the city of New York.* 1863. 22:839–52, 352.0747 N4k.

For bibliography of the West India company and the East India company the student is referred to no. 21–327 in Asher's *Bibliographical and historical essay.* 1854–67.

The bibliography aims to be complete only to December 1898, but important works published since then are included when they have come to the compilers' notice.

CHARLES A. FLAGG
JUDSON T. JENNINGS

ABBREVIATIONS

Abbreviations following entries refer to the libraries in which the books were consulted or sources from which the entries were taken. Call numbers are given for books in the New York state library. Volume and page numbers are separated by a colon: e. g. 3 : 145 means v. 3, p. 145. The following are the principal abbreviations used. Other abbreviations are self-explanatory.

Asher	Asher, G; M. *comp.* Bibliographical and historical essay on the Dutch books and pamphlets relating to New Netherland. 234p. Amst. 1854–67. 016.97 As3
Griffin	Griffin, A. P. C. *comp.* Bibliography of American historical societies, the United States and the dominion of Canada. p. 677–1236. Wash. 1896. 016.973 G871
Grolier club	Grolier club of the city of New York. Catalogue of books printed by William Bradford and other printers in the middle colonies. 100p. N. Y. 1893. 016.094 G89

Exhibited at the Grolier club in commemoration of the bicentennial of the introduction of printing into New York, Ap. 14–21, 1893.

L. I. hist. soc.	Long Island historical society, Brooklyn
Muller	Muller, Frederik, *comp.* Catalogue of books relating to America. 104p. Amst. 1850. 016.97 M91
N. Y. hist. soc.	New York historical society, New York city
N. Y. pub. lib.	New York public library, New York city
N. Y. state lib.	New York state library, Albany

Used for a few books not in new card catalogue.

Prov. pub. lib.	Providence public library, Providence R. I.
Rees	Rees, O. van. Geschiedenis der nederlandsche volkplantingen in Noord-Amerika. 162p. Tiel 1855. 974.7 R25
Sabin	Sabin, Joseph, *comp.* Dictionary of books relating to America. 20v. N. Y. 1868–92. Co16.97 Sa1
Winsor	Winsor, Justin, *ed.* Narrative and critical history of America. 8v. Bost. c1884–89. 973 qW73

BIBLIOGRAPHY
WORKS ANALYZED

The following works have been analyzed and are not elsewhere entered in full.

Albany institute. Transactions. v.1–12. Alb. 1830–93. N. Y. state lib.

American antiquarian society. Proceedings 1849–98. v.1–19. Worcester 1850–98. 906 Am3

American historian and quarterly genealogical record. v.1. Schenectady N. Y. 1876. 973 Am31
Edited by Schenectady historical society. No more pub.

American historical association. Annual report for 1889–98. v. 1–10. Wash. 1890–99. 973 Am33

—— Papers. 5v. N. Y. 1886–91. 973 Am32
No more pub. Subsequent papers appear in the association's reports to congress.

American historical magazine and literary record, monthly. Jan.–June 1836. v. 1. New Haven 1836. 973 Am3
No more pub.

American historical record and repertory of notes and queries, monthly; concerning the history and antiquities of America and biography of Americans. v. 1–19. Phil. c1873–82. 973 qAm3
v. 1–3 ed. by B. J. Lossing. v. 4–19 continued as *Potter's American monthly.* Oct.–Dec. 1882, of v. 19 wanting in New York state library copy and not examined.

American historical register and monthly gazette of the patriotic-hereditary societies of the U. S. of America; ed. by C. H. Browning, Sep. 1894–Ap. 1897. v. 1–5, no. 2. Phil. 1895–97. 973 qAm31

American historical review, quarterly, Oct. 1895–July 1898. v.1–3. N. Y. 1896–98. 973 qAm35

American monthly magazine, July 1892–98. v. 1–13. Wash. 1892–98. 973.3 Am3
Published by the national society of Daughters of the American revolution.

Buffalo historical society. Publications. v.1–4. Buffalo 1879–96. 974.797 B86

Family magazine; or, General abstract of useful knowledge. 1834–40. 8v. N. Y. 1834–40. 051 qF21
Minor variations of title. No more pub.?

Fort Orange monthly, Feb.–Sep. 1886. v. 1–2, no. 3. Alb.
1886. 051 F771
No more pub.?

Goodwin, *Mrs* **Maud (Wilder), Royce, A. C. & Putnam, Ruth,** *ed.*
Historic New York. 2v. N. Y. 1897–99. (Half-moon papers. v.
1–2) 974.71 G63
Same as Half-moon series, but with different paging.

Half-moon series. 1897–98. v. 1–2. N. Y. 1897–98. N. Y. state lib.
Same as Goodwin. *Historic New York*, but with different paging.

Herkimer county historical society. Papers during years 1896–98;
comp. by A. T. Smith. Herkimer 1899. 974.761 H42

Historical magazine concerning America [monthly] 23v. Morrisania N. Y. 1857–75. 973 H62
No more pub. v. 1 pub. in Boston, v. 2-9 in New York. Later volumes
ed. by H: B. Dawson.

Historical record [monthly] devoted to the promotion of historical
research, ed. by the Historical society, Schenectady N. Y. Jan.–Ap.
1872. v. 1, no. 1–4. Schenectady 1872. 974.7 qH62
No more pub.

Holland society of New York. Year book, 1886–97. N. Y.
1886–97. 974.7 qH71

Johns Hopkins university studies in historical and political science;
[monthly]. v. 1–16. Balt. 1883–98. 305 J62

Long Island historical society. Memoirs. v. 1–4. Brooklyn
1867–89. 974.721 L85

Magazine of American history; [monthly]. 30v. N. Y. 1877–93.
973 M27
No more pub. v. 11-29, no. 1 ed. by Mrs M. J. R. (Nash) Lamb.

Magazine of the reformed Dutch church; [monthly]. Ap. 1826–30.
v. 1–4. New Brunswick 1827–29. 205 M27
v. 3-4 pub. in New York.

Magazine of western history; [monthly]. 1884–May 1894. 19v.
Cleveland 1884–94. 973 M271
No more pub. v. 15-19 title reads *National magazine; a journal devoted to
American history.*

Munsell, Joel. Annals of Albany. 10v. Alb. 1850–59. 974.743 M92
—— —— Ed. 2. v. 1–4. Alb. 1869–71. 974.743 M921
—— *pub. anon.* Collections on the history of Albany from its discovery to the present time; with notices of its public institutions and biographical sketches of citizens deceased. 4v. Alb.
1865–71. 974.743 qM92

New England historical and genealogical register; published quarterly under the direction of the New England historic-genealogical society, 1847–98.   v. 1–52.   Bost. 1847–98.   929.1 N422

New England magazine; an illustrated monthly, v. 1–24.   Bost. 1886–Aug. 1898.   051 B34
      v. 1-3 have title *Bay state monthly.*

New Haven colony historical society.   Papers. v. 1–5.   New Haven 1865–94.   974.67 N42

N. Y. (city)–Common council.   Manual of the corporation of the city of New York, 1841–70. 28 v. N.Y. 1841–71. 352.0747 N4k
      v. 2-25 comp. by D: T: Valentine.

N. Y. (state)–Legislature.   Documents relative to the colonial history of the state of New York. v. 1–15. Alb. 1853–87. 974.7 qN421

N. Y. (state)—State, Secretary of. Documentary history of the state of New York; arranged by E. B. O'Callaghan. 4 v   Alb. 1849–51.   974.7 N424
——— ——— 4v.   Alb. 1850–51.   974.7 qN423

New York civil list 1891. Alb. 1891.   351 2 N42

New York genealogical and biographical record; devoted to the interests of American genealogy and biography; issued quarterly, 1870–98. v. 1–29.   N. Y. 1870–98.   929.1 N421
      v. 18-29 are quarto, 929.1 qN421.

New York historical society.   Collections, 1809–30, '41–59.   9v. N. Y. 1811–59.   974.7 N422
No more pub.

——— Collections; publication fund series, 1868–91.   v. 1–24. N. Y. 1868–92.   974.7 N42

——— Proceedings, 1843–49. N. Y. 1844–49.   974.7 N421

O'Callaghan, E. B. *ed.* New York colonial tracts.   v. 1–4.   Alb. 1866–72.   974.7 Oc1

Old New York; a monthly journal relating to the history and antiquities of New York city.   2v.   N. Y. 1890–91.   974.71 qOl1
No more pub.

Oneida historical society, Utica, N. Y. Transactions, 1878–98. Utica N. Y. 1881–98.   974 762 On2

Oud-Holland; nieuwe bijdragen voor de geschiedenis der nederlandsche kunst, letterkunde, nijverheid, enz 1883–98.   v. 1–16. Amst. 1883–98.   059 qOu2

Political science quarterly; a review devoted to the historical, statistical and comparative study of politics, economics and public law; ed. by the faculty of political science of Columbia college. v. 1–13. N. Y. 1886–98. 305 P75

Studies in history, economics and public law; ed. by the faculty of political science of Columbia university in the city of New York v. 1–9. N. Y. 1891–98. 305 St9

Terhune, *Mrs* **M.. V. (Hawes).** Some colonial homesteads and their stories; by Marion Harland. 511p. N. Y. 1897. 973.2 T27

——— More colonial homesteads and their stories; by Marion Harland. 449p. N. Y. 1899. 973.2 T27

Ulster historical society. Collections. v.1. Kingston N. Y. 1860. 974.734 Ul7

BIBLIOGRAPHIES CONSULTED

Asher, G; M. *comp.* Bibliographical and historical essay on the Dutch books and pamphlets relating to New Netherland and to the Dutch West India company and to its possessions in Brazil, Angola, etc. 234p. Amst. 1854–67. 016.97 As3

Including Asher's *List of the maps and charts of New Netherland.*
Contents: Description of New Netherland, p. 1-28, 20 titles; History of New Netherland, p. 180-219, 29 titles.
Titles are translated and there are very full English notes.

——— Bibliographical list containing the books, maps, etc. mentioned in the present work. (*see his* Henry Hudson the Navigator. 1860. p. 258–78) 910.6 H12 v.27

Bibliography and cartography [of Lake George]. (*see* Society for the preservation of scenic and historic places and objects. Annual report. 1900. p. 65–68). N. Y. state lib.

Brooks, E. S. *comp.* Selection of books touching the general story of the state of New York. (*see his* Story of New York. c1888. p. 307–8) 974 7 B79

Includes list of romances and stories illustrating New York history.

Channing, Edward & Hart, A. B. *comp.* Guide to the study of American history. 471 p. Bost. 1896. R016.973 C36

Bibliography of New York, p. 67-69, 112-13, 258-60.

Eastman, F. S. *comp.* Catalogue of authors used. (*see his* History of the state of New York. 1833. p. 7–8) 974.7 Ea7

Fernow, Berthold, *comp.*   Critical essay on the sources of information
[relative to New Netherland]. (*see* Winsor, Justin, *ed.*   Narrative and
critical history of America.   ᶜ1884–89.   4:409–42)   973   qW73

———— Critical essay on the sources of information [relative to the
middle colonies]. (*see* Winsor, Justin, *ed.*   Narrative and critical
history of America.   ᶜ1884–89.   5:231–58)   973   qW73

A few words regarding the falls of Niagara.   (*see* N. Y. (state)—Niagara
reservation, Commissioners of.   Annual report.   1894.   10:72–107)
711   N421
A bibliography of descriptions of Niagara Falls.

Fisher, G: P. *comp.*   Bibliographical note relative to the colonial era in
American history. (*see his* Colonial era.   1892. p.325–35)   973.2 F53

Greene, E. B. *comp.*   List of printed commissions and instructions
to royal and proprietary governors in the English colonies of
North America. (*see* American historical review,   Oct. 1897,
3:170–76)   973   qAm35
Arranged chronologically.

Griffin, A. P. C. *comp.*   Bibliography of American historical societies,
the United States and the Dominion of Canada.   p. 677–1236.
Wash. 1896.   016.973 G871
Also in annual report of American historical association.   1896.   7:675–1236.
Reprinted with additions from annual reports of the American historical
association 1890 and 1892.

———— Index of articles upon American local history in historical
collections in the Boston public library.   225p.   Bost. 1889.
(Boston public library.   Bibliographies of special subjects 3)
Co16.973 qG87
Indexes very fully articles in *Manual of the city of New York; Documents
relative to the colonial history of the state of New York;* and *Documentary history
of the state of New York.*

———— Index of the literature of American local history in collections
published in 1890–95, (with some others).   151p.   Bost.
1896.   016.973 C87
Arranged alphabetically by names of places.

———— [Index to articles in historical collections relating to] New York
city.   11p.   Bost. 1887.   016.9747 qG87
50 copies reprinted from his *Index of articles upon American local history.*

———— Index to articles in historical collections relating to New York,
colony and state.   8p.   Bost. 1887.   016.9747 qG87
50 copies reprinted from his *Index of articles upon American local history.*

Ludewig, H. E. *comp.* The literature of American local history; a _{Biblic} bibliographical essay. 180 p. N. Y. 1846. 016.973 L96 ies co
Bibliography of New York, p. 111-25.

———— ———— 1st supplement: New York. 20p. N. Y. 1848 016.973 L961
30 copies reprinted fr. the *Literary world*, Feb. 19, 1848, 3 : 17.

Muller, Frederik, *comp.* Catalogue of books relating to America; including a large number of rare works printed before 1700 amongst which a nearly complete collection of the Dutch publications on New Netherland from 1612 to 1820. 104p. Amst. 1850. 016.97 M91
New York, p. 37-59.

Munsell, Frank, *comp.* Bibliography of Albany; being a catalogue of books and other publications relating to the city and county of Albany in the state of New York. 72p. Alb. 1883. 016.974742 M92

Murphy, H: C. *comp.* Lijst van stukken betreffende Niew Nederland verschenen in Amerikaansche mengelwerken; 1. 12p. n. t-p. L. I. hist. soc.
A list of documents relating to New Netherland which have been published in different works. It was presented by me to the Netherlands literary society at Leyden, which is engaged in publishing a catalogue of everything that has been written on the subject of Netherlands and its colonies. These sheets are sent to me in advance of the publication. Another list, also presented by me, of publications in this country on the same subject will soon be published by the same society. Ms note by H. C. Murphy, dated Oct. 24, 1864.

North, S. N. D. History and present condition of the newspaper and periodical press of the United States. (*see* U. S. Census, 10th, 1880. [Final reports]. 1883-88. 8:1-446) R317.3 qUn3 v. 10[8]
Newspaper and periodical press, 1639-1783, p. 1-27.
Chronological history of the newspaper press of New York, p. 387-408.

Onderdonk, Henry, jr, *comp.* Bibliography of Long Island. (*see* Furman, Gabriel. Antiquities of Long Island. 1875. p. 435-69)
974.721 F98

Perkins, F : B. *comp.* Check list for American local history; reprinted with additions of the Boston public library. 198p. Bost. 1876. Co16.973 P41

The pilgrim fathers; exhibition of documents from public and private collections at Leiden relating to the Dutch settlements in North America. 22p. Leiden 1888. (*in* Holland society of New York. Year book. 1888-89) 974.7 qH71
Between p. 80 and 81 of the *Yearbook*.

The pilgrim fathers. 32p.   Leiden 1888.   N. Y. pub. lib.
Documents relating to America, p. 19–32.

Publications relating to New York affairs under Governor Cosby. (*see*
N. Y. public library. Bulletin, July 1898, 2:249–55) 027.4747 qN421
Describes the contents of a folio volume in the Lenox library containing
73 documents relating to Cosby's administration, collected by James Alexander, a participator in many of the events in question. 58 of the documents
refer to the dispute between Rip Van Dam and the governor. The remaining
15 relate mainly to Rev. Alexander Campbell. In the list are incorporated
also titles of a few other works in the Lenox library relating to the same
affairs.

Sabin, Joseph, *comp.* Dictionary of books relating to America. 20v.
N. Y. 1868–92.   Co16.97 Sa1
Only 196 p. of v. 20 pub. Ap. 6, 1900; through Smith, Henry.

Satterlee, H. L. *comp.* Authorities. (*see his* Political history of the
province of New York. 1885. p. 106–7)   342.7479 Sa8

Stevens, J: A. *comp.* Critical essay on the sources of information
[relative to the English in New York 1664–1689]. (*see* Winsor,
Justin, *ed.* Narrative and critical history of America. ᶜ1884–89.
3:411-20)   973 qW73

MATTER RELATING TO MANUSCRIPTS

Brodhead, J: R. Address delivered before the New York historical
society at its 40th anniversary 20th Nov. 1844.   107p.   N. Y.
1844.   974.7 B782
Describes his work in transcribing European documents.

———— Communication from Paris July 12, 1842. (N. Y. Assembly doc.
1842. no. 195, doc. C, p. 29–113)   N. Y. state law lib.
Letters requesting increase of appropriation for the transcribing of European documents and giving list of New York documents found in London
archives, followed by Governor Seward's answer.
Also in Senate doc. 1842. no. 106, doc. B, p. 29–113.

———— Communication to the governor, [London, Dec. 2, 1842].
(N. Y. Senate doc. 1843. no. 2, p. 3–4)   N. Y. state law lib.

———— Final report of Brodhead, agent of the state of New York to
procure and transcribe documents in Europe relative to the colonial
history of said state, made to the governor, Feb. 12, 1845.   374p.
Alb. 1845.   016.9747 B78
Contains chronological index to manuscript copies made by Brodhead from
originals in Europe. These manuscripts (80 v.) are now in New York state
library.

Calendar of Holland documents 1611–65; London documents 1614–1782; Paris documents 1631–1778. Matter ing manus

Also in Senate doc. 1845. no. 47.

These documents are published with a general index in *Documents relative to the colonial history of the state of New York.* 1853–61. v. 1–11. **974.7** qN421.

Brodhead, J: R. Report. (N. Y. Senate doc. 1842. no. 2, p. 145–58)
N. Y. state law lib.

Dated, The Hague, Oct. 25, 1841.

Fernow, Berthold. Archives of the state of New York. (*see* New York genealogical and biographical record, July 1889, 20:106–13)
929.1   qN421

—— *comp. & ed.* Calendar of wills on file and recorded in the offices of the clerk of the court of appeals, of the county clerk of Albany and of the secretary of state 1626–1836; comp. under the auspices of the Colonial dames of the state of New York and published by the society. 657p. N. Y. 1896. 929.3   qN42
500 copies printed.

—— Critical essay on the sources of information [relative to New Netherland]. (*see* Winsor, Justin, *ed.* Narrative and critical history of America. ᶜ1884–89. 4:409–38) 973   qW73

—— Manuscript sources of New York history. (*see* Winsor, Justin, *ed.* Narrative and critical history of America. ᶜ1884–89. 5:231–33) 973   qW73

Great Britain—Public record office. Calendar of state papers, colonial series; America and West Indies, preserved in her majesty's public record office; ed. by W. N. Sainsbury. 5 v. Lond. 1880–98. 942   qG792

Contents: v. 1 1661–68.   v. 4 1677–80.
v. 2 1669–74.   v. 5 1681–85.
v. 3 1675–76 and Addenda, 1574–1674.

Jameson, J: F. List of printed guides to and descriptions of archives and other repositories of historical manuscripts. (*see* American historical association—Historical manuscripts commission. Annual reports. 1896. 1:481–512; 1898. 3:573–90) 973   Am37
New York archives, 1:489–91; 3:577–81.

List of documents relating to Ulster county contained in the Clinton papers in the state library at Albany. (*see* Ulster historical society. Collections. 1860. 1:103–5) 974.734   Ul7

N. Y. (state)—Colonial agency, Committee on. Report. 16p.
(N. Y. Senate doc. 1845. no. 111) N. Y. state law lib.

N. Y. (state)—Colonial history of the state, Committee on.
Report of the select committee on so much of the governor's mes-
sage as relates to the colonial history of the state.   11p. (N. Y.
Senate doc. 1844. no. 42)   N. Y. state law lib.

N. Y. (state)—Controller. Reply in answer to a resolution of the senate
adopted Jan. 17, 1853, in relation to the expenses of the colonial history, etc. 14p. (N. Y. Senate doc. 1853. no. 24) N. Y. state law lib.
Including report by E. B. O'Callaghan on binding and preparing manuscripts.

N. Y. (state)—Historical records, Custodian of. General statement of material contained in manuscripts transferred to the state
library from the office of the secretary of state, pursuant to laws of
1881, ch. 120; by Berthold Fernow. (*see* N. Y. (state)–Library.
Annual report.   1882.   64:11–15)   027.5747 N42

—— Report on historical documents; by Berthold Fernow. (*see* N. Y.
(state)—Library. Annual report. 1884. 66:23–24) 027.5747 N42

N. Y. (state)—Legislature. Act *to provide for the publishing of
certain documents relating to the colonial history of the state.* (*see*
N.Y. (state)—Legislature. Laws. 1849. p.236–37) N. Y. state law lib.

N. Y. (state)—Library. Annotated list of the principal manuscripts
in the New York state library.   p. 207–37.   Alb. 1899. (His
tory bulletin *3*)   N. Y. state lib.
Also in 81st annual report of New York state library. 1899. 027.5747 N42.
Including a *Partial bibliography of matter relating to the manuscripts*, comp.
by Charles A. Flagg.

—— Catalogue of manuscripts in the library; supplementary to the
printed list of 1856. (*see* N. Y. (state)—Library.   Annual report.
1874.   56:115–38)   027.5747 N42
Senate doc. 1874. no. 36.

—— Catalogue of the New York state library, 1856; maps, manuscripts, engravings, coins, etc.   Alb. 1867.   016.912 qN42
Manuscripts, p. 93–113.

—— Lists of manuscripts added to the New York state library from
Jan. 1, 1850 to Jan. 1, 1855. (*see* N. Y. (state)—Library. Annual
report. 1855.   37:78–83)   027.5747 N42
Senate doc. 1855. no. 77.

—— Manuscripts received from the office of the secretary of state and
deposited in the state library in pursuance of a joint resolution of
the senate and assembly passed Dec. 15, 1847. (*see* N. Y. (state)—
Library. Catalogue. 1850. p. 1021–54)   027.5747 N42 v.32

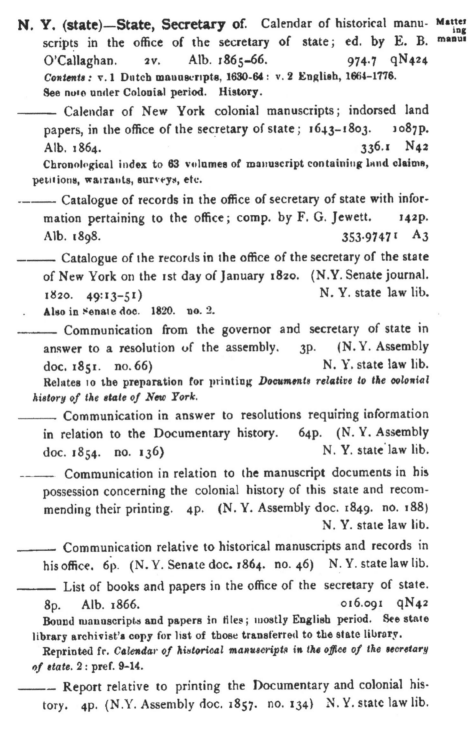

N. Y. (state)—State, Secretary of. Calendar of historical manuscripts in the office of the secretary of state; ed. by E. B. O'Callaghan. 2v. Alb. 1865–66. 974.7 qN424

Matter ing manus

Contents : v. 1 Dutch manuscripts, 1630-64 : v. 2 English, 1664-1776.
See note under Colonial period. History.

———— Calendar of New York colonial manuscripts; indorsed land papers, in the office of the secretary of state; 1643-1803. 1087p. Alb. 1864. 336.1 N42

Chronological index to 63 volumes of manuscript containing land claims, petitions, warrants, surveys, etc.

———— Catalogue of records in the office of secretary of state with information pertaining to the office; comp. by F. G. Jewett. 142p. Alb. 1898. 353.97471 A3

———— Catalogue of the records in the office of the secretary of the state of New York on the 1st day of January 1820. (N.Y. Senate journal. 1820. 49:13–51) N. Y. state law lib.

Also in Senate doc. 1820. no. 2.

———— Communication from the governor and secretary of state in answer to a resolution of the assembly. 3p. (N.Y. Assembly doc. 1851. no. 66) N. Y. state law lib.

Relates to the preparation for printing *Documents relative to the colonial history of the state of New York.*

———— Communication in answer to resolutions requiring information in relation to the Documentary history. 64p. (N. Y. Assembly doc. 1854. no. 136) N. Y. state law lib.

———— Communication in relation to the manuscript documents in his possession concerning the colonial history of this state and recommending their printing. 4p. (N. Y. Assembly doc. 1849. no. 188) N. Y. state law lib.

———— Communication relative to historical manuscripts and records in his office. 6p. (N. Y. Senate doc. 1864. no. 46) N. Y. state law lib.

———— List of books and papers in the office of the secretary of state. 8p. Alb. 1866. 016.091 qN42

Bound manuscripts and papers in files; mostly English period. See state library archivist's copy for list of those transferred to the state library.

Reprinted fr. *Calendar of historical manuscripts in the office of the secretary of state.* 2 : pref. 9-14.

———— Report relative to printing the Documentary and colonial history. 4p. (N.Y. Assembly doc. 1857. no. 134) N. Y. state law lib.

N. Y. (state)—University. Catalogue of historical papers and parchments received from the office of the secretary of state and deposited in the New York state library, made by the regents of the University, Feb. 13, 1849.   55p.   Alb. 1849.   016.9747   N42

Contains rolls of laws passed by legislature 1691-1754: papers have dates from 1664-1814.

Also in Assembly doc. 1849.   no. 148.

O'Callaghan, E. B. *comp.* Index to volumes 1, 2 and 3 of translations of Dutch manuscripts in the office of the secretary of state of the state of New York.   118p.   Alb. 1870.   016.9747   Oc1

v. 4 was also translated and has a manuscript index.   These manuscripts with the originals are in the state library.

Schuyler, G: W. [Description of state archives].   *(see his* Colonial New York.   1885.   1: pref. 4-10)   974.7   Sch8

Versteeg, D. Dutch West India company manuscripts; report on some Dutch papers in possession of the Pennsylvania historical society. *(see* Holland society of New York. Year book. 1892-93. p.150-52)   974.7   qH71

Winsor, Justin. [Archives of] New York. *(see his* Narrative and critical history of America. c1884-89. 8:444-48)   973   qW73

GENERAL HISTORY OF NEW YORK STATE

Anthony, Elliott. Story of the Empire state.   247p.   Chic. 1891.   974.7   An8

Barber, J: W. The history and antiquities of New England, New York and New Jersey.   576p.   Worcester 1841.   974   B23

—— Ed. 3.   624p.   Hartford 1856.   N. Y. pub lib.

—— Pictorial history of the state of New York.   376p. Cooperstown N. Y.   1846.   974.7   B23

Selections from Barber & Howe's *Historical collections of the state of New York*. Chronological table, p. 369-76.

Brooks, E. S. Story of New York.   311p.   Bost c1888.   (Story of the states)   974.7   B79

Told in form of a story; not valuable as history. Bibliography, p. 307-8.

Butler, B: F. Anniversary discourse delivered before the Albany institute Ap. 23, 1830.   88p.   Alb. 1830.   308   B97

Criticism of Smith's, Moulton's, Macauley's and Eastman's histories of New York, p. 9-19.

Carpenter, W: H. & Arthur, T. S. History of New York from its earliest settlement to the present time.   336p.   Phil. 1853. (Lippincott's cabinet histories of the states)   974.7 C21
From discovery to 1848.

Comley, W. J. History of the state of New York.   656p.   N. Y. 1877.   974.7 C73
Contents : New York state, p. 1-74.
          New York city, p. 75-120.
          Brooklyn, p. 121-24.
          Biographical encyclopedia, p. 327-656.
There are no pages numbered 125-326.

Cornell, A. B. The commonwealth.   (see Chadbourne, P. A. & Moore, W. B. ed.   Public service of the state of New York. 1882.   1:1-138)   353.9747 qC34

Eastman, F. S. History of the state of New York from the first discovery of the country to the present time.   279p.   N. Y. 1828.   974.7 Ea71
———— 455p.   N. Y. 1831.   N. Y. pub. lib.
———— 455p.   N. Y. 1832.   N.Y. pub. lib.
———— 455p.   N. Y. 1833.   974.7 Ea7

French, J: H. comp. Gazetteer of the state of New York embracing a comprehensive view of the geography, geology and general history of the state and a complete history and description of every county, city, town, village and locality; with full tables of statistics.   739p. Syracuse 1860.   917.47 qF88

Hendrick, Welland. Brief history of the Empire state; for schools and families.   Ed. 3.   206p.   Syracuse 1892.   974.7 H381

Hough, F. B. comp. Gazetteer of the state of New York embracing a comprehensive account of the history and statistics of the state, with geological and topographical descriptions and recent statistical tables.   745p.   Alb. 1872.   R917.47 H81
Contains brief historical sketch of the state with a description of its government, industries, etc. followed by a condensed history and description of each county; villages and towns are noticed under their counties. A valuable reference book.

Kent, James. Anniversary discourse delivered before the New York historical society Dec. 6, 1828.   40p.   N. Y. 1829.   974.7 K41
A brief sketch of events in state history to 1804 and in the life of Philip Schuyler.

Lossing, B. J: The Empire state, a compendious history of the commonwealth of New York.   618p.   Hartford Ct. 1888.   974.7 qL89

Lucas, F: W: Appendiculae historicae; or, Shreds of history hung on a horn. 216p. Lond. 1891. 974.7 qL96
List of authorities, p. 159–76.

Macauley, James. Natural, statistical and civil history of the state of New York. 3v. N. Y. 1829. 974.7 M11
Contents: v. 1 Geography, geology and natural history; v. 2 Geography, statistics and civil history; v. 3 Civil history.
Specially strong on the physical features of the state; little original matter of a historical nature.

Mather, J. H. & Brockett, L. B. Geography of the state of New York. 432p. Hartford Ct. 1847. 917.47 M42
History of colonial period, p. 48–77. Contains also settlement and early history of various sections.

New York state. (see Willsey & Lewis. Harper's book of facts. 1895. p.562–72) R031 qW68
Gives chronological history of the state, 1524–1894, and list of governors, 1624–1894.

Prentice, W: R. History of New York state for the use of high schools and academies and for supplementary reading. 558p Syracuse 1900. E974.7 P91

Randall, S. S. History of the state of New York for the use of schools. 369p. N. Y. 1870. E974.7 R15

Roberts, E. H: New York; the planting and the growth of the Empire state. 2v. 758p. Bost. 1887. (American commonwealths) 974.7 R54
Paged continuously.

—— —— 2v. Bost. 1892. Cap. 974.7 R541

—— —— 2v. Bost. 1893. N. Y. pub. lib.

Russell, William. Harper's New York class-book; comprising outlines of the geography and history of New York; biographical notices, accounts of public institutions, etc.; arranged as a reading-book for schools. 669p. N. Y. 1847. 974.7 R91
Biographies of persons distinguished in colonial period, p. 305–67.

Seymour, Horatio. A lecture on the topography and history of New York. 41p. Utica 1856. 308 Se91 v.1

Watson, J: F. Annals and occurrences of New York city and state in the olden time. 390p. Phil. 1846. 974.7 W331

—— Historic tales of olden time concerning the early settlement and advancement of New York city and state; for the use of families and schools. 214p. N. Y. 1832. 974.7 W33

GENERAL COLONIAL HISTORY

See also New York city, which was the seat of the colonial government.

Description

Burke, Edmund, *anon.* Account of the European settlements in
America.   2v.   Lond. 1757.   970 B91
> This is the 1st ed.; for a full account of subsequent ed. and translations see
> Sabin. New York state library has also the 5th ed., 1770, and the Italian
> translation 1763.

Earl, Robert. History of lotteries in the state of New York. (*see*
Herkimer county historical society.   Papers for 1896.   p. 69–77)
974.761 H42

Earle, *Mrs* **Alice (Morse).** Colonial days in old New York. 312p.
N. Y. 1896.   Cap. 917.47 Ea7
> Mostly Dutch period.

Edsall, T: H: Something about fish, fisheries and fishermen in New
York in the 17th century. (*see* New York genealogical and biographical record, Oct. 1882, 13:181–200)   929.1 N421

Fisher, S. G: Men, women and manners in colonial times.   2v.
Phil. 1898.   917.3 F531
> Manhattan and the Tappan Zee, v. 2, p. 9–146.

Hoffman, C: F. On the distinctive character of the people of New
York previous to the revolution. (*see* New York historical society.
Proceedings. 1843. p. 95–106)   974.7 N421 v.1
> Extracts from paper read Dec. 5, 1843.

—— Pioneers of New York; an anniversary discourse delivered before
the St Nicholas society of Manhattan, Dec. 6, 1847.   55p.
N. Y. 1848.   974.7 H67
> Institutes a comparison with the pilgrims of Plymouth. Winsor. 4:410.

Houghton, G: W. W. Coaches of colonial New York; a paper
read Mar. 4, 1890 before the New York historical society.   N. Y
1890.   684 qPo

Kipp, W: I. New York society in the olden time. (*see* Putnam's
magazine, Sep. 1870, 16:241–55)   051 P98
> Also in his *Olden time in New York.* 1872. p. 9–42, 917.47 qK62; and in
> W: L. Stone's *History of New York city.* 1872.

General colonial history **Lodge, H: E.** Short history of the English colonies in America. 560p. N. Y. c 1881. 973.2 L82
Best summary of the manners and social and intellectual life of the middle colonies, New York, New Jersey and Pennsylvania.
New York, 1609-1765, p. 285-311; in 1765, p. 312-40.

Lossing, B. J: The Hudson from the wilderness to the sea. 464p. N. Y. 1866. 917.47 L89

Van Rensselaer, *Mrs* M. D. Goede vrouw of Mana-ha-ta at home and in society 1609-1760. 418p. N. Y. 1898. 917.47 V35

Watson, J: F. Manners and customs in colonial times. (*see* N.Y. (city)— Common council. Manual. 1853. 12:457-60) 352.0747 N4k
From his *Historic tales of olden time.*

Wharton, A. H. Colonial days and dames. 248p. Phil. 1895.
Cap. 917.3 W551

History

Baxter, *Mrs* K. S. (Malcolm). A godchild of Washington; a picture of the past. 651p. N. Y. 1897. 974.7 qB33
Sketch of Catharine Van Rensselaer, with notes of men and events from 1650 to the middle of this century.

Beauchamp, W. M. The Iroquois and the colony of New York, (*see* Oneida historical society. Transactions. 1889-92. no. 5, p. 40-59) 974.762 On2

Bonney, *Mrs* C. V. (Van Rensselaer), *comp.* Legacy of historical gleanings. 2v. Alb. 1875. 923.57 V35
Mostly correspondence between men prominent in colonial and revolutionary periods. Colonial period, 1:1-57.

Brodhead, J: R. Address delivered before the New York historical society at its 40th anniversary 20 Nov. 1844; by Brodhead, historical agent of the state of New York to Holland, England and France, with an account of the subsequent proceedings at the dinner given in the evening. 107p. N. Y. 1844. 974.7 B782
Describes his work in transcribing documents.

———— History of the state of New York. 2v. N.Y. 1853-71. 974.7 B78
Contents: v. 1 1609-64; v. 2 1664-91.
At his death Mr Brodhead left material for a 3d volume. The treatment is of the most exhaustive character, and the work is a monument of literary industry and careful execution. The authorities are in all cases given in footnotes. J: A. Stevens in Winsor. 3:413.
Illustrated with a map of New Netherland according to the charters granted by the states general Oct. 11, 1614, and June 3, 1621.

Brodhead, J: R. History of the state of New York. Ed. 2. v.i. Gener nial h
N. Y. 1859, ᶜ53. 974.7 B781
v.1 1609-64.

Butler, Frederick. Complete history of the United States of America embracing the whole period from the discovery of North America down to the year 1820. 3v. Hartford 1821. N. Y. state lib.
New York colonial history, 2: 35-44, 83-107, 200-38, 315-70, 419-26.

Campbell, Douglas. Historical fallacies regarding colonial New York; address before the Oneida historical society, Utica N. Y. Jan 14, 1879. 32p. N. Y. 1879. 974.7 C15

Capen, Nahum. History of democracy; or, Political progress historically illustrated from the earliest to the latest periods. v.i.
Hartford 1874. 321.8 qC17
No more pub.
Colonial New York, p. 188-202.

Chalmers, George. Political annals of the present united colonies from their settlement to the peace of 1763. v.i. Lond.
1780. N. Y. state lib.
No more pub. For continuation of the work see collections of the New York historical society. 1868. Publication fund ser. 1: 1-176, 974.7 N42.
New York to 1691, p. 567-612.

Colden, Cadwallader. History of the five Indian nations depending on the province of New York in America. 119p. N. Y. 1727.
Original edition; only four or five copies known in the United States.
Sabin 4:222.

—— History of the five Indian nations depending on the province of New York; with an introduction and notes by J. G. Shea.
40+141p. N. Y. 1866. 970.3 C673
155 copies reprinted exactly from Bradford's New York ed. 1727. According to Sabin the following work is necessary to complete the 1st ed.

—— History of the five Indian nations of Canada, which are dependent on the province of New York in America and are the barrier between the English and French in that part of the world.
204+283p. Lond. 1747. 970.3 C67

—— History of the five Indian nations of Canada which are the barrier between the English and French in that part of the world.
Ed. 2. 204+283p. Lond. 1750. 970.3 C671

—— History of the five Indian nations of Canada which are dependent on the province of New York in America and are the barrier between the English and French in that part of the world. Ed. 3.
2v. Lond. 1755. 970.3 C672

General colo- **Colden, Cadwallader.** Letters on Smith's History of New York. (*see*
nial history   New York historical society. Collections. 1868–70. Publication
              fund ser. 1:177–235, 2 : 203–12)   974.7 N42

> These letters are supplementary to those contained in collections of the
> New York historical society. 1849. ser. 2, v. 2, 974.7 N242 v.7.

———— Papers relating to an act of the assembly of the province of New
      York, printed and sold by William Bradford. 24p.? N. Y. 1724.

> Mr H. C. Murphy's imperfect copy of this piece is probably unique.
> Sabin. 4:222. It was reprinted with the preceding 3 ed. of his *History of
> the five Indian nations.*

———— **& Smith, William.** Correspondence between Lieut. Gov.
      Cadwallader Colden and William Smith jr the historian respect-
      ing certain alleged errors and misstatements contained in the His-
      tory of New York, with sundry other papers relating to that
      controversy. (New York historical society. Colden papers, v. 4)
      (*see* New York historical society. Collections. 1849. ser. 2,
      2:193–214)   974.7 N422 v.7

De Peyster, Frederic. Address delivered before the New York his-
      torical society on its 60th anniversary, Tuesday, Nov. 22, 1864.
      76p. N. Y. 1865.   974.7 qD44

> Early political history of New York.

Drake, S: A. The making of Virginia and the middle colonies,
      1578–1701. 228p. N. Y. 1893.   973.2 D78

> New York, p. 108–60.

Dunlap, William. History of New York for schools. 2v. N. Y.
      1837.   974.7 D922

———— —— 2v. N. Y. 1844.   974.7 D921

———— —— 2v. N. Y. 1855.   N. Y. pub. lib.

> Conversational style.
> *Contents:* v. 1, Colonial period; v. 2, Revolution.

———— History of the New Netherlands, province of New York and
      state of New York, to the adoption of the federal constitution. 2v.
      N. Y. 1839–40.   974.7 D92

> v. 1 and part of appendix in v. 2 on colonial period.
> Has little merit as historical authority. The main value of the work con-
> sists in the abstracts published as an appendix to the 2d volume. J: A.
> Stevens in Winsor, 3:413.

Fisher, G: P. Colonial era. 348p. N. Y. 1892. (American
      history ser.)   973.2 F53

> New York to 1688, p. 177–93; 1688–1756, p. 241–54.
> Includes a bibliography of colonial era.

Fiske, John. The Dutch and quaker colonies in America.   2v. General
Bost. 1899.   974.7 F54 nial hi

Frost, John, *comp.* The book of the colonies; comprising a history of
the colonies composing the United States from the discovery in the
10th century until the commencement of the revolutionary war.
280p.   N. Y. 1846.   N. Y. state lib.
Settlement of New York and New Jersey, p. 230–44.

—— Remarkable events in the history of America, from the earliest
times to the year 1848.   2v.   Phil. 1848.   N. Y. state lib.
New York colonial history, p. 387–427.

Gordon, T: F. Gazetteer of the state of New York, comprehending its
colonial history.   102+801p.   Phil. 1836.   917.47 G65
History of New York, 102p.

Grahame, James. History of the United States of North America
from the plantation of the British colonies till their assumption of
national independence.   2v.   Phil. 1846.   973.2 G762

—— —— 4v.   Phil. 1845.   973.2 G761
Foundation and progress of New York, book 5.

Hawks, F. L. History of the United States, no. 2; or, Uncle Philip's
conversations with the children about New York.   2v.   N. Y.
1844, °35.   974.7 H31
Mostly on colonial period.

Histoire et commerce des colonies angloises dans l'Amérique septen-
trionale.   336p.   Lond. 1765.   N. Y. state lib.
New York, p. 135–66.

History of British dominion in North America from the first discovery
of that continent by S. Cabot 1497, to the peace of 1763.   297+
275p.   Lond. 1773.   N. Y. state lib.
Province of New York, 82p. book 3.

Hogeboom, J: T. Oration at the centennial celebration at Hudson
N.Y. on the 4th of July, 1876.   32p.   Hudson 1876.   974.739 H861
Discovery and settlement of New York and manors of the patroons, p. 1–15.

Lodge, H: C. A short history of the English colonies in America.
560p.   N. Y. 1881.   973.2 L82
New York, 1609–1765, p. 285–340.

Morse, J. & Parish, E. Compendious history of New England to
which is added a short abstract of the history of New York and New
Jersey.   324p.   Charlestown 1820.   974 M832
New York, p. 292–302.

N. Y. (state)—Legislature.   Documents relative to the colonial history of the state of New York. 15v. Alb. 1853-87. R974.7 qN421

Contents : v. 1-10 Documents procured in Holland, England and France, by J. R. Brodhead agent under an act of the legislature passed May 2, 1839 ed. by E. B. O'Callaghan with a general introduction by the agent.

v.1-2 Holland documents; v. 3-8 London documents; v. 9-10 Paris documents.

v. 11 General index to the documents prepared by E. B. O'Callaghan.

v. 12 Documents relating to the history of the Dutch and Swedish settlements on the Delaware river, trans. and comp. by B. Fernow.

v. 13 Documents relating to the history and settlements of the towns along the Hudson and Mohawk rivers (with the exception of Albany) from 1630-84 trans., comp. and ed. by B. Fernow.

v. 14 Documents relating to the history of the early colonial settlements principally on Long Island ; trans., comp. and ed. by B. Fernow.

v. 15 State archives, v. 1 ed. by Berthold Fernow; New York in the revolution, prepared under direction of the regents of the University of the State of New York.

These volumes are all printed in English, the French and Dutch manuscript being translated by O'Callaghan.

v. 12-15 form new series v. 1-4.

N. Y. (state)—State, Secretary of.   Calendar of historical manuscripts in the office of the secretary of state, Albany N. Y. ed. by E. B. O'Callaghan.   2v. Alb. 1865-66.   974.7 qN424

Contents : v. 1, Dutch manuscripts v. 1-21, 1630-64 ; v. 2, English manuscripts v. 22-101, 1664-1776.

These manuscripts (103 volumes) were transferred to the state library in 1881; last 2 volumes not included in Calendar.

A poor translation by F. A. Van der Kemp of most of the Dutch manuscript is in the state library in 24 manuscript volumes ; for index to them see state archivist's copy of the Calendar.

v. 1-4 of Dutch manuscripts were also translated by E. B. O'Callaghan and an index to the first three printed. (see O'Callaghan, E. B. Index to v. 1, 2 and 3, etc. 016 9747 Oc1) Fourth volume has manuscript index.

The four volumes of Documentary history by O'Callaghan together with v. 12-14 of Documents relating to the colonial history and another volume to be published containing the documents relating to New York city and the relations between the Dutch and English colonies, contain everything of a general and public interest so that the parts not translated anew (referring to Van der Kemp's translation) will refer only to personal matters. B. Fernow in Winsor. 4 : 412.

N. Y. (state)—State, Secretary of. Documentary history of the General
state of New York; arranged by E. B. O'Callaghan.   4v.   Alb.   nial his
1849–51.   974.7 N424

———   4v.   Alb. 1850–51.   947.7 qN423
For contents see Peabody institute. *Catalogue of the library.* 1889.
4:3218, Co19.1 qP31. See also note under preceding entry.

Oldmixon, John, *anon.* British empire in America containing the
history of the discovery, settlement, progress and present state of all
the British colonies on the continent and islands of America.   2v.
Lond. 1708.   970 Ol1
New York, 1:117–33.

——— ——— Ed. 2.   2v.   Lond. 1741.   970 Ol11
New York, 1:236–80.

——— Gross Brittanisches America nach seiner erfindung, bevölck-
erung und allerneuestem zustand aus dem englischen durch Vischer.
879p.   Hamburg 1710.   970 Ol12
New York, p. 168–89.
For translation see two English ed. preceding.

Palfrey, J: G. History of New England.   v.1–3.   Bost. 1858–64.
                                                              974 P177
New York, 1:235–38.

Parton, James. Colonial pioneers.   63p.   N. Y. °1890. (His-
torical classic readings 9)   E973.2 H62
Contents: Peter Stuyvesant, p. 28–34.   Capt. Kid, p. 45–51.
          Sir William Johnson, p. 35–40.   Capt. Henry Hudson, p. 57–63.
Extracted from other works by Parton.

Ruttenber, E: M. History of the Indian tribes of the Hudson river;
their origin, manners and customs; tribal and subtribal organizations;
wars, treaties, etc.   415p.   Alb. 1872.   970.4 R93

Satterlee, H. L. Political history of the province of New York.
107p.   N. Y. 1885.   342.7479 Sa8
Bibliography, 2p.

Schuyler, G: W. Colonial New York; Philip Schuyler and his family.
2v.   N. Y. 1885.   974.7 Sch8
Mostly genealogies of Schuyler and allied families.

A short account of the 1st settlement of the provinces of Virginia,
Maryland, New York, New Jersey and Pennsylvania by the English.
22p.   Lond. 1735.   N. Y. state lib.

Six nations of Indians.   (*see* Civil list and constitutiona. history of the
colony and state of New York by E. A. Werner.   Alb. 1891.
35 : 224–65)   351.2 N42
Relations with the colony and state of New York.

Smith, William.   History of New York, from the 1st discovery to the
year 1732 with a continuation, from the year 1732, to the commencement of the year 1814.   511p.   Alb. 1814.   974.7 Sm62
Supposed to have been edited by J : V. N. Yates.   J : A. Stevens in Winsor
3 : 412.

——— History of the late province of New York, from its discovery
to the appointment of Gov. Colden in 1762.   2v.   N.Y.
1829.   974.7 Sm64

——— ——— 2v.   N. Y. 1829–30.   974.7 Sm65
     Includes the *History of the province of New York from the 1st discovery to the
year* 1732 ; and a continuation in manuscript covering the period 1732–62.
     This was communicated in 1824 to the New York historical society by Wil-
liam Smith, son of the author and printed by them as v. 4–5 of their collections.   974.7 N422 v. 4–5.
     Noticed in *North American review* Jan. 1816, 2 : 150–53.
     Smith was a leader of the dissenting element in New York.

——— History of the province of New York from the 1st discovery.
334p.   Lond. 1776.   974.7 Sm6

——— History of the province of New York from the 1st discovery to
the year 1732.   Ed. 1.   255p.   Lond. 1757. 974.7 qSm6
Discovery to 1664 treated in 1st 23 pages ; English period in remainder.

——— History of the province of New York from the 1st discovery to
the year 1732.   Ed. 2.   276p.   Phil. 1792.   974.7 Sm61

——— Histoire de la Nouvelle-York, depuis la découverte de cette province jusqu'à notre siécle,   traduite de l'Anglois par M . E. ✱ ✱ ✱
415p.   Lond. 1767.   974.7 Sm66
Translated by Marc Antoine Eidous.

Thwaites, R. G.   The colonies, 1492–1750.   301p.   N. Y. 1891.
(Epochs of American history, v.1)   973.2 T42
The middle colonies, p. 195–217 ; Colonies 1700–50, p. 264–85.
Social and economic conditions in the colonies in 1700, p. 218–32.

Warden, D: B.   Chronologie historique de l'Amérique.   10v.   Par.
1826–44.   970 W21
Edited by Marquis de Fortia-d'Urban ; being *L'art de vérifier les dates*. pt 4.
New York colonial history, 10 : 1–123.

Watson, J: F. Annals and occurrences of New York city and state in the olden time; a collection of memoirs, anecdotes and incidents concerning the city, country and inhabitants from the days of the founders. 390p. Phil. 1846. 974.7 W331

—————— Historic tales of olden time, concerning the early settlement and advancement of New York city and state for the use of families and schools. 214p. N. Y. 1832. 974.7 W33

Yates, J: V. N. & Moulton, J. W. History of the state of New York; including its aboriginal and colonial annals. v.1, pt 1–2. N. Y. 1824–26. 974.7 Y2
No more pub.
Sabin says that Moulton is sole author of this scarce book.
Contents: Ante-colonial v. 1 pt 1; Novum Belgium v. 1 pt 2.

Discovery

No attempt has been made to give a complete bibliography of early voyages.

Banvard, Joseph. First explorers of North America; or, Discoveries and adventures in the new world. 334p. Bost. 1874. N. Y. state lib.
Explorations of Hudson and Champlain, p. 194–240.

Belknap, Jeremy. De Monts, Poutrincourt, and Champlain. (*see* Belknap's biographies of the early discoverers of America. n. d. p.92–99) 920.07 qB41
A reprint of the 1st ed. of 1798.

De Costa, B: F. Cabo de Arenas; or, The place of Sandy Hook in the old cartology. (*see* New England historical and genealogical register, Ap. 1885, 39 : 147–60) 929.1 N422

—————— Explorations of the North American coast previous to the voyage of Henry Hudson. (*see* Wilson, J. G. *ed.* Memorial history of the city of New York. 1892–93. 1:1–32) 974.71 qW69

Fiske, John. Discovery of America, with some account of ancient America and the Spanish conquest. 2v. Bost. 1892. 973.1 F54

Heckewelder, *Rev.* **John.** Indian tradition of the 1st arrival of the Dutch at Manhattan Island, now New York. (*see* New York historical society. Collections. 1841. ser. 2, 1 : 69–74) 974.7 N422 v.6

Homes, H: A: The Pompey (N. Y.) stone, with an inscription and date of A. D. 1520; an address before the Oneida historical society on the 11th of November, 1879. 15p. Utica 1881. 908 H75

Howell, G : R.   Evidence of the French discoveries in New York previous to the colonization by the Dutch.   (*see* Albany institute. Transactions. 1887. 11 : 309-16)   N. Y. state lib.

Murphy, H : C.   Voyage of Verrazzano, a chapter in the early history of maritime discovery in America. 198p. N. Y. 1875. N. Y. state lib.

Van Pelt, Daniel.   Were the Dutch on Manhattan Island in 1598 ?   (*see* National magazine, Nov. 1891, 15 : 91-97 ; Jan. 1892, 15:279-85)   973 . M271

Verrazano, John de.   Relation of the land by him discovered in the name of his majestie ; written in Diepe the 8th of July 1524.   (*see* New York historical society. Collections. 1811. 1 : 45-60)   947.7   N422
From *Hakluyt's voyages.* 1600. 2 : 295-300.

────── Verrezano's voyage.   (*see* Reminiscences of the city of New York and its vicinity. 1855. p. 253-63)   974.71   R28

────── Verrazzano's voyage, 1524 [letter] to the king of France.   16p. Bost. n.d.   (Old South leaflets 17)   973   Ol12

Weise, A. J.   Discoveries of America to the year 1525.   380p. N. Y. 1884.   973.1   W43
Gives an account of Verrazano's discovery of New York.

Who discovered the Hudson ?   (*see* Galaxy, July 1869, 8 : 129-33)   051   G13

Wilson, J. G.   Explorations of the North American coast previous to the voyage of Henry Hudson.   (*see* New York genealogical and biographical record, Oct. 1891, 22 : 163-74)   929.1   qN421
From his *Memorial history of the city of New York.*

Winsor, Justin.   Father Louis Hennepin and his real or disputed discoveries.   (*see his* Narrative and critical history of America. c1884-89. 4 : 247-56)   973   qW73

Champlain

Bixby, G. F.   The 1st battle of Lake Champlain ; has current history correctly located its site ? (*see* Albany institute. Transactions. 1893. 12 : 122-36)   N. Y. state lib.

────── The 1st battle of Lake Champlain ; a paper read before the Albany institute, Nov. 5, 1889. 15p. Alb. 1893.   973.2   B55
Regarding the locality of the battle fought by Champlain July 29, 1609.

Champlain, Samuel de. Oeuvres publiées sous le patronage de
l'université Laval par C. H. Laverdière. Ed. 2. 6 v. in 4.
Québec 1870. .917.1 qC35
Discovery of Lake Champlain, p. 184-200.

———— Les voyages de la Nouvelle France occidentale, dicté Canada
depuis l'an 1603 jusques en l'an 1629. 2 v. in 1. Par.
1632. V917.1 C352

———— Voyages; ou, Journal ès découvertes de la Nouvelle France
2v. Par. 1830. 917.1 C35
Discovery of Lake Champlain, 1:188-207.

———— Voyages trans. from the French by C: P. Otis; with historical
illustrations and a memoir of Champlain by E. F. Slafter. 3v.
Bost. 1878-82. (Prince society publications) 917.1 C351
Discovery of Lake Champlain, 2:210-27. 250 copies.

Champlain's expeditions to northern and western New York, 1609-15.
(see N. Y. (state)–State, Secretary of. Documentary history of the
state of New York) 1849-51. 3: 1-24. 974.7 N424
1850-51. 3: 1-15. 974.7 qN423

Notice biographique de Champlain. (see Laverdière. Oeuvres de
Champlain. 1870. 1:pref.9-76) 917.1 qC35

Parkman, Francis. Champlain and his associates; an account of
early French adventure in North America; with introduction and
explanatory notes. 64p. N. Y. °1890. (Historical classic
readings 6) E973.2 H62

———— Pioneers of France in the new world. 420p. Bost. 1865. (see
his France and England in North America. 1865. v.1) 973.1 P23
Champlain's discovery of Lake Champlain in 1609, p. 310-24.

Slafter, E. F. Champlain. (see Winsor, Justin, ed. Narrative and
critical history of America. °1884-89. 4 : 103-34. 973 qW73
Includes a critical essay on the sources of information.

———— Memoir of Samuel de Champlain. (see Champlain, Samuel de.
Voyages. 1878-82. 1 : 1-214) 917.1 C351

Wilmere, Alice. Biographical notice of Champlain. (see Hakluyt
society. Works. 1859. 23 : 2d pref. 1-99) 910.6 H12

Winsor, Justin. Champlain. (see his Cartier to Frontenac. 1894.
p. 77-155) 973.1 W73

Hudson

General his-
tory
Hudson
Asher, G; M. Henry Hudson the navigator; the original documents
in which his career is recorded; collected, partly translated and an-
notated with an introduction.   218+292.   Lond. 1860.   (*in*
Hakluyt society.   Works.   1860.   v. 27)   910.6 H12
Bibliography, p. 258-78.

Contains the following relating to Hudson's 3d voyage and to colonial New
York; The 3d voyage of Master Henry Hudson written by Robert Juet, of
Lime-house.   p. 45-92.

Purchas his pilgrimage.   fol. Lond. 1626. p. 817. VI of Hudson's discoveries
and death.   p. 139-44.

Hudson's 3d voyage (1609) from Van Meteren's *Histoire der Nederlanden.*
fol. Hague 1614, fol. 629a. p. 147-53.

Extracts relating to Hudson's 3d voyage (1609), from J: de Laet's *Nieuwe
Werelt.* fol. Amst. 1625, 1630-31 (from book 3, ch. 7) p. 154-58; from book 3,
ch. 10) p. 159-63.

Extracts containing some original information about Hudson's 3d voyage
from Mr Lambrechtsen van Ritthem's *History of New Netherland.* p. 164-66.

Extracts concerning Hudson's 3d voyage (1609), from Adrian van der
Donck's *Beschryvinge van Nieuw Nederlandt.*   Amst. 1655, 1656.   p. 167-72.

Hessel Gerritz's various accounts of Hudson's last two voyages, from the
Latin and Dutch edition of the *Descriptio et delineatio geographica detectionis
Freti ab. H. Hudsono inventi.*   Amst. 1612, 1613.   p. 181-83.

2 Hudson's 3d and 4th voyage, from the prolegomena to the 1st Latin
ed.   p. 183-84.

3 Hudson's 3d and 4th voyage from the Latin edition of 1612.   An account
of the discovery of the northwest passage which is expected to lead to
China and Japan by the north of the American continent, found by H.
Hudson.   p. 185-88.

4 Hudson's 3d and 4th voyage from the 2d Latin edition of 1613, with notes
indicating the variations of the Dutch edition.   A description and chart of
the strait or passage by the north of the American continent to China and
Japan.   p. 189-96.

———— Henry Hudson the navigator.   (*see* Macmillan's magazine, Oct.
1866, 14:459-71)   052 M22
Also in *Littell's living age,* 17 Aug. 1867, 94:397-407, 051 L71.

———— Sketch of Henry Hudson the navigator.   23p.   Brooklyn
1867.   L. I. hist. soc.
Reprinted for private distribution.

Bardsen, Ivar. Sailing directions of Henry Hudson, prepared for his
use in 1608; from the old Danish of Ivar Bardsen, with an introduction and notes; also a dissertation on the discovery of the Hudson
river; by B: F. DeCosta.   102p.   Alb. 1869.   656 M9

Belknap, Jeremy. Henry Hudson. (*see* Belknap's biographies of the Genera tory early discoverers of America. n.d. p. 113–18)   920.07   qB41 Hudson
Reprint of the 1st ed. of 1798.

Cleveland, H: R. Life of Henry Hudson. (*see* Sparks' library of American biography. 1838. 10 : 185–261)   920.07   Sp2

Ferris, M.. L. D. Henry Hudson the navigator. (*see* Magazine of American history, Sep. 1893, 30:214–36)   973   M27

Higginson, T: W. Henry Hudson and the New Netherlands (A. D. 1609–26). (*see* *his* Book of American explorers. 1877. p.279–307)   973.1   H53
Contents: 1 Discovery of the Hudson river.
          2 Indian traditions of Hudson's arrival.
          3 Last voyage of Hudson.
          4 Dutch settlement of New Netherlands.

Hudson's voyage in 1609; extract from Verhael van de eerste schip-vaert der hollandsche ende zeeusche schepen door 't way-gat by Noorden, Noorwesen, Moscovien, ende Tartarien om, na de con-inckrycken Cathay ende China: etc. 't Amsterdam, voor Joost Hartgers, etc. 1648. Transmitted to the New York historical society by Dr M. F. A. Campbell, at the Hague. Translated by J: R. Brodhead. (*see* New York historical society. Collections. 1849. ser. 2, 2:367–70)   974.7   N422 v.7

Hulsius, Levinus. Zwölfe schiffahrt; oder, Kurze beschreibung der newen schiffahrt Nord Osten ober die Amerische inseln in Chinam and Japponiam von einem Engelander, Heinrich Hudson, newlich erfunden in hochteuchten sprach beschrieben durch M. Gothar-dum Arthusen von Dantzig. 67p. Oppenheim 1627. N. Y. pub. lib.

Juet, Robert. Third voyage of Master Henry Hudson. (*see* Asher, G; M. Henry Hudson the navigator. 1860. p.45–92)   910.6 H12 v.27
Called *Juet's journal*

—— —— (*see* New York historical society. Collections. 1809. 1:102–46)   974.7   N422

—— —— Extract. (*see* New York historical society. Collections. 1841. ser. 2, 1:317–32)   974.7   N422 v.6

—— —— Extract. (*see* Munsell, Joel. Annals of Albany)
          1850–59. 1:9–14. 974.743   M92
          Ed. 2. 1869–71. 1:1–8. 974.743   M921

Juet, Robert.   Discovery of the Hudson river.   20p.   Bost. n. d.
(Old South leaflets 94)   973   Ol12
Extract from Juet's *Third voyage of Master Henry Hudson.*

Laet, Johannes de.   Nieuvve wereldt; ofte, Beschryvinghe van West-
Indien.   510p.   Leyden 1625.   917   qL12
Note on Laet under Dutch period, 1609–64, p. 322.

Meteren, Emanuel van.   Belgische ofte nederlantsche oorlogen ende
gheschiedenissen beginnende van t'jaer 1598 tot 1611, mede verva-
tende enighe haerder gebueren handelinghe.   2v.   Schotlant
buyten Danswyck 1611.   949.203   qM56   v. 2
This ed. the last pub. by the author, is exceedingly scarce.   Appeared
later under the title *Historie der nederlandsche oorlogen.*
  v. 1 wanting in N. Y. state lib.   v.2 p.346 contains the 1st printed account
of Hudson's voyage to the North river.

———— Historie der nederlandscher ende haerder naburen oorlogen ende
geschiedenissen, tot den jare 1612 's Graven-Haghe 1614. Fol. 671.
Full title, and translation of folio 629a on Hudson's voyage to the North river
in Asher. *Henry Hudson the navigator.* 1860. p.274, 147–53, 910.6 H12 v.27.

———— Historie van de oorlogen en geschiedenissen der Nederlanderen
en derzelver naburen, beginnende 1315, en eindigende 1611.
New ed.   10v.   Gorinchem 1748–63.   949.203   M56
First account of Hudson's voyage to the North river, 10:205.

Miller, Samuel.   Discourse designed to commemorate the discovery
of New York by Henry Hudson, delivered before the New York
historical society, Sep. 4, 1809.   28p.   N. Y. 1810.   040 P1 v.55

———— Discourse, designed to commemorate the discovery of New
York by Henry Hudson, delivered before the New York historical
society, Sep. 4, 1809, being the completion of the 2nd century since
that event.   (*see* New York historical society.   Collections.   1809.
1:17–45)   974.7   N422

Murphy, H: C.   Henry Hudson in Holland, an inquiry into the
origin and objects of the voyage which led to the discovery of the
Hudson river with bibliographical notes.   72p.   The Hague
1859.   923.9   H861

Parton, James.   Captain Henry Hudson.   (*see* Parton, James.
Colonial pioneers.   1890.   p.57–63)   E973.2   H62

Purchas, Samuel.   Hakluytus posthumus; or, Purchase his pil-
grimes.   5v.   Lond. 1625–26.   N. Y. state lib.
Hudson's 3d voyage, 3:581–95.
  Asher says we are indebted to Purchas for most of our information about
Hudson.   Described in Sabin, 16:116–24.

Read, J: M. jr. Historical inquiry concerning Henry Hudson, his General history friends, relatives and early life, his connection with the Muscovy Dutch period company and discovery of Delaware bay. 209p. Alb. 1866.

923.9 H86

—— Historical inquiry concerning Henry Hudson, his friends, relatives and early life, his connection with the Muscovy company and and discovery of Delaware bay abridged from the work of Read, and ed. by Edmond Goldsmid. (*see* Clarendon society reprints. 1882–84. ser. 1, p. 143–230) 942 C54

Watson, J: F. Original exploration of the country. (*see his* Annals and occurrences of New York city and state. 1846. p. 37–42)

974.7 W331

Wilson, J. G. Henry Hudson's voyage and its results in trade and colonization. (*see* Wilson, J. G. *ed.* Memorial history of the city of New York. 1892–93. 1 : 108–51) 974.71 qW69

Also in *National magazine*, Jan. 1892, 15 : 221–49, 973 M271.

Dutch period 1609–64

Alphen, D. C. van. Dissertatio historico-politica de Novo Belgio colonia quondam nostratium. Lug. Bat. 1838. British museum

Arnoux, W: H: The discovery and settlement of New York considered in its legal aspect. 24p. N. Y. 1887. N. Y. state law lib.

—— The Dutch in America ; a brief examination into the Dutch claim of sovereignty in America, particularly in New York. 50p. N. Y. 1890. (N. Y. Court of appeals. Brief of counsel in the case of W: P. Abendroth vs N. Y. elevated railway co.) N. Y. state law lib.

Asher, G; M. Bibliographical and historical essay on the Dutch books and pamphlets relating to New Netherland and the Dutch West India company. 234p. Amst. 1854–67. 016.97 As3
Preface and introduction relating to New Netherlands.

Bancroft, George. History of the United States from the discovery of the American continent. Ed. 1–10. 10v. Bost. 1838–74.

N. Y. state lib.

New Netherlands, 2 : 256–315. First 10 ed. printed from same plates.

—— History of the United States of America from the discovery of the continent ; the author's last revision. 6v. N. Y. 1890–91, ᵉ58 84.

973 B221

New Netherlands, 1 : 475–518.

Beekman, J. W: [The founders of New York; an] address delivered before the St Nicholas society of the city of New York, Saturday Dec. 4, 1869.   36p.   Alb. 1870.   974.7 qB39

Bryant, W: C. & Gay, S. H. Popular history of the United States. 5v.   N. Y. 1876-96.   973 qB84
New Netherlands, 1:339-69, 429-75; 2:115-64.

DeWitt, Thomas. New Netherland.   (*see* New York historical society.   Proceedings.   1844.   p. 51-76) 974.7 N421 v.1
Read before the society Jan. 2, 1844.

Dussen-Muilkerk, E. J. Berg van.   Bijdragen tot de geschiedenis onzer kolonisatie in Noord-Amerika.   (*see* Gids, 1848, p. 522-54; 1849, p. 702-20)   059 G36

Early history of New York.   (*see* Family magazine, 1840, 7: 203-5)
                 051 qF21
Dutch period.

Fernow, Berthold. New Netherland; or, The Dutch in North America.   (*see* Winsor, Justin, *ed*.   Narrative and critical history of America.   °1884-89.   4: 395-442)   973 qW73

Hall, C: H: The Dutch and the Iroquois; suggestions as to the importance of their friendship in the great struggle of the 18th century for the possession of this continent; being a paper read before the Long Island historical society, Feb. 21, 1882.   55p.   N. Y. 1882.   970.1 H14

Henderson, J: D. The Dutch in New Netherlands, an address delivered before the Herkimer county historical society, Feb. 8, 1898. 8p.   n. p. 1898.   974.7 H382
Also in papers of Herkimer county historical society.   1898.   p.9-16, 974.761 H42.

Hildreth, Richard. History of the United States of America from the discovery of the continent to the organization of government under the federal constitution.   3v.   N.Y. 1849.   N.Y. state lib.
New Netherlands, 1: 136-49, 413-47.

Hollantse mercurius, 1650-90. v. 1-41. Haerlem 1651-91. 905 H71
This annual publication contains many references to New Netherlands.

Laet, Johannes de. Beschryvinghe van West Indien.   Ed. 2. 622p.   Leyden 1630.   917 qL121
Asher, p. 1, no. 2. New Netherlands, p. 100-9.
De Laet was a director of the West India company and co-patroon of Rensselaerswyck.

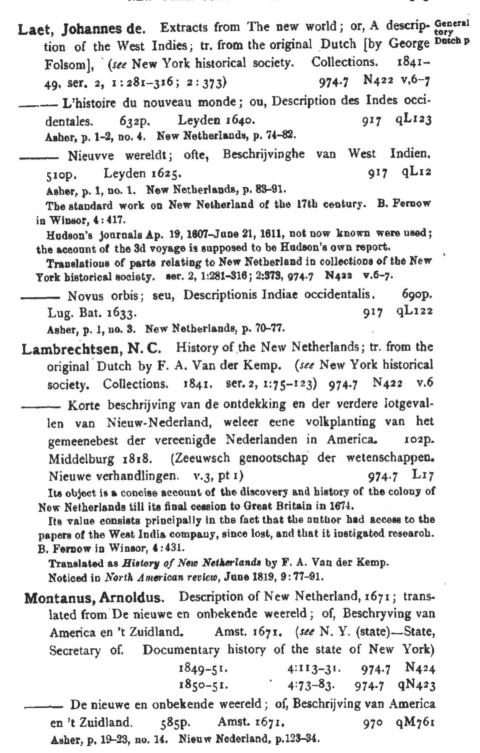

Laet, Johannes de. Extracts from The new world; or, A descrip- ^{General} tion of the West Indies; tr. from the original Dutch [by George ^{Dutch p} Folsom], (*see* New York historical society. Collections. 1841– 49. ser. 2, 1:281–316; 2:373) 974.7 N422 v.6–7

———— L'histoire du nouveau monde; ou, Description des Indes occidentales. 632p. Leyden 1640. 917 qL123
Asher, p. 1-2, no. 4. New Netherlands, p. 74–82.

———— Nieuvve wereldt; ofte, Beschrijvinghe van West Indien. 510p. Leyden 1625. 917 qL12
Asher, p. 1, no. 1. New Netherlands, p. 83–91.
The standard work on New Netherland of the 17th century. B. Fernow in Winsor, 4:417.
Hudson's journals Ap. 19, 1607–June 21, 1611, not now known were used; the account of the 3d voyage is supposed to be Hudson's own report.
Translations of parts relating to New Netherland in collections of the New York historical society. ser. 2, 1:281–316; 2:373, 974.7 N422 v.6–7.

———— Novus orbis; seu, Descriptionis Indiae occidentalis. 690p. Lug. Bat. 1633. 917 qL122
Asher, p. 1, no. 3. New Netherlands, p. 70–77.

Lambrechtsen, N. C. History of the New Netherlands; tr. from the original Dutch by F. A. Van der Kemp. (*see* New York historical society. Collections. 1841. ser. 2, 1:75–123) 974.7 N422 v.6

———— Korte beschrijving van de ontdekking en der verdere lotgevallen van Nieuw-Nederland, weleer eene volkplanting van het gemeenebest der vereenigde Nederlanden in America. 102p. Middelburg 1818. (Zeeuwsch genootschap der wetenschappen. Nieuwe verhandlingen. v.3, pt 1) 974.7 L17
Its object is a concise account of the discovery and history of the colony of New Netherlands till its final cession to Great Britain in 1674.
Its value consists principally in the fact that the author had access to the papers of the West India company, since lost, and that it instigated research. B. Fernow in Winsor, 4:431.
Translated as *History of New Netherlands* by F. A. Van der Kemp.
Noticed in *North American review*, June 1819, 9:77–91.

Montanus, Arnoldus. Description of New Netherland, 1671; translated from De nieuwe en onbekende weereld; of, Beschryving van America en 't Zuidland. Amst. 1671. (*see* N. Y. (state)—State, Secretary of. Documentary history of the state of New York)
1849-51. 4:113-31. 974.7 N424
1850-51. 4:73-83. 974.7 qN423

———— De nieuwe en onbekende weereld; of, Beschrijving van America en 't Zuidland. 585p. Amst. 1671. 970 qM761
Asher, p. 19–23, no. 14. Nieuw Nederland, p.123–34.

Montanus, Arnoldus, *anon.* Die unbekante neue welt; oder, Beschreibung des weltteils Amerika, und des Süd-landes durch O. D.   658p. Amst. 1671.   970 qM76
Neu Niederland, p. 142-53.

O'Callaghan, E. B.   History of New Netherland; or, New York under the Dutch.   2v.   N. Y. 1846-48.   974.7 Oc11
Winsor, 4:431-32.

———— ———— Ed. 2.   2v.   N. Y. 1855.   L. I. hist. soc.

Ogden, J. D.   Founders of New York, being an anniversary address delivered at the Lyceum on the 5th Dec. 1845, before the St Nicholas society.   19p.   N. Y. 1846.   N. Y. pub lib.

Plantagenet, Beauchamp, *anon.*   A description of the province of New Albion.   35p.   Lond. 1648.   (*in* Force, Peter, *ed.* Tracts and other papers relating principally to the origin, settlement and progress of the colonies in North America.   1836-46.   v.2)   N. Y. state lib.
Visit of Sir Samuel Argoll to Manhatas Isle in 1613, p. 18-19.
For criticism see John Pennington.   *An examination of Beauchamp Plantagenet's Description of the province of New Albion.*   (see Pennsylvania historical society.   Memoirs.   1840.   v. 4, pt 1, p. 133-65, 974.8 P383.

Rees, O. van.   Geschiedenis der nederlandsche volkplantigen in Noord-Amerika, beschouwd uit het oogpunt der koloniale politiek ; drie voorlezingen, gehouden in de afdeeling koophandel der maatschappij Felix Meritis, te Amsterdam op. 8, 15 en 22 Feb. 1855.   162p.   Tiel 1855.   974.7 R25

Scisco, L. D.   Garrison of Fort Amsterdam.   (*see* American historical register, May-June 1896, 4:255-62, 372-77)   973 qAm31

Stanwood, J. R.   Sketch of events incident to the settlement of the province of New Netherland.   (*see* New England historical and geneological register, July 1882, 36:233-41)   929.1 N422

———— ———— (*see his* Direct ancestry of the late Jacob Wendell.   1882. p. 7-17)   929.2 qW483

Valentine, D: T: Notable women of olden times.   (*see* Munsell, Joel. Annals of Albany.   1850-59.   7:86-93)   974.743 M92
Contents :

Elizabeth Van Es	Lysbet Van Voorhuydt
Helena Teller	Geertruyd Schuyler
Johanna De Laet	Machtelde Willemsen
Katrijn Roelofs	Lysbet Greveraet
Annetje Jans	

Wassenaer, Nicolaes van. Historisch verhael alder ghedenck-
weerdichste geschiednisse die hier en daer in Europa van den
beginne des jaers 1621 tot [1632] voorgevallen syn.   21v.in 5.
Amst. 1622-35.   940.7   W28
> Asher, p. 180-81, no. 330. Description and contents in Muller, p. 53-59.
> v. 18-21 continued by Barent Lampe.
> Records all the information that could be gathered from America.
> Brodhead speaks of the work at some length in his *History of the state of New York*. 1853. 1:46, 157.
> Wassenaer's description and 1st settlement of New Netherland is reprinted in *Collectanea adamantea*, v. 27.

Watson, J: F. The first colonists. (*see his* Annals and occurrences of New York city and state. 1846. p. 42-45) 974.7 W331

Yates, J: V. N. & Moulton, J. W. History of the state of New York; including its aboriginal and colonial annals.   v.1, pt 1-2.
N. Y. 1824-26.   974.7   Y2
> No more pub. Sabin says Moulton is the sole author of this scarce book.
> *Contents*: Ante-colonial, v. 1, pt 1. Novum Belgium, v. 1, pt 2.

Trading companies 1609-26

Agreement between the managers and principal adventurers of the West India company made with the approbation of the states general. (*see* O'Callaghan, E. B. History of New Netherland. N. Y. 1846-48. 1:408-10)   947.7 Oc11

Banta, T. M. Who founded New York? (*see* Holland society of New York. Yearbook. 1895. p. 119-33)   947.7 qH71

Brief relation of the discovery and plantation of New England.   36p.
Lond. 1622.   N. Y. pub. lib.
> Contains account of Capt. Darmer's meeting with Holland traders at Hudson river.

A brief relation of the discovery and plantation of New England and of sundry events therein occurring from 1607 to the present 1622.
Lond. 1622. (*see* Massachusetts historical society. Collections.
1822. ser. 2, 9:1-25)   974.4 M38 v.19
> On p. 11 occurs the 1st mention in English of the Dutch colony.

Brodhead, J: R. Memoir on the early colonization of New Netherland. (*see* New York historical society. Collections. 1849.
ser. 2, 2:355-66)   974.7 N422 v.7

De Forest, J. W. The founder of New York, [Jesse de Forest].
(*see* American historical register, May 1895, 2:881-90, 1172-80)   973 qAm31

Dozy, C. M. Jesse de Forest, founder of New Amsterdam. (*see* The pilgrim fathers. 1888. p. 20–22, *in* Holland society of New York. Yearbook. 1888–89)   974.7 qH71
Between p. 80 and 81 of the *Yearbook.*

Folsom, George, *anon.* Expedition of Capt. Samuel Argall to the French settlements in Acadia and Manhattan Island, A. D. 1613. (*see* New York historical society. Collections. 1841. ser. 2, 1 : 333–42)   974.7 N422 v.6

Heckewelder, John. Indian tradition of the first arrival of the Dutch at Manhattan Island, now New York. (*see* New York historical society. Collections. 1841. ser. 2, 1 : 68–74) 974.7 N422 v.6

Howell, G: R. Date of the settlement of the colony of New York, 15p.   Alb. 1897.   (Founders and patriots of America–New York society.   Publications 1)   · 974.7 F82

Lamb, *Mrs* **M. J. R. (Nash).** Origin of New York ; glimpse of the famous Dutch West India company. (*see* Magazine of American history, Oct. 1887, 18 : 273–88)   973 M27

Miller, E. J. West India company and the Walloons. (*see* Albany institute. Transactions. 1893. 12 : 53–68)   N. Y. state lib.

Netherlands—States general. Charter given to the West India company, dated the 3d of June 1621. (*see* O'Callaghan, E. B. History of New Netherland. 1846–48. 1 : 399–407) 974.7 Oc11

—— Generael octroy voor de ghene die eenighe nieuwe passagien haavenen, landen of plaetsen sullen ontdecken. n. p. 1614.
Asher, p. 180, no. 329.

—— Octroy by de hooghe mogende heeren staten generael verleent aende West-Indische compagnie, in dato den 3. Juni 1621 Ed. 1.   24p.   s'Gravenhage 1621.
Murphy, p. 51, no. 475.

—— Octroy by de hooghe mogende heeren staten generael verleent aende West Indische compagnie in date den derden Junii 1621. Mette ampliatien van dien ende het accoort tusschen de bevint-hebberen ende hooft-participanten vande selve compagnie. Na de copie ghedruckt in'sGraven-haghe. Tot Middeburgh, by de weduwe ende erffgenamen van Symon Moulert, ordinaris drucker vande 'Ed: Mog: hoeren staten van Zeelandt. 1623.
Grollier club, p. 85, no. 254. A reprint of the 2d edition of the Dutch West India company charter.

Netherlands—States General. Ordres and articles granted by the Gener
high and mighty lords the states generael. Lond. 1621. tory,
Dutch

Murphy, p. 51, no. 476. Very rare translation of the *Ootroy* of 1621.

Olden time in New York ; discovery and early settlement. (*see* N. Y.
(city)–Common council. Manual. 1848. 7 : 372–75) 352.0747 N4k

Van Pelt, Daniel. Antecedents of New Netherland and the Dutch
West India company. (*see* Wilson, J. G. *ed.* Memorial history of
the city of New York. 1892–93. 1 : 55–107) 974.71 qW69

———— The Dutch West India company the founders of Manhattan colony.
(*see* National magazine, Dec. 1891, 15 : 109–35) 973 M271
From Wilson's *Memorial history of the city of New York.*

Wassenaer, Nicolaes van. Description and first settlement of New
Netherland. (*see* N. Y. (state)–State, Secretary of. Documentary
history of the state of New York) 1849–51. 3:25–63. 974.7 N424
1850–51. 3:19–31. 974.7 qN423

Translated from his *Historie van Europa*, 1621-22.

Dutch colony 1626–64

For contemporaneous occupation of Long Island by the English, see Suffolk
county, p. 454, and its towns. Southampton, Southold and others were settled
in 1640 or soon after.

Description

Beschryvinghe van Virginia, Nieuw Nederlandt, Nieuw Engelandt en
d'eylanden Bermudes, Berbados en S. Christoffel. 6op. Amst. 1651.
Asher, p. 2-3, no. 6.

Castell, William. Extract from Castell's Discoverie of America, 1644.
(*see* New York historical society. Collections. 1857. ser. 2,
3 : 231–36) 974.7 N422 v.8

De Rasieres, Isaack. New Netherland in 1627. (*see* New York
historical society. Collections. 1849. ser. 2, 2 : 339–54)
974.7 N422 v.7

Letter to Samuel Bloomaert found in the Royal library at the Hague, and
tr. by J: R. Brodhead.

Donck, Adriaen van der. Beschrijvinge van Nieuvv-Nederlant,
gelijck het tegenwoordigh in staet is, begrijpende de nature, aert,
gelegentheyt en vruchtbaerheyt van het selve lant. 1oop.
Amst. 1655. L. I. hist. soc.

Asher, p. 4, no. 7. Translated by Jeremiah Johnson under title *Description of New Netherlands.* v.6.

Donck, Adriaen van der. Beschryvinge van Nieuvv-Nederlant, gelijck het tegenwoordigh in staet is, begrijpende de nature, arte gelegentheyt en vruchtbaerheyt van het selve landt.   Ed. 2. 100p.   Aemsteldam 1656.   V917.47   D71
Asher, p. 4–5, no. 8.

—————— Description of New Netherlands.   N. Y. 1841.
Griffin. p. 1023.   Translated by Jeremiah Johnson.

—————. Description of the New Netherlands; tr. from the original Dutch by Jeremiah Johnson. (*see* New York historical society. Collections. 1841. ser. 2, 1:125–242)   974.7   N422 v.6

—————- Description of the New Netherlands.   24p.   Bost. n. d. (Old south leaflets 69)   973   Ol12

Dunlap, William. Review of Van der Donck's account of New Netherlands. (*see* Dunlap, William. History of the New Netherlands. 1839–40. 2 : apx. 72–88)   974.7   D92

Earle, *Mrs* **Alice (Morse).** Colonial days in old New York.   312p. N. Y. 1896.   Cap. 917.47   Ea7

Father Isaac Jogues, S. J. (*see* Catholic world, Oct. 1872, 16 : 105–21)   205   C28

The first apostle to the Iroquois. (*see* Month, Mar. 1874, 20 : 306–24)   052   M76
Father Jogues.

Gerbier, Balthasar. Sommier verhael van sekere Amerikaensche voyagie gedaen door den ridder Balthasar Gerbier. n. p. 1660.
Asher, p. 11, no. 11.

Hall, C: H. Speech at 7th annual dinner in reply to the toast Colbert and the Corlaer. (*see* Holland society of New York. Year book. 1892–95. p. 66–74)   974.7   qH71

Hooper, Joseph. Pere Jogues and Domine Megapolensis. (*see his* History of Saint Peter's church in the city of Albany. 1900. p. 485–87)   283.747   Al17

Jogues, Isaac. Description of New Netherland in 1644. (*see* N. Y. (state)–State, Secretary of. Documentary history of the state of New York)   1849–51. 4 : 19–24.   974.7   N424
                          1850–51. 4 : 15–17.   974.7   qN423

Jogues, Isaac. The Jogues papers, translated and arranged, with a General
memoir by J: G. Shea, (*see* New York historical society. Collections. 1857. ser. 2, 3: 161–229) 974.7 N422 v.8

> *Contents:* 1 Narrative of his captivity among the Mohawks from a Latin
> manuscript preserved at Montreal, and in Algambe.
> 2 Account of his escape, from the *Relation of 1642-43.* p. 284.
> 3 Description of New Netherland from his original manuscript.
> 4 His last letters in 1646, from the *Relation of 1646-47.*
> 5 Captivity and death of René Goupil, from his original
> manuscripts.
> 6 Letters of Gov. Kieft announcing his death, from an attested
> copy preserved at Montreal.

—— Narrative of a captivity among the Mohawk Indians and a
description of New Netherland in 1642–3 by Jogues with a memoir of
the holy missionary by J: G. Shea. 69p. N.Y. 1856. 922.27 J591

—— Novum Belgium; an account of New Netherland in 1643–4;
with a facsimile of his original manuscript, his portrait, a map and
notes by J: G. Shea. 53p. N. Y. 1862. N. Y. state lib.

> Jogues was in New Netherland from August 1642 to November 1643; and
> the original manuscript is preserved in the Hôtel Dieu at Quebec. Fernow
> in Winsor, 4:421.

—— Novum Belgium; description de Nieuw Netherland et notice sur
René Goupil. 44p. N. Y. 1862. V917.47 qJ59

> 100 copies printed.

Keye, Otto. Het waere onderscheyt tusschen koude en warme landen
aengewesen in de nootsakelyckheden die daer vereyscht worden voorgestelt en vergeleken met Nieu-Nederlant, als synde een koudt landt
en Guajana synde een warm landt. 178p. 's Graven-Hage 1659.

> Asher, p. 11, no. 10. Same work published in 1660 under title *Beschryvinge
> van het heerlijcke ende Gezegen de landt Guajana.*

—— Kurtzer entwurff von Neu Niederland und Guajana einander
entgegen gesetzt um den unterschied zwischen warmen und kalten
landen herauss zu bringen; auss dem holländischen ins hochteutsche
versetzt durch T. R. C. S. C. S. 144p. Lpz. 1672. V917.47 K52

Kort verhael van Nieuw Nederlants gelegentheit, deughden, natuerlyke
voorrechten en byzondere bequaemheidt ter bevolkingh. 84p.
n. p. 1662. N. Y. pub. lib.

> Asher, p. 14–19, no. 13. Contents in Muller, p. 48–49.
> Reissued in 1663 under title *Zeekere vrye-voorslagen, en versoeken, tot be-
> vorderingh van een bestandige, voor Hollandt hoognutte vrye nolk uitzetting,
> in Nieuw-Nederlandt.* 84p.

Martin, Felix. The life of Father Isaac Jogues, missionary priest of the Society of Jesus, with Father Jogues' account of the captivity and death of his companion René Goupil tr. from the French by J: G. Shea. 263p. N. Y. 1885. 922.27 J59

Schagen, P. Old Dutch letter relating to the settlers in the New Netherlands. (*see* Holland society of New York. Yearbook. 1890–91. p. 152–53) 974.7 qH71
Dated at Amsterdam, Nov. 5, 1826. Dutch original and English translation.

Stevenson, T. B. Père Jogues. (*see* Sunday magazine, May 1893, 29:322–27) 205 Su7

Verheerlickte Nederland door d'herstelde zee-vaart klaerlyck voorgestelt, ontdeckt en aengewesen door manier van't samensprekinge van een boer ofte landtman, een burger ofte stee-man, een schipper ofte zee-man. 68p. n. p. 1659.
Asher, no. 9, p. 5–10.

Withrow, W. H. Adventures of Isaac Jogues, S. J. (*see* Royal society of Canada. Proceedings and transactions. 1886. v. 3, sec. 2, p. 45–53) 061 qR81

History

Amsterdam-Burgermeesteren. Conditien die door de heeren burgermeesteren der stadt Amstelredam. volgens't gemaeckte accoprdt met de West-Indische compagnie, ende d'approbatie van de heeren staten generael daer op gevolght, gepresenteert werden aen alle de gene, die als coloniers na Nieuw-Nederlandt willen vertrecken. 14p. Amst. 1656. N. Y. pub. lib.
This is not the ed. appended to the 2d ed. of Van der Donck.

Atkins, T: A. Adriaen Van der Donck; an address delivered before the Westchester county historical society at White Plains N. Y. Nov. 2, 1888. 26p. Yonkers 1888. L. I. hist. soc.

Brodhead, J: R. Dutch governors of Nieuw Amsterdam. (*see* International magazine, Dec. 1851, 4:597–93) 051 In81

Concerning New Netherland or Manhattan. (*see* New York historical society. Collections. 1869. Publication fund ser. 2:1–14) 974.7 N42

Correspondence between the colonies of New Netherland and New Plymouth, from Gov. Bradford's letter book. (*see* Massachusetts historical society. Collections. 1794. 3:27–76) 974.4 M38
1624–30.

—— Extract. (*see* New York historical society. Collections. 1841. ser. 2, 1:355–68) 974.7 N422 v.6

Daly, C: P. Speech at the 6th annual dinner.   (*see* Holland society <small>Genera</small>
of New York.   Yearbook.   1890–91.   p. 217–27)   974.7   qH71 <small>tory
Dutch</small>
Chiefly on the Dutch governors. `

Dexter, F. B. Early relations between New Netherland and New
England.   (*see* New Haven colony historical society.   Papers.
1882.   3 : 443–69)   974.67   N42

Donck, Adriaen van der *& others.* Remonstrance of New Netherland and the occurrences there, addressed to the high and mighty
lords states general of the United Netherlands by the people of
New Netherland on the 28th July 1649.   (*see* N. Y. (state)–Legislature.   Documents relative to the colonial history of the state of
New York.   1853–87.   1 : 271–318)   R974.7   qN421

—— Remonstrance of New Nederland and the occurrences there,
addressed to the high and mighty lords states general of the United
Netherlands, on the 28th July 1649, with Secretary Van Tienhoven's
answer, translated from a copy of the original Dutch manuscript by
E. B. O'Callaghan.   65p.   Alb. 1856.   974.7   qD711
Reprinted from *Documents relative to the colonial history of the state of New
York.*   1 : 271-318.

—— *anon.* Representation of New Netherland, concerning its location, productiveness and poor condition; presented to the states
general of the United Netherlands, and printed at the Hague in
1650; translated from the Dutch for the New York historical society
with notes by H: C. Murphy.   88p.   N. Y. 1849.   974.7   D71

—— *anon.* Representation of New Netherland, concerning its location, productiveness and poor condition; translated from the Dutch
for the New York historical society with explanatory notes by H: C.
Murphy.   (*see* New York historical society.   Collections.   1849.
ser. 2, 2 : 251–338)   974.7   N422 v.7

—— *anon.* Vertoogh van Nieu-Nederland, weghens de gheleghent-
heydt vruchtbaerheydt en soberen staet desselfs.   49p.   'sGraven-
hage.   1650.   V974.7   D711
Asher, p. 2, no. 5. Probably written by Van der Donck.
A contemporaneous relation of events in New Netherland, signed by 11
residents of New Amsterdam.
For translation see his *Representation of New Netherland.*
Entire history of this important work in O'Callaghan. *History New Nether-
land,* 2:90-99, 111-26; and, Brodhead. *History of the state of New York.*
Ed. 2. 506-7, 511, 512.

Donck, Adriaen van der *& others. anon.* Vertoogh van Nieu Nederland; and, Breeden raedt aende vereenichde nederlandsche provintien [by Cornelis Melyn]: two rare tracts printed in 1649–50, relating to the administration of affairs in New Netherland, translated from the Dutch by H: C. Murphy. 190p. N. Y. 1854.   974.7 qD71

Breeden raedt has been translated with title *Broad advice to the United Netherland provinces.*

Early history of New York. (*see* American historical magazine and literary record)   973   Am3

Jan. 1836, 1:36–37	Ap. 1836, 1:154–57
Feb. " 1:71–72	May " 1:185–95
Mar. " 1:102–4	June " 1:221–30

Copy of a series of documents bearing date Fort William Henry, 1639–50.

Folsom, George, *anon.* A few particulars concerning the directors general, or governors of New Netherlands. (*see* New York historical society. Collections. 1841. ser. 2, 1:449–56)   974.7 N422 v.6

Portrait of Stuyvesant opposite p. 453.

Hazard, Ebenezer. Documents relating to the Dutch colonial history, 1646–56. (*see* New York historical society. Collections. 1811. 1:189–303)   974.7 N422

From his *Historical collections,* v. 2.

——— Historical collections consisting of state papers and other authentic documents, intended as material for an history of the United States of America. 2v. Phil. 1792–94.   N. Y. state lib.

For journal kept by the commissioners, Cornelis Van Ruyven, Burgomaster Van Cortlandt and Mr John Lawrence, citizen and inhabitant of the city of New Amsterdam on their voyage to Hartford in 1663, see 2:623–33.

List of patents issued by the Dutch government from 1630 to 1664 rendered as complete as the books of patents and town records now admit. (*see* O'Callaghan, E. B. History of New Netherland. 1846–48. 2:581–93)   974.7 Oc11

Melyn, Cornelis, *anon.* Breeden raedt aende vereenighde Nederlandsche provintien, gemaeckt uyt ware memorien door I. A. G. W. C. 45p.   Antwerpen 1649.   N. Y. pub. lib.

First book printed treating of New Netherlands. Extracts in English in Muller, p. 38–46. Full account in Asher, p. 183–200.

——— Broad advice to the United Netherland provinces translated from the Dutch by H: C. Murphy. (*see* New York historical society. Collections. 1857. ser. 2, 3:237–84.   974.7 N422 v.8

Translation of *Breeden raedt.*

Melyn, Cornelis, *anon.* Broad advice to the United Netherland General provinces made and arranged from divers true and trusty memories Dutch eq by I. A. G. W. C. Antwerp 1649.   (*see* Donck, Adriaen van der, *anon.*   Vertoogh van Nieu Nederland; and, Breeden raedt. 1854.   p. 125–90)·   974.7 qD71

—————— Extracts from a work called Breeden raedt aen de vereenighde nederlandsche provintien, printed in Antwerp in 1649; translated from the Dutch original by Mr C.   (*see* N. Y. (state)- State, Secretary of.   Documentary history of the state of New York)

1849–51.   4:99–112.   974.7 N424
1850–51.   4:63–71.   974.7 qN423

—————— Extracts from a work called Breeden raedt aen de vereenighde nederlandsche provintien; printed in Antwerp 1649, translated from the Dutch original by Mr C.   14p.   Amst. 1850. 974.7 M49

Stilwell, B: M. Early memoirs of the Stilwell family, comprising the life and times of Nicholas Stilwell and incidentally a sketch of the history of Manhattan Island and its vicinity under the Dutch. 289p.   N. Y. 1878.   929.2 St58

Tienhoven, Cornelis van. Brief statement or answer to some of the points contained in the written remonstrance laid by Adriaen van der Donck cum sociis before the states general.   (*see* Donck, Adriaen van der.   Remonstrance of New Netherland.   1856. p. 53–65)   974.7 qD711

Valentine, D: T: Indian wars in and about New Amsterdam.   (*see* N. Y. (city)—Common council.   Manual.   1863.   22:533–58)

352.0747 N4k

Vries, D. P. de. Extracts from the voyages of David Pieterzen de Vries; translated from a Dutch manuscript by G. Troost.   (*see* New York historical society.   Collections.   1841.   ser. 2, 1:243–80)   974.7 N422 v.6

—————— Korte historiael ende journaels aenteyckeninge van verscheyden voyagiens in de vier deelen des wereldts-ronde als Europa, Africa, Asia ende Amerika gedaen.   190p.   Hoorn 1655.   V910 V96 **Asher, p. 201-2, no. 336.**

—————— Korte historiael ende journaels aenteyckeninge van verscheyden voyagiens inde vier deelen des wereldts-ronde, als Europa, Africa, Asia, ende Amerika gedaen.   Hoorn 1688. **Muller, p. 47.**

Vries, D. P. de. Voyages from Holland to America, A. D. 1632 to 1644; translated from the Dutch by H: C. Murphy.   199p. N. Y. 1853.   917.3   qV96

Translation of the part of the foregoing work relating to New Netherland. Extracts from the voyages are printed in collections of the New York his-historical society. 1841. ser. 2, 1:243-80, 974.7 N422 v.6.

————— Voyages from Holland to America, A. D. 1632-1644; translated by H: C. Murphy. (*see* New York historical society. Collections. 1857. ser. 2, 3:1-136)   974.7   N422 v.8

West Indische compagnie. Articulen met appobatie vande staten generael provisioneeljie beraemt by bewinthebberen van de compagnie. Hier zijn achter by gedruckt de vryheden van Nieu-Nederlant.   Amsterdam 1631.
Grolier club, p. 85, no. 255.

————— Freedoms and exemptions granted by the board of the 19 of the incorporated West India company to all those who will plant colonies in New Netherland. Amst. 1630. (*see* N. Y. (state)—Legislature. Documents relative to the colonial history of the state of New York. 1853-87. 2:551-57)   R974.7   qN421

Wilson, J. G. Peter Minuit and Walter Van Twiller, 1626-37. (*see his* Memorial history of the city of New York. 1892-93. 1:152-94)   974.71   qW69
Also in *National magazine*, Feb. 1892, 15:337-70,   973   M271.

Minuit 1626-32

Correspondence between the colonies of New Netherlands and New Plymouth, 1627, from the letter book of William Bradford. (*see* New York historical society. Collections. 1841. ser. 2, 1:355-68)
974.7   N422 v.6

Delaware—General assembly. Memorial services in honor of Peter Minuit, 1st governor of New Netherlands, 1626-1632, and of New Sweden 1638, held Tuesday, Ap. 23, 1895, in the court house, Dover Del. under the auspices of the general assembly.   43p. Dover 1895.   923.27   M66

Gorges, Ferdinando. Letter to Capt. Mason about an expedition on the Dutch, Ap. 6, 1632. (*see* O'Callaghan, E. B. History of New Netherland. 1846-48. 1:416-17)   974.7   Oc11
From London documents, v. 1.

Kapp, Friedrich. Peter Minnewit aus Wesel am Rhein,   (*see* Kapp,
Friedrich.   Geschichte der Deutschen im staate New York.   1869.
p. 11–33)   325.243 K14

Mason, John. Letter relative to the Dutch in New Netherland, Ap. 2,
1632. (*see* O'Callaghan, E. B.   History of New Netherland.
1846–48.   1 : 415–16)   974.7 Oc11
From London documents, v. 1.

Mickley, J. J. Some account of William Usselinx and Peter Minuit.
27p.   Wilmington Del. 1881.   (Delaware historical society.
Papers. v. 3)   975.1 D37
Minuit, p. 22–27.

Moore, J. B. Notes for a memoir of Peter Minuit, one of the early
directors of New Netherland. (*see* New York historical society.
Proceedings. 1849. p. 73–82)   974.7 N421

Sardemann, J. E. Peter Minuit, 1st governor of New Netherlands;
letter to Friedrich Kapp. (*see* Historical magazine, Ap. 1868, ser.
2, 3 : 205–9)   973 H62 v.13

West Indische compagnie. Charter of liberties and exemptions of
1629 ; privileges and exemptions for the patroons, masters or particular persons who shall settle any colony or bring cattle therein, in
New Netherland, considered for the service of the General West
India company in New Netherland and for the advantage of the
patroons, masters and particular persons. (*see* Yates, J: V. N. &
Moulton, J. W.   History of the state of New York.   1824–26.   v. 1,
pt 2, p. 389–98)   974.7 Y2
Translated 1762 by Abraham Lott jr.

——— Charter of liberties and exemptions of 1629 ; privileges and
exemptions for the patroons, masters and private individuals who
shall settle any colony or bring cattle therein, in New Netherlands,
considered for the service of the General West India company in
New Netherlands and for the advantage of the patroons, masters
and private individuals. (*see* New York historical society. Collections. 1841. ser. 2, 1 : 370–77)   974.7 N422 v.6

——— Vryheden by de vergaderinghe van de negenthiene van de
geoctroyeerde West-Indische compagnie vergunt aen allen den
ghenen, die eenighe colonien in Nieuw Nederlandt sullen planten.
16p.   Amst. 1630.   N. Y. pub. lib.
Asher, p. 181–82, no. 331.

General his-
tory
Van Twiller

West Indische compagnie. Articulen met approbatie ven de Ho: mog: heeren staten generael der Vereenichde Nederlanden provisioneelijc beraemt by bewinthebberen van de generale geoctroyeerde West-Indische compagnie hier zijn achter by ghedruckt de Vryheden van Nieu-Nederlant. 24p. Amst. 1631. N. Y. pub. lib.
Asher, p. 182, no. 332.

Wilson, J. G. Peter Minuit and Walter Van Twiller, 1626–37. (*see* Wilson, J. G. *ed.* Memorial history of the city of New York. 1892–93. 1 : 153–94) 974.71 qW69

Van Twiller 1633-37

Curler, Arent van. Account of the quarrel between himself and Van der Donck. (*see* O'Callaghan, E. B. History of New Netherland. 1846–48. 1 : 469–70) 974.7 Oc11

Frey, S. L. Notes on Arendt Van Corlaer's journal of 1634. (*see* Oneida historical society. Transactions. 1898. no. 8, p. 42–48) 974.762 On2

Griffis, W: E. Arendt van Curler, 1st superintendent of Rensselaerwyck, founder of Schenectady and of the Dutch policy of peace with the Iriquois. (*see* Albany institute. Transactions. 1887. 11 : 169–80) N. Y. state lib.

———— ————— 12p. Alb. 1884.
Griffin, p. 1000.

Wilson, J. G. Arent van Curler and his journal of 1634–35. (*see* American historical association. Annual report. 1896. 7 : 79–101) 973 Am33

———— Peter Minuit and Walter Van Twiller, 1626–37 (*see* Wilson, J. G. *ed.* Memorial history of the city of New York. 1892–93. 1 : 153–94) 974.71 qW69

Kieft 1637-47

C, V. W. Trou-hertighe onderrichtinge aen alle hooft participanten en lief-hebbers vande ge-octroyeerde West-Indische compagnie, nopende het open stellen vanden handel op de cust van Africa mitsgaders de Marignian, Nieu Nederlant ende West-Indien. n. p. 1643.
Asher, p. 182-83, no. 333.

Gerard, J. W. Administration of William Kieft, 1638–47. (*see* Wilson, J. G. *ed.* Memorial history of the city of New York. 1892–93. 1 : 195–242) 974.71 qW69
Also in *National magazine*, Mar. 1892, 15 : 447-77, 973 M271.

Journal of New Netherland 1647; written in the years 1641–46. (*see* General h
   N. Y. (state)–State, Secretary of. Documentary history of the state Kieft
   of New York) 1849–51.   4 : 1–17.   974.7   N424
                  1850–51.   4 : 1–11.   974.7   qN423

Journal of New Netherland written in the years 1641–46. (*see* N. Y.
   (state)-Legislature. Documents relative to the colonial history of
   the state of New York. 1853–87. 1 : 179–88)   R974.7   qN421

Redfield, A. A. A case of laesea majestatis in New Amsterdam in
   1647. (*see* New York state bar association. Proceedings. 1899.
   22 : 68–81)   N. Y. state law lib.
   Relates to the prosecution and conviction of Cornelis Melyn and Jochem
   Pietersen Kuyter.

Report and advice on the condition of New Netherland, drawn up from
   documents and papers placed by commission of the assembly, dated
   Dec. 15, 1644, in the hands of the general chamber of accounts.
   (*see* O'Callaghan, E. B. History of New Netherland. 1846–48.
   1 : 418–24)   974 7   Oc11

West India company. Commissions of Vice-director Dinclage and
   H. van Dyck, schout-fiscaal of New Netherland; and, Instructions
   for Hendrick van Dyck, fiscaal of the general privileged West India
   company in New Netherland. (*see* O'Callaghan, E. B. History of
   New Netherland. 1846–48. 2 : 561–64)   974.7   Oc11
   Dated 1645.

——— Instructions of the commissioners of the general privileged West
   India company to the director and council of New Netherland.
   (*see* O'Callaghan, E. B. History of New Netherland. 1846–48.
   2 : 559–60)   974.7   Oc11
   Dated 1645.

Stuyvesant 1647-64

For conquest by the English in 1664, see Nicolls p. 344

Abbott, J: S. C. Peter Stuyvesant, the last Dutch governor of New
   Amsterdam. 362p. N. Y. 1873. (Abbott, J: S. C. American pioneers and patriots)   974.7   Ab2

Aitzema, Leo de. Extracts from Aitzema's "History of the United
   provinces," relating to New Netherland. (*see* New York historical
   society. Collections. 1849. ser. 2, 2 : 374–80) 974.7 N422 v.7

Amsterdam-Burgermeesteren. Conditien die door de heeren burgermeesteren der stadt Amsteredam volgens 't gemaeckte accoordt
met de West-Indische compagnie ende d'approbatie van hare Hog.
mog. de heeren staten generael der Vereenighde Nederlanden daer
op gevolght, gepresenteert werden aen alle gene, die als coloniers na Nieuw-Nederlant willen vertrecken.   14p.   Amst.
1656.   N. Y. pub. lib.

Atkins, T. A. Indian wars and the uprising of 1655; Yonkers depopulated : a paper read before the Yonkers historical and library association, Mar. 18, 1892.   14p.   Yonkers 1892.

Augustine Heerman. (*see* New York genealogical and biographical
record, Jan. 1891, 22 : 1–3)   929.1   qN421
A prominent opponent of Gov. Stuyvesant.

Beverningk, Hieronymus van *& others.* Verbael gehouden door
de heeren H. van Beverningk, W. Nieuport, J. van de Perre en A.
P. Jongestal als gedeputeerden en extraordinaris ambassadeurs van
de heeren staeten generael der Vereenigde Nederlanden aen de
republyk van Engelandt waer in omstandighlyck gevonden werdt
de vredehandelinge met gemelde republyk onder het protectoraet
van Cromwell.   716p.   's Gravenhage 1725.   942,964   B46
Asher, p. 201, no. 335.

The *Verbael* treats on the negotiations of Dutch ambassadors with the
English republic in 1651 and 1652 and contains also the speeches and reports
on that question.

Bogaert, Johannes. Two original letters relating to the expedition
of Gov. Stuyvesant against Fort Casimir on the Delaware. (*see*
Historical magazine, Sep. 1858, 2 : 257–59)   973   H62

Brief and true narrative of the hostile conduct of the barbarous natives
towards the Dutch nation ; translated by E. B. O'Callaghan.
48p.   Alb. 1863.   974.7   B76
The original Dutch manuscript (a petition dated Oct. 31, 1655) is contained
in *Colonial manuscripts,* v. 6, in New York state library.

Cist, L: J. Memorials of Gov. Stuyvesant. (*see* Historical magazine,
July, 1864, 8 : 228–30)   973   H62

Dyck, Hendrik van. Defence of Hendrik van Dyck, fiscal in New
Netherland, dated Dec. 18, 1652. (*see* N. Y. (state)—Legislature.
Documents relative to the colonial history of the state of New
York. 1853-87. 1 : 489–518)   R974.7   qN421

Fernow, Berthold. Peter Stuyvesant, the last of the Dutch directors, General t tory
1647–64. (*see* Wilson, J. G. *ed.* Memorial history of the city of Stuyvesan
New York. 1892–93. 1:243–306)   974.71 qW69
With portrait. Also in *National magazine*, Ap. 1892, 15:571–602, 973 M271.

Journal kept by the commissioners Cornelius Van Ruyven, Burgomaster Van Cortlandt, and Mr John Lawrence, citizen and inhabitants of New Amsterdam, on their voyage to Hertford, 1663.
(*see* Blue laws of New Haven colony comp. by an antiquarian.
1838.   p. 245–60)   N. Y. state lib.
Translated from the Dutch. Said to be the 1st diplomatic embassy in this
country. Also printed in Hazard. *Historical collections.* 1792–94. 2:623–33.

Kreiger, Martin. Journal of the 2d Esopus war; with an account of
the massacre at Wildwyck, now Kingston, and the names of those
killed, wounded and taken prisoners by the Indians on that occasion,
1663. (*see* N. Y. (state)—State, Secretary of.   Documentary history of the state of New York) 1849–51. 4:37–98. 974.7   N424
1850–51. 4:27–62. 974.7   qN423

Moore, C: B. Biographical sketch of Capt. Bryan Newton, the military officer of Peter Stuyvesant.   (*see* New York genealogical and
biographical record, July 1876, 7:97–110)   929.1   N421

Netherlands–States general.   Gov. Stuyvesant's   commission.
1646. (*see* Historical magazine, Ap. 1859, 3:116)   973   H62

———— Order for the West India company concerning the division of
boundaries in New Netherland, dated the 23d Jan. 1664; and,
Letter to the villages situated in New Netherland. (*see* O'Callaghan, E. B. History of New Netherland. 1846–48. 2:579–80)
974.7   Oc11

Ordinances, etc. of the director-general and the council of New Netherlands. (*see* N. Y. (city)—Common council.   Manual.   1861.
20:669–93)   352.0747   N4k

Original document—Letter of the board of nine men, accrediting
delegates to Holland, 1649. (*see* National magazine, Oct. 1892,
16:692–95)   973   M271

Parton, James. Peter Stuyvesant. (*see* Parton, James. Colonial
pioneers. 1890. p.28–34)   E973.2   H62

Second part of the Amboyna tragedy; or, A faithful account of a bloody, treacherous and cruel plot of the Dutch in America, purporting the total ruin and murder of all the English colonists in New England, 1653. (*see* O'Callaghan, E. B. History of New Netherland. 1846-48. 2:571-72)   974.7 Oc11

Stuyvesant, *Mrs* **Judith.** Will, 1678-79; translated. (*see* Old New York, Nov. 1889, 1:254-60)   974.71 qOl1

Stuyvesant, *Gov.* **Peter.** Answer of the Hon. Peter Stuyvesant, late director-general of New Netherland to the observations of the West India company on his Report on the surrender of that country to the English. n. p. 1866. (*see* N. Y. (state)—Legislature. Documents relative to the colonial history of the state of New York. 1853-87. 2:427-47)   R974.7 qN421

——— Gov. Stuyvesant's journey to Esopus 1658; verbal and written report concerning the occurrences and affairs at the Esopus. (*see* Magazine of American history, Sep. 1878, 2:540-48)   973 M27

——— Letters to Gov. John Winthrop. (*see* Massachusetts historical society. Collections. 1863. ser. 4, 6:533-35)   974.4 M38 v.36

——— Report of Hon. Peter Stuyvesant, late director-general of New Netherland, on the causes which led to the surrender of that country to the English. n. p. 1665. (*see* N. Y. (state)—Legislature. Documents relative to the colonial history of the state of New York. 1853-87. 2:363-70)   R974.7 N421

Tienhoven, Cornelis van. Information relative to taking up land in New Netherland, in the form of colonies or private boweries. 1650. (*see* N. Y. (state)—State, Secretary of. Documentary history of the state of New York) 1849-51. 4:25-36.   974.7 N424
                              1850-51. 4:19-26.   974.7 qN423

Tuckerman, Bayard. Peter Stuyvesant, director general for the West India company in New Netherland. 193p. N. Y. 1893. (Makers of America)   Cap. 923.27 St9

West Indische compagnie. Naeder klagh-vertoogh aende Ho: Mo: heeren staten generael, wegens de bewinthebberen vande generale geoctroyeerde West-Indische compagnie ter sake vande onwettelijke, ende grouwelijcke proceduren der Engelsche in Nieu Nederlant, met versoeck van hulp, ende assistentie vande macht van 'tlant, tegens de selve. 8p. n. p. 1664.   N. Y. pub. lib.
Translation of part relating to New Netherland in Asher, p. 210-13.

West Indische compagnie. Remonstrantie van de bewinthebberen der Nederlantsche West Indische compagnie aende d'heeren staten generael over verscheyde specien van tyrannye ende gewelt door de Engelsche in Nieuw-Nederlant aende onderdanen van haer Hoogh Mog. verrecht, en hoe sy reparatie ende justitie versoecken. 1663.

Asber, p. 208-10, no. 310.

——— Reply of the West India company to the Answer of the Hon. Peter Stuyvesant, late director-general of New Netherland, with appendices. n. p. 1666. (*see* N. Y. (state)—Legislature. Documents relative to the colonial history of the state of New York. 1853-87. 2 : 489-510)   R974.7 qN421

English period, conquest to revolution, 1664-1776

Bancroft, George. History of the United States from the discovery of the American continent. Ed. 1-10. 10v. Bost. 1838-74.   N. Y. state lib.

New York as an English colony, 2:320-25, 405-26; 3:50-65; 4:24-55, 144-48.

——— History of the United States of America from the discovery of the continent; the author's last revision. 6v. N. Y. 1890-91, °58-84.   973 B221

New York as an English colony, 1:518-27; 2:34-46, 253-54, 339, 399-401.

Bryant, W: C. & Gay, S. H. Popular history of the United States. 5v. N. Y. 1876-96.   973 qB84

New York as an English colony, 2:319-51; 3:222-53.

Douglass, William. Summary, historical and political of the first planting, progressive improvements and present state of the British settlements in North America. 2v. Bost. 1755. N. Y. state lib.

"Concerning the province of New York," 2 : 220-66.

English colonial governors. (*see* Howell, G: R. & Tenney, Jonathan. Bicentennial history of Albany. 1886. p. 379-82) 974.742 qH83

Gives name, date of service, rank and character.

Fernow, Berthold. The middle colonies. (*see* Winsor, Justin, *ed.* Narrative and critical history of America. °1884-89. 5 : 189-258)   973 qW73

1689-1769.

Hildreth, Richard. History of the United States of America from the discovery of the continent to the organization of government under the federal constitution. 3v. N. Y. 1849. N. Y. state lib.
New York as an English colony, 1: 445-47; 2: 44-57, 76-77, 87, 116, 130, 138-40, 182-92, 200-4, 226, 246-49, 263-66, 315-18, 357-61, 391-94, 408.

Hulsemann, J; G; Geschichte der democratie in den Vereinigten Staaten von Nord America. 388p. Göttingen 1823. N. Y. state lib.
New York as an English colony, p. 53-56, 66-80.

Johnson, Rossiter. A history of the French war, ending in the conquest of Canada, with a preliminary account of the early attempts at colonization and struggles for the possession of the continent. 381p. N. Y. ᶜ1882. (Minor wars of the United States) N. Y. state lib.

Kapp, Friedrich. Die land und seereise im vorigen jahrhundert. (*see his* Geschichte der Deutschen im staate New York. 1869. p. 280-307) 325.243 K14

Levermore, C: A. The whigs of colonial New York. (*see* American historical review, Jan. 1896, 1: 238-50) 973 qAm35

Marshall, O. H. The New York charter, 1664 and 1674. (*see* Magazine of American history, Jan. 1882, 8: 24-30) 973 M27
Largely on boundary troubles.

—— New York charter, 1664 and 1674. (*see his* Historical writings. 1887. p. 321-32) N. Y. state lib.

N. Y. (state)-Historian. Annual report. v. 2-3. Alb. 1897-98.
974.7 N425
v. 2-3 called *Colonial series* v. 1-2; this series has for its purpose the printing of the English volumes of the *New York colonial mss* of which v. 22-24 have been already issued. These two volumes also include all the muster rolls to be found in the same series of manuscripts with a full index of names.

Papers relating to the trade and manufactures of the province of New York, 1705-57. (*see* N. Y. (state)-State, Secretary of. Documentary history of the state of New York)
1849-51. 1: 709-36. 974.7 N424
1850-51. 1: 483-99. 974.7 qN423

Pearson, Jonathan. Indian wars on the border, 1662-1713. (*see his* History of the Schenectady patent. 1883. p. 231-43, 271-89)
974.744 qSch2

Stevens, J: A. English in New York, 1664–1689. (*see* Winsor, Jus- _{Genera} tin, *ed*. Narrative and critical history of America. c1884–89. _{English} 3 : 385–420)   973   qW73

Bibliography, p. 411-20.

Period 1664-74

Blome, Richard. Brittania; or, A geographical description of the kingdoms of England, Scotland and Ireland with the isles and territories thereto belonging.   464p.   Lond. 1673.   914.2 B62

Title page wanting in New York state library copy. New York, p. 327-28.

Denton, Daniel. Brief description of New York, formerly called New Netherlands with the places thereunto adjoyning; likewise a brief relation of the customs of the Indians there.   21p.   Lond. 1670.

V917.47 D451

First account of the province of New York printed in English. Winsor, 3 : 420.

—— Brief description of New York formerly called New Netherlands with the places thereunto adjoining; likewise a brief relation of the customs of the Indians there; a new edition with an introduction and copious historical notes by Gabriel Furman.   79 p.   N. Y. 1845. (Gowans' bibliotheca Américana, 1)   917.47   D43

—— Brief description of New York, formerly called New Netherlands with the places thereunto adjoining, together with the manner of its scituation, fertility of the soyl, healthfulness of the climate and the commodities thence produced; also some directions and advice for such as shall go thither. Lond. 1760. 16p. n. p. 1845. (*in* Pennsylvania historical society, Bulletin. 1848. v. 1)   974.8 P384

Partly reprinted in Stedman. *Library of American literature.* 1880-90. 1 : 419-26, R810.8 qSt3.

Description exacte de tout ce qui s'est passé dans les guerres entre le roy d'Angleterre, le roy de France, les estats des provinces unies du Pays-bas, et l'evesque de Munster, 1664–1667.   241 p. Amst. 1668.   942.066 D45

Ogilby, John. America : being a description of the new world containing the conquest of Mexico and Peru and other provinces with the several European plantations in those parts. 674p. Lond. 1671.   917 fOg4

New Netherland, now called New York, p. 168-82.

Nicolls 1664-68

General his-
tory
Nicolls

Articulen van vrede ende verbondt tusschen Karel de tweede van dien
naem, koningh van Groot Britannien ter eenre; ende de staten
general der Vereenighde Nederlantsche provintien ter andere zijde
geslooten.   24p.   'sGravenhage 1667.   N. Y. pub. lib.
Asber, p. 219, no. 357.

This is the treaty of Breda which established the right of Great Britain
to New Netherland.

Capitulation by the Dutch to the English, 1664. (*see* N. Y. (state)—
Legislature. Laws revised and passed at the 36th session of the
legislature. 1813. 2: apx. 1-2)   · N. Y. state law lib.
Also called *Articles of surrender.*

Also printed in Smith. *History of New York.* 1829. 1: 28; *New York
colonial history.* 2:250; O'Callaghan. *History of New Netherland.* 2:532;
Munsell. *Annals of Albany.* 4:28; and New York state library bulletin;
history 2. p. 95 98.

The Clarendon papers: copied from the original ms in the Bodleian library at Oxford Eng. by G: H. Moore. (*see* New York historical society. Collections. 1870. Publication fund ser. 2:1–
162)   974.7 N42

Downing, *Sir George.* A discourse vindicating his royal master
from the insolencies of a scandalous libel, printed under the title
of "An extract out of the register of the states general of the
United Provinces, upon the memorial of Sir George Downing,
envoy, etc.," whereunto is added a relation of some former and
later proceedings of the Hollanders, by a meaner hand.   171p.
Lond. 1672.   942.066 D75

——— Sommiere aenteyckeninge ende deductie ingestelt by de gedeputeerden van de Ho: Mog: heeren staten general der Vereenighde
Nederlanden.   29p.   'sGravenhage 1665.

Translation of titles and description of this and following work in
Catalogue of library of J: C. Brown. 1882. 2:386, 391, 016.97 qB811.
Asber, p. 215-17, no. 345-52.

This was the first energetic protest of the Dutch government against the
capture of New Netherland by the English.

——— Verdere aenteyckeninge of duplyque op seeckere replyue vanden Heer George Downing, extraordinaris envoyé vanden coningh
van Groot Brittagne, jegens de Remarques vande gedeputeerden
vande Ho: Mo: heeren staten generael der Vereenighde Nederlanden: ingestelt 30 Dec. 1664.   256p.   'sGravenhage 1666.

See notes under immediately preceding entry.

Kort en bondigh verhael van't geene in den oorlogh tusschen den Genern
koningh van Engelant etc. en de H. M. heeren staten der vrije Nicolle
Vereenighde Nederlanden en den bisschop van Munster is voorgevallen beginnende in den jare 1664 en eyndigende met het sluiten
van de vrede tot Breda in 't jaer 1667. 255p. Amst.
1667. V949,204 K84
Asher, p. 217, no. 353.
A French edition was printed at Amsterdam in 1688: now very rare.

Lawrence, Eugene. Richard Nicolls, the first English governor,
1664-68. (*see* Wilson, J. G. *ed.* Memorial history of the city of
New York. 1892-93. 1: 307-40) 974.71 qW69
Also in *National magazine*, May 1892, 16: 1-27, **973 M271.**

N. Y. (state)—Library. Colonial records: General entries, v. 1,
1664-65, transcribed from manuscripts in the state library.
p. 51-204. Alb. 1899. N. Y. state lib.
Also in 81st annual report of New York state library. 1899. **027.5747 N42.**

New York historical society. Commemoration of the conquest of
New Netherland on its 200th anniversary. 87p. N. Y. 1864.
N. Y. state lib.
Contents: Oration on the conquest of New Netherland, J: R. Brodhead,
p. 5-58.
Translation of the 1st New Netherland charter, granted 1614,
p. 59-60.
Translation of the commission of Stuyvesant, p. 62-63.
Copy of the duke of York's commission to Richard Nichols,
p. 63-64.
Official documents relating to the surrender of New Netherland,
1664, p. 64-69.
Translation of a letter of Sec. Van Ruyven to Dutch villages on
Long Island announcing the surrender, p. 69.
Translation of a letter from officials of New Amsterdam to the
West India company, p. 70-71.
Translation of a letter from Rev. Samuel Drisius to the classis of
Amsterdam, dated 15 Sep. 1664, p. 72-73.

Nichols, *Gov.* **Richard.** Gov. Nichols' answer to the several queries
relating to the planters in the territories of the duke of York in
America. (*see* N. Y. (state)—State, Secretary of. Documentary
history of the state of New York) 1849-51. 1: 87-88. 974.7 N424
1850-51. 1: 59. 974.7 qN423
Made about 1669.

Seizure of New Netherland by the English. (*see* Holland society of New York. Yearbook. 1899. p. 69–77)   974.7 qH71

Extracts from Mrs Lamb's *History of the city of New York*; and, Brodhead's *History of the state of New York*.

Treaty between Col. Richard Nicolls, governor of New York and the Esopus Indians, 1665. (*see* Ulster county historical society. Collections. 1860. 1 : 59–65)   974.734 Ul7

Lovelace 1668–73

Vermilye, A. G. Francis Lovelace and the recapture of New Netherland, 1668–74. (*see* Wilson, J. G. *ed*. Memorial history of the city of New York. 1892–93. 1 : 341–62)   974.71 qW69

Also in *National magazine*, June 1892, 16 : 129–48, 973 M271.

Dutch occupation 1673–74

Dyre, William. Some proposition concerning ye ill consequence of New Yorke being in ye hands of ye Dutch. (*see* Historical magazine, May 1867, ser. 2, 1 : 299–300)   973 H62 v.11

Sharpe, John. Surrender of New York to the Dutch. (*see* Massachusetts historical society. Collections. 1889. ser. 6, 3 : 436–44)   974.4 M38 v.53

Period 1674–1719

Description

Beschryvinge van eenige voorname kusten in Oost en West Indien; als Zueriname, Nieuw-Nederland; Florida, van haar gelegentheyd, aart en gewoonte dier volkeren, hun koophandel, godsdienst en zelzaame voorvallen, door verscheidene liethebbers gedaen.   150p. Leeuwarden 1716.

Asber, p. 27, no. 19.

Blome, Richard. A description of the island of Jamaica, with the other isles and territories in America to which the English are related. 88p. Lond. 1678.   917.29 B62

New York, p. 76–78.

————' The present state of his majesties isles and territories in America with new maps of every place, together with astronomical tables from the year 1686 to 1700. 262p. Lond. 1687.   917.3 B621

New York, p. 201–9.

Blome, Richard. L'Amérique anglaise; ou, Description des isles et ^{General} terres du roi d'Angleterre dans Amérique traduite de l'Anglais. 331p.   Amst. 1688.   917.3   B62
Nouvelle York, p. 256-57.

Burton, R. The English empire in America; or, A view of the dominions of the crown of England in the West Indies with an account of the discovery, situation, product and other excellencies and rarities of these countries. Ed. 5. 191p. Lond. 1711. N.Y. state lib.
New York, p. 90-96.

Dankers, Jasper & Sluyter, Peter. Journal of a voyage to New York and a tour in several of the American colonies in 1679-80; tr. from the original manuscript in Dutch for the Long Island historical society and edited by H: C. Murphy. 440p. Brooklyn 1867. (*in* Long Island historical society. Memoirs. 1867. v. 1)
                                                            974.721 L85

Duyckinck, E. A. A peep into New Netherland 200 years ago. (*see* Putnam's magazine, Ap. 1868. 11 : 479-87)   051   P98
Description of the above journal of Dankers and Sluyter.

Knight, *Mrs* **Sarah** (**Kemble**). Journals of Madam Knight and Rev. Mr Buckingham, from the original mss written in 1704 and 1710. 129p. N. Y. 1825.   917.4   K741
Contents: Private journal kept by Madam Knight on a journey from Boston to New York in the year 1704, p. 3-76.
Diary of the land expedition against Crown Point in the year 1711, kept by Rev. John Buckingham, p. 101-29.

———— Private journal of a journey from Boston to New York in the year 1704. 92p. Alb. 1865.   917.4   K74

Lacroix, A. P. de. Algemeene weereld-beschryving nae de rechte verdeeling der landschappen, plaetsen, zeeën, rivieren, &c. geographisch, politisch, historisch, chronologisch en genealogisch in't fransch beschreeven, in de hoogduitsche tael overgebraght met veel' aenmerkingen en verbeteringen door Hieronymus Dicelius; nu vertaeld nae den tweeden druk met veel' aenmerkenswaerdige byvoegzelen opgehelderd door S. de Vries met landkaarten van N. Sarson. 3v. Amst. 1705.   910 L112
Asher, p. 27-28, no. 20.
This description is remarkable by the fact that it contains the same statement regarding the foundation of New Amsterdam as was made by Stuyvesant in his letter to Nicholls in 1664, viz, that the town was founded in 1623.
New Netherland, 3:338-39.

Lodwick, Charles. New York in 1692; letter from Lodwick to Mr Francis Lodwick and Mr Hooker dated May 20, 1692 read before the Royal society of London; copied from the original in the British museum. (*see* New York historical society, Collections. 1849, ser. 2, 2:241–50)   974.7   N422   v.7

Melton, Edward. Aenmerkenswaardige en zeldzame West Indische zee- en landreizen door de Carabische eylanden, Nieuw-Nederland, Virginien en de Spaanische West-Indien.   96p.   Amst. 1705.

Asher, p. 26–27, no. 18.   Reprint from his *Zee en land reizen;* continuing it from 1682 to the death of the author, who was in New York during the quarrel between England and Holland.

New Netherland, p. 16–46.

——— Edward Meltons zeldzaame en gedenkwaardige zee-en land reizen door Egypten, West-Indien, Perzien, Turkyen, Oost-Indien aangevangen in den jaare 1660 en geëindigd in den jaare 1677. Amst. 1681.   910.4   M49

Asher, p. 24, no. 16.

New Netherland, p. 136–51.

Contents of the part concerning New Netherland, in Muller, p. 49–50.

——— Eduward Meltons zeldzaame en gedenkwaardige zee-en land reizen door Egypten, West Indien, etc. aangevangen in den jaare 1660 en geëindigd in den jaare 1677.   495p.   Amst. 1702.   N. Y. pub. lib.

Asher, p. 24–26, no. 17.

Exact reprint of 1st edition, 1681.

Miller, John. Description of the province and city of New York with plans of the city and several forts as they existed in the year 1695; now first printed from the original manuscript; to which is added a Catalogue of an extensive collection of books relating to America, on sale by the publisher Thomas Rood.   43+115p.   Lond. 1843.   917.47   M611

——— Description of the province and city of New York with plans of the city and several forts as they existed in the year 1695; a new edition with an introduction and copious historical notes by J: G. Shea.   127p.   N. Y. 1862.   (Gowans' bibliotheca Americana 3)   917.47   M61

Partly reprinted in Stedman. *Library of American literature.* 1888–90. 2:209–10, R810.8 qSt3.

Pitman, Henry. A relation of the great sufferings and strange adventures of Henry Pitman, chyrurgion to the late duke of Monmouth, containing an account: 1 Of the occasion of his being engaged in the duke's service; 2 Of his tryal, condemnation and General tory transportation to Barbadoes, etc. How he made his escape in a Andros small open boat with some of his fellow captives, etc. Lond. 1689. Grolier club, p. 89, no. 270.

History

Lamb, *Mrs* **M. J. R. (Nash).** Career and times of Nicholas Bayard, the son of an exiled Huguenot. (*see* Huguenot society of America. Proceedings. 1891. 2 : 27–57) N. Y. state lib.

Morris, J: J. Captain Silvester Salisbury. (*see* Magazine of American history, Mar. 1888, 19 : 233–44) · 973 M27
Came to New York at the time of the English conquest and held important offices.

Van Rensselaer, *Mrs* **Sarah.** Nicholas Bayard and his times. (*see* her Ancestral sketches. 1882. p.63-127) 923.27 qV35

Beginning of constitutional government
1674-88

Papers relating to the restoration of New York to the English, and to the charges against Captain Manning for its previous surrender to the Dutch, 1674, 1675. (*see* N. Y. (state)–State, Secretary of. Documentary history of the state of New York)

1849–51.	3 : 65–100.	974.7	N424
1850–51.	3 : 43–65.	974.7	qN423

Andros 1674-83

Andros, *Gov.* **Edmund.** Answers of Gov. Andros to enquiries about New York, 1678. (*see* N. Y. (state)–State, Secretary of. Documentary history of the state of New York)

1849–51.	1 : 88–92. ·	974.7	N424
1850–51.	1 : 60–62.	974.7	qN423

Charles 2, *king of Great Britain.* Charter of libertys and privileges granted by his royal highness to the inhabitants of New York and its dependencies, 1683. (*see* Munsell, Joel. Annals of Albany)

	1850–59.	4 : 32–39.	974.743 M92
. Ed. 2.	1869–71.	4 : 25–32.	974.743 M921

Ferguson, Henry. Sir Edmund Andros. 32p. n.p. n.d.
923.27 An23

An address delivered before the Westchester county historical society, Oct. 28, 1892.

Moore, J. B. Sir Edmund Andros. (*see* American quarterly register, Feb. 1841, 13 : 273–75)   37c.5   Am35

——Sir Edmund Andros. (*see* Moore, J. B.   Memoirs of American governors. 1846, 1 : 403–22)   923.27   M78
Only v. 1 published : also appeared under title *Lives of the governors of New Plymouth and Massachusetts Bay, 923.27 M781.*

Sir Edmund Andros. (*see* N. Y. (city)—Common council, Manual. 1869. 27 : 768–71)   352.0747   N4k

Stone, W: L. Administration of Sir Edmund Andros, 1674–82. (*see* Wilson, J. G. *ed.* Memorial history of the city of New York. 1892–93. 1 : 363–98)   974.71   qW69
Also in *National magazine*, July 1892, 16:249–74, **973** M271.

Whitmore, W: H. Sir Edmund Andros. (*see* Whitmore, W: H. *ed.* Andros tracts. 1868–74. 1 : pref. 5–49)   974.4   W59

Dongan 1683-88

Benjamin, Marcus. Thomas Dongan and the granting of the New York charter, 1682–88. (*see* Wilson, J. G. *ed.* Memorial history of the city of New York. 1892–93. 1 : 399–452)   974.71   qW69
Also in *National magazine*, Aug. 1892, 16:373–97, **973** M271.

Brodhead, J: R. The duke of York's approval of the New York bill of rights, 1684. (*see* Historical magazine, Aug. 1862, 6 : 233)   973   H62

Clarke, R. H. Hon. Thomas Dongan, governor of New York. (*see* Catholic world, Sep. 1869, 9 : 767–82)   205   C28

Danaher, F. M. Address delivered before the Dongan club of Albany, N. Y. July 22, 1889. 55p. Alb. 1889.   923.27   qL62
Sketch of Gov. Dongan.

Dealey, P. F. The great colonial governor. (*see* Magazine of American history, Feb. 1882. 8 : 106–11)   973   M27
Thomas Dongan.

Dongan, *Gov.* **Thomas.** Gov Dongan's report to the committee of trade on the province of New York, dated 22d Feb. 1687. (*see* N. Y. (state)—State Secretary of. Documentary history of the state of New York) 1849–51. 1 : 145–89.   974.7   N424
1850–51.   1 : 93–118.   974.7   qN423
Also in *Manual of the city of New York.* 1850. 9:456–86, 352.0747 **N4k.**

Moore, C: B. Laws of 1683; old records and old politics. (*see* New
York genealogical and biographical record, Ap. 1887, 18:49-63)

929.1   qN421

Winsor, Justin. Denonville and Dongan. (*see his* Cartier to Frontenac. 1894. p. 326-40)   973.1   W73

King William's war 1688-98

For French and Indian expedition of 1690 and the burning of Schenectady,
see Schenectady county, p. 497.

Beyard, Nicholas & Lodowick, Charles. Journal of the late
actions of the French at Canada. 55p. N. Y. 1868. N. Y. pub. lib.
Reprint of London ed. of 1693.

———— Journal of the late actions of the French at Canada, with the
manner of their being repuls'd by his excellency, Benjamin Fletcher,
their majesties gouvernour of New York, to which is added: 1 An
account of the present state and strength of Canada; 2 The examination of a French prisoner; 3 His excellency, Benjamin Fletcher's
speech to the Indians; 4 An address from the corporation of
Albany. 22p. Lond. 1693.   V974.7   B46

Brodhead, J: R. The government of Sir Edmund Andros over New
England in 1688 and 1689; read before the New York historical
society Dec. 4 1866. 40p. Morrisania N. Y. 1867. N. Y. state lib.
Also in *Historical magazine*, Jan. 1867, ser. 2, 1:1-14, 973   H62 v.11.
New England as used here included all the territory (except Pennsylvania)
between Maryland and Canada.

De Peyster, J. W. Benjamin Fletcher, colonial governor of the
province of New York 30th Aug. 1692 to 13th Ap. 1698; a biographical sketch or address to be read before the Oneida county
historical society. 118p. N. Y.
Address proper, and 112 p. of notes. 30 copies printed.
Griffin, p. 1042.

Ford, W. C. Sketch of Sir Francis Nicholson. (*see* Magazine of
American history, May 1893, 29:499-513)   973   M27

Journall of what passed in the expedition of Coll. Benjamin Fletcher
governor in chiefe of the province of New York, etc. to Albany to
renew the covenant chain with the five canton nation of Indians.
(*see* N. Y. (state)—State, Secretary of. Documentary history of
the state of New York)   1849-51. 1:346-55.   974.7   N424
                             1850-51. 1:220-25.   974.7   qN423

Papers relating to the invasion of New York and burning of Schenectady by the French, 1690. (*see* N. Y. (state)—State, Secretary of.
Documentary history of the state of New York)

1849–51. 1:283–312.   974.7 N424
1850–51. 1:177–95.   974.7 qN423

Contents: Project of the Chevalier de Callieres, governor of Montreal,
Jan. 1689.

Memoir of instructions to Count de Frontenac, June 1689.

Account of the most remarkable occurrences in Canada from
Nov. 1689 to Nov. 1690, by M. de Monseignat.

Receipt of news of burning of Schenectady in Albany.

List of people killed and taken prisoners.

Letters: Jacob Leisler to Maryland; Jacob Leisler to the bishop
of Salisbury; Robert Livingston to Sir Edmond Andros; Jacob
Leisler to the governor of Barbadoes; Mr Van Courtlandt to Sir
Edmond Andros; Mr Livingston to Capt. Nicholson.

The red sea men. (*see* N. Y. (city)—Common council. Manual.
1857. 16:455–79)   352.0747 N4k

Schuyler, John. Journal of Capt. John Schuyler on his expedition to
Canada and Fort La Prairie during the latter part of Aug. 1690; tr.
by S. Alofson, from the original Dutch manuscript. (*see* New
Jersey historical society. Proceedings. 1845–46. 1 : 72–74)

974.9 N421

Shea, J: G. Early New York history from Canadian sources; the
New York expedition of 1690. (*see* Historical magazine, May
1868, ser. 2, 3 : 263–65)   973 H62 v.13

Todd, C: B. Benjamin Fletcher and the rise of piracy, 1692–98. (*see*
Wilson, J. G. *ed.* Memorial history of the city of New York. 1892–
93. 1 : 489–522)   974.71 qW69

Also in *National magazine*, Oct. 1892, 16: 625–51, 973 M271.

Leisler 1689–91

Brooks, E. S. Jacob Leisler in The Begum's daughter. (*see* Critic,
June 7, 1890; 16: 288)   051 qC86

Chandler, P. W. Trial of Jacob Leisler before a special court of oyer and
terminer for high treason, New York, 1691. (*see* Chandler, P. W.
American criminal trials. 1841–44. 1 : 255–66) N. Y. state law lib.

Documents relating to the administration of Jacob Leisler. (*see* New
York historical society. Collections. 1868. Publication fund
ser. 1 : 237–426)   974.7 N42

Hoffman, C: F. Administration of Jacob Leisler, a chapter in Ameri-   General tory
can history. (*see* Spark's library of American biography. 1844. Leisler
13 : 179–238)   920.07 Sp2

Kapp, Friedrich. Jacob Leisler aus Frankfurt am Main. (*see*
Kapp, Friedrich. Geschichte der Deutschen im staate New York.
1869. p.34-57)   325.243 K14

Leisler's grave. (*see* N. Y. (city)—Common council. Manual. 1856.
15 : 439-41)   352.0747 N4k

Letter from a gentleman of the city of New York to another concerning the troubles which happened in that province at the time of the
late happy revolution. 24p. N. Y. 1698. Printed by William
Bradford.   N. Y. pub. lib.

——— (*see* N. Y. (state)—State, Secretary of. Documentary history of
the state of New York) 1849-51. 2 : 423-35.   974.7   N424
                         1850-51. 2 : 243-49.   974.7   qN423
Against Leisler. Only three copies known. Also reprinted in *Collectanea-
adamentea.* v. 23.

Loyalty vindicated; being an answer to a late false, seditious and
scandalous pamphlet entitled A letter from a gentleman, etc. 28p.
Bost. 1698.
Winsor, 5:240. Reprinted in collections of the New York historical society. 1868. Publication fund ser. 1:365-94, 974.7 N42.

Marriage of Jacob Milborne and Mary Leisler. (*see* N. Y. (city)—Common council. Manual. 1869. 27 : 737-48)   352.0747 N4k
Includes sketch of the Leisler troubles.

A modest and important narrative of several grievances, and great
oppressions that the peaceable and most considerable inhabitants of
their majesties province of New York in America, lie under, by the
extravagant and arbitrary proceedings of Jacob Leysler and his
accomplices. n.p. n.d.
Grolier club, no. 9, p. 10; Winsor, 5 : 240.

Myers, T. B. Jacob Leisler. (*see* Historical magazine, Jan. 1872,
ser. 3, 1 : 18-20)   973 H62 v.21

Papers relating to the administration of Lieut. Gov. Leisler, 1689–91.
(*see* N. Y. (state)—State, Secretary of. Documentary history of
the state of New York) 1849-51. 2 : 1-438. 974.7 N424
                         1850-51. 1 : 1-250. 974.7 qN423

Purple, E. R. Genealogical notes relating to Lieut. Gov. Jacob
Leisler and his family connections in New York. 24p. N. Y.
1877.   929.2 qL535

75 copies reprinted, with additions from the *New York genealogical and
biographical record.*

Schuyler, G: W. Jacob Leisler. (*see* Schuyler, G: W. Colonial
New York. 1885. 1 : 337–80)   974.7 Sch6

Seymour, C: C. B. Jacob Leisler. (*see* Seymour, C: C. B. Self-
made men. 1858. p. 23–29)   920.02 Se9

Smith, William. Rule of Jacob Leisler and his fate. (*see* Stedman,
E. C. & Hutchinson, E. M. *comp.* Library of American literature.
1888–90. 2 : 478–84)   R810.8 qSt3
From his *History of the province of New York.*

Vermilye, A. G. Leisler troubles in 1689; an address delivered before
the Oneida historical society. (*see* Old New York, Mar. 1891,
2:369–403)   974.71 qOl1

———— Period of the Leisler troubles, 1688–92. (*see* Wilson, J. G. *ed.*
Memorial history of the city of New York. 1892–93. 1:453–88)
974.71 qW69
Also in *National magazine*, Sep. 1892, 16:505–28, **973 M271.**

The wife of Jacob Leisler. (*see* N. Y. (city)—Common council.
Manual. 1860. 19:594–95)   352.0747 N4k

Queen Anne's war 1698–1719

Colden, Cadwallader. Affairs of New York and New Jersey under
the joint governors. (*see* New Jersey historical society. Proceedings. 1860–64. 9 : 92–94)   974.9 N421
This communication to Zenger's paper is an interesting exposition of the
characteristics of several early governors.

Bellomont 1698–1701

Campbell, W: W. An historical sketch of Robin Hood and Capt.
Kidd. 263p. N. Y. 1853.   398.2 C15
William Kidd, p. 97–263.

De Costa, B: F. Captain Kidd; why he was hung. (*see* Galaxy,
May 1869, 7 : 742)   051 G12

De Peyster, Frederic. Life and administration of Richard, earl of
Bellomont, governor of the provinces of New York, Massachusetts
and New Hampshire from 1697–1701, an address before the New
York historical society at its 75th anniversary 18 Nov. 1879.
59p. N. Y. 1879.   923.27 qB41

Earl, Robert. Piracy in its relation to the colony of New York. (*see* Generatory Herkimer county historical society. Papers for 1898. 1899. Bellomp.32–34) 974.761 H42

—— Piracy in its relation to the colony of New York an address delivered before the Herkimer county historical society May 14, 1898. (*see his* John Jost Herkimer. 1898. p. 5–7) 920 H42

Felt, J. B. Captain Kidd. (*see* New England historical and genealogical register, Jan. 1852, 6 : 77–84) 929.1 N422

Full account of the proceedings in relation to Capt. Kidd in two letters written by a person of quality to a kinsman of the earl of Bellomont in Ireland. 51p. Lond. 1701. 923.9 K53

Journal of the voyage of the sloop Mary from Quebeck, together with an account of her wreck off Montauk Point, L. I. anno 1701 with introduction and notes by E. B. O'Callaghan. 17+50p. Alb. 1866. (*in* O'Callaghan, E. B. New York colonial tracts. 1866–72. v. 1) 974.7 Oc1

Montague, John. Arguments offer'd to the right honourable the lords commissioners for trade and plantation relating to some acts of assembly past at New-York in America. 23p. N. Y. 1701. N. Y. pub. lib.

A memorial on behalf of several land owners and inhabitants of New York protesting against three acts: 1 Committing Ebenezer Williams and Samuel Burt for refusal to render an account of what they had formed the excise for; 2 Act for vacating, breaking and annulling of several extravagant grants of land, etc.; 3 Act for granting £1500 to the earl of Bellomont, £500 to John Nanfan, lieutenant governor.

Murphy, H: C. The piracy of Captain Kidd. (*see* Littell's living age, Jan. 31, 1846, 8 : 201–7) 051 L71

Parsons, C: W. Bellomont and Rasle in 1699. (*see* Magazine of American history, Ap. 1885, 13 : 346–52) 973 M27

Parton, James. Captain Kid. (*see* Parton, James. Colonial pioneers. 1890. p. 45–51) E973.2 H62

The piracy of Captain Kidd. (*see* Hunt's merchants magazine, Jan. 1846, 14 : 39–51) 332 M53

T. A cruise with Kidd. (*see* Belgravia, Oct. 1874, 24 : 473–79) 052 B41

Taking the oath of allegiance, 1699. (*see* Munsell, Joel. Annals of Albany) 1850–59. 3 : 273–80. 974.743 M92
Ed. 2. 1869–71. 3 : 197–201. 974.743 M921

List of those signing in Albany, Schenectady, manor of Rensselaerwyck, Kinderhook, Catskill, etc.

Todd, C: B. Captain William Kidd. (*see* Lippincott's magazine, Ap. 1882, 29 : 380–89)   •   051 L66

Vermilye, A. G. The earl of Bellomont and suppression of piracy, 1698–1791. (*see* Wilson, J. G. *ed.* Memorial history of the city of New York. 1892–93. 2 : 1–49)   974.71 qW69
Also in *National magazine*, Nov. 1892. 17 : 1–34, 973 M271.

Wooley, Charles. A two years journal in New York and part of its territories in America.   90p.   Lond. 1701.   N. Y. pub. lib.

———— A two years journal in New York and part of its territories in America; a new edition with an introduction and copious historical notes by E. B. O'Callaghan.   97p.   N. Y. 1860.   (Gowan's bibliotheca Americana 2)   917.47 W88
Partly reprinted in Stedman. *Library of American literature.* 1888–90. 2 : 48–51, R810.8 qSt3.

Nanfan 1701–2

Account of the commitment, arraignment, tryal and condemnation of Nicholas Bayard, esq. for high treason in endeavoring to subvert the government of the province of New York in America by his signing and procuring others to sign scandalous libels, called petitions or addresses to his late majesty, King William, the parliament of England and the Lord Cornbury, now governour of that province. 31p.   Lond. 1703.   N. Y. pub. lib.

Account of the illegal prosecution of Col. Nicholas Bayard in the province of New York for supposed high treason in the year 170½; collected from several memorials taken by divers persons privately, the commissioners having strictly prohibited the taking of the tryal in open court.   44p.   N. Y. 1702.   N. Y. pub. lib.
Only three copies known.

Case of William Atwood, esq. by the late King William constituted chief justice of the province of New York in America and judge of the admiralty there and in neighboring colonies; with a true account of the government and people of that province, particularly Bayard's faction and the treason for which he and Hutchins stand attainted.   23p.   Lond. 1703.   N. Y. pub. lib.

———— (*see* New York historical society. Collections. 1881. Publication fund ser. 13 : 239–319)   974.7 N42

Chandler, P. W. Trial of Nicholas Bayard before a special court of oyer and terminer for high treason, New York 1702.   (*see* Chandler, P. W.   American criminal trials.   1841–44 1 : 267–94)
N. Y. state law lib.

Deed to King George the first reciting the surrender by the five General: nations of their beaver hunting country. (*see* N. Y. (state)–State, Lovelace Secretary of.   Documentary history of the state of New York)

1849–51.   1 : 773–74.   974.7   N424

1850–51.   1 : 525.   974 7   qN423

Dated July 19, 1701.

Trial of Colonel Nicholas Bayard, in the province of New York for high treason, 1702. (*see* Howell, T. B. *comp.* Complete collection of state trials. 1809–16. v. 14, col. 471–516)   N. Y. state law lib. v. 1-10 of this work known as *Cobbett's complete collection of state trials.*

Cornbury 1702–8

For Rev. Francis Makemie's imprisonment, 1707, see New York city, Religious history, p. 433.

Brodhead, J: R.   Impeachment of Lord Cornbury as a forger. (*see* Historical magazine, Nov. 1863, 7 : 329–31)   973   H62 Relates to the Makemie affair.

—— Lord Cornbury. (*see* Historical magazine, Feb. 1868, ser. 2, 3 : 71–72)   973   H63 v. 13   .

Clarke, George.   Voyage to America, with introduction and notes by E. B. O'Callaghan. 81+126p. N. Y. 1867. (*in* O'Callaghan, E. B. New York colonial tracts. 1866–72. v. 2)   974.7   Oc1 · Secretary of the province 1703–43 : biographic, including will and genealogy.

Lord Cornbury. (*see* N. Y. (city)—Common council. Manual. 1869.   27 : 763–64)   352.0747   N4k

Sharp, John.   Sermon preached at Trinity church in New York in America Aug. 13, 1706 at the funeral of the Rt Hon. Katherine Lady Cornbury.   16p.   Lond. 1708.   923.27   C811

Stone, W: L.   Administration of Lord Cornbury. (*see* Wilson, J. G. *ed.* Memorial history of the city of New York. 1892–93. 2 : 55–92)   974.71   qW69 Also in *National magazine*, Dec. 1892, 17 : 95–119, 973   M271.

Lovelace 1708–10

Wilson, J. G.   Lord Lovelace and the second Canadian campaign 1708–10. (*see* Wilson, J. G. *ed.* Memorial history of the city of New York. 1892–93.   2 : 93–120)   974.71   qW69 Also in *National magazine*, Jan. 1893, 17 : 189–212, 973   M271; and in annual report of the American historical association. 1892. 3 : 267–97, 973   Am33.

Hunter 1710-19

For Palatine immigration, see Palatines, p. 502; for the negro plot of 1712, see New York city, English period, p. 415.

Buckingham, John. Diary of the land expedition against Crown Point in the year 1711. (*see* Knight, *Mrs* Sarah (Kemble). Journals of Madam Knight and Rev. Mr Buckingham. 1825. p. 101-29)

917.4 K741

Mulford, Samuel. Memorial of several grievances and oppressions of his majesty's subjects in the colony of New York in America. (*see* American historical association. Annual report. 1892. 4:45-52)

973 Am33

Copy of a tract relating to America found in Bodleian library by Prof. J. E. T. Rogers; same as following.

———— Representations against the government of New York; a memorial of several aggrievances, etc. (*see* N. Y. (state)–State, Secretary of. Documentary history of the state of New York)

1849-51. 3:363-83. 974.7 N424
1850-51. 3:220-32. 974.7 qN423

O'Callaghan, E: B. David Jamison, attorney general of the province of New York, 1710. (*see* Magazine of American history, Jan. 1877, 1:21-24)

973 M27

Todd, C: B. Robert Hunter and the settlement of the palatines, 1710-19. (*see* Wilson, J. G. *ed.* Memorial history of the city of New York. 1892-93. 2:121-50)

974.71 qW69

Period 1719-53

Description

Colden, Cadwallader. Observations on the situation, soil, climate, water communications, boundaries, etc. of the province of New York. 1738. (*see* N. Y. (state)—State, Secretary of. Documentary history of the state of New York)

1849-51. 4:169-79. 974.7 N424
1850-51. 4:109-15. 974.7 qN423

Kalm, Pehr. Beschreibung der reise die er nach dem nördlichen Amerika auf den befehl [der schwedischen akademie der wissenschaften] und öffentliche kosten unternommen hat; eine übersetzung. 3v. Göttingen 1754-64.

917.4 K12

Travels in New York, 1748 and 1749, 2:377-409; 3:194-341.

Kalm, Pehr. Travels into North America; containing its natural his- ᴳ
tory and a circumstantial account of its plantations and agriculture ᵗᶜ
in general, with the civil, ecclesiastical and commercial state of the
country tr. into English by J: R. Forster. 3v. Warrington
1770–71. 917.4 K122
Travels in New York 1748 and 1749, 1:235–72; 2:223–352; 3:1–51.

—— —— Ed. 2. 2v. Lond. 1772. 917.4 K121
Travels in New York 1748 and 1749, 1:183–212; 2:71–217.

—— —— (*see* Pinkerton, John, *ed.* General collection of voyages.
1808–14. 13:374–700) 910.8 qP65
From 2d ed. Lond. 1772. Travels in New York 1748 and 1749, p. 452–64,
573–619.

Murray, James. Description of New York, 1737. (*see* Wilson,
J. G. *ed.* Memorial history of the city of New York. 1892–93.
2:202–4) 974.71 qW69

Quinby, Josiah. Short history of a long journey; it being some
account of the life of Josiah Quinby, until he came to enter the 48th
year of his age, with remarks and reflections upon his own past
actions. 61p. N. Y. 1740. N. Y. pub. lib.
A quaker merchant of Westchester county.

Representation of the lords commissioners for trade and plantations
to the king on the state of the British colonies in North America.
42p. n. p. 1727. N. Y. state lib.

State of New York in 1721. (*see* N. Y. (state)—Legislature. Documents relative to the colonial history of the state of New York.
1853–87. 5:600–2) R974.7 qN421

State of the province of New York 1738; 20 queries from the lords of
trade with reports in answer. (*see* N. Y. (state)—State, Secretary
of. Documentary history of the state of New York)
1849–51. 4:163–241. 974.7 N424
1850–51. 4:105–56. 974.7 qN423

History

Delafield, M. M. William Smith, judge of the supreme court of the
province of New York. (*see* Magazine of American history, Ap.
1881, 6:264–82) 973 M27
Includes an account of his family.

O'Callaghan, E. B. Biographical sketch of Francis Harison. (*see* New York genealogical and biographical record, Ap. 1878, 9: 49–51)
929.1   N421

——— John Chambers; one of the justices of the supreme court of the province of New York. (*see* New York genealogical and biographical record, Ap. 1872, 3: 57–62)   929.1   N421

Freedom of the press 1719-36

For troubles between Rev. William Vesey and Alexander Campbell 1732; and for Rev. Louis Rou's disputes with the French church 1726; see New York city, Religious history, p. 433.

Administrations of William Cosby and George Clarke, 1732–1743. (*see* National magazine, May 1893, 18: 1–16)   973   M271

Alexander, James. [Denial that he ever advised or consented to the Hon. George Clarke's taking on him the administration of this government, dated] N. Y. Mar. 24, 173⅚.   1p.   N. Y. 1736.
V974.7   qN428

Bobin, Isaac. Letters of Isaac Bobin, esq. private secretary of Hon. George Clarke, secretary of the province of New York, 1718–30. 196p.   Alb. 1872. (*in* O'Callaghan, E. B. New York colonial tracts. 1866–72. v. 4)   974.7   Oc1

Campbell, Alexander. Maxima libertatis custodia est, ut magna imperia diuturna non sint, et tempora modus imponatur quibus juris imponi non potest.   2p.   N. Y. 1732.   N. Y. pub. lib.
A political handbill on the dissolution of the assembly by the governor maintaining the necessity of frequent elections. Printed by John Peter Zenger.

Clarke, *Gov.* **George.** A proclamation in council [announcing the death of Gov. Cosby; and charging all officers to continue to exercise their offices until his majesty's pleasure shall be known] given this 10th day of Mar. 1735.   1p.   N. Y. 1735.   Printed by W: Bradford.   N. Y. pub. lib.

——— Proclamation [Oct. 1, 1736.]   Broadside 38x31 cm. N. Y. 1736.   V974.7   qN428
Against Rip Van Dam.

De Peyster, Frederic. Memoir of Rip Van Dam. 26p. N. Y. 1865.   923.27   qV28
With portrait.

Dissolution, Robt. *pseud.* Letter from a gentleman in the country to a friend in town [protesting against the long session of the assembly without a dissolution].   1p.   N. Y. 1732.   N. Y. pub. lib.

George 2, *king of Great Britain.* His majesty's royal commission to General hi tory Freedom of the press
William Cosby, for the government of the province of New York.
8p. N. Y. 1736. V974.7 qN428

George Clarke. (*see* N. Y. (city)—Common council. Manual. 1869.
27 : 764–66) 352.0747 N4k

Harison, Francis. To the right worshipful, the mayor, aldermen
and commonalty of the city of New York. 9p. N. Y. 1734.
V974.7 qN428
Defense of Harison against the accusation of Mr Alexander.

Hon. Rip Van Dam. (*see* N. Y. (city)—Common council. Manual.
1865. 24 : 713–25) 352.0747 N4k

Moore, J. B. William Burnett. (*see* American quarterly register, Feb.
1842, 14 : 290–95) 370.5 Am35

Morris, Lewis. Petition to the king in behalf of the inhabitants of
New York for a redress of grievances. (*see* Historical magazine,
Feb. 1867, ser. 2, 1 : 68–79) 973 H62 v.11

Murray, Joseph. Mr Murray's opinion relating to the courts of justice in the colony of New York, delivered to the general assembly
12 June 1734. 44p. N. Y. 1734. N. Y. pub. lib.

Nelson, William. Administration of William Burnet, 1720–28. (*see*
Wilson, J. G. *ed.* Memorial history of the city of New York.
1892–93. 2 : 151–78) 974.71 qW69
Also in *National magazine*, Mar. 1893, 17 : 399–421, 973 M271.

——— Original documents relating to the life and administration of
William Burnet, governor of New York and New Jersey 1720–28,
and of Massachusetts and New Hampshire 1728–29. 217p.
Paterson N. J. 1897. 923.27 B93
Edition of 50 copies.

N. Y. (province)-Chief justice. The opinion and argument of the
chief justice of the province of New York concerning the jurisdiction of the supream court of the said province to determine causes in
a course of equity. Ed. 2 corrected. N. Y. Printed and sold by
J. Peter Zenger. 1733. N. Y. 15p. folio. N. Y. pub. lib.
This opinion on one of the points raised in the quarrel over their fees
between Governor Cosby and Rip Van Dam the acting governor, led to the
summary removal of Lewis Morris from the chief justiceship.

——— ——— Ed. 3. 15p. N. Y. 1733. N. Y. pub. lib.

P, P. Letter from a gentleman in New York to his friend in London.
3p. N. Y. 1733. V974.7 qN428

Publications relating to New York affairs under Governor Cosby. (*see* N. Y. public library. Bulletin. July 1898. 2 : 249–55)

027.4747   qN421

Describes the contents of a folio volume in the Lenox library containing 73 documents relating to Cosby's administration collected by James Alexander, a participator in many of the events in question. 58 of the documents refer to the dispute between Rip Van Dam and the governor. The remaining 15 relate mainly to Rev. Alexander Campbell. In the list are incorporated also titles of a few other works in the Lenox library relating to the same affairs.

Report of the committee of his majesty's council to whom it was referred to examine and make inquiry touching a letter found in the house of Mr Alexander in New York on the 1st day of Feb. 1733¾ in order to make the fullest discovery concerning the author of the same. N. Y. Printed and sold by William Bradford in New York. 1734.   Folio 11p.   V974.7   qN428

Sentiments of a principal freeholder, offered to the consideration of the representatives of the province of New York who are now called to meet and sit the 14th of September, 1736.   4p.   N. Y. 1736.

N. Y. pub. lib.

Smith, William. Mr Smith's opinion humbly offered to the general assembly of the colony of New York 7 June 1734, at their request occasioned by sundry petitions of the inhabitants of the city of New York, Westchester county and Queens county to the said general assembly, praying an establishment of courts of justice within the said colony by act of the legislature.   45p.   N. Y. 1734.

N. Y. pub. lib.

——— **& Alexander, James,** *anon.* Arguments of the council for the defendant in support of a plea to the jurisdiction pleaded to a bill filed in a course of equity at the suit of the attorney general complainant against Rip Van Dam defendant, in the supream court of New York.   73p.   N. Y. 1733.   V974.7   qN428

Contents: Proceedings of Rip Van Dam, esq. in order for obtaining equal justice of his excellency, William Cosby, esq. p. 53–63.

Farther proceedings concerning the case of Rip Van Dam, esqr. at the suit of the attorney general, being for the use of his excellency, Coll. Cosby, governour of this province, in the equity side of the exchequer, p. 65–68.

Heads of articles of complaint, made by Rip Van Dam, esq. on Thursday the 30th of May, 1734, to the committee of grievances appointed by the general assembly for the province of New York reduced to writing by order of the said committee; who also ordered that a copy thereof be served on the chairman and Mr Justice Phillipse, p. 69–71.

To all to whom these presents shall come or may any way concern; Rip Van Dam sendeth greeting, p. 69–73.

Pages are numbered incorrectly. There are two each of pages 69, 70 and 71.

To F.-H. [Francis Harison] esq: I am very much oblig'd to you for your sincere wishes. 4p. N. Y. 1732. Printed by J: P: Zenger.

N. Y. pub. lib.

Letter in answer to Andrew Fletcher's letter to Mr A. C. defending the positions maintained in his former publication; stating that Mr C. (Alexander Campbell) had nothing to do with the paper signed Robt. Dissolution nor any others, except one signed M. B. maintaining the advantages of annual elections.

To Mr A. C. [Alexander Campbell]: While you were pleased to bring your private affairs upon the carpet. 3p. N. Y. 1732.

N. Y. pub. lib.

An open letter dated Aug. 22, 1732, in answer to three papers by him protesting against the present support of his majesty's government in the province, and urging an immediate dissolution of the assembly, after the Oswego bill and the excise bill have been passed. Probably by Francis Harison.

Van Dam, Rip. Copy of a letter dated Ap. 26, 1736 to the several members of that general assembly of New York that stood adjourned to the last Tuesday of Mar. 1736. 4p. N. Y. 1736?

V974.7 qN428

Including action of the general assembly on the letter.

———— Heads of articles of complaint, by Rip Van Dam, esq. against his excellency, Governor William Cosby, governor of New York; to which is prefixed Mr Vandam's letter sent to his excellency with a copy of those articles; as also a letter from some of the gentlemen of the council of New York to the duke of Newcastle in answer to the several articles of complaint; and, A reply to those answers of the gentlemen of the council. 28p. Bost. 1734. V974.7 qN428

Arranged in 3 parallel columns.

Van Pelt, Daniel. The city [New York] under Gov. John Montgomerie, 1728–32. (*see* Wilson, J. G, *ed.* Memorial history of the city of New York. 1892–93. 2 : 179–208) 974.71 qW69

Also in *National magazine*, Ap. 1893, 17 : 493–516, 973 M271.

A vindication of James Alexander, one of his majesty's council for the province of New York and of William Smith, attorney at law, from the matters charged and suggested against them in two pamphlets lately published. The one a paper addressed to the mayor, aldermen and commonalty of the city of New York by the honourable Francis Harison. The other a report of the committee of his majesty's council touching a letter found in the house of Mr Alexander. To which is added a supplement containing a brief account of the case of William Trusdell, against the honourable Francis

Harison,   Printed by John Peter Zenger, and to be sold by him at his house in Broad street, near the upper end of the long bridge in New York. 1733. Folio 20p. N. Y. 1733.   V974.7 qN428

Wheelwright, Timothy, *pseud.* [Letter from brother tradesmen, with his answer,] dated Sep. 12, 1734. 3p. n.p. 1734. V974.7 qN428

Willes, J. Case of Lewis Morris, late chief justice of the province of New York who was removed from the said office by William Cosby, governor of the said province. 8p. n. p. 1735. V974.7 qN428

Word in season.   2p. F.   N. Y. 1736.   V974.7 qN428
    Dated N. Y. Sep. 28, 1736 and printed by Zenger. Concerning the trouble between the rival governors Rip Van Dam and George Clarke.

Zenger

Alexander, James & Smith, William. The complaint to the committee of the *general assembly of the colony of New York*, etc. 19p.   N. Y. 1735?   V974.7 qN428
    Alexander and Smith, counsel for Zenger, having raised a point as to the legality of the court, were immediately disbarred.

Fisher, J. F. Andrew Hamilton, esq. of Pennsylvania. (*see* Pennsylvania magazine of history and biography, Ap. 1892, 16:1–27)
                                                                 974.8 P382
    Zenger's counsel.

Freedom of the press vindicated. (*see* Harper's magazine, July 1878, 57:293–98)   051 H23
    Relates to Zenger.

Kapp, Friedrich. Johann Peter Zenger, der Deutsche drucker; ein pressprozess aus dem jahre 1735. (*see* Kapp, Friedrich. Geschichte der Deutschen im staate New York. 1869. p.171–99) 325.243 K14

Lawrence, Eugene. Freedom of the press in New York in 1733–35. (*see* National magazine, July, 1893, 18:113–27)   973   M271

—— William Cosby and the freedom of the press, 1732–36. (*see* Wilson, J. G. *ed.* Memorial history of the city of New York. 1892–93. 2:209–58)   974.71 qW69

N. Y. (province)—Chief justice. The charge of the Hon. James De Lancey, esq; chief justice of the province of New York, to the gentlemen of the grand jury for the city and county of New York on the 15th day of January, 1733, New York. Printed and sold by William Bradford. N. Y. 1733.   Folio 6p.   V974.7   qN428
    This charge is mainly devoted to the subject of libels, and may be looked upon as the first step in the prosecution of Zenger.

N. Y. (province)—Chief justice. Charge of the Hon. James De _{General hi} Lancey, chief justice to the gentlemen of the grand jury for the _{tory} _{Zenger tria} city and county of New York the 15th of October 1734. 8p. N. Y. 1734. V974.7 qN428

N. Y. (province)—Governor. Proclamation [offering £20 reward for the discovery of the authors of two scandalous songs or ballads lately dispersed in the city of New York.] 1p. N. Y. 1734. N. Y. pub. lib.

———— Proclamation [offering £50 reward for the discovery of the authors of the scandalous, virulent, and seditious reflections contained in no. 7, 47, 48 and 49 of Zenger's N. Y. weekly journal] 6 Nov. 1734. 1p. N. Y. 1734. V974.7 qN428

Some observations on the charge given by the honourable James D. Lancey, esq: chief justice of the province of New York to the grand jury the 15th day of January, 1733. [Colophon] New York. Printed and sold by John Peter Zenger. 18p. N. Y. 1734. V974.7 qN428

Song made upon the election of new magistrates for this city. Also A song made upon the foregoing occasion. 1p. N. Y. 1734. N. Y. pub. lib.

These are the two " virulent, scandalous and seditious" songs brought into question when Zenger was arrested Nov. 17, 1734.

Steiner, B. C. Andrew Hamilton and John Peter Zenger. (*see* Pennsylvania magazine of history and biography, Oct. 1896, 20:405-8) 974.8 P382

Watson, J: F. Presentation of the freedom of the city of New York to Andrew Hamilton of Philadelphia. (*see* Pennsylvania historical society. Collections. 1853. 1:79–80) 974.8 P385

Accounts of Zenger trial

The trial of John Peter Zenger in 1735, was the germ of American freedom—the morning star of that liberty which subsequently revolutionized America. *Gouverneur Morris to Dr John W. Francis*

Chandler, P. W. Trial of John Peter Zenger before the supreme court of New York for two libels on the government, New York 1735. (*see* Chandler, P. W. American criminal trials. 1841–44. 1 : 151–209) N. Y. state law lib.

———— Trial of Zenger in New York, in the year 1735. (*see* N. Y. (city)- Common council. Manual. 1856. 15 : 452–61) 352.0747 N4k

From *Chandler's criminal trials.*

Chandler, P. W. Trial of Zenger in New York in the year 1735.
(*see* Reminiscences of the city of New York and its vicinity.
1855.   p. 202–11)   974.71   R28
From Chandler's criminal trials.

Remarks on Zenger's tryal, taken out of the Barbados gazette's for the
benefit of the students in law and others in North America by Indus
Britannicus.   Printed by Andrew Bradford.   Phil. 1737.
71p.   N. Y. pub. lib.
no. 466–69 of the *Pennsylvania gazette* contain an answer to this written by
James Alexander. N. Y. pub. lib.
This and the following work are attributed by Hildeburn to Jonathan
Blenman, king's attorney in Barbados.

Remarks on Zenger's trial, taken out of the Barbados gazette, for the
benefit of the students in law and others in North America.   53p.
N. Y. 1770.   Reprinted by H. H. Gaine.

Remarks on Zenger's trial by Anglo-Americanus. (*see* Caribbeana.
1741.   2 : 198–221).   N. Y. state lib.

Remarks on Zenger's trial by Indus-Britannicus. (*see* Caribbeana.
1741.   2 : 225–41)   N. Y. state lib.
These two papers were published together as *Remarks on the trial of John
Peter Zenger*. Lond. 1738.

Remarks on the trial of John Peter Zenger, printer of the N. Y.
weekly journal, who was lately try'd and acquitted for printing and
publishing two libels against the government of that province.
Printed for J. Roberts. 27p. Lond. 1738.   N. Y. state law lib.
By two eminent lawyers in one of our colonies. *Preface.* Criticized in
Caribbeana, 2 : 264–73.

Zenger, J: P: Brief narrative of the case and tryal of Zenger, printer
of the New York weekly journal. 42p. N. Y. 1736; printed by J:
P: Zenger. Ed. 1.   V974.7 qN428

———— Tryal of John Peter Zenger of New York, printer, who was lately
try'd and acquitted for printing and publishing a libel against the
government. 32p. Lond. printed for J. Wilford 1738.

——— ——— Ed. 2. 32p. Lond. printed for J. Wilford 1738

——— ——— Ed. 3. 32p.   "   "   1738

——— ——— Ed. 4. 32p.   "   "   1738
Ed. 1–4 in N. Y. pub. lib.; ed. 4 in N. Y. state law lib.

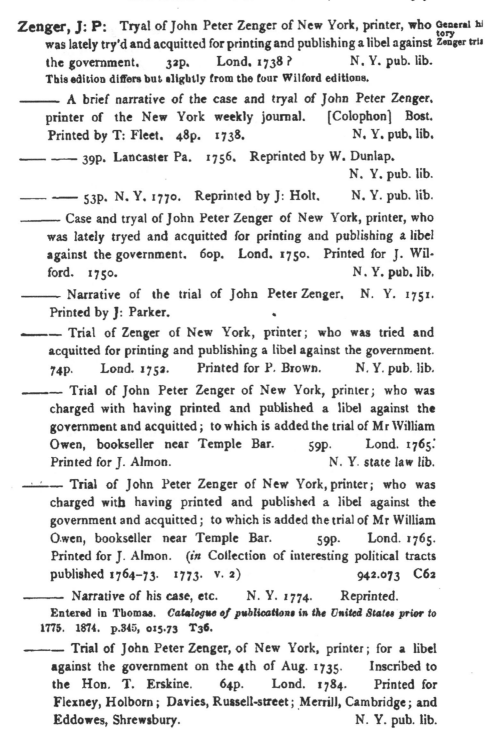

Zenger, J: P: Tryal of John Peter Zenger of New York, printer, who General hi
tory
Zenger tri was lately try'd and acquitted for printing and publishing a libel against the government. 32p. Lond. 1738? N. Y. pub. lib. This edition differs but slightly from the four Wilford editions.

—— A brief narrative of the case and tryal of John Peter Zenger, printer of the New York weekly journal. [Colophon] Bost. Printed by T: Fleet. 48p. 1738. N. Y. pub. lib.

—— —— 39p. Lancaster Pa. 1756. Reprinted by W. Dunlap. N. Y. pub. lib.

—— —— 53p. N. Y. 1770. Reprinted by J: Holt. N. Y. pub. lib.

—— Case and tryal of John Peter Zenger of New York, printer, who was lately tryed and acquitted for printing and publishing a libel against the government. 60p. Lond. 1750. Printed for J. Wilford. 1750. N. Y. pub. lib.

—— Narrative of the trial of John Peter Zenger. N. Y. 1751. Printed by J: Parker. .

—— Trial of Zenger of New York, printer; who was tried and acquitted for printing and publishing a libel against the government. 74p. Lond. 1752. Printed for P. Brown. N. Y. pub. lib.

—— Trial of John Peter Zenger of New York, printer; who was charged with having printed and published a libel against the government and acquitted; to which is added the trial of Mr William Owen, bookseller near Temple Bar. 59p. Lond. 1765. Printed for J. Almon. N. Y. state law lib.

—— Trial of John Peter Zenger of New York, printer; who was charged with having printed and published a libel against the government and acquitted; to which is added the trial of Mr William Owen, bookseller near Temple Bar. 59p. Lond. 1765. Printed for J. Almon. (*in* Collection of interesting political tracts published 1764–73. 1773. v. 2) 942.073 C62

—— Narrative of his case, etc. N. Y. 1774. Reprinted. Entered in Thomas. *Catalogue of publications in the United States prior to 1775.* 1874. p.345, 015.73 T36.

—— Trial of John Peter Zenger, of New York, printer; for a libel against the government on the 4th of Aug. 1735. Inscribed to the Hon. T. Erskine. 64p. Lond. 1784. Printed for Flexney, Holborn; Davies, Russell-street; Merrill, Cambridge; and Eddowes, Shrewsbury. N. Y. pub. lib.

General history
King George's war

Zenger, J: P: The trial of Mr John Peter Zenger, of New York, printer, for printing and publishing a libel against the government at New York, on Aug. 4, 1735; including, Remarks on the trial of John Peter Zenger by two eminent lawyers in one of the colonies. (*see* Howell, T. B. *comp.* Complete collection of state trials. 1809-26. v.17, col. 675–764)　　　N. Y. state law lib.
v.1-10 of this work known as *Cobbett's complete collection of state trials.*

King George's war 1736-53

For the negro plot of 1741, see New York city, English period, p.415.

Gitterman, J: M. George Clinton and his contest with the assembly, 1743–53. (*see* Wilson, J. G. *ed.* Memorial history of the city of New York. 1892–93. 2 : 259–86)　　　974.71　qW69
Also in *National magazine*, Sep. 1893, 18 : 209–30, 973 M271.

A Letter from some of the representatives in the late general assembly of the colony of New York to his excellency, Gov. C . . . . . n, principally in answer to his message of the 13th of October last and his dissolution speech.　30p.　n. p. 1747.　N. Y. state law lib.

Morris, *Gov.* **Lewis.** [Letters of Gov. Morris] to Sir Charles Wager. (*see* New Jersey historical society. Collections. 1852. 4 : 40–46, 60–69)　　　974.9　N422
Includes his opinion on affairs in New York.

Norris, Isaac. Journal of Isaac Norris (afterward speaker of the Pennsylvania assembly) during a trip to Albany in 1745, and an account of a treaty held there in October of that year.　31p. Phil. 1867.　　　923.27　qN79
Commissioner from Pennsylvania to attend the Indian treaty. Edition of 80 copies.

Treaty between his excellency the Hon. George Clinton, governor of the province of New York, and the six united Indian nations depending of the province of New York; held at Albany in August and September 1746.　N. Y. 1746.　　　N. Y. pub. lib.

Valentine, D: T: Extracts from the earliest newspapers of the city. (*see* N. Y. (city)—Common council. Manual. 1862. 21 : 695–737)
352.0747　N4k
New York, 1733–48.

Period 1753-76
Description

American gazetteer, containing a distinct account of all the parts of the new world, the whole intended to exhibit the state of things in that part of the globe and the views and interests of the powers who have possession.   3v.   Lond. 1762.   917 Am3
New York is alphabeted under York, New.

General story, 175

Burnaby, Andrew. Travels through the middle settlements in North America in the years 1759 and 1760, with observations upon the state of the colonies.   Ed.2.   198p.   Lond. 1775.   917.3 B931
New York, p. 104-16.

—— —— (*see* Pinkerton, John, *ed.*   General collection of voyages. 1808-14.   13:701-52)   910.8 qP65
From ed. 3, Lond. 1798.   New York, p. 736-39.

Cluny, Alexander. The American traveller; or, Observations on the present state, culture and commerce of the British colonies in America by an old and experienced trader.   122p.   Lond. 1769.   917.3 qC62
New York, p. 73-76.

Hare, Robert. Memoranda on a tour through a part of North America in company with Mr William Allen.   (*see* Pennsylvania historical society.   Collections.   1853.   1 : 363-76)   974.8 P385
Chiefly, New York, 1774.

Izard, Ralph, *anon.* An account of a journey to Niagara, Montreal and Quebec in 1765; or, " 'Tis 80 years since."   30p. N. Y. 1846.
917.1 I21
From New York city to Albany; thence westward to Niagara.

Lott, Abraham. Journal of a voyage to Albany, etc. made by Abraham Lott, treasurer of the colony of New York 1774.   (*see* Historical magazine, Aug. 1870, ser. 2, 8 : 65-74).   973 H62 v.18

Rogers, Robert. A concise account of North America, containing a description of the several British colonies on that continent.   264p. Lond. 1765.   917.3 R63
Province of New York, p. 59-72.

Taylor, G. Voyage to North America performed by G. Taylor of Sheffield in the years 1768 and 1769.   248p.   Nottingham 1771.   917.3 T21
New York, p. 66-90.

Thompson, Edward. New York in 1756. (*see* Wilson, J. G. *ed.*
Memorial history of the city of New York. 1892-93. 2:314-15)
974.71   qW69

Also in *Old New York*, Feb. 1890, 2:36-38, 974.71 qOl1.

History

Annual register; or, A view of the history, politics and literature for the
year 1758-76.   Lond. 1761-88.   905 An72

v. 1-19, 1758-76 contain accounts of the relations of Great Britain with her
colonies.

Biographical memoir of Cadwallader Colden, M. D. F. R. S.
lieutenant governor of the colony of New York. (*see* Analectic
magazine, Oct. 1814, 4:307-12)   051 An1

Biographical sketch of Cadwallader Colden, formerly lieutenant-
governor of New York. (*see* Family magazine, 1838.   5:334-36)
051 qF21

Burdge, Franklin. Second memorial of Henry Wisner. 38p.
N. Y. 1898.   N. Y. state lib.

Cadwallader Colden. (*see* Historical magazine, Jan. 1865, 9:9-13)
973   H62

The Colden papers. (*see* New York historical society. Collections.
1877-78. Publication fund ser. v.9-10)   974.7 N42
Gov. Colden's official letter book, 1760-1775.

Delafield, M. M. William Smith, the historian, chief justice of New
York and Canada. (*see* Magazine of American history, June 1881,
6:418-39)   973 M27

DeLancey, E: F. Memoir of the Hon. James DeLancey, lieutenant
governor of the province of New York. (*see* N. Y. (state)—State,
Secretary of. Documentary history of the state of New York)

1849-51.   4 : 1035-59.   974.7 N424
1850-51.   4 : 625-40.   974.7 qN423

De Peyster, J: W. Life and misfortunes and the military career of
Brig.-Gen. Sir John Johnson, bart. 168p. N. Y. 1882. 923.57 J62
Sir John Johnson was the son of Sir William Johnson and adhered to the
British cause in the revolution.
Genealogy of the Johnson family, p. 1-10.

Duyckinck, E. A: Philip Schuyler. (*see* Duyckinck, E. A: National
portrait gallery of eminent Americans. c1862. 1:264-71) 920.07 qD95

Grant, *Mrs* **Anne (Macvicar).** Memoirs of an American lady ^{Gener.}_{tory, 1} [Madame Philip Schuyler]; with sketches of manners and scenery in America as they existed previous to the revolution.   2v.   Lond. 1808.   920.7   Sch8

—— —— 2v.   Bost. 1809.   W920.7   Sch82

—— —— 344p.   N. Y. 1809.   N. Y. pub. lib.

—— —— 354p.   N. Y. 1836.

—— —— 295p.   N. Y. 1846.   920.7   Sch83

—— —— with a memoir of Mrs Grant by James Grant Wilson.   377p. Alb. 1876.   920.7   Sch81

Griffis, W : E. Sir William Johnson and the six nations.   227p. N. Y.ᶜ 1891.   (Makers of America)   923.27   J635

Halsey, *Mrs* **C : H.** Sketches of celebrated women; Mrs Catharine Schuyler, wife of General Philip Schuyler.   (*see* Potter's American monthly, Jan. 1876, 6: 29–30)   973   qAm3

Headley, J. T. Major General Schuyler.   (*see* Headley, J. T. Washington and his generals.   1847.   1: 229–59)   923.57   H341

Humphreys, M.. G. Catherine Schuyler.   251p.   N. Y. 1897. (Women of colonial and revolutionary times)   Cap. 920.7   Sch831

Jones, Thomas. History of New York during the revolutionary war, and of the leading events in the other colonies at that period, ed. by E : F. De Lancey.   2v.   N. Y. 1879.   N. Y. state lib. New York, 1752–75, p. 1–54 ; editor's notes, p. 391–437.

Kent, James. Biographical sketch of Gen. Philip Schuyler.   (*see* Munsell, Joel. Annals of Albany.   1850–59.   1:250–57)   974.743   M92

Lossing, B. J : Life and times of Philip Schuyler.   2v.   N. Y. ᶜ1860.   923.57   Sch8

McKnight, Charles. Sir William Johnson, bart. (*see* Lippincott's magazine, June 1879, 23 : 731–40)   051   L66

Manuscripts of Sir William Johnson.   (*see* N. Y. (state) – State, Secretary of.   Documentary history of the state of New York)
1849–51.   2 : 543–1009   974.7   N424
1850–51.   2 : 315–584   974.7   qN423

Nearly all the manuscripts known as the Sir William Johnson papers, including a list of manuscripts missing since they were deposited in secretary of state's office, 1801.

General his-
tory, 1753-76
Montresor, John. Journals of Capt. John Montresor, 1757–78. (*see* New York historical society. Collections. 1881. Publication fund ser. 14: 113–520)   974.7 N42

Parton, James. Sir William Johnson. (*see* Parton, James. Colonial pioneers. 1890. p.35–40)   E973.2 H62

Pratt, D. J. Biographical notice of Peter Wraxall, secretary of Indian affairs for the province of New York and of the first provincial congress held in Albany in 1754.   6p.   n.p. n.d.
Sabin, 15 : 395.

Purple, E. R. Genealogical notes of the Colden family in America. 24p.   N. Y. 1873.   929.2 qC674
With additions from the *New York genealogical and biographical record*, Oct. 1873, 4 : 161-83.

———— Notes, biographical and genealogical, of the Colden family and some of its collateral branches in America. (*see* New York genealogical and biographical record, Oct. 1873, 4 : 161–83) 929.1 N421
Sketch of Cadwallader Colden, p. 161-68.

Shea, J: G. Introduction. (*see* Colden, Cadwallader. History of the five Indian nations. 1866. pref. p. 3–40)   970.3 C673
Biographical sketch of Colden.

Stevens, J: A. jr. Colonial New York; sketches biographical and historical 1768–84.   172p.   N. Y. 1867.   (*in* Colonial records of the New York chamber of commerce)   381 qN42

Stone, W: L. The life and times of Sir William Johnson, bart. 2v.   Alb. 1865.   N. Y. state lib.

Thurmàn, John, jr. Extracts from letterbooks. (*see* Historical magazine, Dec. 1868, ser. 2, 4 : 283–97)   973 H62 v.14
Letters dated at New York, 1760-88.

French and Indian war 1753-65

For campaigns of Ticonderoga and Crown Point, see also Lakes George and Champlain, p. 508.

For campaigns of Oswego and Niagara, see also Central New York, p. 510 and Lake Erie and Niagara, p. 511 respectively.

Alexander, William, *anon.* The conduct of Major Gen. Shirley, late general and commander in chief of his majesty's forces in North America, briefly stated.   130p.   Lond. 1758.   973.2 Sh6
1755-56.

Banyar, Goldsbrow. Diary of Goldsbrow Banyar, deputy secretary ^{Gene} of the province of New York, Aug. 5 to 20, 1757. (*see* Magazine of American history, Jan. 1877, 1:25–33)   973   M27

Clarke, William. Observations on the late and present conduct of the French with regard to their encroachments upon the British colonies in North America together with remarks on the importance of these colonies to Great Britain; to which is added, wrote by another hand Observations concerning the increase of mankind, peopling of countries, etc.   54p.   Bost. 1755.

N. Y. state lib.

Defence of New York against the slanders of New England. (*see* N. Y. (city)—Common council. Manual. 1870. 28:892–97)   352.0747   N4k

Supplement to the *New York mercury* Feb. 23, 1756.

Dunlap, William. Treaty of peace of 1763: Indian hostilities after the peace. (*see his* History of the New Netherlands. 1839–40. 2:apx.69–72)   974.7   D92

Dwight, Timothy. Travels in New England and New York.   4v. New Haven 1821–22.   917.4   D96

Battles near Lake George, 1755–57, 3:361–86.

An impartial account of Lieut. Col. Bradstreet's expedition to Fort Frontenac, to which are added a few reflections on the conduct of that enterprize and the advantages resulting from its success; by a volunteer on the expedition. 6op. Lond. 1759.   N. Y. state lib.

Johnson, *Sir* **William.** Account of conferences held and treaties made between Major General Sir William Johnson, bart. and the chief sachems and warriors of the Indian nations in North America at their meetings on different occasions at Fort Johnson in the county of Albany, in the colony of New York in the years 1755 and 1756; with a letter from the Rev. Mr Hawley to Sir William Johnson, written at the desire of the Delaware Indians and a preface giving a short account of the six nations, some anecdotes of the life of Sir William Johnson, and notes illustrating the whole; also an appendix containing an account of conferences between several quakers in Philadelphia and some of the heads of the six nations in April 1756.   12+77p.   Lond. 1756.   970.4   J63

Journal of a provincial officer in the campaign in northern New York in 1758. (*see* Historical magazine, Aug. 1871, ser. 2, 10: 113–22)   973   H62   v.20

Journals of Sir William Johnson's scouts, 1755–56. (*see* N. Y. (state) — State, Secretary of. Documentary history of the state of New York) 1849–51. 4 : 257–87. 974.7 N424
1850–51. 4 : 167–85. 974.7 qN423

Kennedy, Archibald, *anon.* Serious considerations on the present state of the affairs of the northern colonies. 24p. N. Y. 1754.
973.2 K38 ·

Lamb, *Mrs* **M. J. R. (Nash).** Governor Robert Monckton. (*see* Magazine of American history, June 1887, 17 : 470–73) 973 M27

Mante, Thomas. History of the late war in North America. 542p. Lond. 1772. 971 qM31

Montresor, James. Journals of Col. James Montresor, 1757–59. (*see* New York historical society. Collections. 1881. Publication fund ser. 14 : 11–111) 974.7 N42

Review of the military operations in North America from the commencement of the French hostilities on the frontier of Virginia in 1753 to the surrender of Oswego on the 14th of August 1756; interspersed with various observations, characters and anecdotes, necessary to give light into the conduct of American transactions in general and more especially into the political management of affairs in New York in a letter to a nobleman. 144p. Lond. 1757.
N. Y. state lib.

Review of the military operations in North America from the commencement of the French hostilities on the frontiers of Virginia in 1753 to the surrender of Oswego on the 14th of August 1756; in a letter to a nobleman. (*see* Massachusetts historical society. Collections. 1801. 7 : 67–163) - 974.4 M38
Said to have been written by Gov. Livingston and his friends Messrs W. Smith and Scott, lawyers, New York.

Stark, Caleb. Memoirs and official correspondence of Gen. John Stark, with notices of several other officers of the revolution, also, a biography of Capt. Phinehas Stevens and of Col. Robert Rogers, with an account of his services in America during the " seven year's war ". 495p. Concord N. H. 1860. 923.57 St25

Thompson, Samuel. Diary while in the service in the French · 1758, with notes by W : R. Cutter. 60p. Bost. 1896. 973.2
50 copies printed for private distribution. Thompson partici Abercrombie's expedition against Ticonderoga.

Walker, J. B.   Robert Rogers, the ranger.   (*see* Bay state monthly, Gener tory Prerev ary
Jan. 1885, 2 : 211–25)   974.4   qB34

Wilson, J. G.   Sir Danvers Osborn and Sir Charles Hardy, 1753–61.
(*see* Wilson, J. G. *ed.*   Memorial history of the city of New York.
1892–93.   2 : 287–313)   974.71   qW69

Winslow, *Gen.* **John.**   Gen. John Winslow's letter to the earl of Hali-
fax, relating to his conduct and that of the troops under his command
on the Ticonderoga expedition in 1756   (dated Bost. Dec. 30, 1756).
(*see* Massachusetts historical society.   Collections.   1800.   6 : 34–39)
                                                974.4   M38

Woodhull, Nathaniel.   Journal kept when colonel of the 3d regiment New York provincials, in the expedition to Montreal in 1760.
(*see* Historical magazine, Sep. 1861, 5 : 257–60)   973   H62

Prerevolutionary 1765–76

Almon, John, *ed.*   Collection of interesting, authentic papers relative
to the dispute between Great Britian and America, shewing the
causes and progress of that misunderstanding from 1764 to 1775.
280+202p.   Lond. 1777.   N. Y. state lib.
Known as the Prior documents.
Contents: Letters from Sec. Conway to Lieut. Gov. Colden, p. 43.
          Gov. Moore's letter to Sec. Conway 27 May 1766, p. 94.
              "   "   "   20 June 1766, p. 94.
              "   speech to New York council and assembly 12 June
          1766, p. 95.
          Address of council of New York to Gov. Moore with his reply
          14–16 June 1766, p. 96.
          Address of assembly of New York to Gov. Moore with his reply
          16 June 1766, p. 97.
          Gov. Moore's two messages to the assembly of New York and the
          answers 13–23 June 1766, p. 97.
          Extract from a letter of Lieut. Gov. Colden to Sec. Conway 24
          June 1766, p. 99.
          Extract from a letter of Gen. Gage to Sec. Conway 15 July
          1766, p. 101.
          Extract of a letter from Gen. Gage to the duke of Richmond 25

Extract of a letter from Lieut.-Gov. Colden to the earl of Shelburne, 26 Dec. 1766, p. 124.

Extract of a letter from Gen. Gage to the earl of Shelburne 17 Jan. 1767, p. 124.

Act to furnish barracks in cities of New York and Albany with firewood, etc. 10 July 1766, p. 125.

Extract of a letter from Gen. Gage to the earl of Shelburne 10 Feb. 1767, p. 130.

Extracts from the manuscript journal of the general assembly of New York laid before parliament 10 Nov.-19 Dec. 1766, p. 144.

Gov. Pownall's speech against suspending the government of New York 15 May 1767, p. 162.

Petition of merchants of New York to the house of commons, p. 163.

Authentic account of the proceedings of the congress held at New York in 1765 on the subject of the American stamp act.   37p.   n.p. 1767.   N. Y. state lib.

Colden, Cadwallader. State of the province of New York. (*see* New York historical society. Collections. 1877. Publication fund ser. 10:68-78)   974.7   N42

Dated Dec. 6, 1765.

Conduct of Cadwallader Colden, esq. lieutenant governor of New York relating to the judges' commissions, appeals to the king and the stamp duty.   56p.   N. Y. 1767.   V974.7

———— (*see* New York historical society. Collections. 1877. Publication fund ser. 10:431-67)   974.7   N42

The assembly made every effort to discover the author but in vain. see Sedgwick. *Memoir of William Livingston.* 1833. p.124, 923.27 L761; and, *Analectic magazine,* Oct. 1814, 4:307.

Dawson, H: B. Sons of liberty in New York; a paper read before the New York historical society, May 3, 1859.   118p.   N. Y. 1859.
974.7   D32

Printed for private circulation. Sons of liberty was the name given to the organized opposition to the crown which started about the time of the Zenger trial and flourished specially just preceding the revolution.

Deed executed at Fort Stanwix Nov. 5, 1768, establishing a boundary line between the whites and Indians of the northern colonies. (*see* N. Y. (state) – State, Secretary of. Documentary history of the state of New York)   1849-51.   1:587-91.   974.7   N424
1850-51.   1:377-81.   974.7   qN423

Dix, J: A. John Cruger, mayor of New York, speaker of New York General tory
assembly. (*see* Magazine of American history, Mar. 1877, 1: 172– Prerevol ary
74) 973 M27

Earl, Robert. A historical mistake corrected. (*see* Herkimer county
historical society. Papers 1896. p. 91–93) 974.761 H42
Concerning the first liberty pole in the colony of New York, 1766.

Great Britain—Parliament. The stamp act, 1765. 34p. N. Y.
1895. (American history leaflets colonial and constitutional 21)
973 Am34

Hildeburn, C: S. R. Notes on the stamp act in New York and Virginia.
(*see* Pennsylvania magazine of history and biography, 1878, v.2,
no. 3, p.296–302) 974.8 P382

Lamb, *Mrs* M. J. R. (Nash). Golden age of colonial New York.
(*see* Magazine of American history, July 1890, 24: 1–30) 973 M27
The year 1768.

Lodge, H: C. A short history of the English colonies in America.
Rev. ed. 560p. N. Y. °1881. 973.2 L82
New York, 1765, p. 312–40.

Sedgwick, Theodore. Memoir of the life of William Livingston.
449p. N. Y. 1833. 923.27 L761
Career before the revolution, p. 45–178.
Noticed in *American monthly review*, Sep. 1833, 4 : 177–92.

Stebbins, Calvin. Edmund Burke; his services as agent of the province of New York. (*see* American antiquarian society. Proceedings. 1893–94. new ser. 9: 89–101) 906 Am3 v.16
Burke was chosen agent in 1770.

Stevens, J: A. The part of New York in the stamp act troubles, 1761–
68. (*see* Wilson, J. G. *ed.* Memorial history of the city of New
York. 1892–93. 2: 325–90) 974.71 qW69
Also in *National magazine*, Dec. 1893–Ap. 1894, 19: 113–37, 229–50, 323–46,
973 M271.

—— Second non-importation agreement and the committees of correspondence and observation 1769–75. (*see* Wilson, J. G. *ed.*
Memorial history of the city of New York. 1892–93. 2: 391-444)
974.71 qW69

—— Stamp act in New York. (*see* Magazine of American history,
June 1877, 1: 337–71) 973 M27
Including copies of non-importation agreements of the merchants of New
York and Philadelphia.

Tryon, *Gov.* **William.** Report on the state of the province of New
York. 1774. (*see* N. Y. (state)—State, Secretary of. Documentary
history of the state of New York.) 1849–51. 1 : 737–72. 974.7 N424
1850–51. 1 : 501–23. 974.7 qN423

Van Shaack, H: C. Life of Peter Van Shaack ; embracing selections
from his correspondence and other writings.   490p. N. Y. 1842.
923.47 V362

Special topics

Constitutional history

Assembly. (*see* Civil list and constitutional history of the colony and
state of New York by E. A. Werner. 1891. 35:432–36) 351.2 N42

Bishop, C. F. History of elections in the American colonies. 297p.
N. Y. 1893. (*in* Studies in history, economics and public law,
ed. by the university faculty of political science of Columbia
college. 1893. v.3, no.1)   305 St9

Butler, B: F. Outline of the constitutional history of New York, an
anniversary discourse delivered at the request of the New York
historical society. 75p.   N. Y. 1848.   342.7479 B97

—— —— (*see* New York historical society. Collections. 1849. ser. 2,
2:9–75)   974.7 N422 v.7

Constitutional history of the colony of New York. (*see* Civil list and
constitutional history of the colony and state of New York by E. A.
Werner. 1891. 35:3–116)   351.2 N42
Much of this material is found in the earlier volumes as well.
Contents: New Netherland   Constitution of the colony
Constitutional history   Colonial confederacies
Proprietary governments

The councils. (*see* Civil list and constitutional history of the colony and
state of New York by E. A. Werner. 1891. 35:406–9) 351.2 N42
Includes list of members.

Cumming, R. C. Historical note. (*see* N. Y. (state)—Legislature.
Colonial laws of New York. 1894–96. 1 : pref. 9–21)
N. Y. state law lib.
On the development of representative government in the colony.

Elting, Irving. Dutch village communities on the Hudson river.
68p. Balt. 1886. (*in* Johns Hopkins university studies. 1886. v.4)
305 J62

Fowler, R. L. Constitutional and legal history of New York in the 17th century. (*see* Wilson, J. G. *ed.* Memorial history of the city of New York. 1892–93. 1: 523.69)   974.71   qW69   General history
Constitutional history

——— Constitutional and legal history of New York in the 18th century. (*see* Wilson, J. G. *ed.* Memorial history of the city of New York. 1892–93. 2: 575–630)   974.71   qW69

——— Historical introduction. (*see* N. Y. (colony)—General assembly. Facsimile of the laws and acts of the general assembly for their majesties province of New York printed and sold by William Bradford. 1894. pref. p. 1–104)   N. Y. state law lib.
Legislative history, 1609–94.

Gitterman, J: M. Council of appointment in New York. (*see* Political science quarterly, Mar. 1892, 7: 80–115)   305   P75
Appointing power in the province of New York, p.81–86.

Greene, E. B. The provincial governor in the English colonies of North America. 292p. N. Y. 1898. (Harvard historical studies, v.7)   342.73   G83

Hill, H : W. Development of constitutional law in New York state and the constitutional convention of 1894. (*see* Buffalo historical society. Publications. 1896. 4: 163–201)   974.797   B86

Hutchins, S. C. Introduction to the civil list and constitutional history of the colony and state of New York. 128p. Alb. 1879.   342.7479   H97

N. Y. (colony)—General assembly. Journal of the votes and proceedings of the general assembly of the colony of New York. 2v. N. Y. 1764–66.   N. Y. state law lib.
Contents: v. 1, Ap. 9, 1691–Sep. 27, 1743.
     v. 2, Nov. 8, 1743–Dec. 23, 1765.

N. Y. (colony)—Legislative council. Journal of the legislative council of the colony of New York. 2v. 2078p. Alb. 1861.   N. Y. state law lib.
Contents: v. 1, Ap. 9, 1691–Sep. 27, 1743.
     v. 2, Dec. 8, 1743–Ap. 3, 1775.

North, S. N. D. Constitutional development of the colony of New York. (*see* Magazine of American history, Mar. 1879, 3: 161–74)   973   M27

O'Callaghan, E. B. Historical introduction. (*see* N. Y. (colony) — Legislative council. Journal. 1861. 1: 3–27)   N. Y. state law lib.

General his-
tory
Law

O'Callaghan, E. B. Origin of legislative assemblies in the state of New York, including titles of the laws passed previous to 1691.   39p.   Alb. 1861.   328.7479 qOc1 1664-91.

Osgood, H. L. The proprietary province as a form of colonial government. (*see* American historical review)   973   qAm 35 July 1897, 2:644–64   Jan. 1898, 3:244–65 Oct. " 3:31–55

Reasons in support of triennial elections in the province of New York with the king's veto on the triennial act. 1738. (*see* N. Y. (state) — State, Secretary of. Documentary history of the state of New York) 1849-51.   4:243–56.   974.7   N424 1850-51.   4:157–65.   974.7   qN423

Representatives in colonial assemblies. (*see* Civil list and constitutional history of the colony and state of New York by E. A. Werner. 1891.   35:445–52)   351.2   N42

Law

No editions of colonial laws are included except O'Callaghan. *Laws and ordinances of New Netherland*; and, N. Y. (state)—Legislature. *Colonial laws of New York.*

For bibliography of New York laws, see Tower. *The Charlemagne Tower collection of colonial laws.* 298p. Phil. 1890. p.168-81,o16, 345 qT65.

Brooks, J. W. History of the court of common pleas of the city and county of New York with full reports of all important proceedings. 253p.   N. Y. 1896.   N. Y. hist. soc.

Daly, C: P. Historical sketch of the judicial tribunals of New York from 1623 to 1846.   68p.   N. Y. 1855.   N. Y. state law lib.

———— Judiciary of the early Dutch period. (*see* Stone, W: L. History of New York city.   1872.   apx. p. 41–54)   N. Y. pub. lib.

———— The nature, extent and history of the jurisdiction of the surrogates court of the state of New York, opinion of Daly in the matter of the estate of J. W. Brick, deceased; printed by order of the board of supervisors.   54p.   N. Y. 1863.   L. I. hist. soc.

———— State of jurisprudence during the Dutch period, 1623–74. (*see* McAdam, David & others, *ed.* History of the bench and bar of New York. 1897. 1:1–34)   N. Y. state law lib.

Fowler, R. L. History of the law of real property in New York, an essay introductory to the study of the New York revised statutes. 229p.   N. Y. 1895.   N. Y. state law lib.

Fowler, R. L. Observations on the particular jurisprudence of New Generalt tory Law York. (*see* Albany law journal, 1879–82, v.20–26) N.Y. state law lib.

——— Organization of the supreme court of judicature of the prov-ince of New York. (*see* Albany law journal, 1879, v.19–20)

N. Y. state law lib.

——— Historical gossip about the New York court of sessions. (*see* Historical magazine, Nov. 1864, 8 : 359–66)   973 H72

Hill, H : W. Development of constitutional law in New York. (*see* Buffalo historical society.   Publications.   1896.   4 : 163–201)

974.797   B86

The judiciary. (*see* Civil list and constitutional history of the colony and state of New York by E. A. Werner. 1891. 35 : 362–401)

351.2 N42

Includes history of the various colonial courts and lists of officials.

Murray, Joseph. Mr Murray's opinion relating to the courts of justice in the colony of New York; delivered to the general assembly of the said colony at their request, the 12th of June 1734. 44p. n. t–p.   N. Y. state law lib.

Includes "Appendix at a council held at Fort George, Nov. 25, 1727," p. 33–44.

N. Y. (state)-Legislature. Colonial laws of New York from the year 1664 to the revolution.   5v.   Alb. 1894–96.   N. Y. state law lib.

Contents: v. 1 Cummings, R. C. Historical note, pref. p. 9–21.

1st grant to the duke of York, p. 1–5.

Duke of York's laws, 1665–75, p. 6–100.

Nicoll's proclamation, revoking the Dutch and establishing the English form of government, 1665, p. 100–1.

Restoration of Dutch government, p. 101–2.

Colve's charter, p. 102–4.

2d grant to the duke of York, 1674, p. 104–5.

Commission of Andros as governor, 1674, p. 106–7.

Orders to put the duke's laws in force, 1674, p. 107.

Proclamation of Gov. Andros, 1674, p. 107–8.

Instructions to Gov. Dongan, 1683, p. 108–10.

Acts of general assemblies, 1683–85, p. 111–77.

Commission of Gov. Dongan, 1686, p. 177–78.

Instruction to Gov. Dongan, 1686, p. 178–80.

Dongan charter of the city of New York, 1686, p. 181–95.

Dongan charter of the city of Albany, 1686, p. 195–216.

Commission of Sir Edmund Andros, 1688, p. 216–17.

Instructions for Sir Edmund Andros, 1688, p. 217–18.

General assembly, 24 Ap. to 15 Sep. 1690, Jacob Leisler, lieutenant governor, p. 218–20.

Commission of Gov. Henry Sloughter, p. 221–22.

v. 1, p. 223–v. 5. Laws passed by assemblies 1 to 31, 1691–1775.

O'Callaghan, E. B. *comp.* Laws and ordinances of New Netherland, 1638–74; comp. and tr. from the original Dutch records in the office of the secretary of state, Albany N. Y.   602p.   Alb. 1868.   N. Y. state law lib.

Redfield, A. A. English colonial polity and judicial administration, 1664–1776. (*see* McAdam, David & others, *ed.* History of the bench and bar of New York. 1897. 1:35–93)   N. Y. state law lib.

Seymour, Horatio. Influence of New York on American jurisprudence. (*see* Magazine of American history, Ap. 1879, 3:217–30)
973   M27

Smith, William. Mr Smith's opinion humbly offered to the general assembly of the colony of New York on the 7th of June 1734 at their request, occasioned by sundry petitions of the city of New York, Westchester county and Queens county praying an establishment of courts of justice within the said colony by act of the legislature.   45p.   N. Y. 1734.   N. Y. state law lib.

Civil lists

List of all the officers employed in civill offices in the province of New York the 20th of April, 1693, and of their salaries. (*see* N. Y. (state)– State, Secretary of. Documentary history of the state of New York)
1849–51.   1:313–18.   974.7   N424
1850–51.   1:197–202.   974.7   qN423

Lists of colonial officers. (*see* Civil list and constitutional history of the colony and state of New York by E. A. Werner. 1891. v.35)
351.2   N42

Contents: Colonial executives, p. 206.
Auditors general, p. 216.
Treasurers, p. 217.
Schout-fiscals and attorneys general, p. 219.
Surveyors, p. 221.
Officers of the port of New York, p. 222.
Commissioners of Indian affairs, p. 263.
County judges, p. 533–41.
Surrogates, p. 544–51.
Sheriffs, p. 561–79.
County clerks, p. 580–90.

O'Callaghan, E. B. The register of New Netherland, 1624 to 1674, 198p.   Alb. 1865.   351.2   qOc1
List of officials, colonial and local.

Classes of settlers

For Huguenots, see also Newpaltz, p. 480, and New Rochelle, p. 469. For palatines, see Palatines, p. 502. For English on Long Island, see Suffolk county, p. 454 and its towns.

Baird, C : W. Histoire des réfugiés Huguenots en Amérique ; traduit de l'Anglais par N. E. Meyer et de Richemond. Toulouse 1886.

———— Huguenot emigration to America. 2 v. N. Y. 1885.

284.5 B162

New Netherland, 1 : 148–200.

DeWitt, Thomas. On the sources of settlements in New York. (*see* New York historical society. Proceedings. 1848. p. 72–88)

974.7 N421

Disosway, G. P. The Huguenots in America. (*see* Smiles, Samuel. ' Huguenots,; their settlements, churches and industries in England and Ireland. 1868. p. 427-42)
284.542 Sm4
Huguenots in New York, p. 429-33.

———— Huguenots of Staten Island. (*see* Continental monthly, June 1862, 1 : 683–88)
051 C76

Holland society of New York. Year book. 1886–98. N. Y. 1886–98.
974.7 qH71

Kapp, Friedrich. Geschichte der deutschen einwanderung in Amerika. Ed. 3. v.1, 416p. N. Y. 1869.
325.243 K14
v.1 *Geschichte der deutschen im staate New York bis zum anfange des 19 ten jahrhunderts.* No more published.

Knevels, J. W. Our Dutch progenitors. (*see* New York historical society. Proceedings. 1849. p. 182–220)
974.7 N421

Lefevre, Ralph. Huguenots of Ulster county. (*see* Historical society of Newburgh bay and the Highlands. Papers. 1894. p. 41-55.)
N. Y. state lib.

Vermilye, A. G. Huguenot element among the Dutch. 23p. Schenectady n. d.
284.5 V59

———— ———— (*see* Reformed church in America. Centennial discourses. 1877. p.139-61.)
285.7 R25

———— Mingling of Huguenot and Dutch in early New York. (*see* Huguenot society of America. Abstract of proceedings. n. d. 1 : 24-31.)
N. Y. state lib.

Waldron, W: W. Huguenots of Westchester and parish of Fordham.
126p.   N. Y. 1864.   284.5747   W52

Wittmeyer, A. V. Huguenots in America and their connection with
the church. (*see* Perry, W: S. History of the American episcopal church. 1885. 2:407–36)   283.73   qP42

Lists of immigrants

For settlers in a particular locality, see name of county or town under
Local colonial history.

Baudartius, Gulielmus. First emigrants to New Netherland, 1624;
translated from Gedenkwaardige geschiedenissen zo kerkelyke als
wereldlyke.   Arnhem 1624. (*see* N. Y. (state)—State, Secretary of. Documentary history of the state of New York)
                    1849–51.   4:131–32.   974.7   N424
                    1850–51.   4:84.   974.7   qN423

Bergen, T. G. List of early immigrants to New Netherland, 1654–64
alphabetically arranged. (*see* New York genealogical and biographical record)   929.1   N421
Oct. 1883, 14:181–90   Ap. 1884, 15:72–77
Jan. 1884, 15:34–40

Early immigrants to New Netherland, 1657–64. (*see* N. Y. (state)—
State, Secretary of. Documentary history of the state of New York)
                    1849–51.   3:52–63.   974.7   N424
                    1850–51.   3:33–42.   974.7   qN423
Also in Holland society of New York. *Year book.* 1896. p.141–58, 974.7 qH71.

Early immigrants to New Netherland. (*see* Holland society of New
York. Year book. 1896. p.124–29)   974.7   qH71
Mentions lists that have been published.

List of citizens of New York admitted as freemen between the years
1683 and 1740. (*see* Wilson, J. G. *ed.* Memorial history of the
city of New York. 1892–93. 2:204–8)   974.71   qW69

O'Callaghan, E. B. Early highland immigration to New York. (*see*
Historical magazine, Oct. 1861, 5:301–4)   973   H62
Alphabetic list of Scotch highlanders coming to New York, 1738–42.

Selyns, Henricus. List of church members and their residences in
1686, kept by Selyns, pastor of the Dutch reformed church. (*see*
Wilson, J. G. *ed.* Memorial history of the city of New York.
1892–93. 1:446–52)   974.71   qW69

Settlers in Rensselaerwyck from 1630–46, compiled from the books ~General tory~ of monthly wages and other mss. (*see* Holland society of New ~Genealo~ York. Yearbook. 1896. p. 130–40) 974.7 qH71
From O'Callaghan. *History of New Netherland.* 1846–48. 1 : 430–41.

Census population

For enumerations of the whole colony. Census of a special locality is found with its history.

Dexter, F. B. Estimates of population in the American colonies. (*see* American antiquarian society. Proceedings. 1887–88. new ser. 5 : 22–50) 906 Am3 v.12
New York, p. 33–35.

Hough, F. B: History of the census in New York and plan proposed for the state census of 1865. (*see* Albany institute. Transactions. 1867. 5 : 196–228) N. Y. state lib.

List of inhabitants of province by counties, 1738. (*see* N. Y. (state)— State, Secretary of. Documentary history of the state of New York)
1849–51. 4 : 184–88. 974.7 N424
1850–51. 4 : 118–22. 974.7 qN423
All counties except Westchester.

Livingston, R. R. Census of state of New York at different periods since 1731. (*see* Society for the promotion of useful arts. Transactions. 1807. 2 : 216–18) 630.6 F92a
Enumeration by counties in 1731, 1771, 1786, 1791, 1801.

Statistics of population of province of New York, 1647–1774. (*see* N. Y. (state)–State, Secretary of. Documentary history of the state of New York) 1849–51. 1 : 687–97. 974.7 N424
1850–51. 1 : 465–74. 974.7 qN423

Genealogy

Genealogies of special places will be found with their local history. Histories of single families are not included.

Bergen, T. G. Register of early settlers of Kings county, Long Island, N. Y., from its 1st settlement by Europeans to 1700; with contributions to their biographies and genealogies. 452p. N. Y. 1881. 929.1 B45

Bunker, M.. P. Long Island genealogies, being kindred descendants of Thomas Powell. 530p. Alb. 1895. (Munsell's historical ser. v. 24) 929.1 B88

Griffin, Augustus. Griffin's journal; 1st settlers of Southold; the names of the heads of those families, being only 13 at the time of their landing; 1st proprietors of Orient, biographical sketches, etc. etc. 312 p. Orient, L. I. 1857.   929.1   G87

Holgate, J. B. American genealogy, being a history of some of the early settlers of North America and their descendants from their 1st emigration to the present time. 244 p. Alb. 1848.   929.1   qH71
Mostly New York families.

Latting, J. J. Genealogical fragments. (*see* New York genealogical and biographical record)   929.1   N421

    Oct. 1879, 10 : 170–77   Ap. 1880, 11 : 70–74
    Jan. 1880, 11 : 12–24   Oct. 1880, 11 : 168–71

New York genealogical and biographical record, 1870–98. v. 1–29. N. Y. 1870–98.   929.1   N421
    v. 18–29 are quarto, 929.1 qN421.

Pearson, Jonathan, *comp.* Contributions for the genealogies of the descendants of the 1st settlers of the patent and city of Schenectady from 1662 to 1800. 324p. Alb. 1873.   929.1   P311

——— Contributions for the genealogies of the 1st settlers of the ancient county of Albany from 1630 to 1800.   182 p.   Alb. 1872.
929.1   P31

———Contributions to the history of the ancient Dutch families of New York. (*see* New York genealogical and biographical record)
929.1   N421

    Jan. 1871, 2 : 22–23   July 1871, 2 : 139–41
    Ap. 1871, 2 : 68–70   Oct. 1871, 2 : 190–92

Purple, E. R. Contributions to the history of the ancient families of New York. (*see* New York genealogical and biographical record)
929.1   N421

    Ap. 1876, 7 : 49–64   Jan. 1878, 9 : 3–16
    July 1876, 7 : 117–24   Ap. 1878, 9 : 52–62
    Oct. 1876, 7 : 145–51   July 1878, 9 : 113–25
    Jan. 1877, 8 : 11–20   Oct. 1878, 9 : 153–60
    Ap. 1877, 8 : 67–73   Jan. 1879, 10 : 35–43
    July 1877, 8 : 124–33

Talcott, S. V. *comp.* Genealogical notes of New York and New England families. 747 p. Alb. 1883.   929.1   T14

Wills, marriage licenses, etc.

Ancient New York wills. (*see* New York genealogical and boigraphical ^{General h} record) 929.1 N421 ^{Wills, mar} ^{licenses}

Jan. 1871, 2 : 39–40	Oct. 1871, 2 : 202–5
Ap. 1871, 2 : 103	Oct. 1872, 3 : 190–92
July 1871, 2 : 155–56	

Cornbury, *Gov.* New York marriage licenses granted, 1702-6. (*see* New York genealogical and biographical record) 929.1 'N421

Jan. 1870, 1 : 3	Jan. 1871, 2 : 25–28
Ap. 1870, 1 : 13	

Fernow, Berthold, *comp. & ed.* Calendar of wills on file and recorded in the offices of the clerk of the court of appeals, of the county clerk at Albany and of the secretary of state, 1626–1836; compiled under the auspices of the Colonial dames of the state of New York and published by the society. 657p. N. Y. 1896. 929.3 qN42
500 copies printed.

Gleanings from the surrogate's office. (*see* Old New York) 974.71 qOl1

Sep. 1889, 1 : 131–36	Jan. 1890, 1 : 417–22
Oct. 1889, 1 : 176–84	Ap. 1890, 2 : 202–4
Nov. 1889, 1 : 269–76	

Moore, C: B. English and Dutch intermarriages. (*see* New York genealogical and biographical record, Jan. 1873, 4 : 13–20; July 1873, 4 : 127–39) 929.1 N421

N. Y. (state)—Library. Supplementary list of marriage licenses. 48p. Alb. 1898. (Bulletin: history 1) 929.3 N42 v.2
Also in 81st annual report of New York state library. 1899. 027.5747 N42.
Supplementary to *Names of persons for whom marriage licenses were issued.* 1860.

N. Y. (state)—State, Secretary of. Names of persons for whom marriage licenses were issued by the secretary of the province of New York previous to 1784; printed by order of G. J. Tucker. 480p. Alb. 1860. 929.3 N42

New York marriage licenses, 1686–88. (*see* New York genealogical and biographical record, Oct. 1874, 5:174) 929.1 N421

New York marriage licenses, 1691–93 from v.4 of Records of wills, surrogate's office, New York. (*see* New York genealogical and biographical record, Jan. 1873, 4:31–32) 929.1 N421

General history
Manors

O'Callaghan, E. B.   New York marriage licenses; supplementary list for the years 1756 and 1758. (*see* New York genealogical and biographical record, Oct. 1871, 2:194-200)   929.1   N421

Philadelphia, Friends society.   New York marriages, from the Friends' records of Philadelphia. (*see* New York genealogical and biographical record, Jan. 1872, 3:51-52)   929.1   N421

Manors

See also Rensselaerswyck, p. 483; Philipse manor in Westchester county, p. 463.

Anthony, Elliott.   The patroons. (*see* National magazine, Dec. 1891, 15:194-96)   973   M271

Colden, Cadwallader.   Letter to the governor of New York. (*see* Historical magazine, Oct. 1867, ser. 2, 2:226-27) 973   H62 v.12

———— State of lands in the province of New York in 1732 by Cadwallader Colden, surveyor-general.   (*see* N. Y. city)–Common Council. Manual. 1851.   10:454-61)   352.0747 N4k·

———— ———— (*see* N. Y. (state)–State, Secretary of.   Documentary history of the state of New York)   1849-51.   1:375-89.   974.7   N424

1850-51.   1:247-55.   974.7   qN423

De Lancey, E: F.   Manors in province of New York and in county of Westchester.   160p.   N. Y. 1886.   New York pub. lib.
From Scharf. *History of Westchester county.*

———— ———— (*see* Scharf, J: T: Westchester county. 1886.   1:31-160f.)
974.727   qSch1

Schuyler, G: W.   New Netherland and the patroons. (*see his* Colonial New York.   1885.   1:1-33)   974.7   Sch8

Whitmore, W: H.   Manors of New York and their lords. (*see* Heraldic journal, Ap. 1867, 3:69-82)   929   H411

Names

Beauchamp, W: M.   Indian names in New York with a selection from other states and some Onondaga names of plants, etc.   148p. Fayetteville N. Y. 1893.   929.4   B38

Benson, Egbert.   Memoir read before Historical society of state of New York, 1816.   72p.   N. Y.   1817.   929.4   B44
Indian, Dutch and English names of places in New York state.

Benson, Egbert. Ed. 2.   127p.   Jamaica 1825.   929.4   B441

—— —— 72p.   N. Y. 1848.   929.4   B442
    Reprinted from a copy with the author's last corrections.

—— —— (*see* New York historical society. Collections. 1849. ser.
    2, 2:77–148)   974.7   N422 v.7

Cooper, S. F.   Hudson river and its early names. (*see* Magazine of
    American history, June 1880, 4 : 401–19)   973 M27

Davis, W: T.   Staten Island names; ye olde names and nicknames,
    with map by C: W. Leng.   p.20–76.   New Brighton 1896.
                                              917.4726 D29
    Being special no. 21 of the proceedings of the Staten Island natural science
    association.

DeKay, J. E.   Indian names on Long Island.   12p.   Oyster Bay
    1851.   929.4   D36

Dutch and Indian names for Albany and vicinity. (*see* Munsell, Joel.
    Annals of Albany)   1850–59.   2 : 226–33.   • 974.743 M92
          Ed. 2.   1869–71.   2 : 311–19.   974.743 M921

Fernow, Berthold.   New Amsterdam family names and their origin.
    p.209–40.   N. Y. ᶜ1898.   (Half moon ser. v.2, no. 6)
                                              N. Y. state lib.

—— —— (*see* Goodwin, *Mrs* Maud (Wilder) & *others*. Historic New
    York.   1899.   2 : 209–40)   974.71   G63

Field, T: W.   Indian, Dutch and English names of localities in
    Brooklyn and its vicinity. (*see his* Historic and antiquarian scenes
    in Brooklyn. 1868. p.49–60)   974.723 qF45

Flint, M. B.   Study of names. (*see her* Early Long Island.   1896.
    p.60–75)   974.721 F64

Harris, G: H.   Notes on the aboriginal terminology of the Genesee
    river.   10p.   n.t–p.   n.p.1889?   929.4   H24

—— —— (*see* Rochester historical society. Publications.   1892.
    1:9–18)   974.789 R58

Historical sketches of the origin and changes of names of New York
    city. (*see* Reminiscences of the city of New York and its vicinity.
    1855.   p.71–88)   974.71   R28

Marshall, O. H. Niagara frontier embracing sketches of its early history and Indian, French and English local names. 46p. n.p.n.d.

974.798 M35

Read before the Buffalo historical society Feb. 27, 1865.

—— —— (*see* Munsell, Joel. Historical series. 1887.   15:275–320)

N. Y. state lib.

Matthes, Susanna. Van and von; some facts about Dutch names and titles which are not generally understood. (*see* New York genealogical and biographical record, Oct. 1893, 24:170–73)

929.1 qN421

Obsolete names of localities on Manhattan Island. (*see* N. Y. (city)— Common council. Manual. 1856.   15:465–76)   352.0747 N4k

—— (*see* Reminiscences of the city of New York and its vicinity. 1855. p.215–26)   974.71 R28

Obsolete names of New York. (*see* American historian and quarterly genealogical record)   .   973   Am31

July 1875, 1 : 30–36   Jan. 1876, 1 : 113–17
Oct. 1875, 1 : 66–73   Ap. 1876, 1 : 154–60

Through the letter G.

Purple, E. R. Dutch aliases and names spelt in two or more ways. (*see* New York genealogical and biographical record, Jan. 1879, 10 : 38–43)   929.1 N421

Purple, S: S. Dutch aliases. (*see* Holland society of New York. Yearbook. 1896.   p.190–98)   974.7 qH71

Nearly all the aliases of males in the baptismal records of the reformed Dutch church in the city of New York, 1639-1756.

Schoolcraft, H: R. Comments on the aboriginal names and geographical terminology of the state of New York, part first, Valley of the Hudson. (*see* New York historical society. Proceedings. 1844.   p.77–115)   974.7 N421

Thompson, B: F. Paper upon Indian names of Long Island. (*see* New York historical society. Proceedings. 1845. p.125–31)

974.7 N421

Tooker, W: W. Indian place-names in East Hampton town, L. I. with their probable significations. Sag Harbor 1889. L. I. hist. soc.

—— —— (*see* Easthampton, N. Y.   Records of. 1889.   4 : pref. 1–10)   974.725 Ea71

Tooker, W: W. Some Indian names of places on Long Island, N. Y. Genera tory and their correspondences in Virginia. (*see* Magazine of New England Militar history, July 1891, 1 : 154–58) 929 M27

Trumbull, J. H. Indian names of places on Long Island derived from esculent roots. (*see* Magazine of American history, June 1877, 1 : 386–87) 973 M27

Military history

Fletcher, *Gov.* **Benjamin.** State of militia in province of New York in America, Ap. 1693. (*see* N. Y. (state)—State, Secretary of. Documentary history of the state of New York) .

1849–51.	1 : 318–19.	974.7 N424
1850–51.	1 : 202–3.	974.7 qN423

List of officers and soldiers in various militia companies 1738. (*see* N. Y. (state)–State, Secretary of. Documentary history of the state of New York) 1849–51. 4 : 208–39. 974.7 N424

1850–51. 4 : 136–55. 974.7 qN423

Also in *Manual of the city of New York.* 1852.11:498–504. 352.0747 N4k.

List of officers of militia of province of New York. 1700. (*see* N. Y. (state)–State, Secretary of. Documentary history of the state of New York). 1849–51. 1 : 357–64. 974.7 N424

1850–51. 1 : 227–35. 974.7 qN423

Also in *Manual of the city of New York.* 1851.10:475–80, 352.0747 N4k.

Muster rolls of New York provincial troops, 1755–64. (*see* New York historical society. Collections. 1892. Publication fund ser. v. 24) 974.7 N42

Muster rolls of the several companies of the burgher corps of New Amsterdam, 1653. (*see* O'Callaghan, E. B. History of New Netherland. 1846–48. 2 : 569) 974.7 Oc11

N. Y. (state)–Historian. Muster rolls of a century; from 1664 to 1760. (*see his* Annual report. 1897–98. 2 : 371–956; 3 : 437–1130) 974 7 N425

Ruttenber, E: M. Provincial and revolutionary military organizations. (*see* Historical society of Newburgh bay and the Highlands. Papers. 1894. p.8–22) N. Y. state lib.
Read before the society Dec. 7, 1885.

Scisco, L. D. Rural militia of the New Netherland. (*see* American historical register, Nov. 1895, 3 : 335–39) 973 qAm31

Vail, H: H. Some records of the French and Indian war. (*see* New York genealogical and biographical record, Ap. 1895, 26 : 73–79)

929.1 qN421

Includes muster roll of Capt. Thomas Terry's company of Long Island troops, 1759.

Religious history

For particular churches, see name of the place under Local colonial history.

Baird, C: W. Churches in the province of New York in the year 1700. (*see* Magazine of American history, Oct. 1879, 3 : 625) 973 M27

Disosway, G. P. The earliest churches of New York and its vicinity. 416p. N. Y. 1865. 277.471 D63

Earl, Robert. Religion in the colony of New York; address before the Herkimer county historical society, Dec. 14, 1897. 11p. n.p. 1897? 277.47 Ea7

Also in Herkimer county historical society. Papers 1897. p.131–41, 974.761 H42.

Holland society of New York. Transcript of church records in possession of the society. (*see its* Year book. 1898. p.206–9)

974.7 qH71

Hopkins, A. G. Early protestant missions among the Iroquois. (*see* Oneida historical society. Transactions. 1885–86. p.5–28)

974.762 On2

Papers relating principally to the conversion and civilization of the six nations of Indians, interspersed with letters on other subjects of public interest. (*see* N. Y. (state)–State, Secretary of. Documentary history of the state of New York)

1849–51.	4 : 289–504.	974.7	N424
1850–51.	4 : 187–312.	974.7	qN423

Papers relating to the state of religion in the province, 1657–1712. (*see* N. Y. (state)–State, Secretary of. Documentary history of the state of New York)

1849–51.	3 : 101–30.	974.7	N424
1850–51.	3 : 67–84.	974.7	qN423

Sprague, W: B. Annals of the American pulpit; or, Commemorative notices of American clergymen of various denominations from the early settlement of the country to the close of 1855; with historical introductions. 9v. N. Y. 1857–69. 922 Sp7

For contents see Boston athenaeum. *Catalogue.* p. 2839.

Stiles, Ezra. Brief view of the state of religious liberty in the colony General of New York read before the reverend general convention of the Episcopal delegates from the consociated churches of Connecticut and the synod of New York and Philadelphia, met at Stanford, September 1, 1773. (*see* Massachusetts historical society. Collections. 1814. ser. 2, 1 : 140–57) 974.4 M38 v.11

Including *Account of the dissenting interest in the middle states, A. D. 1759 in letter from Elihu Spencer to Dr Stiles.*

Catholic

For Father Jogues, see Dutch colony 1626–64 ; Description, p.327.

Courcy de Laroche-Héron, Henry de. The catholic church in the United States, a sketch of its ecclesiastical history; translated and enlarged by J: G. Shea. 594p. N. Y. 1856. 282.73 C83

Colonial church in New York, p. 314–44.

Mullany, J: F. Pioneer church of the state of New York with other essays. 140p. Syracuse 1897. 282.747 M91

Murray, J: O. Popular history of the catholic church in the United States. Ed 3. 619p. N. Y. 1876. 282.73 M96

Father Isaac Jogues, p.111–18.
Colonial church, New York, p.150–54.
Hon. Thomas Dongan, 1st catholic governor of New York, p. 155–58.

O'Gorman, Thomas. History of the Roman catholic church in the United States. 515p. N. Y. 1895. (American church history) 282.73 Og6

Colonial church in New York, p.230–31, 243–44.

Shea, J: G. History of the catholic church within the limits of the United States from the first attempted colonization to the present time. 4v. N. Y. 1886–92. 282.73 qSh3

Colonial church in New York, 1:87–99, 356–58, 396–400, 433.

Episcopal

Anderson, J. S. M. History of the church of England in the colonies and foreign dependencies of the British empire. 3v. Lond. 1845–56. 283 An21

—— —— Ed.2. 3v. Lond. 1856. 283 An2

Church in New York, 2 : 436–40; 3 : 286–336, 460–73.

DeCosta, B: F. Centennial of the diocese of New York: and, Church and state during the colonial period. (*see* Wilson, J. G. *ed.* Centennial history of the protestant episcopal church in the diocese of New York. 1886. p.46–103) 283.747 W69

Establishment of the church of England in New York. (*see* Historical magazine, May, 1861, 5 : 153–55) 973 H62

Humphreys, David. Historical account of the incorporated Society for the propagation of the gospel in foreign parts. 356p. Lond. 1730. 266.3 H88

Includes accounts of the missionary work in the colony of New York and of the negro riots in New York city.

Inglis, Charles. State of the Anglo-American church in 1776. (*see* N. Y. (state)–State, Secretary of. Documentary history of the state of New York) 1849–51. 3 : 1047–66. 974.7 N424
1850–51. 3 : 635–46. 974.7 qN423

Keith and Talbot. (*see* Protestant episcopal historical society. Collections. 1851. 1: pref. 1–43, p.1–86) 283.73 P94

Includes *Journal of travels* by George Keith.

The letters of these agents of the Society for the propagation of the gospel in foreign parts furnish a very full account of the general religious aspect of the colonies.

McConnell, S: D. History of the American episcopal church from the planting of the colonies to the end of the civil war. 392p. N. Y. 1890. 283.73 M13

Church in colonial New York, p.59–68, 93–95, 191–94.

Perry, W: S. History of the American episcopal church, 1587–1883. 2 v. Bost. 1885. 283.73 qP42

Beginnings of the church in New York, 1 : 148–74 ; Mission of Keith and Talbot. 1 : 206–22.

Protestant episcopal historical society. Collections. 1851. v.1. 283.73 P94

State of the protestant episcopal church in New York and Long Island in letter from Dr Bray about 1740, p.99–106.

List of persons licensed by the bishops of London, to Albany and New York city, 1745–84, p.107, 116.

List of parishes in 1724, p.125.

Tiffany, C: C. History of the protestant episcopal church in the United States of America. 593p. N. Y. 1895. (American church history) 283.73 T44

Colonial church in New York, p.162–89.

Wilson, J. G. *ed.* Centennial history of the protestant episcopal church in the diocese of New York, 1785–1885. 454p. N. Y. 1886. 283.747 W69

Parish histories, p.201–365.

Huguenot

See Classes of settlers, p. 383.

Lutheran

Jacobs, H: E. History of the evangelical Lutheran church in the United States 539p. N. Y. 1893, (American church history)
284.17 J15

Lutherans of New Netherlands, p. 46–61.
Dutch churches from Falckner to Muhlenberg, p. 118–32.

Lintner, G. A. Early history of the Lutheran church in the state of New York, discourse delivered before the Hartwick synod in the Lutheran church of Richmondville, N. Y. Sep. 21, 1867. 24p. Alb. 1867.   Providence pub. lib.

Schaeffer, C: W. Early history of the Lutheran church in America from the settlement of the Swedes on the Delaware to the middle of the 18th century. 143p. Phil. 1857.   284.173 Sch1

Dutch, p.61–69.

Wolf, E. J. Lutherans in America; a story of struggle, progress, influence and marvelous growth. 544p. N.Y. 1890. 284.17 W83

Dutch, p.107–32.

Moravian

Kapp, Friedrich. Die herrnhuter in Schekomeko. (*see his* Geschichte der Deutschen im staate New York. 1869. p.200–29) 325.243 K14

Moravians in New York including names of persons in New York and on Long and Staten Islands attached to the brethren's church in 1744. (*see* Moravian historical society. Transactions. 1876. 1 : 419–26)   284.6 M791

Papers relating to Quakers and Moravians. (*see* N. Y. (state)–State, Secretary of. Documentary history of the state of New York)
1849–51.   3 : 997–1030.   974.7 N424
1850–51.   3 : 603–24.   974.7 qN423

Presbyterian

Alexander, S. D. Presbytery of New York, 1738 to 1888. 198p. N. Y. n.d.   L. I. hist. soc.

Baird, C: W. Civil status of the presbyterians in the province of New York. (*see* Magazine of American history, Oct. 1879, 3 : 593–628)
973 M27

Briggs, C: A: American presbyterianism; its origin and early history. 373+142p.   N. Y. 1885.   285.1 B76

Hodge, Charles. Constitutional history of the presbyterian church in the United States of America, pt 1–2. Phil. 1839–41. 285.173 H66
     Contents: pt 1, 1705–41, pt 2, 1741–88.

Macoubrey, A. R. Relation of presbyterianism to the revolutionary sentiment in the province of New York, an address delivered before the Westchester county historical society, Oct. 28, 1890. 46p. n.p.1891.
     Griffin, p.1047.

Presbyterian church in the U. S.—General assembly. Records. 548p. Phil. 1841. 285.1 P922
     Contents: Presbytery of Philadelphia, 1706–16, p.7–44.
         Synod of Philadelphia , 1717–58, p.45–231.
         "   New York, 1745–58, p.232–84.
         "   New York and Philadelphia, 1758–88, p.285–548.

Thompson, R. E. History of the presbyterian churches in the United States. 424p. N. Y. 1895. (American church history) 285.17 T37

Webster, Richard. History of the presbyterian church in America from its origin until the year 1760; with biographical sketches of its early ministers. 720p. Phil. 1857. 285.17 W39

Puritan

Briggs, C: A: Puritanism in New York, its origin and growth till the middle of the 18th century. (*see* Magazine of American history, Jan. 1885, 13 : 39–58) 973 M27

Quaker

Bowden, James. History of the society of friends in America. 2v. Lond. 1850–54.
     Sabin, 2 : 363.

Bowne, John. Persecution of an early friend or quaker, copied from his journal by Henry Onderdonk. (*see* American historical record, Jan. 1872, 1 : 4–8) 973 qAm3

First settlement of the society of friends in New York. (*see* Historical magazine, June 1862, 6 : 193–94) 973 H62

Keith, George. Journal of travels from New Hampshire to Caratuck on the continent of North America. 92p. Lond. 1706. 289.67 K26
     Keith spent some time in the vicinity of New York and preached against the quakers.

    ———— ———— (*see* Protestant episcopal historical society. Collections. 1851. 1 : 1–54) 283.73 P94

Onderdonk, Henry, jr. Friends on Long Island and in New York, Genera tory Reform church
1657–1826. (*see his* Annals of Hempstead. 1878. p.93–104)
974.724 H37

Papers relating to quakers and Moravians. (*see* N. Y. (state)–State,
Secretary of. Documentary history of the state of New York)
1849–51. 3 : 997–1030. 974.7 N424
1850–51. 3 : 603–24. 974.7 qN423

Reformed

Buddingh, Derk. De hervormde hollandsche kerk in de
Vereenigde Staten van Noord-Amerika. 167p. Utrecht 1853.
(*in his* Kerk, school en watenschap. 1853.) 285.7 B85

Corwin, E: T. The Amsterdam correspondence. p.81–107.
N. Y. 1897. 285.77 C811
Reprinted from American society of church history. *Papers.* v. 8. 270 Am3.

——— Character and development of the reformed church in the colonial period. 66p. (*see* Reformed church in America. Centennial
discourses. 1877. p. 41–106) 285.7 R25

——— Manual of the reformed church in America, 1628–1878. Ed. 3.
676p. N. Y. 1879. 285.773 C812
An alphabetic list of ministers with biographic and bibliographic
information, p. 161–570.
Alphabetic list of churches with list of ministers and bibliographic
data, p.571–646.

——— Report of the general synod's agent on his searches in the ecclesiastical archives of Holland, 1897–98. 8p. N. Y. 1898.

——— **Dubbs, J. H. & Hamilton, J. T.** History of the reformed
church Dutch, the reformed church German, and the Moravian
church in the United States. 525p. N. Y. 1895. (American
church history) 285.77 C81
Reformed church Dutch, p.1–212.

Demarest, D: D. History and characteristics of the reformed
protestant Dutch church. 221p. N. Y. 1856. 285.7 D39
New York before the revolution, p.60–100.

——— Reformed church in America, its origin, development and characteristics. 210p. 1889.
Noted in Corwin. *History of the reformed church.* 1895. p.14, 285.77 C81.

General his-
tory
Reformed
church

DeWitt, Thomas. List of ministers of the reformed Dutch church in North America, in chronological order from 1633 to 1800. (*see his* Discourse delivered in the North reformed Dutch church 1857. p.71–79)   285.77471 N811

Gunn, Alexander. Memoirs of the Rev. John H. Livingston, prepared in compliance with a request of the general synod of the reformed Dutch church in North America. 540p. N. Y. 1829.   922.57 L76
New York before the revolution, p.77–155.

—— Memoirs of the Rev. John Henry Livingston, first professor of theology in the reformed protestant Dutch church in North America. New ed. 404p. N. Y. 1856.   922.57 L761

History of the origin and progress of the protestant reformed Dutch church in the United States. (*see* Magazine of the reformed Dutch church)   205 M27
  Nov. 1827, 2:247–50   Jan. 1828, 2:312–15
  Feb. 1828, 2:344–48

Holland society of New York. List of Dutch reformed churches organized before 1800, with their records. (*see* Hackensack (N. J.) Reformed Dutch church. Records of the reformed Dutch churches of Hackensack and Schraalenburgh, N. J. 1891. 1:pref. 9–15)   929.3 qH11

—— —— (*see* Holland society of New York. Year book. 1892–93. p.21–29)   974.7 qH71

Names of the ministers of the Dutch reformed churches in New York and New Jersey, 1758 and 1796. (*see* N. Y. (state)—State, Secretary of. Documentary history of the state of New York)
          1849–51.   1:625–26.   974.7 N424
          1850–51.   1:406–7. · 974.7 qN423

Ordination of the first clergyman in the reformed protestant Dutch church in North America. (*see* Historical magazine, Nov. 1865, 9:325–26)   973 H62
Rev. Petrus Tesschenmaecker, 1679.

Reformed church in America — General synod. Acts and proceedings, vol. 1, embracing the period from 1771 to 1812; preceded by the Minutes of the coetus, 1738–54 and the Proceedings of the conferentie, 1755–67. 493p. N. Y. 1859.   285.773 R25

Rev. John H. Livingston. (*see* Old New York, Sep. 1889, 1:94–105)   974.71 qOl1

Slavery

Census of slaves, 1755. (*see* N. Y. (state)–State, Secretary of. Documentary history of the state of New York)

1849–51.   3 : 843–68.   974.7   N424
1850–51.   3 : 503–21.   974.7   qN423
Under names of masters.

Cruger, John. Experience on a slave-ship, 1698–1700. (*see* Wilson, J. G. *ed.* Memorial history of the city of New York, 1892–93. 2 : 285–86)   974.71   qW69

DuBois, W: E: B: The suppression of the African slave trade to the United States of America, 1638–1870.   335p.   N. Y. 1896. (Harvard historical studies 1)   326.1   D85
Slavery and the slave trade in New York, p.17–20.

Earl, Robert. Slavery in the colony and state of New York; an address delivered before the Herkimer county historical society, Oct. 12, 1897.   12p.   n.t-p.   n.p. 1897.   326.9747   Ea7
Also in Herkimer county historical society. Papers for 1897. p.103–14, **974.761   H42.**

Historical notes on slavery in the northern colonies and states; New York. (*see* Historical magazine, Aug. 1866, 10 : 237–38)   973   H62

Mather, F: G. Slavery in the colony and state of New York. (*see* Magazine of American history, May 1884, 11 : 408–20)   973   M27

Morgan, E. V. Slavery in New York.   30p.   N. Y. ᶜ1898. (Half moon ser. v.2, no.1)   N. Y. state lib.

—— —— (*see* Goodwin, *Mrs* Maud (Wilder) & *others.* Historic New York. 1899.   2 : 1–30)   974.71   G63

——— Slavery in New York; the status of the slave under the English colonial government. (*see* American historical association. Papers. 1891.   v.5, pt 4, p.3–16)   973   Am32

——— ——— Abstract. (*see* American historical association. Annual report. 1891.   2 : 87–88)   973   Am33

Northrup, A. J. Slavery in New York, a historical sketch.   p. 243–313.   Alb. 1900. (New York state library bulletin: history no. 4)   N. Y. state lib.

Slavery in Albany county. (*see* Howell, G. R. & Tenny, Jonathan. Bicentennial history of Albany.   1886.   p. 300–3)   974.742   qH83

Valentine, D: T: Slaves and the slave trade in New Amsterdam. (*see* N. Y. (city)—Common council. Manual. 1863. 22:581–94) · 352.0747 N4k

Voyages of the slavers, St John, and Arms of Amsterdam, 1659, 1663, together with additional papers illustrative of the slave trade under the Dutch; translated from the original mss with an introduction and index by E. B. O'Callaghan. (*in* O'Callaghan, E. B. New York colonial tracts. 1866–72. v. 3) 974.7 Oc1

Williams, G: W. History of the negro race in America, from 1619 to 1880. 2 v. in 1. N. Y. 1885. 326.973 W67
Colony of New York, 1628–1775, p. 134–71.

Printing

See also Zenger, p. 364.

Bicentennial anniversary of the introduction of printing into the middle colonies. (*see* Pennsylvania magazine of history and biography, 1886, 10:78–85) 974.8 P382

Boardman, G: D. Early printing in the middle colonies; address delivered before the historical society of Pennsylvania, Dec. 11, 1885. (*see* Pennsylvania magazine of history and biography, 1886. 10:15–32) 974.8 P382

The Bradford bicentenary. (*see* Critic, Ap. 15, 1893, 22:236–37) 051 qC86

Colonial printers in New York. (*see* Book buyer, Feb. 1896, 23:8–10) 015.73 B64

Early history of the printing and newspaper press in Boston and New York. (*see* Continental monthly, Sep. 1863, 4:256–68) 051 C76

The first book printed in New York. (*see* Bookworm, Feb. 1890, 3:89–92) 010.5 B64

Hildeburn, C: S. R. *comp.* List of the issues of the press in New York, 1693–1752. 28p. Phil. 1889. 015.747 H54

—— List of the issues of the press in New York, 1693–1784. (*see* Pennsylvania magazine of history and biography) 974.8 P382
　　Jan. 1889, 12:475–82　　Ap. 1889, 13:90–99
　　July " 13:207–15

—— Additions to A list of the issues of the press in New York, 1693–1752. (*see* Old New York, Feb. 1890, 2:23–27) 974.71 qOl1

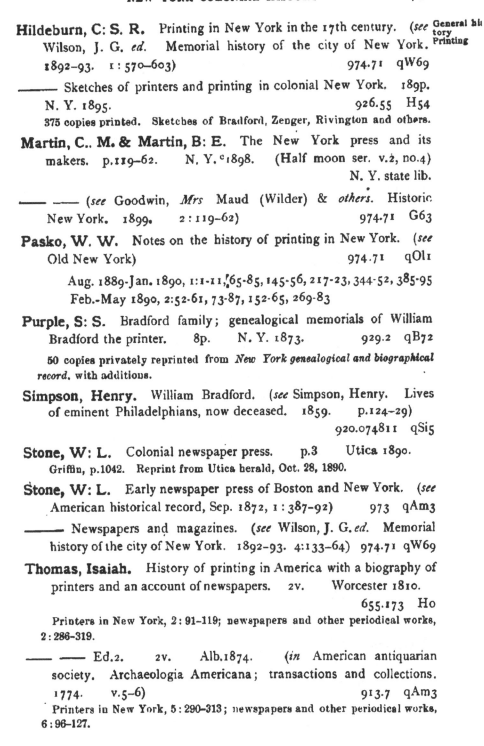

Hildeburn, C: S. R. Printing in New York in the 17th century. (*see* General history
Wilson, J. G. *ed*. Memorial history of the city of New York. Printing
1892–93. 1 : 570–603) 974.71 qW69

————— Sketches of printers and printing in colonial New York. 189p.
N. Y. 1895. 926.55 H54
375 copies printed. Sketches of Bradford, Zenger, Rivington and others.

Martin, C.. M. & Martin, B: E. The New York press and its
makers. p.119–62. N. Y. ᶜ1898. (Half moon ser. v.2, no.4)
N. Y. state lib.

————— ————— (*see* Goodwin, *Mrs* Maud (Wilder) & *others*. Historic
New York. 1899. 2 : 119–62) 974.71 G63

Pasko, W. W. Notes on the history of printing in New York. (*see*
Old New York) 974.71 qOl1
Aug. 1889-Jan. 1890, 1:1-11, 65-85, 145-56, 217-23, 344-52, 385-95
Feb.-May 1890, 2:52-61, 73-87, 152-65, 269-83

Purple, S: S. Bradford family; genealogical memorials of William
Bradford the printer. 8p. N. Y. 1873. 929.2 qB72
50 copies privately reprinted from *New York genealogical and biographical
record*. with additions.

Simpson, Henry. William Bradford. (*see* Simpson, Henry. Lives
of eminent Philadelphians, now deceased. 1859. p.124–29)
920.074811 qSi5

Stone, W: L. Colonial newspaper press. p.3 Utica 1890.
Griffin, p.1042. Reprint from Utica herald, Oct. 28, 1890.

Stone, W: L. Early newspaper press of Boston and New York. (*see*
American historical record, Sep. 1872, 1 : 387–92) 973 qAm3

————— Newspapers and magazines. (*see* Wilson, J. G. *ed*. Memorial
history of the city of New York. 1892-93. 4:133–64) 974.71 qW69

Thomas, Isaiah. History of printing in America with a biography of
printers and an account of newspapers. 2v. Worcester 1810.
655.173 Ho
Printers in New York, 2: 91-119; newspapers and other periodical works,
2: 286-319.

————— ————— Ed.2. 2v. Alb.1874. (*in* American antiquarian
society. Archaeologia Americana; transactions and collections.
1774. v.5–6) 913.7 qAm3
Printers in New York, 5: 290-313; newspapers and other periodical works,
6: 96-127.

Wallace, J: W: Address delivered at the celebration by the New York historical society, May 30, 1863, of the 200th birthday of Mr William Bradford who introduced the art of printing into the middle colonies. 114p. Alb.1863. 926.55 B72

Newspapers

The following list of newspapers printed in New York state before 1775 has been carefully revised by Mr Wilberforce Eames of the Lenox library. The books immediately following have also been consulted.

Grolier club of the city of New York. Catalogue of books printed by William Bradford and other printers in the middle colonies. 100p. N. Y. 1893. 016.094 G89

Martin, C.. M. & Martin, B: E. The New York press and its makers. p.119–62, N. Y.ᶜ 1898. (Half moon ser. v.2, no.4) N. Y. state lib.

—— —— (*see* Goodwin, *Mrs* Maud (Wilder) & *others.* Historic New York. 1899. 2 : 119–62) 974.71 G63

North, S. N. D. History and present condition of the newspaper and periodical press of the United States. (*see* U. S. Census, 10th, 1880. Final reports. 1883–88. 8 : 1–446) R 317.3 qUn3 v.10⁸ New York newspapers, p.387–408.

Thomas, Isaiah. History of printing in America. 2 v. Alb. 1874. (*in* American antiquarian society. Archaeologia Americana ; transactions and collections. 1874. v.5–6) 913.7 qAm3

Newspapers arranged chronologically

New York gazette (weekly)

Printed by William Bradford, 1725–44.
1st newspaper in New York city.
Partial files at :
New York society library (1726–29)
New York historical society (1730–38)
Lenox library (1733–40)
Pennsylvania historical society (1736–40)

New York weekly journal.

Printed by John Peter Zenger, 1733–52?
2d newspaper in New York city.
Partial files at :
Lenox library (1733–44)
Antiquarian society, Worcester (later than 1744)

New York gazette or weekly postboy (successor to Gazette)

Printed by James Parker, 1743–73.

3d newspaper in New York city.

Partial files at:

New York historical society (1744–)

Lenox library (1744–66)

New York evening post (weekly)

Printed by Henry De Foreest, 1744–51.

4th newspaper in New York city.

Partial file at:

New York historical society (1750–51)

New York mercury (weekly)

Printed by Hugh Gaine, 1752–83.

Afterward called New York gazette and weekly mercury.

5th newspaper in New York city.

Partial files at:

Pennsylvania historical society.

Lenox library (nearly complete file after 1755)

New York gazette (weekly)

Printed by William Weyman, 1759–67.

6th newspaper in New York city.

Nearly complete file at Lenox library.

American chronicle.

Printed by Samuel Farley, 1761–62.

7th newspaper in New York city.

No copies found.

New York pacquet.

Printed by Benjamin Mecon; one or more numbers issued, 1763.

8th newspaper in New York city.

Lenox library has first number.

New York journal or general advertiser.

Printed by John Holt, 1766–98 or not long after.

Published in Kingston, 1777 and in Poughkeepsie, 1777–83; several changes in title after 1783.

9th newspaper in New York city.

This paper was intended to succeed the New York gazette or weekly post-boy and so numbered, but the latter was published till 1773.

Lenox library has 1766–75, 1787–89.

New York chronicle.

Published by Alex. & James Robertson, 1769–70.

Publishers removed to Albany in 1770.

10th newspaper in New York city.

Lenox library has one number.

Rivington's New York gazetteer; or the Connecticut, New Jersey, Hudson's river and Quebec weekly advertiser.

Printed by James Rivington, 1773–75, 1777–83.
Discontinued from Nov. 1775 to Oct. 1777; changes of title after 1777.
11th newspaper in New York city.
Lenox library has 1773–75, 1779–80.

Constitutional gazette.

Printed by John Anderson.
Published for a few months in 1775.
12th newspaper in New York city.
Lenox library has one number.

Independent reflector; or weekly essays.

Printed by James Parker, 1752–53.
52 numbers form a set.
Complete file at Lenox library.

Albany gazette.

Printed by Alex. & James Robertson, 1771–75.
1st newspaper in Albany.

Occasional reverberator.

Printed by James Parker, New York.
September, 1753, no. 1–2.
No more published.
Complete file at Lenox library.

Instructor.

" J. Parker & William Weyman, New York, 1755, no. 1–6.

John Englishman.

" Parker & Weyman, April–July 1755, no. 1–10.
Lenox library has all but no. 9.

Medicine

Beck, J. B. Historical sketch of the state of American medicine before the revolution.   35p.   Alb. 1842.   610.8 H7
Annual address before the New York state medical society, Feb. 1, 1842.

———— ———— Ed. 2. Alb. 1850.   N. Y. state lib.

Curtis, F: C. Glimpses of early medicine in Albany. (*see* Albany medical annals, Oct. 1886, 7: 289-300)   610.5 Oo

McNaughton, James. Progress of medicine in New York state. (*see* New York state medical society. Transactions. 1836-37. p. 53-81)   610.6 G9a

Wyckoff, R. M. Early medicine in New York: a centennial contribution. (*see* New York state medical society. Transactions. 1876. p. 278-97)   610.6 G9a

Commerce and manufactures

Colden, Cadwallader. Papers relating to an act of the assembly of General h
tory
Commerce the province of New York for encouragement of the Indian trade and for prohibiting the selling of Indian goods to the French. 24p.　N. Y. 1724.　　　　　　　　　　　　　　N. Y. pub. lib.

> *Contents :* 1 Petition of London merchants against act.
> 2 Reference of petition to lords commissioners.
> 3 Extract from minutes of lords commissioners.
> 4 Report of lords commissioners on petition.
> 5 Report of committee of council of New York.
> 6 Memorial concerning fur trade of New York.

Edsall, T: H: Something about fish, fisheries and fishermen in New York in the 17th century. (*see* New York genealogical and bio-graphical record, Oct. 1882, 13 : 181-200)　　　929.1　N421

Hasenclever, Peter. The case of Peter Hasenclever.　97p. n.t-p.　　　　　　　　　　　　　　　　　　923.843　H27

> Narrative of the establishment by him of iron foundries in various parts of New York, 1764-69, and his subsequent failure.

Histoire et commerce des colonies Angloises dans l'Amérique septen-trionale.　336p.　Lond. 1765.　　　　　　　N. Y. state lib.

> New York, p. 135-66.

Homes, H: A: Notice of Peter Hasenclever ; an iron manufacturer of 1764-69.　8p.　Alb. 1875.　　　　　　　　　908　H75

———— Notice of Peter Hasenclever ; an early iron manufacturer. (*see* Albany institute. Transactions. 1876. 8 : 199-206) N. Y. state lib.

Kennedy, Archibald. Report on trade and production, 1738. (*see* N. Y. (state)-State, Secretary of. Documentary history of the state of New York)　1849-51.　4 : 182-83.　974.7　N424
　　　　　　　　　　　　　1850-51.　4 : 117.　974.7　qN423

Papers relating to the trade and manufactures of the province of New York, 1705-57. (*see* N. Y. (state)-State, Secretary of. Docu-mentary history of the state of New York)
　　　　　　　　1849-51.　1 : 709-36.　974.7　N424
　　　　　　　　1850-51.　1 : 483-99.　974.7　qN423

> Also in *Manual of the city of New York.* 1852, 11:441-49, 352.0747 N4k.

Statistics of revenue, imports, exports, etc.　1691-1768.　(*see* N. Y. (state)-State, Secretary of. Documentary history of the state of New York)　　1849-51.　1 : 699-707.　974.7　N424
　　　　　　　　　　　　1850-51.　1 : 475-82.　974.7　qN423

Tariff of 1655. (*see* N. Y. (state)-Legislature. Documents relating to the colonial history of the state of New York.　1853-87.　1 : 572-73)
　　　　　　　　　　　　　　　　　　　　　　R974.7　qN421

LOCAL COLONIAL HISTORY

Barber, J: W. & Howe, Henry. Historical collections of the state
of New York.   608p.   N. Y. 1841.   974.7 B231
Outline history of the state, p.13-41: remainder of volume contains short
sketches of the counties in alphabetic order.

Fernow, Berthold, *tr. & ed.* Documents relating to the history and
settlements of the towns along the Hudson and Mohawk rivers,
with the exception of Albany, from 1630 to 1684, and also illustrating the relations of the settlers with the Indians.   617p.
Alb. 1881.   (*in* N. Y. (state)-Legislature. Documents relative
the colonial history of the state of New York. 1853-87.   v. 13)
                 R974.7 qN421

Powell, L. P. *ed.* Historic towns of the middle states.   439p.
N. Y. 1899.   (American historic towns)   974.7 P87

New York city and vicinity
New York city

Bartram, F. S. Retrographs; comprising a history of New York city
prior to the revolution.   196p.   N. Y. °1888.   N. Y. pub. lib.

Belden, E. P. New York; past, present and future; comprising a
history of the city of New York, a description of its present condition and an estimate of its future increase.   125p   N. Y. 1849.
                 974 71   B41

Colonial history, p.11-20.
—— —— Ed. 3   153p.   N. Y. pub. lib.

Bernheim, A. C. Relations of the city and the state of New York.
(*see* Political science quarterly, Sep. 1894, 9:377-402)   305   P75
Colonial period, p.377-86.

Black, G: A. History of municipal ownership of land on Manhattan
Island to 1844.   83p.   N. Y. 1891.   (*in* Studies in history,
economics and public law, ed. by the university faculty of political science of Columbia college. 1891-92. v.1, no. 3)   305   St9

Booth, M.. L. History of the city of New York, from its earliest set-
tlement to the present time.   846p.   N. Y. 1859.   974.71 B64
Prerevolutionary period, p.21-509.
—— History of the city of New York.   2v.   892p.   N. Y. 1867.
                 N. Y. pub. lib.

Paged continuously.
—— —— 920p.   N. Y. 1880. °67.   N. Y. pub. lib.

Chronological sketch of the progress of the city of New York till the
close of the revolutionary war. (*see* Reminiscences of the city of
New York and its vicinity. 1855. p. 280–90)   974.71 R28
Also in Manual of the city of New York. 1856. 15 : 530–40, 352.0747 N4k.

Chronology of New York, 1609–1835. (*see* Old New York, Nov. 1889,
1 : 276–88)   974.71 qOl1

Clark, Emmons. The New York military. (*see* Wilson, J. G. *ed.*
Memorial history of the city of New York. 1892–93. 4 : 263–96)
974.71 qW69

Colton, J. H. *pub.* Summary historical, geographical and statistical
view of the city of New York together with some notices of Brooklyn,
Williamsburgh, etc. in its environs. 46p. N.Y. 1836. 917 47 C72

Curry, Daniel, *anon.* New York; a historical sketch of the rise and
progress of the metropolitan city of America, by a New Yorker.
339p.   N. Y. 1853.   974.71 C93
Colonial history, p.13–120.

Darling, C. W. New Amsterdam, New Orange, New York; with
chronological data. 43p.   n.p.1889.   N. Y. state lib.

DeForest, T. R. *anon.* Olden times in New York by those who
knew. 54p.   N. Y. 1833.   974.71 D36
17th and 18th centuries.

Digest of city ordinances, prior to the revolution. (*see* N. Y. (city)—
Common council. Manual. 1858. 17 : 531–90)   352.0747 N4k

Disturnell, John, *comp.* New York as it was and as it is; giving an
account of the city from its settlement to the present time, forming
a complete guide to the great metropolis of the nation, including the
city of Brooklyn and the surrounding cities and villages. 296p.
N. Y. 1876.   917.471 D63
First 50 pages describe New York city as it was.

Durand, E: D. Finances of New York city. 397p. N. Y. 1898.
352.1 D93
Finances before 1784, p. 7–26.

The Dutch in New York. (*see* National magazine, June 1858, 12 :
494–501)   051 N21

Early state of medical science and practice in the city of New York.
(*see* N. Y. (city)—Common council. Manual. 1849. 8 : 378–81)
352.0747 N4k

Extracts from the ancient records, commencing from the year 1647, and continuing to about the period of 1797. (*see* N. Y. (city)—Common council. Manual. 1844-45. 4 : 293-324) 352.0747 N4k

Extracts from the official records in early times. (*see* N. Y. (city)— Common council. Manual. 1847. 6 : 342-71) 352.0747 N4k
1645-97.

Gerard, J. W. Impress of nationalities on New York city. (*see* Magazine of American history, Jan. 1890, 23 : 40-59) 973 M27

Gilder, J. B. New York, the cosmopolitan city. (*see* Powell, L. P. *ed.* Historic towns of the middle states. 1899. p.169-211) 974.7 P87

Goodwin, *Mrs* **Maud (Wilder), Royce, A. C. & Putnam, Ruth,** *ed.* Historic New York; being the 1st and 2d series of the Half moon papers. 2v. N. Y. 1897-99. 974.71 G63
Eva P. Brownell, a fourth joint editor of v.2.

Gowans, William. Western memorabilia. (*see* Old New York, Mar.– May 1890, 2 : 130-37, 177-84, 226-42) 974.71 qOl1
Chronology of New York city, 1631-1851.

Griffin, A. P. C. New York city. 11p. Bost. 1887. 016.9747 qG87
50 copies reprinted from his *Index of articles upon American local history.*

Hardie, James. Description of the city of New York, to which is prefixed a brief account of its first settlement by the Dutch in the year 1629; and of the most remarkable events which have occurred in its history from that to the present period. 360p. N. Y. 1827.
917.471 H21
History, p.1-144.

History of the government of New York. (*see* N. Y. (city)—Common council. Manual. 1854. 13 : 537-46) 352.0747 N4k

History of the poor in the city of New York, 1699-1816. (*see* N. Y. (city) — Common council. Manual. 1862. 21 : 658-60)
352.0747 N4k

Honeyman, A. V. *comp.* Joannes Nevius, schepen and 3d secretary of New Amsterdam under the Dutch, 1st secretary of New York city under the English; and his descendants A. D. 1627–1900. 732p. Plainfield N. J. 1900. 929.2 qN414

Jameson, J: F. Origin and development of the municipal government of New York city. (*see* Magazine of American history, May 1882, 8 : 315-30, Sep. 1882, 8 : 598-611) 973 M27

Lamb, *Mrs* **M. J. R. (Nash).** History of the city of New York; its origin, rise and progress. 2v. N. Y. ᶜ1877–80. 974.71 qL16
   Contents: v.1 The period to 1776..
         v.2 Century of national independence, closing in 1876.

—— —— Externals of modern New York by Mrs Burton Harrison; being v.2 ch.21, of Mrs Martha J. Lamb's History of the city of New York. p.789–874. N. Y. ᶜ1896. 974.71 qL16 v.3
   This volume and the two of the previous entry were published as a new edition of Mrs Lamb's history in 1896.

List of the members of the city government from its incorporation, 1653, up to the present time; arranged alphabetically. (*see* N. Y. (city)—Common council. Manual. 1854. 13:400–38) 352.0747 N4k
   Continued in later volumes.

Lossing, B. J: History of New York city embracing an outline sketch of events from 1609–1830, and a full account of its development from 1830–84. 2v. 881p. · N. Y. ᶜ1884. 974.71 L89
   Paged continuously. Colonial period, p.1–39.

Mayors of the city of New York. (*see* N. Y. (city)—Common council. Manual. 1869. 27:772–75) 352.0747 N4k

Members of the city council from 1655 to 1842. (*see* N. Y. (city)—Common council. Manual. 1841. 1:91–180) 352.0747 N4k
   Continued in later volumes.

Mines, J: F. Walks in our church yards; old New York, Trinity parish, by Felix Oldboy. 181p. N. Y. 1896. 917.471 M661

Mitchell, S: L. Historical summary of the several attacks that have been made upon the city of New York and of the measures that have been adopted for its defence, from 1613 until 1812. (*see* N.Y. (city)—Common council. Manual. 1868. 26:864–83) 352.0747 N4k

—— An historical summary of the several attacks that have been made upon the city of New York since its first settlement, and of the measures that have been adopted from time to time for its defence. 40p. N. Y. 1812. L. I. hist. soc. ·

Moss, Frank. American metropolis from Knickerbocker days to the present time; New York city life in all its various phases. 3v. N. Y. 1897. 974.71 M851

Local history
New York city **N. Y. (state)-N. Y. city charter, Commissions to amend.**
Charter of the city of New York from 1686 to 1857, inclusive, and the amendments thereto; also various acts of the legislature relative to the city of New York. 222p.   N. Y. 1861.   N. Y. state law lib.
Dongan charter 1686, p. 1-20.
Montgomerie charter 1730, p. 21-85.
Confirming act of 1732, p. 85-87.

New York city. (*see* Willsey & Lewis. Harper's book of facts. 1895.
p. 572-75)   Ro31   qW68
Chronological history of the city, 1626-1894, and list of mayors, 1665-1895.

New York privateers, 1704-1815. (*see* N. Y. (city)—Common council.
Manual. 1870. 28 : 867-73)   352.0747   N4k

Old New York. (*see* Munsey's magazine, Ap. 1898, 19 : 43-56)   051   M92

Olden time in New York; early city settlement. (*see* N. Y. (city)—
Common council. Manual. 1849. 8 : 336-37)   352.0747   N4k

Papers relating to the city of New York. (*see* N. Y. (state)—State,
Secretary of. Documentary history of the state of New York)
                    1849-51.   1 : 593-626.   974.7   N424
                    1850-51.   1 : 383-407.   974.7   qN423
Contents : First application for municipal form of government, 1649.
            Provisional order for the government, 1650.
            Communication from West India company to director and council, 1652.
            Instruction for the sheriff, 1652-53.
            Nicolls's charter, 1665.
            Mayor and aldermen's commission, 1665.
            Benckes and Evertsen's charter, 1673.
            Instructions for under sheriff and schepens of suburbs, 1673.
            Colve's charter, 1674.
            Census about 1703.
            Ministers of Dutch reformed church 1758 and 1796.

Population of the city, at various periods. (*see* N. Y (city)—Common
council. Manual. 1842. 2 : 248)   352.0747   N4k
Population in 1696, 1731, 1756, 1773.

Reminiscences of the city of New York and its vicinity.   350p.
N. Y. 1855.   974.71   R28
Papers written for *Manual of the city of New York*, collected and 50 copies printed; mostly on colonial period. No index.

Richmond, J. F. New York and its institutions, 1609-1873.   Ed. 7.
608p.   N. Y. 1873, c71.   917.471   R41
71 pages relating to colonial period.

Roosevelt, Theodore. New York.   232p.   Lond. 1891.   (Historic towns)   974.71 R67
Colonial period, p. 1-104.

Ruttenber, E: M. Native inhabitants of Manhattan and its Indian antiquities. (*see* Wilson, J. G. *ed.* Memorial history of the
city of New York. 1892-93. 1:33-54)   974.71 qW69

Sketches of the mayors of New York from 1665-1834. (*see* N. Y.(city)—
Common council. Manual. 1853. 12:379-426)   352.0747 N4k

Stone, W: L. Centennial history of New York city from the discovery to the present day.   252p.   N. Y. 1876.   974.71 St7
Same work as his *History of New York city.* 1868.

———— History of New York city from the discovery to the present day.
252p.   N. Y. 1868.   974.71 St71
Colonial period, p. 1-144.

———— ———— 658+136p.   N. Y. 1872.   N. Y. pub. lib.
Dutch period, p. 9-246.
Judiciary of the early Dutch period by C: P. Daly,   apx. p. 41-54.
New York society in the olden time by W: I. Kipp,   "   93.

Todd, C: B. Story of the city of New York.   478p.   N. Y. 1888.
(Great cities of the republic)   · 974.71 T56
Colonial period, p. 1-282.

Valentine, D: T: Financial history of the city of New York from the
earliest period. (*see* N. Y. (city)—Common council. Manual.
1859. 18:496-537)   352.0747 N4k

———— History of the city of New York. 404p. N. Y. 1853. 974.71 V23
From earliest discovery to 1750.
Includes list of freemen 1683-1740, lists of inhabitants, landowners, etc.

———— *comp.* Reminiscences and history of the city of New York.
264p. N. Y. 1857-58.   974.71 V231
No title page.
Transfer of land, early ordinances, general description, etc. relating chiefly
to the period before the revolution.
Extracts from his *Manual* 1857-58.

Van Pelt, Daniel. Leslie's history of the greater New York.   3v.
N. Y. ᶜ1898.   974.71 qV34
Contents : v. 1 New York to the consolidation.
        v. 2 Brooklyn and the other boroughs.
        v. 3 Encyclopedia of New York biography and genealogy.

Van Rensselaer, *Mrs* **Sarah.** The Bayards of New York and the
early history of the city. (*see her* Ancestral sketches. 1882.
p.29–61)   923.27 qV35
1647-73.

———— The growth of the city of New York from 1626. (*see her* Ancestral sketches. 1882. p. 159–82)   923.27 qV35

Watson, J: F. Historic tales of olden time, concerning the early settlement and advancement of New York city and state for the use of
families and schools. 214p. N. Y. 1832.   974.7 W33

———— New York city. (*see his* Annals and occurrences of New York
city and state in the olden time. 1846. p.141–390) 974.7 W331

———— Olden time; researches and reminiscences of New York city.
(*see his* Annals of Philadelphia. 1830.   apx.p.1–78)
                                                974.811 W332

Wilson, J. G. *ed.* Memorial history of the city of New York from
its first settlement to the year 1892.   4v. N. Y. 1892–93.
                                                974.71 qW69

———— Old New York. (*see* Cosmopolitan, Jan. 1892, 12:313–23) 051 qC82

Winthrop, B: R. Old New York. (*see* N. Y. (city)—Common council. Manual. 1862. 21:686–94)   352.0747 N4k
Read before the New York historical society Feb. 4, 1862.

Dutch period

For first settlement of Manhattan Island, see Trading companies, p. 325.

Account of Anneke Janse and her family; also the will of Anneke
Janse in Dutch and English. 31p. Alb. 1870.   040 P v.2541
150 copies printed.

Anneke Jans Bogardus and her farm. (*see* Harper's magazine,
May 1885, 70:836–49)   051 H23

Anneke Janse. (*see* Munsell, Joel. Collections on the history of
Albany. 1865–71. 2:422–27; 3:459–64)   974.743 qM92
Contains a partial genealogy of her descendants.

Antiquities of New York. (*see* Catholic world, Aug. 1869, 9:652–60)
                                                205 C28

The beginning of the city. (*see* N. Y. (city)—Common council.
Manual. 1853. 12:427–41)   352.0747 N4k

Biographical sketches of all the magistrates of New Amsterdam. (*see* Local hist
New York
Dutch peri
N. Y. (city)—Common council. Manual. 1852. 11:378–400)
352.0747 N4k

Burgomasters of New Amsterdam 1653–74. (*see* Wilson, J. G. *ed.*
Memorial history of the city of New York. 1892–93. 2:49)
974.71 qW69

Davis, Asahel. History of New Amsterdam; or, New York as it was,
in the days of the Dutch governors together with papers on events
connected with the American revolution, and on Philadelphia in
the times of William Penn. 240p. N.Y. 1854. 974.71 D29
Albany, Schenectady, Esopus and Newpaltz, apx. p. 93–111.

Durand, E: D. City chest of New Amsterdam p. 209–38. N. Y.
^c1897. (Half moon ser. v. 1, no. 7)   N. Y. state lib.

———— ———— (*see* Goodwin, *Mrs* Maud (Wilder), & *others.* Historic
New York. 1897. 1:159–90)
974.71 G63

The Dutch on Manhattan. (*see* Harper's magazine, Sep. 1854,
9:433–53)
051 H23

The Dutch records of New York. (*see* Old New York) 974.71 qOl1
     May 1890, 2:251–61   Dec. 1890, 2:337–42
     Mar. 1891, 2:462–70
    Contents: Ordinances of Gov. Stuyvesant; inordinate drinking to be sup-
       pressed, goats and hogs must be kept out of the highway, ob-
       servance of the sabbath, no liquor to be sold to the Indians,
       trading by foreigners forbidden.

Goodwin, *Mrs* **Maud (Wilder).** Fort Amsterdam in the days of the
Dutch.   p. 239–74. N. Y. ^c1897. (Half moon ser. v. 1, no. 8)
N. Y. state lib.

———— ———— (*see* Goodwin, *Mrs* Maud (Wilder) & *others.* Historic
New York. 1897. 1:1–37)
974.71 G63

Historical minutes of the times of the Dutch. (*see* N. Y. (city)—
Common council. Manual. 1860. 19:612–19) 352.0747 N4k

McManus, Blanche. How the Dutch came to Manhattan. 82p.
N. Y. 1897. (Colonial monographs) 974.71 M22
New Amsterdam from settlement through 2d occupation by the Dutch.

Megapolensis, Johannes. Original letter. (*see* Old New York, Ap.
1890, 2:145–51) 974.71 qOl1
Dated 15 Aug. 1648: relating to Bogardus and Anneke Jans.

Nash, S. P. Anneke Jans Bogardus; her farm and how it became the
property of Trinity church, New York; an historic inquiry. 105p.
N. Y. 1896. 283.7471 T733

New Amsterdam. Proceedings of the burgomaster and schepens
(*see* N. Y. (city)—Common council. Manual)   352.0747   N4k

1845, 5:340–71	1849, 8:382–434	1852, 11:473–98
1847, 6:371–86	1850, 9:487–546	1853, 12:472–99
1848, 7:376–84	1851, 10:421–50	

—— Records of New Amsterdam from 1653 to 1674, A. D. ed. by
Berthold Fernow. 7v.   N. Y. 1897.   974.71   N424

Contents: Minutes of the court of burgomasters and schepens.

v.1 1653–55	v.2 1656–58	v.3 1658–61
v.4 1662–63	v.5 1664–66	v.6 1666–73

v. 7 1673–74, p. 1–139; Administrative minutes, p. 140–267;
Index, p. 269–352.

—— Records of the city of New Amsterdam, ed. by H: B. Dawson.
(*see* Historical magazine)   973   H62   v.11–13

Jan.–Ap. 1867, ser. 2, 1:32–41, 108–12, 170–75, 224–29
June   "   "   1:354–64   Jan. 1868, ser. 2, 3:39–45
July   "   "   2:30–34   Mar. "   "   3:168–71
Administration of Gov. Stuyvesant.

—— Records of the city of New Amsterdam in New Netherland, *ed.*
by H: B. Dawson. v. 1, 79p.   Morrisania N.Y. 1867. 974.71 D32

No more published. 100 copies reprinted with changes from *Historical
magazine*, v. 11. Chiefly orders of Gov. Stuyvesant and council selected
from the early Dutch records, 1747–59.

New York city in 1661: the story of an old map. (*see* American bibliopolist, Dec. 1871, 3:497–98)   010.5   Am3

Noyes, J. O. The Dutch in New Amsterdam. (*see* National magazine, May 1858, 12:443–48)   051   N21

Paulding, J. K. *comp.* Affairs and men of New Amsterdam, in the
time of Governor Peter Stuyvesant; comp. from Dutch manuscript
records of the period. 161p.   N. Y. 1843.   974.71   P28

Schaghen, P. Original document; letter announcing purchase of New
York city. (*see* National magazine, Sep. 1892, 16:586–90) 973 M271

Scisco, L. D. The burgher guard of New Amsterdam. (*see* American historical register, Ap. 1895, 2:737–47)   973   qAm31

—— Garrison of Fort Amsterdam.   (*see* American historical register,
May–June 1896, 4:255–62, 372–77)   973   qAm31

Stilwell, B: M. Early memoirs of the Stilwell family with a sketch
of the history of Manhattan Island and its vicinity under the Dutch.
289p.   N. Y. 1878.   929.2   St58

Valentine, D: T: Cornelis Steenwyck, burgomaster of New Amster- Local his Now Yor dam, mayor of New York. (*see* N. Y. (city)—Common council. *English p* Manual. 1864. 23 : 648–64) 352.0747 N4k

——— Law and lawyers in New Amsterdam. (*see* N. Y. (city)—Common council. Manual. 1863. 22 : 569–80) 352.0747 N4k

Van Rensselaer, *Mrs* **Schuyler.** The mother city of Greater New York. (*see* Century magazine, May 1898, 56 : 138–46) 051 Scr31

Watson, J: F. First settlement of the city of New York. (*see his* Annals and occurrences of New York city and state. 1846. p.9–13) 974.7 W331

English period

American divines: the Rev. Samuel Johnson, D. D. (*see* Christian observer, Dec. 1832, 32 : 763–76, apx. 829–36) 205 C462

Andrews, W: L. The Bradford map; the city of New York at the time of the granting of the Montgomerie charter; a description to accompany a [reduced] facsimile of an actual survey made by James Lyne and printed by William Bradford in 1731. 115p. N. Y. 1893. 917.471 An2

Only two copies of the original are known to exist.

Beardsley, E. E: Life and correspondence of Samuel Johnson, D. D. missionary of the church of England in Connecticut and first president of Kings college, New York. Ed. 2. 380p. N. Y. 1874.

923.77 J63

The burghers of New Amsterdam and the freemen of New York 1675–1866. (*see* New York historical society. Collections. 1886. Publication fund ser. v. 18) 974.7 N42

Capture of the city of New Amsterdam by the English. (*see* N. Y. (city)–Common council. Manual. 1861. 20:603–21) 352.0747 N4k

Carpenter, D. H. New York's first mayor. (*see* New York genealogical and biographical record, Oct. 1887, 28: 190–96) 929.1 qN421

Thomas Willett, mayor 1665.

Carther, E. Letter describing the stamp act riot in New York. (*see* New York mercantile library. New York city in the American revolution. 1860. p. 41–49) N. Y. state lib.

Chandler, P. W. Trials of certain negroes and others before the supreme court of New York for a conspiracy to burn the city and murder the inhabitants, 1741. (*see his* American criminal trials. 1841–44. 1 : 211–54) N. Y. state law lib.

Chandler, T:B. Life of Samuel Johnson, D. D. the first president of Kings (now Columbia) college in New York. 208p. N. Y. 1805. 923.77 J632

City affairs after the capture of the city by the English, 1665–1672. (*see* N. Y. (city)-Common council. Manual. 1869. 27:887–90) 352.0747 N4k

City of New York in 1673. (*see* Family magazine, 1835–36, 3 : 162–68) 051 qF21

Clarke, Jo. New York in 1672–73; A letter·written by Jo. Clarke of Fort James, N. Y. to Silvester Salisbury, commander of Fort Albany. (*see* Historical magazine, Feb. 1860, 4 : 50–51) 973 H62

Condition of New York in 1757. (*see* Old New York, Ap.1890, 2:166–77) 974.71 qOl1

Condition of the city fortifications, from a survey in 1688. (*see* Reminiscences of the city of New York and its vicinity. 1855. p. 123–25) 974.71 R28

Court of lieutenancy, 1686–96. (*see* New York historical society. Collections. 1881. Publication fund ser. 13 : 389–438) 974.7 N42

DeWitt, Edward. Map of the city of New York showing the original high water line and the location of the different farms and estates; with an explanation. (*see* N. Y. (city)-Common council. Manual. 1855. 12 : 436–41) . 352.0747 N4k

The duke of York's present to the common council of New York. (*see* N.Y. (city)—Common council. Manual. 1849. 8:343) 352.0747 N4k

Execution of persons engaged in the negro plot in the city of New York in the year 1741. (*see* N. Y. (city)—Common council. Manual. 1866. 25:810–20) . 352.0747 N4k

Extracts from early newspapers, 1726–27. (*see* Old New York, Aug. 1889, 1:37–41) 974.71 qOl1

Extracts from early newspapers, 1733–34. (*see* Old New York, Dec. 1889, 1:357–59) 974.71 qOl1

The first negro plot in the city of New York, 1712. (*see* N. Y. (city)— Common council. Manual. 1869. 27:775–76) 352.0747 N4k

Gerard, J. W. Dongan charter of the city of New York. (*see* Magazine of American history,. July 1886, 16:30–49) 973 M27
New York city, 1664–88.

Grim, David. Memorandum. (*see* Reminiscences of the city of New York and its vicinity. 1855. p. 156–58)   974.71   R28   Local hist
New York
English pe
1741–55.

Headley, J. T. Negro riots of 1712–41 ; and, Stamp act riot of 1765.
·   (*see his* Great riots of New York 1712 to 1873. 1873. p. 24–55)
     974.71   H34

Hoes, R. R. Negro plot of 1712. (*see* New York genealogical and biographical record, Oct. 1890, 21:162–63)   929.1   qN421

Horsmanden, Daniel. Journal of the proceedings in the detection of the conspiracy formed by some white people in conjunction with negro and other slaves for burning the city of New York in America and murdering the inhabitants, by the recorder of the city of New York.   205p.   N. Y. 1744.   N. Y. pub. lib.

———— ———— 425.   Lond. 1747.   N. Y. pub. lib.

———— Negro conspiracy in the city of New York in 1741 ; ed. by W: B. Wedgwood.   96p.   N. Y. 1851.   N. Y. hist. soc.

———— New York conspiracy ; or, A history of the negro plot with the journal of the proceedings against the conspirators at New York in the years 1741–42. Ed. 2.   385p.   N. Y. 1810.   326.9747   H78
List of editions of this work in Winsor, 5 : 242.

———— Trial of John Ury " for being an ecclesiastical person, made by authority pretended from the see of Rome and coming and abiding in the province of New York " and with being one of the conspirators in the negro plot to burn the city of New York, 1741.   58p.
Abridged from *The New York conspiracy ; or, A history of the negro plot.* 100 copies printed.

Interesting selections of olden times. (*see* N. Y. (city)—Common council. Manual. 1849. 8:338–43)   352.0747   N4k
Includes stamp act, population, commerce, taxes, etc.

Interesting selections of the doings of our city fathers in early times. (*see* N. Y. (city)—Common council. Manual. 1848. 7 :402–6)
     352.0747   N4k
1684–91.

Leach, J. G. Major William Dyre of New York. (*see* American historical register, Sep. 1894, 1 : 37–43)   973   qAm31

Marshall, O. H. New York charter, 1664 and 1674. (*see* Magazine of American history, Jan. 1882, 8 : 24–30)   973   M27

Mementoes of the olden time. (*see* N. Y. (city)—Common council.
  Manual. 1869.   27:850–63)   352.0747 N4k
  1676–1790.

Moulton, J. W. New York 170 years ago; with a view and explanatory notes. 24p.   N. Y. 1843.   974.71 M861
  1673. Not the same as his *View of the city of New Orange*.

—— View of the city of New Orange (now New York) as it was in the
  year 1673, with explanatory notes. 40p. N.Y. 1825.   974.71 M86

The negro execution, 1741. (*see* N. Y. (city)—Common council.
  Manual. 1856.   15:448–51)   352.0747 N4k

Negro executions, 1741. (*see* Reminiscences of the city of New York
  and its vicinity. 1855.   p.198–201)   974.71 R28

Negro plot in New York in 1741. (*see* National magazine, July 1893,
  18:128–31)   973 M271

N. Y. (city)—Common council. Petition for a new charter, 1730.
  (*see* Reminiscences of the city of New York and its vicinity. 1855.
  p.343–47)   974 71 R28
  Includes report of the committee on the petition.

N. Y. (city), Protestants. Petition to King William 3. (*see* Reminiscences of the city of New York and its vicinity. 1855.
  p.170–71)   .   974.71 R28

Newspaper correspondence on public matters in the city of New York
  from 1704–1708. (*see* N. Y. (city)—Common council. Manual.
  1869.   27:796–837)   352.0747 N4k
  Signed J. S.

Old times; New York in 1673. (*see* N. Y. (city)—Common council.
  Manual. 1850.   9:420–22)   352.0747 N4k

Papers relating to the city of New York. (*see* N. Y. (state)—State,
  Secretary of. Documentary history of the state of New York)
                    1849–51.   3:395–538.   974.7 N424
                    1850–51.   3:239–324.   974.7 qN423
  1671–1769.

Papers relating to the restoration of New York to the English. (*see*
  N. Y. (city)—Common council. Manual.   1852. 11:415–38)
                                                        352.0747 N4k

Parsons, C: W. First mayor of New York city; Thomas Willett. (*see*
  Magazine of American history, Mar. 1887, 17:233–42)   973 M27

Particulars of the riot, soon after the capture of the city of New York Local his
New York
English p
by the English in 1665. (*see* N. Y. (city)—Common council. Man-
ual. 1869. 27:890–91) 352.0747 N4k

Petition of the common council of New York for a free trade with
Holland, 1669. (*see* N. Y. (city)—Common council. Manual.
1850. 9:423) 352.0747 N4k

Political disputes of the year 1701 in New York city. (*see* N. Y. (city)—
Common council. Manual. 1857. 15:515–28) 352.0747 N4k

Random extracts from city records. (*see* N. Y. (city)—Common
council. Manual. 1856. 15:515–19) 352.0747 N4k
1752-93.

Samuel Johnson. (*see* American journal of education, July 1877,
27:449–58) 370 5 Am31
Also in same journal Dec. 1859, 7:461-70.

Shannon, J. City of New York, 1753–4, compiled from the newspapers of the day. (*see* N. Y. (city)—Common council. Manual.
1868. 26:884–905) 352.0747 N4k
Signed J. S.

Sharpe, *Rev.* **John.** Proposals for erecting a school, library and chapel
at New York, 1712–13. (*see* New York historical society. Collections. 1881. Publication fund ser. 13:339–63) 974.7 N42

Shea, J:G. New York negro plot of 1741. (*see* N. Y. (city)—Common council. Manual. 1870. 28:764–71) 352.0747 N4k

Thompson, Edward. New York in 1756. (*see* Old New York,
Feb. 1890, 2:36–38) 974.71 qOl1
Letter dated Aug. 15, 1756.

Translation of a letter sent by the burgomasters and schepens of New
Amsterdam to the West India company, describing the taking of
the city by the English in 1664. (*see* N. Y. (city)—Common council.
Manual. 1860. 19:592–93) 352.0747 N4k

Valentine, D:T: Caleb Heathcote, mayor of New York, 1711–13.
(*see* N. Y. (city)—Common council. Manual. 1864. 23:665–68)
352.0747 N4k

———— The city of New York 1730–52, compiled from the newspapers
of the day. (*see* N. Y. (city)—Common council. Manual.
1864–66) 352.0747 N4k
23:672–739, 1730–36 24:726–848, 1737–49 25:617–724, 1850–52

Van Pelt, Daniel. The city under Governor John Montgomerie, 1728–32. (*see* Wilson, J. G. *ed.* Memorial history of the city of New York. 1892–93. 2 : 179–202)   974.71 qW69

Localities, buildings

Baptist church in Gold street. (*see* Old New York, May 1890, 2 : 242–50)   974.71 qOl1

Bellamy, B. W. Governors island. p.141–81. N. Y. ᶜ1897. (Half moon ser. v.1, no. 5)   N. Y. state lib.

—— —— (*see* Goodwin, *Mrs* Maud (Wilder) & *others.* Historic New York. 1897. 1 : 365–457)   974.71 G63

Bisland, Elizabeth. Old Greenwich. p.275–301. N. Y. ᶜ1897. (Half moon ser. v. 1, no. 9)   N. Y. state lib.

—— —— (*see* Goodwin, *Mrs* Maud (Wilder) & *others.* Historical New York. 1897. 1 : 263–91)   974.71 G63

The bowery. (*see* N. Y. (city) — Common council. Manual. 1866. 25 : 573–89)   352.0747 N4k

Bowling green. (*see* N. Y. (city) — Common council. Manual. 1858. 17 : 633–38)   352.0747 N4k

Caldwell, A. B. A lecture; the history of Harlem with appendix of history of New York from 1589 to 1674, also a business directory of Harlem. 49p. N. Y. 1882.   974.71 C12
Delivered at Harlem April 24, 1882.

Cutting, E.. B. Old taverns and posting inns. p. 241–76. N. Y. ᶜ1898. (Half moon ser. v. 2, no. 7)   N. Y. state lib.

—— —— (*see* Goodwin, *Mrs* Maud (Wilder) & *others.* Historic New York. 1899. 2 : 241–76)   974.71 G63

Daly, C; P. First theater in New York. (*see* Historical magazine, July 1864, 8 : 232–37)   973 H62

Dawson, H: B. The park and its vicinity. (*see* N. Y. (city) — Common council. Manual. 1855. 14 : 433–85)   352.0747 N4k
Events during stamp act troubles and the revolution.

—— —— (*see* Reminiscences of the city of New York and its vicinity. 1855. p.5–57)   974.71 R28

—— —— 95p. Morrisania N. Y. 1867. (Gleanings from the harvest field of American history) pt1   974.71 qD32
250 copies printed.

Descriptive parts of early grants and deeds on this island, specifying the localities to which they applied. (*see* Valentine, D : T : History of the city of New York. 1853. p. 307–12) 974.71 V23

Earle, *Mrs* **Alice (Morse).** Stadt huys of New Amsterdam. 29p. N. Y. ᶜ1896. (Half moon ser. v. 1, no. 1) N. Y. state lib.

—— —— (*see* Goodwin, *Mrs* Maud (Wilder) & *others*. Historic New York. 1897. 1 : 39–73) 974.71 G63

Early history of some of the streets of New York. (*see* N. Y. (city)—Common council. Manual. 1849. 8 : 347–55) 352.0747 N4k

Edsall, T: H. History of the town of Kings Bridge, now part of the 24th ward, New York city, with index. 102p. N. Y. 1887.
974.71 qEd7

Fletcher, *Gov.* **Benjamin.** Patent to Samuel Bayard, 1697. (*see* New York genealogical and biographical record, July 1887, 18 : 135–37) 929.1 qN421

The fort at the battery. (*see* N. Y. (city)—Common council. Manual. 1869. 27 : 749–55) 352.0747 N4k

Gerard, J. W. The old stadt huys of New Amsterdam; a paper read before the New York historical society, June 15, 1875. 59p. N. Y. 1875. 974.71 G31

Quarrels and law suits among the colonists in the 17th century.

—— Old streets of New York under the Dutch; a paper read before the New York historical society, June 2, 1874. 52p. N. Y. 1875.

Griffin, p.1035.

—— —— 65p. N. Y. 1874. N. Y. pub. lib.

Hazen, William. Old Chelsea. (*see* Old New York, Dec. 1890, 2 : 361–63) 974.71 qOl1

Hewitt, E: R. & Hewitt, M.. A. The bowery. p.371–406. N. Y.ᶜ 1867. (Half moon ser. v. 1, no. 12) N. Y. state lib.

—— —— (*see* Goodwin, *Mrs* Maud (Wilder) & *others*. Historic New York. 1897. 1 : 357–94) 974.71 G63

Hill, G: E. & Waring, G: E. jr. Old wells and watercourses of the island of Manhattan. 2 no. p.303–70. N. Y.ᶜ 1897. (Half moon ser. v. 1, no. 10–11) N. Y. state lib.

—— —— (*see* Goodwin, *Mrs* Maud (Wilder) & *others*. Historic New York. 1897. 1 : 191–262) 974.71 G63

Historical sketch of the islands in the East river and New York harbor. (*see* N. Y. (city) — Common council. Manual. 1855. 14 : 493-98) 352.0747 N4k

—— —— (*see* Reminiscences of the city of New York and its vicinity. 1855. p. 65-70) 974.71 R28

Historical sketches of its origin and changes of names of the streets of the city. (*see* N. Y. (city)—Common council. Manual. 1855. 14 : 499-516) 352.0747 N4k

Holland society of New York. Commemorative tablets. (*see its* Year book. 1890-91. p.15-36) 974.7 qH71
New York city.

House with a history. 10p. N. Y. 1882. N. Y. pub. lib.
Col. Roger Morris's fine old mansion.

Importance of the Long Island ferry question in old times. (*see* Reminiscences of the city of New York and its vicinity. 1855. p. 129-32) 974.71 R28

An interesting historical mansion. (*see* Spirit of '76, Feb. 1895, 1 : 114-15) 369.1 qA
Col. Roger Morris's house.

Jones, W: A. Names of streets in New York city. (*see* New York genealogical and biographical record, Ap. 1889, 20 : 65-66) 929.1 qN421

King's arms tavern, New York. (*see* Historical magazine, Oct. 1860, 4 : 303-5) 973 H62

Lamb, *Mrs* **M. J. R. (Nash).** Historic homes and landmarks, their significance and present condition. (*see* Magazine of American history) 973 M27
      Jan. 1889, 21 : 1-23   Mar. 1889, 21 : 177-207
      Sep. 1889, 22 : 177-203
New York city.

—— Wall street in history. 95p. N. Y. 1883. 974.71 L16
Colonial period, p. 9-38.
Papers written for the *Magazine of American history,* May-July, 1883.

Memorials of the ancient condition of this city. (*see* N. Y. (city)—Common council. Manual. 1852. 11 : 401-6) 352.0747 N4k

Obsolete names of localities on Manhattan Island. (*see* N. Y. (city)—Common council. Manual. 1856. 15 : 465-76) 352.0747 N4k

—— (*see* Reminiscences of the city of New York and its vicinity. 1855. p. 215-26) 974.71 R28

The old graveyard of New Amsterdam.   (*see* N. Y. (city)—Common
council.   Manual.   1856.   15:444-47)   352.0747   N4k

———— (*see* Reminiscences of the city of New York and its vicinity.
1855.   p. 194-97)   974.71   R28

Onderdonk, Henry, jr.   Old meeting houses of the society of friends in
the city of New York.   (*see* American historical record. Mar. 1872,
1 : 117-23)   973   qAm3

The original grants of village plots below Wall street.   (*see* N. Y. (city)—
Common council.   Manual.   1857.   16:495-514)   352.0747   N4k

Papers relating to the swamp.   (*see* N. Y. (city)—Common council.
Manual.   1854.   13:529-35)   352.0747   N4k

The park and its neighborhood in former times.   (*see* N. Y. (city)—
Common council.   Manual.   1856.   15:426-39)   352.0747   N4k

———— (*see* Reminiscences of the city of New York and its vicinity.
1855.   p. 176-89)   974.71   R28

Pearl street.   (*see* Old New York, Feb. 1890, 2:1-23)   974.71   qOl1

Post, J: J.   Old streets, roads, lanes, piers and wharves of New York,
showing the former and present names together with a list of altera-
tions of streets.   76p.   N. Y. 1882.   917.471   qP84

Public buildings and churches in the city erected within different
intervals.   (*see* Reminiscences of the city of New York and its
vicinity.   1855.   p.145-47)   974.71   R28

Public buildings; the ancient and modern city halls.   (*see* N.Y. (city)—
Common council.   Manual.   1845.   5:336-37)   352.0747   N4k
Selected from the *New York mirror.*

Putnam, Ruth.   Annetje Jans' farm.   p.61-98.   N. Y. ©1897.   (Half
moon ser. v.1, no.3)   N. Y. state lib.

———— —— (*see* Goodwin, *Mrs* Maud (Wilder) & *others.*   Historic New
York.   1897.   1 : 119-58)   974.71   G63

Riker, James.   Harlem (city of New York); its origin and early
annals; prefaced by notices of its founders before emigration;
also, sketches of numerous families, and the recovered history of the
land titles.   636p.   N. Y. 1881, ©'79.   974.71   R44
Earliest time to 1687.

Rodenbough, T. F.   Governors island.   (*see* Wilson, J. G. *ed.*
Memorial history of the city of New York.   1892-93.   4:38-43)
                                                        974.71   qW69

Roosevelt, Jacobus. Will. (*see* Old New York, Dec. 1889, 1 : 360–69) 974.71 qOl1

Smith, W. C. Roger Morris house. (*see* Magazine of American history, Feb. 1881, 6 : 89–104) 973 M27

Stephenson, John. The Bowery under Dutch rule. (*see* Independent, Feb. 17, 1898, v. 50, pt 1, p.208–9) 205 fIn2

────── The Bowery under English rule. (*see* Independent, Jan. 27, 1898, v. 50, pt 1, p.109–10) 205 fIn2

Terhune, *Mrs* **M. . V. (Hawes).** The Jumel mansion, on Washington Heights, New York city. (*see her* Some colonial homesteads. 1897. p.276–326) 973.2 T27

Tillou, F. R. Trinity church yard. (*see* N. Y. (city)—Common council. Manual) 352.0747 N4k
1861, 20 : 622–28   1862, 21 : 679–85   1864, 23 : 740–47

Trask, Spencer. Bowling green. 84p. N. Y. 1898. 974.71 T69

── ── p.163–208. N. Y. c1898. (Half moon ser. v. 2, no. 5) N. Y. state lib.

── ── (*see* Goodwin, *Mrs* Maud (Wilder) & *others.* Historic New York. 1899. 2 : 163–208) 974.71 G63

Valentine, D: T: The first establishment of the village of Harlem. (*see* N. Y. (city)—Common council. Manual. 1863. 22 : 610–18) 352.0747 N4k

────── Historical : public improvements previous to the revolution. (*see* N. Y. (city)—Common council. Manual. 1862. 21 : 499–555) 352.0747 N4k

────── History of Broadway. (*see* N. Y. (city)—Common council. Manual. 1865. 24 : 509–655) 352.0747 N4k

────── History of the fort in New York. (*see* N. Y. (city)—Common council. Manual. 1864. 23 : 624–47) 352.0747 N4k

────── History of Wall street to the commencement of the present century. (*see* N. Y. (city)—Common council. Manual. 1866. 25 : 533–70) 352.0747 N4k

────── *ed. anon.* Original grants of village plots below Wall street. p.495–571. N. Y. 1857. 917.471 V23
Extracted from *Manual of the city of New York.* 1857.

Villard, O. G. Early history of Wall street. p.99–140. N. Y. °1897 *Local hi*
(Half moon ser. v. 1, no 4) N Y. state lib. *New Yor* *Residents* *church re*

—— —— (*see* Goodwin, *Mrs* Maud (Wilder) & *others.* Historic New
York. 1897. 1 : 75–118) 974.71 G63

Willers, Diedrich, jr. Land titles in New York city. (*see* Old New
York, Mar. 1890, 2 : 123–29) 974.71 qOl1

Winthrop, B: R. Old New York; read before the New York histori-
. cal society Feb. 4, 1862. (*see* N. Y. (city)—Common council.
Manual. 1862. 21 : 686–94) 352.0747 N4k

List of residents, church records, etc.

Ballard, F. W. Huguenot settlers of New York city and its vicinity.
(*see* N. Y. (city)—Common council. Manual. 1862. 21 : 743–61)
352.0747 N4k

Census of the city of New York about the year 1703. *(see* N. Y.
(state)—State, Secretary of. Documentary history of the state of
New York) 1849–51. 1 : 611–24. 974.7 N424
1850–51. 1 : 395–405. 974.7 qN423
Names of heads of families.

Citizens of New Amsterdam in 1657. (*see* Wilson, J. G. *ed.* Memorial history of the city of New York. 1892–93. 1 : 305–6) 974.71 qW69

Copy of a poll list of New York city; election for assembly, February
1761. (*see* Wilson, J. G. *ed.* Memorial history of the city of New
York. 1892–93. 2 : 317–24) 974.71 qW69

Directory of the citizens of New York of Dutch descent in 1687. (*see*
N. Y. (city)—Common council. Manual. 1869. 27 : 872–79)
352.0747 N4k

Directory of the city of New York in 1665. (*see* Wilson, J. G. *ed.*
Memorial history of the city of New York. 1892–93. 1 : 338–40)
974.71 qW69

Directory of the city. in 1665. (*see* N. Y. (city)—Common council.
Manual. 1849. 8 : 356–59) 352.0747 N4k
From the records of the Dutch magistrates. Also in *National magazine,*
May 1892, 16 : 28–31. 973 M271.

Fernow, Berthold. Genealogical data gathered from Albany county
and New York city records. (*see* New York genealogical and biographical record, Oct. 1890, 21 : 170–72) 929.1 qN421

Gleanings from the surrogate's office. (*see* Old New York)   974.71 qOl1

 Sep. 1889, 1 : 131–36 Nov. 1889, 1 : 269–76
 Oct. " 1 : 176–84 Jan. 1890, 1 : 417–22

Huguenots of New York city. (*see* Continental monthly, Aug. 1862,
 2 : 193–98)   051 C76

Huling, R. G. *ed.* Rhode Islanders at Manhattan in the 17th century. (*see* Narragansett historical register, July 1890, 8 : 241–73)
               974.5 N16
  Extracts from O'Callaghan. *Calendar of (Dutch) historical manuscripts concerning residents of Rhode Island.*

List of citizens admitted as freemen of the city of New York from 1749
 to 1775. (*see* Reminiscences of the city of New York and its vicinity. 1855. p. 227–52)   974.71 R28

List of citizens of New York admitted as freemen between the years
 1680 and 1740. (*see* Wilson, J. G. *ed.* Memorial history of the city
 of New York. 1892–93. 2 : 204–8)   974.71 qW69

List of citizens of New York admitted as freemen of the city between
 the years 1683 and 1740. (*see* Valentine, D : T : History of the
 city of New York. 1853. p. 366–78) 974.71 V23
 Arranged alphabetically.

List of freemen continued from and including the year 1740, to and in-
 cluding 1748. (*see* Valentine, D : T : History of the city of New
 York. 1853. p. 385–93)   974.71 V23
 Arranged by years.

List of inhabitants of the city in 1703. (*see* Valentine, D : T : History
 of the city of New York. 1853. p. 344-65) 974.71 V43

List of inhabitants who offered loans for erecting the city palisades in
 1653. (*see* Valentine, D : T : History of the city of New York.
 1853. p. 313-14)   974.71 V23

List of members of the Dutch church in this city in the year 1686. (*see*
 Valentine, D : T : History of the city of New York. 1853.
 p. 331-43)   974.71 V23
 From the manuscript of Domine Selynus by Rev. Dr De Witt; also in Holland society of New York. *Year book.* 1896. p. 178–89, 974.7 qH71.

List of the owners of houses and lots in the city about the year 1674,
 at the final cession to the English with the national descent of the
 persons named and their estimated wealth. (*see* Valentine, D : T :
 History of the city of New York. 1853. p. 319–30) 974.71 V23
 Also in Holland society of New York. *Year book.* 1896. p. 167-77,
974.7 qH71.

List of the wealthier citizens of New Amsterdam, 1653.   (*see* New   Local hist
New York
York historical society. Collections. 1841. ser. 2,   1 : 386)   *Residents,*
church reco

974.7   N422 v.6

Marriages in the Dutch church. (*see* N. Y. (city)—Common council.
Manual. 1861. 20 : 640–68)   352.0747 N4k

Names of attorneys practicing in the city of New York between the
year 1695 and the revolutionary war. (*see* Valentine, D : T : History of the city of New York. 1853. *p*.394–95)   974.71 V23

Names of physicians and surgeons practicing in the city between the
year 1695 and the revolutionary war. (*see* Valentine, D : T : History of the city of New York. 1853. p.396–97)   974.71 V23

Names of schoolmasters, teaching in the city, between the year 1659
and the revolutionary war. (*see* Valentine, D : T :   History of the
city of New York. 1853. p. 398)   974 71 V23

Names of the principal male inhabitants of New York [city] anno 1774.
(*see* N. Y. (city)—Common council. Manual. 1850. 9 : 427–42)

352.0747 N4k

New York (city). Copy of the poll list of the election for representatives for the city and county of New York alphabetically
made. 3v.   N. Y. 1880.   N. Y. pub. lib.
1761, 1768, 1769.
Edition of 50 copies.

—— New York marriage licenses communicated by J. J. Latting
(*see* New York genealogical and biographical record, Jan. 1873,
4 : 31–32)   .   929.1 N421
From v.4 of *Records of wills.*

—— New York marriage licenses 1692–1701. (*see* New York
genealogical and biographical record)   929.1 N421
   July 1871, 2 : 141–42   Ap. 1872, 3 : 91–94
   Oct. 1872, 3 : 192–95

—— Rato or taxacon made this 24th day of July 1677 by ye mayoe
and aldermen. (*see* N. Y. (city)—Common council. Manual.
1848.   7 : 391–401)   352.0747 N4k

—— Tax list of New York city in the year 1676. (*see* New York genealogical and biographical record, Jan. 1871, 2 : 36–38)   929.1 N421

New York (city), Eglise Francoise. Register of the births,
marriages and deaths of the Eglise Françoise à la Nouvelle York
from 1688 to 1804; ed. by Rev. A. V. Wittmeyer; and, Historical

documents relating to the French protestants in New York during the same period. 431p. N. Y. 1886. (*in* Huguenot society of America. Collections. 1886. v.1)   284.57 qH87

New York (city), First and Second presbyterian churches.
Records of marriages, 1756-1813. (*see* New York genealogical and biographical record)   929.1 N421

Ap.-July 1880, 11 : 83-88, 120-24
Jan. 1881, 12 : 32-36
July 1881, 12 : 134-41
Jan.-Ap. 1882, 13 : 43-47, 87-91
Jan.-Oct. 1883, 14 : 40-42, 90-95, 118-23, 169-72
Jan.-July 1884, 15 : 31-33, 89-92, 132-37
Jan.-July 1885, 16 : 40-41, 86, 114

New York (city), First presbyterian church.
Record of births and baptisms, 1728-83. (*see* New York genealogical and biographical record)   929.1 N421

Ap.-Oct. 1873, 4 : 98-103, 140-43, 195-99 .
Jan.-Ap. 1874, 5 : 35-37, 100-2
Oct. 1874, 5 : 183-86
Jan. 1875, 6 : 48-52
Jan.-Oct. 1876, 7 : 35-38, 65-68, 135-40, 169-72
Jan.-Ap. 1877, 8 : 20-24, 74-79
Jan.-Ap. 1878, 9 : 16-19, 80-85
Oct. 1878, 9 : 169-73
Jan.-Oct. 1879, 10 : 44-46, 93-96, 127-33, 177-81
Jan. 1880, 11 : 29-33

New York (city), Friends society.
Record of the society of friends of New York and vicinity, from 1640 to 1800. (*see* New York genealogical and biographical record)   929.1 N421

Oct. 1872, 3 : 184-90
Jan.-Ap. 1873, 4 : 32-39, 94-98
Oct. 1873, 4 : 190-94
Jan.-Ap. 1874, 5 : 38-41, 102-7
Oct. 1874, 5 : 186-90
Ap. 1875, 6 : 97-107
Oct. 1875, 6 : 192-93
Jan. -Ap. 1876, 7 : 39-43, 85-90
Births, marriages and deaths.

New York (city), Reformed Dutch church. Baptisms in the Dutch Local hi
New Yo
Resident
church re church prior to 1697; prepared by D: T: Valentine. (*see* N.Y. (city)– Common council. Manual. 1863. 22 : 738-834) 352.0747 N4k

——— Baptisms in the Dutch church from 1697–1720, arranged by D: T: Valentine. (*see* N. Y. (city)–Common council. Manual. 1864. 23 : 767-837) 352.0747 N4k

——— Marriages in the Dutch church before the revolutionary war, prepared by D: T: Valentine. (*see* N. Y. (city)–Common council. Manual. 1862. 21 : 556-651) 352.0747 N4k

——— Record of births and baptisms, 1639–1773. (*see* New York genealogical and biographical record, v.5–29) 929.1 N421
A part of the record printed in nearly every number of the periodical.

——— Record of marriages, 1639–1731. (*see* New York genealogical and biographical record) 929.1 N421
    Jan.-Oct. 1875, 6 : 32-39, 81-88, 141-48, 184-91
    Jan.-Ap. 1876, 7 : 27-34, 77-84
    Jan. 1877, 8 : 33-40
    July 1879, 10 : 119-26
    Ap.-Oct. 1880, 11 : 75-82, 125-32, 172-80
    Jan.-Oct. 1881, 12 : 37-44, 84-91, 124-31, 187-94
    Jan.-Ap. 1882, 13 : 16-23, 77-84
    July 1885, 16 : 123-30

——— Record of members, 1649–83. (*see* New York genealogical and biographical record) 929.1 N421
    Jan.-Oct. 1878, 9 : 38-45, 72-79, 140-47, 161-68

——— Records of the reformed Dutch church in New Amsterdam and New York; marriages from 11 Dec. 1639 to 26 Aug. 1801; ed. with an introduction by S: S. Purple. 351p. N. Y. 1890. (*in* New York genealogical and biographical society. Collections. v.1) 929.3 qN421

New York (city), Trinity church. Earliest Trinity church marriages, 1746–1800. (*see* New York genealogical and biographical record, Oct. 1888, 19 : 147-49) 929.1 qN421

——— Early records. (*see* Historical magazine) 973 H62 v. 21, 23
    Jan.-Feb. 1872, ser. 3, 1 : 10-14, 73-77
    Ap.-May 1873, ser. 3, 1 : 218-22, 285-88
    June 1873, ser. 3, 1 : 351-55
    Jan.-Mar. 1874, ser. 3, 3 : 10-12, 101-5, 167-69
    Ap. 1875, ser. 3, 3 : 267-70

Notable women of olden times in this city. (*see* N. Y. (city)–Common council. Manual. 1855. 14: 517–38) 352.0747 N4k

───── (*see* Reminiscences of the city of New York and its vicinity. 1855. p.89–110) 974.71 R28

Record of burials in the Dutch church, New York. (*see* Holland society of New York. Year book. 1899. p.139–211) 974.7 qH71

Residences and stores of the merchants of New York, 1768. (*see* Wilson, J. G. *ed.* Memorial history of the city of New York. 1892–93. 2:466–68) 974.71 qW69
From Holt's *New York journal* and Gaines's *New York mercury.*

Selyns, Henry. Catalogue of the members of the Dutch church with the names of the streets in the city of New York, 1686. (*see* New York historical society. Collections. 1841. ser. 2, 1.: 389–400) 974.7 N422 v.6

Tax and contribution list, raised in 1655 to defray the debt for constructing the city defences. (*see* Valentine, D: T: History of the city of New York. 1853. p.315–18) 974.71 V23
This list embraces all the taxable inhabitants of the city at that time.

Tax list of New Amsterdam, 1674. (*see* New York historical society. Collections. 1841. ser. 2, 1:387–88) 974.7 N422 v.6

Tax list of New York city in the year 1676. (*see* New York genealogical and biographical record, Jan. 1871, 2:36–38) 929.1 N421

Tax list of New Orange (New York) in 1674, during the occupation by the Dutch. (*see* Wilson, J. G. *ed.* Memorial history of the city of New York. 1892–93. 1:362) 974.71 qW69

Tax list of 1674. (*see* N. Y. (city)–Common council. Manual. 1866. 25:805–9) 352.0747 N4k

Valentine, D: T: Biographical sketches of the principal public men in the city of New York, during the English colonial era. (*see* N.Y. (city)–Common council. Manual. 1864. 23:563–623) 352.0747 N4k

───── Notices of some of the marriages of this city in the times of the Dutch. (*see* N. Y. (city)–Common council. Manual. 1862. 21:762–75) 352.0747 N4k

Description

Advantages of New York as set forth a century ago. (*see* N. Y. (city)–Common council. Manual. 1869. 27:755–62) 352.0747 N4k
Reprint of a newspaper article of 1753.

Alden, *Mrs* **C. M. (Westover).** Manhattan, historic and artistic; a six day tour; the greater New York guide book. New ed. 275p. N. Y. ᶜ1897.

Bosworth, F. H. The doctor in Old New York, p. 277-317. N. Y. ᶜ1898. (Half moon ser. v. 2, no. 8) · N. Y. state lib.

—— —— (*see* Goodwin, *Mrs* Maud (Wilder), & *others.* Historic New York. 1899. 2 : 277-317) 974.71 G63

Condition of New York in 1757. (*see* Old New York, Ap. 1809, 2 : 166-77) · 974.71 qOl1

Dawson, H : B. Introduction; New York city in 1767. (*see* New York mercantile library. New York city in the American revolution. 1860. p. 9-40) N. Y. state lib.

Facilities of travel between New York and Philadelphia at different intervals. (*see* Reminiscences of the city of New York and its vicinity. 1855. p. 141-44) . 974.71 R28

History of the domestic affairs of the inhabitants of New York, anterior to the time of the revolutionary war. (*see* N. Y. (city)— Common council. Manual. 1858. 17 : 493-529) 352.0747 N4k

Inventories of the wardrobes of various persons, 1685-92. (*see* Reminiscences of the city of New York and its vicinity. 1855. p. 111-16) 974.71 R28

Janvier, T : A. In old New York. 285p. N. Y. 1894. Cap. 917.471 J26

Kalm, Peter. Description of the city of New York in the year 1748. (*see* N. Y. city)—Common council. Manual. 1869. 27 :837-49) 352.0747 N4k

King, Moses, *ed.* King's handbook of New York city; an outline history and description of the American metropolis. Ed. 2. 1008p. Bost. 1893. R917.471 K58
A guide book. Colonial period, p. 1-28 : contains reproductions of early maps.

Knight, *Mrs* **Sarah (Kemble).** Description of New York in the year 1704-5. (*see* Wilson, J. G. *ed.* Memorial history of the city of New York. 1892-93. 2:89) 974.71 qW69

Lamb, *Mrs* **M. J. R. (Nash).** Christmas season in Dutch New York. (*see* Magazine of American history, Dec. 1883, 10 : 471-74) 973 M27

Lewis, E.. D. Old prisons and punishments. p. 81–118. N. Y. °1898.   (Half moon ser. v. 2, no. 3)   N. Y. state lib.

—— —— (*see* Goodwin, *Mrs* Maud (Wilder), & *others*.   Historic New York. 1899.   2:81–118)   974.71 G63

Mackraby, Alexander. Letters to Sir Philip Francis, 1768. (*see* Wilson, J. G. *ed*. Memorial history of the city of New York. 1892–93. 2:465–66)   974.71 qW69

Michaëlius, Jonas. First minister of the Dutch reformed church in the United States; letter from Jonas Michaëlius from Manhatas in New Netherland, 11 Aug. 1628; translated and printed for private distribution by H: C. Murphy. 25p.   Hague 1858.   N. Y. pub. lib.

—— First minister of the Dutch reformed church in the United States. (*see* N. Y. (state)–Legislature. Documents relative to the colonial history of the state of New York. 1853–87.   2:757–70)
                    R974.7 qN421
Letter of Michaëlius to Rev. Adrianus Smoutius, ed. by H: C. Murphy.

—— The first minister of the reformed protestant Dutch church in North America ; letter of Domine Jonas Michaëlius to Domine Adrianus Smoutius, dated at Manhattan, 11 Aug. 1628; translated from the Dutch with a preface and notes by H: C. Murphy. (*see* New York historical society. Collections. 1881. Publication fund ser. 13:365–87)   974.7 N42
Including a facsimile of the original letter.
Reprinted from the *Yearbook of the Collegiate reformed church of New York*. 1896.

—— Jonas Michaëlius, eerste predikant der Nederduitsche hervormde gemeente op Manhattans of Nieuw-Amsterdam, het latere New York, in Noord-Amerika ; medegedeeld door Mr J. T. Bodel Nijenhuis. (*see* Kerkhistorisch archief. 1857.   1:365–88)
                    N. Y. state lib.

—— Jonas Michaëlius, the first minister of the Dutch reformed church in the United States, facsimile of his letter, the only extant, written during the first years of the settlement of New York with transcript, preface and English translation by the late H: C. Murphy. 22+5p. Amsterdam 1883.

Mines, J: F. A tour around New York ; and, My summer acre, being the recreation of Mr Felix Oldboy. 518p. N. Y. 1893. 917.471 M66
Contains illustrations of colonial buildings and description of life in the early days of the city.

Old New York revived. (*see* Historical magazine) 973 H62 v. 10–12
1866, 10 : sup. 11–14, 38–43, 73–77, 108–13, 143–44
Jan–Ap. 1867, ser. 2, 1 : 42–44, 105–8, 166–67, 214–15
Aug. 1867, ser. 2, 2 : 110–113
Nov. 1867, ser. 2, 2 : 291–94
Mar. 1868, ser. 2, 3 : 166–68

Picture of New York and stranger's guide. 492p. N. Y. °1828.
917.471 P58

First 135 pages, chronologic record of the city's progress.

Prime, B: Y. New York in 1770; extract from a letter. (*see* New York mercantile library. New York city in the American revolution. 1860. p. 50–52)   N. Y. state lib.

Sketch of the origin of the fire department. (*see* Reminiscences of the city of New York and its vicinity. 1855. p. 271–79) 974.71 R28

Stevens, J: A. Life in New York at the close of the colonial period. (*see* Wilson, J. G. *ed.* Memorial history of the city of New York. 1892–93. 2 : 445–64)   974.71 qW69

———— Old New York coffee-houses. (*see* Harper's magazine, Mar. 1882, 64 : 481–99)   051 H23

———— Old New York taverns. (*see* Harper's magazine, May 1890, 80 : 842–64)   051 H23

Value of property in New York city in early times. (*see* Reminiscences of the city of New York and its vicinity. 1855. p. 117–18)
974.71 R28

1643–1705.

Religious history

From the great mass of literature, controversial and other, touching Trinity church, only that has been included which seems fullest and most important in its bearing on the colonial period.

Baird, C: W. Pierre Daillé, the first Huguenot pastor of New York. (*see* Magazine of American history, Feb. 1877, 1 : 91-97) 973 M27

Bayley, J. R. Brief sketch of the early history of the catholic church on the island of New York. Ed. 2. 242p. N. Y. 1870. 282.7471 B34
Colonial period, p. 13-49.

Berrian, William. Historical sketch of Trinity church. 386 p. N. Y. 1847.   283.7471 T731

Bowen, L. P. Days of Makemie ; or, The vine planted A. D. 1680-1708, with an appendix. 558p. Phil. 1885. 922.57 M28

Campbell, Alexander. Protestation. 4p. N. Y. 1733. N. Y. pub. lib.
Before Richard Nicolls, Mar. 26, 1733, against Rev. William Vesey's exam-
ining certain charges made to the bishop of London against him.

—— Supplement to the vindication of Mr Alexander Campbell:
wherein all the objections made to the said vindication are answered,
particularly those in a late paper called Mr Noxon's observations,
etc. 35p. N. Y. 1732. N. Y. pub. lib.

—— True and just vindication of Mr Alexander Campbell from the several aspersions cast upon him, and that load of undeserved calumny
and reproach he at present lyes under. In a letter directed to
Edmund lord bishop of London. 14p. N. Y. 1732. V922.37 C15

The case of the Scotch presbyterians of the city of New York. N Y. 1733.
Entered in Thompson. *History of the presbyterian churches in the United
States.* 1895. pref. p. 16.

Clarke, R : H. Catholic church in New York. (*see* Wilson, J. G. *ed.*
Memorial history of the city of New York. 1892-93. 4 : 634-48)
974.71 qW69

Collection of some papers concerning Mr Lewis Rou's affair. 34p.
N. Y. 1725. N. Y. pub. lib.
Contents : 1 Acts of the French consistory in the city of New York passed
against him the 13th and 20th of Sep. 1724.
2 Petition of several heads of families to the governor in council.
3 Order of the council about the petition.
4 Answer of the consistory to said petition.
5 Mr Rou's reply to this answer.
6 The two reports of the committee of the council, with the
orders of that board concerning the same.

Daly, C : P. Settlement of the Jews in North America; ed. with notes
and appendices by M. J. Kohler. 171p. N. Y. 1893. 296 D17
New York, p. 1-58.

De Costa, B : F. Early Huguenots of Manhattan. (*see* Wilson,
J. G. *ed.* Memorial history of the city of New York. 1892-93.
4 : 371-79) 974.71 qW69

DeLancey, W : H. Title, parish rights and property of Trinity
church New York from the appendix to Bishop De Lancey's 20th
conventional address, delivered in Oswego, Aug. 19, 1857. 23p.
Utica 1857. 283.7471 T732 v.4

DeWitt, Thomas. Discourses delivered in the North reformed
Dutch church (collegiate) in the city of New York on the last sab-
bath in August 1856. 100p. N. Y. 1857. 285.77471 N811
History of the reformed church in New York city.

Dix, Morgan. Historical recollections of St Paul's chapel : to which is prefixed an account of the celebration of its centennial anniversary. Oct. 28, 29 and 30, 1866. 64p. N Y. 1867. 283.7471 Sa21

———— History of Trinity parish. (*see* Wilson, J. G. *ed.* Memorial history of the city of New York. 1892-93. 4 : 188-207) 974.71 qW69

———— History of the parish of Trinity church in the city of New York. v.1. N.Y. 1898. 283.7471 qT731
In 3 volumes.

———— Old Trinity, New York and its chapels. (*see* Perry, W: S. *ed.* History of the American episcopal church. 1885. 2 : 473-84) 283.73 qP42

Dunshee, H: W. *anon.* History of the school of the collegiate reformed Dutch church in the city of New York, from 1633 to 1883. Ed.2. 284p. N. Y. 1883. 373.747 N4E

Dyer, A. M. Points in the first chapter of New York Jewish history (*see* American Jewish historical society. Publications. 1894. 3 : 41-60) 296 Am3

———— Pulpit censorship in New Amsterdam. (*see* American historical register, Feb. 1895, 1 : 507-14) 973 qAm31

Early Dutch reformed church in Nassau street in the city of New York. (*see* American historical record, Sep. 1872, 1 : 400-32) 973 qAm

Early history of the catholic church on the island of New York. (*see* Historical magazine, Oct.-Nov. 1869, ser. 2, 6 : 229-33, 271-79) 973 H62 v.16
From *Catholic world*, Dec. 1869, 10 : 413-20, 515-25, 205C28.

A familiar conversational history of the evangelical churches of New York. 222p. N. Y. 1838. 277.471 F21

Foote, W: H: Rev. Francis Makemie and his associates. The confinement and trial of Makemie for preaching a sermon in New York, 1707. (*see* Foote, W: H: Sketches of Virginia. 1850. 1 : 40-84) 285 1755 F73

Greenleaf, Jonathan. A history of the churches of all denominations in the city of New York from the first settlement to the year 1846. 379p. N. Y. 1846. 277.471 G84

———— Ed.2. 429p. N. Y. 1850. 277.471 G841

Harrison, W: H. *anon.* Trinity church title ; an exposure of Miller's letter, with documents, etc. addressed to the late commissioners of the land office. 46p. Alb. 1856. 283.7471 T732 v.3

Historical documents relating to the French protestants in New York. 1686-1804. (*see* Huguenot society of America. Collections. 1886. 1:327-431)   284.57 qH87

Induction of the Rev. William Vesey. (*see* Old New York, Jan. 1890, 1:401-17)   974.71 qOl1

Introduction of methodism. (*see* Old New York, Aug. 1889, 1:41-45)
                      974.71 qOl1

Isaacs, A. S. The Jews of New York. (*see* Wilson, J. G. *ed.* Memorial history of the city of New York. 1892-93. 4:380-85) 974.71 qW69

Kemp, R. M. *comp.* Old St Paul's chapel, Trinity parish, New York, names and histories that have clustered round it in four generations. 24p.   N. Y. 1896.   N. Y. pub. lib.

Kohler, M. J. Beginnings of New York Jewish history. (*see* American Jewish historical society. Publications. 1893. 1:41-48)   296 Am3

———— Civil status of the Jews in colonial New York. (*see* American Jewish historical society. Publications. 1897. 6:81-106)   296 Am3

———— Phases of Jewish life in New York before 1800. (*see* American Jewish historical society. Publications. 1893-94. 2:77-100; 3:73-86)   296 Am3

Makemie, Francis. A good conversation; a sermon preached at the city of New York, January 18, 1706/7.   36p.   Bost. 1707.
Sabin, 11:136.
For preaching this sermon the author was imprisoned.

———— ———— (*see* New York historical society. Collections. 1871. Publication fund ser. 3:411-53)   974.7 N42

———— Narrative of a new and unusual American imprisonment of two presbyterian ministers and prosecution of Mr Francis Makemie, one of them, for preaching one sermon at the city of New York, by a learner of the law and lover of liberty. 47p.   Bost. 1707.   N. Y. pub. lib.

———— ———— 52p. N. Y.   1755.   N. Y. pub. lib.

———— ———— (*in* Force, Peter, *ed.* Tracts and other papers. 1846. v.4, no. 4)   N. Y. state lib.

Memorial with accompanying documents of inhabitants of the city of New York in communion with the protestant episcopal church in the state of New York praying the repeal or amendment of an act entitled "An act to alter the name of the corporation of Trinity church in New York and for other purposes", passed Jan. 25, 1814. 48p.   N. Y. 1846.   283.7471 T732 v.1
Appended are 579 manuscript signatures.

Miller, R. G. Letter and documentary evidence in relation to the *Local hist New York* Trinity church property in the city of New York submitted to the *Religious history* commissioners of the land office, June 21, 1855.   86p.   Alb. 1855.   283.7471   T732 v.3

Moore, G: H. Notes on the maintenance of the ministry and poor in New York, the colonial ministry acts; the vestry of the city of New York, the minister of the city; Trinity church and its first resident rector. (*see* Historical magazine, June–July 1867, ser. 2, 1:321–33; 2:9–15)   973   H62 v. 11–12

New York (city), Collegiate reformed church. Bicentenary of the charter of the reformed protestant Dutch church of the city of New York, May 11, 1896.   87p.   N. Y. 1896.   N. Y. pub. lib.
Contents: Historical address by E: B. Coe, p. 17–39.
        Addresses by H: M. Baird, J. B. Remensnyder, Morgan Dix, C. C. Tiffany, D. J. Burrell, p. 4–75.
        The charter, p. 76–87.

———— Collegiate Dutch church proceedings at the centennial anniversary of the dedication of the north Dutch church, May 25, 1869 and also at the laying of the corner stone of the new church on 5th avenue, corner 48th street, on the same day.   76p.   N. Y. 1869.
                                           285.77471   N812

———— Historical sketch of the origin and organization of the reformed church in America and of the Collegiate church of the city of New York.   48p.   N. Y. 1896.   285.77471   C681

———— ———— 54p.   n. p.   1899.   285.77471   C68

New York (city), Reformed Dutch church. Records of the reformed Dutch church in New Amsterdam and New York; marriages from 11 Dec. 1639 to 26 Aug. 1801, edited with an introduction by S: S. Purple.   351p.   N. Y. 1890. (*in* New York genealogical and biographical society.   Collections.   1890.   v. 1)
                                           929 qN42
Edition of 100 copies.

New York (city), Trinity church. Charter, etc. of Trinity church in the city of New York.   30p.   N. Y. 1846.   283.7471   T732 v.3

———— Trinity church bicentennial celebration, May 5th, 1897.   38p. 1897.   283.7471   qT73

Noxon, Thomas. Mr Noxon's observations upon Parson Campbell's vindication.   1p.   N. Y. 1732.   N. Y. pub. lib.

Old New York and Trinity church. (*see* New York historical society. Collections. 1871. Publication fund ser. 3 : 145–408)   974.7 N42

Parkinson, William. Jubilee : a sermon, containing a history of the origin of the First baptist church in the city of New York delivered Jan. 1, 1813.   52p.   N. Y. 1813.   286.17471 F51

Pollock, Allan. History of Trinity church and its graveyard.   32p. N. Y. 1880.   283.7471 T73

Potter, H : C. Protestant episcopal church.   (*see* Wilson, J. G. *ed.* Memorial history of the city of New York.   1892–93.   4 : 620–34)
                                                            974.71 qW69

Rev. Mr Doughty.   (*see* O'Callaghan, E. B.   History of New Netherland.   1846–48.   1 : 427–28)   974.7 Oc11
From *Vertoogh van Nieu Nederland* by Adriaen van der Donck, and *Cort bericht* by Van Tienhoven.

Rou, Louis.   Difficulties in the French protestant church, New York. (*see* N. Y. (state,—State, Secretary of.   Documentary history of the state of New York)   1849–51.   3 : 1159–77.   974.7 N424
                       1850–51.   3 : 703–13.   974.7 qN423

Sandford, L : H. Bogardus vs Trinity church ; opinion in the case of Nathaniel Bogardus and others vs the rector, church-wardens and vestrymen of Trinity church, June 28, 1847.   40p.   N. Y. 1847.
                                                        283.7471 T732 v.2

Sharpe, Rev. John. Proposals for erecting a school, library and chapel at New York, 1712–13. (*see* New York historical society. Collections.   1880.   Publication fund ser. 13 : 337–63) 974.7 N42

Spence, Irving. Letters on the early history of the presbyterian church in America.   199p.   Phil. 1838.   285.173 Sp3
Prosecution of Rev. Francis Makemie in New York, p.69–74.

To the Rev. William Vesey and his two subalterns, viz Tom Pert, the Beotian, and Clumsy Ralph, the Cimmerian.   4p.   N. Y. 1732. Printed by J : P. Zenger.   N. Y. pub. lib.
A letter supporting Alexander Campbell in his differences with Rev. William Vesey.

The true state of Mr Rou's case ; or, A short discourse concerning his difference with the present consistory of the French church in New York.   Printed and sold by William Bradford in the city of New York.   1726.
Grolier club, p. 27, no. 69.   Rev. Louis Rou's statement of his side of the question in the unsuccessful attempt to remove him.

Valentine, D : T : Dominie Bogardus. *(see* N. Y. (city)—Common
council. Manual. 1863. 22 : 595–609)   352.0747 N4k

Van Pelt, Daniel. Pictures of early church life in New York city. 81p.
N. Y. n. d.   L. I. hist. soc.

White, F : C. & Terry, Roderick, *comp. anon.* Historical sketch
of the South church reformed, of New York city.   57p.   N. Y.
1887.   N. Y. pub. lib.
    First church in New York city, reformed protestant Dutch, p. 7–13.

Winslow, F. E. Trinity church and its 200 years.   *(see* Outlook,
May 8, 1897.   56 : 112–15)   205 C4622

Commercial

Devoe, T : F. Market book; containing a historical account of the
public markets in the cities of New York, Boston, Philadelphia and
Brooklyn.   2v.   N. Y. 1862.   643 M2
    Public markets of New York, v. 1.

———— Old Fly market butchers. *(see* N. Y. (city)—Common council.
Manual.   1868.   26 : 841–63)   352.0747 N4k

King, Charles. History of the New York chamber of commerce with
notices of some of its most distinguished members. *(see* New York
historical society.   Collections.   1849. ser. 2, 2 : 381–446)
     974.7 N422 v. 7

New York chamber of commerce. Centennial celebration at
Irving hall, Ap. 6, 1868; report of proceedings. 44p. N. Y. 1868.
     N. Y. pub. lib.

———— Charter and bylaws; with a history of the Chamber of commerce
of the state of New York. 104p. N. Y. 1849.   381 N422

———— ———— 160p   N. Y. 1855.   381 N421

———— Colonial records, 1768–1784 with historical and biographical
sketches by J: A. Stevens jr. 404+172p. N. Y. 1867. 381 qN42

Stevens, J: A., jr. Commercial history of the city of New York. *(see*
Wilson, J. G. *ed.* Memorial history of the city of New York.
1892–93.   4 : 498–550)   974.71 qW69

———— Merchants of New York, 1765–1775. *(see* Galaxy, June 1875,
19 : 787–800)   051 G13

Long Island

The eastern part was settled by the English from New England and the towns included in the present county of Suffolk and part of Queens placed themselves under the jurisdiction of New Haven. By the treaty of Hartford in 1650, the west line of Oyster Bay was made the boundary between the Dutch and English claims. In 1664 on the conquest of the duke of York, the whole island became part of his dominion.

Agreement between John Scott and Gov. Stuyvesant, 1663-4. (*see* O'Callaghan, E. B. History of New Netherland. 1846-48. 2 : 578) 974.7 Oc11

Scott was "president of the English of ye townes of Gravesend, Ffolstone, Hastings, Crafford, Newark and Hempsted".

Bunker, M.. P. Long Island genealogies being kindred descendants of Thomas Powell. 530p. Alb. 1895. (Munsell's historical ser. v. 24) 929.1 B88

Colve, *Gov.* **Anthony.** Charter to the several towns on Long Island, anno 1673. (*see* N. Y. (state)—State, Secretary of. Documentary history of the state of New York)

1849-51.	1 : 655-58.	974.7 N424
1850-51.	1 : 426-27.	974.7 qN423

DeKay, J. E. Indian names on Long Island. 12p. Oyster Bay 1851. 929.4 D36

Fernow, Berthold, *tr.* & *ed.* Documents relating to the history of the early colonial settlements, principally on Long Island, with a map of its western part made in 1666. 800p. Alb. 1883. (*in* N. Y. (state)—Legislature. Documents relative to the colonial history of the state of New York. 1853-87 *v.* 14) R974.7 N421

Flint, M. B. Early Long Island, a colonial study. 549p. N. Y. 1896. 974.721 F64

Limited letter press ed. containing a bibliography.
Prerevolutionary, p. 1-384.

Furman, Gabriel. Antiquities of Long Island. 478p. N. Y. 1875. 974.721 F98

General history of Long Island. (*see* History of Suffolk county, N. Y. 1882. p. 16-48) 974.725 qH62

Jones, W: A. Long Island. 23p. N. Y. 1863.

Griffin, p. 1012. Read before Long Island historical society, Nov. 5, 1863.

—— —— (*see* Historical magazine, Mar. 1864, 8 : 89-98) 973 H62

Moore, C: B. Laws of 1683; old records and old politics. (*see* New York genealogical and biographical record, Ap. 1887, 18 : 49-63) 929.1 qN421

Contains much information about Long Island towns.

Moore, C: B. Shipwrights, fishermen, passengers from England. (*see* Local hi Long Isl
New York genealogical and biographical record, Ap. 1879, 10 : 66-76,
Oct. 1879, 10 : 149-55) 929.1 N421
Mainly settlers on Long Island.

Mulrenan, Patrick. Brief historical sketch of the catholic church
on Long Island. 129p. N. Y. 1871. 282.747 L86

Nicoll, E : H. Early settlement of Long Island. (*see* Magazine of
American history, Mar. 1884, 11 : 239-43) 973 M27

Onderdonk, Henry, jr. Bibliography of Long Island. (*see*
Furman, Gabriel. Antiquities of Long Island. 1875. p. 435 69)
974.721 F98

———— Historic and anterevolutionary churches of Long Island. (*see*
Perry, W : S. *ed.* History of the American episcopal church. 1885.
1 : 598-99) 283.73 qP42

Prime, N. S. History of Long Island from its first settlement by
Europeans to the year 1845, with special reference to its ecclesiastical concerns. 420p. N. Y. 1845. 974.721 P93

Rate lists of Long Island, 1675, 1676 and 1683. (*see* N. Y. (state)—
State, Secretary of. Documentary history of the state of New
York) 1849-51. 2 : 439-542. 974.7 N424
1850-51. 2 : 251-314. 974.7 qN423

Contents : List of Easthampton, 1675.
List of estate of Huntington, 1675.
Southold's estimate. 1675.
Valuation of estates at Flushing, 1675.
Valuations of Flushing, Gravesend, Hempstead and Jamaica, 1675.
List of the estate of Newtown, 1675.
Valuation for Brookhaven. 1675.
Assessment rolls of the five Dutch towns in King's county;
Flatbush, Brooklyn. Bushwick, New Utrecht and Flatlands, 1676.
Rate list of Bushwick, 1683.
Rate list of Flatlands, 1683.
Valuation of Brooklyn, 1683.
Rate list of Flatbush, 1683.
Rate list of New Utrecht, 1683.
List of persons, lands and cattle ratable, Gravesend, 1683.
Rate list of Newtown, 1683.
Flushing estimations, 1683.
List of town estate of Jamaica, 1683.
Valuation o estates of Hempstead, 1683.
List of estates of Oyster Bay, 1683.

List of ratable estate of Huntington, 1683.

Smithtown estimations, 1683.

Valuation of ratable estate, Brookhaven, 1683.

Estimate of Southold, 1683.

Estimate of Southampton, 1683.

Estimate of Easthampton, 1683.

Society for the propagation of the gospel in foreign parts.
Extracts from the early and original records of the society, made
by R. R. Hoes. (*see* New York genealogical and biographical
record, July 1891, 22 : 127–32)   929.1   qN421

Thompson, B: F.   History of Long Island; containing an account of
the discovery and settlement, with other important and interesting
matters to the present time. 536p. N. Y. 1839.   974.721   T37

——— History of Long Island, from its discovery and settlement to the
present time. Ed. 2. 2v. N. Y. 1843.   974.721   T371
Includes genealogy and biographic sketches of the early settlers.

Tooker, W : W.   Some Indian names of places on Long Island, N. Y.
and their correspondences in Virginia. (*see* Magazine of New
England history, July 1891, 1 : 154–58)   929   M27

Townshend, C : H.   Early history of Long Island sound and its
approaches. (*see* New Haven colony historical society. Papers.
1895. 5 : 275–305)   974.67   N42

Trumbull, J. H.   Indian names of places on Long Island derived from
esculent roots. (*see* Magazine of American history, June 1877
1 : 386–87)   973   M27

Watson, J : F.   Early settlement and incidents at Brooklyn and Long
Island. (*see his* Annals and occurrences of New York city and
state. 1846. p. 34–37)   974.7   W331

Wood, Silas.   Sketch of the first settlement of the several towns on
Long Island with their political condition to the end of the American revolution.   66p.   Brooklyn 1824.   974.721   W85

——— ——— New ed.   111p.   Brooklyn 1826.   974.721   W851

——— ——— New ed.   181p.   Brooklyn 1828.   974.721   W852
First historian of Long Island after Denton's mention of it in 1670.

——— Sketch of the first settlement of the several towns on Long
Island with their political condition to the end of the American
revolution; with a biographical memoir and additions by A. J.
Spooner.   206p.   Brooklyn 1865.   N. Y. pub. lib.
Edition of 250 copies.

Kings county

Assessment rolls of the five Dutch towns in Kings county, L. I. 1675, Local ¦ translated from the original Dutch ms. (*see* N. Y. (state)—State, Kings ¢ Secretary of. Documentary history of the state of New York)

1849–51.   4 : 139–61.   974.7 N424

1850–51.   4 : 89–104.   974.7 qN423

Bergen, T. G. Contributions to the history of the early settlers of Kings county, N. Y. (*see* New York genealogical and biographical record)   929.1 N421

July 1878, 9 : 126–29   Ap. 1880, 11 : 62–70

Ap. 1879, 10 : 85–86   Oct. 1880, 11 : 159–67

Oct. 1879, 10 : 155–61

—— *comp.* Register in alphabetical order of the early settlers of Kings county, Long Island, N. Y. from its first settlement by Europeans to 1700 with contributions to their biographies and genealogies compiled from various sources   452p.   N. Y. 1881.   929.1 B45

Flint, M. B. The five Dutch towns. (*see her* Early Long Island. 1896.   p 76–103)   974 721 F64

Furman, Gabriel. Antiquities of Long Island, to which is added a bibliography by Henry Onderdonk jr; ed. by Frank Moore.   478p. N. Y. 1875.   974 721 F98

Reprint of edition of 1824 : contains his *Notes geographical and historical relating to the town of Brooklyn.*

Kings county genealogical club. Collections. v.1, no. 1–6. N. Y. 1882–88.   929.5 K61 no. 1–4

L I. hist. soc. no. 5–6

Contents : no. 1 Inscriptions on tombstones in the cemetery of the reformed Dutch church, New Utrecht L. I. p. 1–15.

no. 2 Inscriptions on tombstones in and around the churchyard. Flatlands, L. I. p. 17–29.

no. 3 Inscriptions on the tombstones in and around the churchyard, Gravesend, p. 31–43.

no. 4 Tombstone inscriptions in the burial ground of the old Bushwick church, p. 45–52 ; baptisms in the reformed Dutch church of Brooklyn, 1660–79, p. 53–60.

no. 5–6 Brooklyn baptismal record, 1679–1719; marriages, 1660–96, p. 61–96.

List of all the inhabitants of towns in Kings county, 1738. (*see* N. Y. (state)—State, Secretary of. Documentary history of the state of New York)	1849–51.	4 : 188–200.	974.7	N424

1850–51.	4 : 122–31.	974.7	qN423

Contents: Flatbush, Brooklyn, Flatlands, Bushwyck, Gravesend.

Papers relating to Kings county, L. I. (*see* N. Y. (state)—State, Secretary of. Documentary history of the state of New York)	1849–51.	3 : 131–85.	974.7 · N424

1850–51.	3 : 85–116.	974.7	qN423

Contents: List of all freeholders within Kings county about 1698.

Documents relating to troubles in the Dutch reformed churches, 1702–11.

List of officers and soldiers belonging to the regiment of militia, 1715.

Proctor, L. B. History of the bench and bar of Kings county; and, History of the board of supervisors, 1714–1884. (*see* Stiles, H: R. Civil, political, professional and ecclesiastical history of the county of Kings. 1884. 1 : 338–414a)	974.722	qSt5

List of county officials, p.366–69.	Legislative officers, p.372–77.

Roll off those who haue taken the oath off allegiance in the Kings county 26–30 day off Sep. 1687. (*see* N. Y. (state)—State, Secretary of. Documentary history of the state of New York)	1849–51.	1 : 659–61.	974.7	N424

1850–51.	1 : 429–32.	974.7	qN423

Also in Holland society of New York. *Year book.* 1896.	p.159–66, 974.7	qH71.

Stiles, H: R. Ecclesiastical history of Kings county, 1628–1800. (*see his* Civil, political, professional and ecclesiastical history of the county of Kings. 1884. 1 : 327–37)	974.722	qSt5

Brooklyn
Including Bushwick and Williamsburg

Bailey, J. T. Historical sketch of the city of Brooklyn and the surrounding neighborhood; including the village of Williamsburgh and the towns of Bushwick, Flatbush, Flatlands, New Utrecht and Gravesend, to which is added an interesting account of the battle of Long Island. 72p. Brooklyn 1840.	974.723	B15

Baker, C: D. First reformed Dutch church, Brooklyn, N. Y. (*see* Magazine of American history, Oct. 1887, 18 : 336–38)	973	M27

Barnes, S : C. Wallabout and the Wallabouters; lecture in 1856 at the Local h
Brookly Wallabout presbyterian church. 21p. N. Y. 1888. L. I. hist. soc.

Beekman, A. J. History of the corporation of the reformed Dutch church of the town of Brooklyn; known as the first reformed Dutch church; compiled from the original records. 20p. Brooklyn 1886. L. I. hist. soc.

Brooklyn, Reformed Dutch church. Baptisms in the reformed Dutch church of Brooklyn, as translated by T. G. Bergen. (*see* Kings county genealogical club. Collections. 1888. 1 : 53-60) 929.5 K61
1660-79.

—— —— (*see* Brooklyn—Common council. Manual. 1869. p. 448-504) 352.0747 B7k

—— First book of records, 1660-1719 (*see* Holland society of New York. Year book. 1897. p. 133-94) 974.7 qH71
Contents : Members, p. 133-38; marriages, p. 139-44; baptisms, p. 144-94.

Civil list of officers of the town and village of Brooklyn, 1671-1833. (*see* Stiles, H : R. Civil, political, professional and ecclesiastical history of the county of Kings. 1884. 1 : 423ᵃ-24ᵃ) 974.722 qSt5

Devoe, T : F. Reminiscences of old Brooklyn. (*see* Historical magazine, Nov.-Dec. 1867, ser. 2, 2 : 257-66, 340-47) 973 H62 v. 12

Drowne, T. S. Commemorative discourse delivered on the occasion of celebrating the completion of the tower and spire of the church of the Holy Trinity, Brooklyn, L. I., Dec. 19, 1867, with illustrative historical notes. 78p. N. Y. 1868. 283.747 B791
Early churches of Brooklyn, p. 35-55.

Field, T : W. Historic and antiquarian scenes in Brooklyn and its vicinity with illustrations of some of its antiquities. 96p. Brooklyn 1868. 974.723 qF45
Editon of 110 copies.
Indian, Dutch and English names of localities in Brooklyn, p. 49-60.

Furman, Gabriel. Notes geographical and historical relating to the town of Brooklyn in Kings county on Long Island. 114p. Brooklyn 1824. 974.723 F98
Almost entirely in 17th and 18th centuries.
Reprinted in his *Antiquities of Long Island.* 1875. p. 273-434 974.721 F98.

Furman, Gabriel. Notes geographical and historical relating to the town of Brooklyn on Long Island; with notes and a memoir of the author. 116+42p. Brooklyn 1865. 974.723 F981

120 copies reprinted from the 1824 edition, for the Faust club.

Howard, H: W. B. *ed.* The Eagle and Brooklyn, the record of the progress of the Brooklyn daily eagle with the history of the city of Brooklyn from its settlement to the present time, ed. by Howard, assisted by A. N. Jervis. 1195p. Brooklyn 1893. 974.723 qH83

Johnson, Jeremiah. Olden times. (*see* Magazine of the reformed Dutch church, May 1828, 3: 51-55) 205 M27

Sketch of the reformed Dutch church of Brooklyn.

Ostrander, S. M. History of the city of Brooklyn and Kings county; ed. by Alexander Black. 2 v. Brooklyn 1894. 974.723 Os7

Edition limited to 500 copies.

Includes biography of Francis Lewis read before Long Island historical society, Feb. 1, 1881, 2: 235-57.

Putnam, Harrington. Brooklyn; the town of freedom's battle field. (*see* Powell, L. P. *ed.* Historic towns of the middle states. 1889. p. 213-49) 974.7 P87

—— Origin of Breuckelen. p. 385-405. N. Y. ᶜ1898. (Half moon ser., v. 2, no. 11) N. Y. state lib.

—— —— (*see* Goodwin, *Mrs* Maud (Wilder) & *others.* Historic New York. 1899. 2: 385-405) 974.71 G63

Reynolds, Samuel. History of the city of Williamsburgh. 85p. (*in* Reynolds' Williamsburgh city directory for 1852) 917.4723 W67

—— History of the city of Williamsburgh; containing an account of its early settlement, growth and prosperous condition. 137p. Williamsburgh 1852. 974.722 W67

Prerevolutionary civil and religious history of the town of Bushwick from which Williamsburg was set off, p. 9-17, 35-38.

Stiles, H: R. Brooklyn ferry and ferry rights. (*see his* Civil, political, professional and ecclesiastical history of the county of Kings. 1884. 1: 425-46) 974.722 qSt5

—— The city of Brooklyn. (*see* Wilson, J. G. *ed.* Memorial history of the city of New York. 1892-93. 4: 1-26) 974.71 qW69

—— Civil, political, professional and ecclesiastical history and commercial and industrial record of the county of Kings and the city of Brooklyn, N. Y. from 1683-1884. 2v. ᶜ1884. 974.722 qSt5

Paged continuously.

Bushwick, p. 270-91.

Stiles, H: R. History of the city of Brooklyn, including the old town Local his and village of Brooklyn, the town of Bushwick and the village and Gravesenc city of Williamsburgh. 3v. Brooklyn 1867–70. 974.723 St5

Flatbush

Flatbush Dutch church records. (*see* Holland society of New York. Year book. 1898. p. 87–152) 974.7 qH17

List of all the inhabitants of the township of Flatbush, 1738. (*see* N. Y. (state)—State, Secretary of. Documentary history of the state of New York) 1849–51. 4 : 188–91. 974.7 N424
1850–51. 4 : 122–24. 974.7 qN423

Schenck, P. L. Historical sketch of the Zabriskie homestead, removed 1877, Flatbush, L. I. with biographical accounts of some of those who have resided on it. 100p. Brooklyn 1881. N. Y. pub. lib.

Strong, R. G. History of the town of Flatbush, N. Y. 46p. Brooklyn 1884. 974.722 qF61
50 copies reprinted from Stiles. *Civil, political, professional and ecclesiastical history of the county of Kings.* 1: 213–54, 974.722 qSt5.
First 12 pages colonial period.

Strong, T : M. History of the town of Flatbush in Kings county, Long Island. 178p. N. Y. 1842. 974.722 F61

Vanderbilt, *Mrs* **G. L. (Lefferts),** *anon.* History of the reformed church, Flatbush; published by the consistory. 49p. n. p. 1890. W285.7747 F61

——— Social history of Flatbush and manners and customs of the Dutch settlers in Kings county. 351p. N. Y. 1882. 917.4722 V281
Largely prerevolutionary period.

Flatlands

Dubois, Anson. History of the town of Flatlands. (*see* Stiles, H : R. Civil, political, professional and ecclesiastical history of the county of Kings. 1884. 1 :64–79) 974.722 qSt5

Gravesend

Abstract of title to lots 49 to 56 inclusive and Coney Island point. 28+26p. n. p. n. d. L. I. hist. soc.
Appendix including Kieft charter 1645, Nicolls charter 1668, Lovelace charter 1670, Dongan patent of the land 1686.

Flint, M. B. Lady Moody's plantation. (*see* Flint, M. B. Early Long Island. 1896. p. 104–15) 974.721 F64

Gerard, J. W. Lady Deborah Moody; a discourse delivered before the New York historical society, May 1880. 40p. N. Y. 1880.
Griffin, p. 1036.

Gravesend. Marriage records, 1664–1702, copies by T. G. Bergen. (*see* New York genealogical and biographical record, Oct. 1873, 4 : 199–200)   929.1 N421

Gravesend, Friends society. Record of births, 1665–84. (*see* New York genealogical and biographical record, Jan. 1873, 4 : 39–40)
929.1 N421

Kieft, *Gov.* **Wilhelm.** Director Kieft's patent to the town of Gravesend, anno 1645. (*see* N. Y. (state)—State, Secretary of. Documentary history of the state of New York)
1849–51. 1 : 629–32.   974.7 N424
1850–51. 1 : 411–12.   947.7 qN423

Onderdonk, Henry, jr. Friends' meeting house at Gravesend (*see* American historical record, May 1873, 2 : 209–12)   973 qAm3

Stillwell, W : H. History of Coney Island. (*see* Stiles, H : R. Civil, political, professional and ecclesiastical history of the county of Kings. 1884. ·1 : 189–212)   974.722 qSt5

———— History of the reformed protestant Dutch church of Gravesend, Kings county, N. Y. 88p.   Gravesend 1892.   285.7747 G78
Registers of baptisms, marriages and deaths, p. 54–88.

Stockwell, A. P. Gravesend, L. I. old and new. (*see* New York genealogical and biographical record, July 1885, 16 : 97–110) 929.1 N421

———— History of the town of Gravesend. (*see* Stiles, H : R. Civil, political, professional and ecclesiastical history of the county of Kings. 1884. 1 : 156–88)   974.722 qSt5

The story of Manhattan beach; a practical and picturesque delineation of its history, development and attractions, also an account of Coney Island. 61p. N. Y. 1879.   L. I. hist. soc.

Was Anthony Jansen Van Salee a Huguenot? (*see* Historical magazine, June 1862, 6:172–75)   973 H62

New Lots

Andros, *Sir* **Edmund.** New Lots patent. (*see* Historical magazine, July 1863, 7:223)   973 H62
Formerly a part of Flatbush.

New Utrecht

Bergen, T. G. Address on the annals of New Utrecht; and list of elders and deacons in the protestant reformed Dutch church of New Utrecht, L. I. (*see* Sutphen, D: S. Historical discourse delivered on the 18th of October, 1877. 1877. p. 33–59)

285.7747 N421

———— History of the town of New Utrecht. (*see* Stiles, H:R. Civil, political, professional and ecclesiastical history of the county of Kings. 1884. 1:255–69) 974.722 qSt5

Description of the founding or beginning of New Utrecht with the names of officers and magistrates from the year 1657, also short abstracts of proclamations or edicts relating to misdemeanors, translated by T. G. Bergen. (*see* N. Y. (state) – State, Secretary of. Documentary history of the state of New York)

1849–51. 1:633–55. 974.7 N424
1850–51. 1:413–25 974.7 qN423

Onderdonk, Henry, jr. Church and ministers at New Utrecht, L. I. *see* American historical record, Sep. 1872, 1:385–87) 973 qAm3 Dutch reformed.

Sutphen, D: S. Historical discourse delivered on the 18th of Oct. 1877 at the celebration of the 200th anniversary of the reformed Dutch church of New Utrecht, L. I. and an historical address by T. G. Bergen. 59p. Brooklyn 1877. 285.7747 N421

Queens county

Flint, M. B. North riding of Yorkshire. (*see her* Early Long Island. 1896. p.116–23) 974.721 F64 Includes Queens and Westchester counties.

———— Other Queens county towns, Newtown, Flushing, Oyster Bay, Jamaica. (*see her* Early Long Island. 1896. p. 162–215)

974.721 F64

History of Queens county, N. Y. with illustrations, portraits and sketches of prominent families and individuals. 576p. N. Y. 1882.

974.724 qH62

Onderdonk, Henry, jr. Queens county in olden times; being a supplement to the several histories thereof. 122p. Jamaica N. Y. 1865. 974.724 qOn1 Events before the revolution, p. 3–49.

Papers relating to the churches in Queens county. *(see* N. Y. (State)—
State, Secretary of. Documentary history of the state of New York)

1849–51.	3: 187–340.	974.7	N424
1850–51.	3:117–206.	974.7	qN423

Flushing

An exact list of all ye inhabitants names wthin ye town of ffiushing and
p'cincts, of old and young ffreemen and seruants white and blacke,
etc. 1698. *(see* N. Y. (state)—State, Secretary of. Documentary
history of the state of New York)

1849–51.	1:661–65.	974.7	N424
1850–51.	1:432–37.	974.7	qN423

Mandeville, G. H: Flushing, past and present; a historical sketch.
180p. Flushing 1860.   974.724 F67
Colonial period, p. 9-55.

Onderdonk, Henry, jr. Friends' meeting house at Flushing, L. I.
(see American historical record, Feb. 1872, 1 : 49–53)   973 qAm3

Smith, J. C. History of St George's parish, Flushing, Long Island.
146p. Flushing 1897.   N. Y. hist. soc.

Waller, H: D. History of the town of Flushing, Long Island, N. Y.
287p. Flushing 1899.   974.724 F671

Hempstead
Including North Hempstead

Carmichael, W: M. Rise and progress of St George's church,
Hempstead; including short biographical sketches of the missionaries
of the same; being a discourse delivered Jan. 1, 1841. 55p.
Flushing 1841.   283.747 H39

Flint, M. B. Stamford migration. *(see her* Early Long Island.
1896.   p. 124–61)   974.721 F64
Settlement of Hempstead.

Forbush, W: B. Wantagh, Jerusalem and Ridgewood, 1644–1892.
16p. Wantagh 1892.   L. I. hist. soc.

Friends meeting house at Jerusalem. *(see* American historical record,
Feb. 1873, 2 : 53–54)   973 qAm3

George 2, *king of England.* Patent and charter of St George's
church, Hempstead, Queens co. Long Island, granted by King
George II in 1735, printed directly from the original parchment
patent issued by order of the king, now in possession of the church.
8p.   Hempstead 1878.   L. I. hist. soc.

Hart, Seth.   Sermon in St George's church, Hempstead, Sep. 21, Local hi
1823.   N. Y. 1823.   Hempste
Entered in *American bibliopolist*, 4 : 540.   Historical sketch prefixed.

Hempstead, St George's church.   Record of baptisms, 1725–71 *(see*
New York genealogical and biographical record)   929.1   N421

    Oct. 1878, 9 : 182–87   Jan.–Ap. 1880, 11 : 47–51, 88–93
    Jan.–July 1879, 10 : 16–19, 89–92, 133–39

———— Record of marriages, 1725–86.   (*see* New York genealogical and
biographical record)   929.1   N421

    July 1880, 11 : 133–36 Jan.–July 1881, 12 :45–46, 78–83, 141–45
    Ap.–July 1882, 13 : 93–95, 140–43
    Jan.–July 1883, 14 : 43–44, 70–73, 116–18
    Ap.–Oct. 1884, 15 : 77–80, 111–13, 176–77 Ap. 1893, 24 :79–80

Hoes, R. R.   Extracts from the early and original records of the
Society for the propagation of the gospel in foreign parts, London.
(*see* New York genealogical and biographical record, July 1891,
22 : 127–32)   929.1   qN421
Relating chiefly to Hempstead.

Moore, C: B.   Early history of Hempstead, L. I.   (*see* New York genealogical and biographical record, Jan. 1879, 10 : 5–16)   929.1   N421

———— ——— 14p.   N. Y. 1879.   L. I. hist. soc.
Reprinted from *New York genealogical and biographical record*.

———— Genealogical and biographical sketch of Capt. John Seaman of
Hempstead, L. I.   (*see* New York genealogical and biographical
record, Oct. 1880, 11 : 149–55)   929.1   N421

Moore, W: H.   History of St George's church, Hempstead, Long
Island, N. Y.   308p.   N. Y. 1881.   L. I. hist. soc.

Names of inhabitants of the town of Hempstead, 1673. (*see* N. Y.
(state)—State, Secretary of.   Documentary history of the state of
New York)   1849–51.   1 : 658.   974.7   N424
             1850–51.   1 : 427–28.   974.7   qN423

North Hempstead—Town board.   Records of the towns of North
and South Hempstead, Long Island, N. Y.   v.1.   Jamaica
N. Y. 1896.   974.724   N81

Onderdonk, Henry, jr, *comp.* Annals of Hempstead, 1643–1832; also, the rise and growth of the society of friends on Long Island and in New York, 1657–1826. 107p. Hempstead 1878. 974.724 H37

Annals before the revolution, p.15–79; quakers at Hempstead, p.5–14; friends on Long Island and in New York, p.93–104.

———— Antiquities of the parish church, Hempstead, including Oyster Bay and the churches of Suffolk county illustrated from letters of the missionaries and other authentic documents. 63p. Hempstead 1880. N. Y. pub. lib.

———— An historical sketch of ancient agriculture, stockraising and manufactures in Hempstead, county of Queens. p.43–63. Jamaica 1867. L. I. hist. soc.

———— Westbury monthly meeting. (*see* American historical record, July–Aug. 1872, 1 : 289–93, 360–64) 973 qAm3

Westbury, Friends society. Record of births. (*see* New York genealogical and biographical record. Oct. 1885, 16 : 171–75, July 1886, 17 : 218–22) 929.1 N421

Woodbridge, Sylvester, jr. Historical discourse delivered Nov. 29, 1840 at the dedication of Christ's 1st church chapel in Raynor South, Hempstead, L. I. 21p. N. Y. 1840. L. I. hist. soc.

Jamaica

Betts, B. R. Inscriptions from tombstones in the parish churchyard at Jamaica, L. I. (*see* New York genealogical and biographical record, Jan. 1876, 7 : 18) 929.1 N421

1738–1831.

Field, T: W. Two British occupations of the presbyterian church of Jamaica; by Lord Cornbury and General Howe. (*see his* Historic and antiquarian scenes in Brooklyn and its vicinity. 1868 p.9–16) 974.723 qF45.

Garretson, G. J. A discourse delivered in the reformed Dutch church, Jamaica, N. Y. Feb. 15 and repeated in Newtown, Feb. 20, 1842, at the quadragenian anniversary of the ministry of the Rev. Jacob Schoonmaker. 29p. Flushing 1842. L. I. hist. soc.

McDonald, J. M. Sketch of the history of the presbyterian church in Jamaica, L. I. 138p. N. Y. 1847. 285.1747 J221

McDonald, J. M. Two centuries in the history of the presbyterian church, Jamaica, L. I. the oldest existing church of the presbyterian name in America. 329p. N. Y. 1862. 285.1747 J22

Onderdonk, Henry, jr. Antiquities of the parish church of Jamaica, including Newtown and Flushing, illustrated from letters of the missionaries and other authentic documents, with a continuation of the history of Grace church to the present time. 162p. Jamaica 1880. 283.747 J22

——— History of the First reformed Dutch church of Jamaica, L. I. with an appendix by Rev. W: H. DeHart, the pastor. 207p. Jamaica 1884. 285.7747 J22

Poyer, Thomas. Register book for the parish of Jamaica, kept by Rev. Thomas Poyer, rector from 1710 to 1732. (*see* New York genealogical and biographical record, Jan.-Ap. 1888, 19:5-12, 53-59) 929.1 qN421

Van Slyke, J. G. The reformed church of Jamaica, Long Island; an historical discourse delivered July 2, 1876. 43p. N. Y. 1876. L. I. hist. soc.

Long Island City

Kelsey, J. S. History of Long Island city, N. Y. a record of its early settlement and corporate progress. 202p. n.p. 1896. 974.721 qK29

Newtown

Kieft, *Gov.* Wilhelm. Patent of Mespath or Newton, L. I. (*see* O'Callaghan, E. B. History of New Netherland. 1846-48. 1:425-26) 974.7 Oc11

Moore, C: B. Sketch of the life of Rev. John Moore of Newton, L. I. (*see* New York genealogical and biographical record, Jan.-Ap. 1880, 11:5-12, 92-97) 929.1 N421

Riker, James. Annals of Newtown, in Queens county, N. Y.; containing its history from its first settlement with many facts concerning the adjacent towns; also, a particular account of numerous Long Island families. 437p. N. Y. 1852. 974.724 N48

Waters, I: S. Extracts from records of the reformed church of Newtown, L. I. translated from the Dutch language. (*see* Putnam's monthly historical magazine, 1893-94, ser. 2, 2:115-18) 929.1 qSa31 v.4

Oyster Bay

Clapham, G. M. Colonial neighbors. (*see* New England magazine,
Oct. 1893, ser. 3, 9: 201-7) 051 B34 v.15
Rev. Benjamin Woolsey of Glen Clove L. I.

Glen Clove. Address at the celebration of the second centennial anniversary of the settlement of that village by H: J. Scudder, May 25,
1868; with an appendix. 195p. Glen Clove 1868. 974.724 G48

Onderdonk, Henry, jr. Friends meeting house. (*see* American
historical record) 973 qAm3
Bethpage, Feb. 1873, 2: 73-76 Matinecock, June, 1872, 2: 257-61
Jericho, Nov. 1872, 1: 500-2 Oyster Bay, May, 1872, 1: 219-23

Wightman, C: S. History of the baptist church of Oyster Bay, L. I.
14p. Oyster Bay 1873. L. I. hist. soc.

Suffolk county

Bayles, R: M. Historical and descriptive sketches of Suffolk county,
and its towns, villages, hamlets, scenery, institutions and important
enterprises; with a historical outline of Long Island, from its first
settlement by Europeans. 424p. Port Jefferson 1874. 974.725 B34
Historical outline of Long Island, p. 1-91.

—— History of Suffolk county. (*see* History of Suffolk county, New
York. 1882. p. 49-82) 974.725 qH62

Flint, M. B. The Connecticut towns. (*see her* Early Long Island.
1896. p. 244-60) 974.721 F64

Hedges, H: P. Development of agriculture in Suffolk county. (*see*
Suffolk county. Bicentennial; history of Suffolk county. 1885.
p. 39-54) 974.725 Su2

Herrick, S: E. Religious progress and Christian culture of Suffolk
county. (*see* Suffolk county. Bicentennial; history of Suffolk county.
1885. p. 29-38) 974.725 Su2

History of Suffolk county, New York with illustrations, portraits and
sketches of prominent families and individuals. v. p. N. Y. 1882.
974.725 qH62

List of freeholders in Suffolk county, 1737. (*see* N. Y. (state)—State,
Secretary of. Documentary history of the state of New York)
1849-51. 4: 200-4. 974.7 N424
1850-51. 4: 132-34. 974.7 qN423

Moore, C: B. Inventories, Suffolk county, L. I. 1668–92. (*see* New York genealogical and biographical record, July 1881, 12: 132–34)

929.1 N421

Nicoll, Henry. Early history of Suffolk county, L. I. a paper read before the Long Island historical society Nov. 16, 1865. 18p. Brooklyn 1866.

N. Y. pub. lib.

Papers relating to Suffolk county. (*see* N. Y. (state)–State, Secretary of. Documentary history of the state of New York)

1849–51. 3: 341–94. 974.7 N424
1850–51. 3: 207–38. 974.7 qN423

Pelletreau, W: S. Early Long Island wills of Suffolk county, 1691–1703; an unabridged copy of the manuscript volume known as "The Lester will book;" being the record of the prerogative court of the county of Suffolk, N. Y. with genealogical and historical notes. 301p. N. Y. 1897.

929.3 Su21

Reeves, H: A. Commerce, navigation and fisheries of Suffolk county. (*see* Suffolk county. Bicentennial; history of Suffolk county. 1885. p. 55–78)

974.725 Su2

Scudder, H: J. Formation of the civil government of Suffolk county. (*see* Suffolk county. Bicentennial; history of Suffolk county. 1885. p. 19–28)

974.725 Su2

Stiles, H: R. Notes on the graveyards of Long Island; tombstone inscriptions from the churchyards of Southold, Sag Harbor and Southampton. (*see* New York genealogical and biographical record, Jan. 1871, 2: 29–32)

929.1 N421

Suffolk county. Bicentennial: history of Suffolk county, comprising the addresses delivered at the celebration of the bicentennial of Suffolk county, N. Y. in Riverhead, Nov. 15, 1883. 125p. Babylon 1885

974.725 Su2

Whitaker, Epher. Growth of Suffolk county in population, wealth and comfort. (*see* Suffolk county. Bicentennial; history of Suffolk county. 1885. p. 9–18)

974.725 Su2

Brookhaven

Bayles, R: M. Brookhaven. 101p. (*in* History of Suffolk county, N. Y. 1882)

974.725 qH62

Brookhaven. Records up to 1800 as compiled by the town clerk. 219p. Patchogue 1880.

974.725 B79

Most important and valuable parts of the old records.

Chichester, Daniel & others vs W. H. Smith & Peter Ruland.
New York supreme court; case upon exceptions directed to be
heard in the first instance at general term. 55p. n.p. 1856.
L. I. hist. soc

Suit brought to try the title of the town of Brookhaven to the fisheries in
Great South bay. Question as to validity of letters patent granted by Gov.
Nicolls, Dongan and Fletcher and will of William Smith, dated 1704.

Petty, J. H. Abstracts of Brookhaven, L. I. wills on record in the
surrogate's office at New York. (*see* New York genealogical and
biographical record) .   929.1 N421

    Jan. 1880, 11 : 24–29   July 1883, 14 : 140–42
    Jan. 1881, 12 : 46–49   Ap. 1893, 24 : 88–90
    Oct. " 12 : 198–99   July " 24 : 142–44

Rev. James Lyons and his church at Setauket. (*see* New York
genealogical and biographical record, Oct. 1888, 19 : 150–51)
    929.1 qN421

Trial for witchcraft of Ralph Hall of Brookhaven and Mary, his wife,
1665. (*see* N. Y. (state) – State. Secretary of. Documentary
history of the state of New York)

    1849–51. 4 : 133–36.   974.7   N424
    1850–51. 4 : 85–86.   974.7   qN423

Easthampton
Including Gardiners Island

Beecher, Lyman. Sermon containing a general history of the town
of East-Hampton, L. I.; from its first settlement to the present
time, delivered at East-Hampton, Jan. 1, 1806. 40p. Sag
Harbor 1806.   974.725 Ea7

—— —— 24p. Lyons Ia. 1886.   L. I. hist. soc.

Buell, Samuel. Faithful narrative of the remarkable revival of religion in the congregation of Easthampton on Long Island in
1764. N. Y. 1766.   L. I. hist. soc.

—— Faithful narrative of the remarkable revival of religion in the
congregation of Easthampton on Long Island 1764; with some
reflections; to which are added sketches of the author's life
144p. Sag Harbor 1808.   269 B86.

Buell, Samuel. Import of the Saint's confession that the times of men are in the hand of God; exhibited to view in an anniversary, euchar- istical and half century sermon delivered at East-Hampton Jan. 1, 1792. 52p. New London n. d. 240 B86

Colton, H : E. East Hampton and its old church. (*see* Appleton's journal, Mar. 25, 1871, 5 : 346-50) 051 qAp5

Easthampton. Records of the town of East Hampton, Long Island, Suffolk county, N. Y. with other ancient documents of historic value. v. 1-4. Sag Harbor 1887-89. 974.725 Ea71
Contents : v. 1 1639 to 1679-80. v. 3 1701-1734.
v. 2 1679-80 to 1701-2. v. 4 1734 to 1849.

Flint, M. B. Lion Gardiner. (*see her* Early Long Island. 1896. p. 216-23) 974.721 F64

Gardiner, C. C. *ed.* Papers and biography of Lion Gardiner, 1559-1663, with an appendix. 106p. St Louis 1883. 926.2 qG16

—— —— (*see his* Lion Gardiner and his descendants. 1890. p. 1-75)
929.2 qG16

Gardiner, David. Chronicles of the town of Easthampton, county of Suffolk, N. Y. 121p. N. Y. 1871. 974.725 Ea73
Published in the *Corrector* newspaper about 1840 : largely on colonial times.

—— Gardiner family and the lordship and manor of Gar- diner's island. (*see* New York genealogical and biographical record, Oct. 1892, 23 : 159-90) 929.1 qN421

Gardiner, J: L. East Hampton. (*see* New York historical society. Collections. 1870. Publication fund ser. 2 : 223-76) 974.7 N42

—— Lordship and manor of Gardiner's island. (*see* New York genealogical and biographical record, Jan. 1886, 17 : 32-34)
929.1 N421

—— Notes and observations on the town of East Hampton, L. I. Ap. 1798. (*see* N. Y. (state)—State, Secretary of. Documentary history of the state of New York) 1849-51. 1 : 674-86. 974.7 N424
1850-51. 1 : 457-63. 974.7 qN423

Hedges, H: P. Address delivered on the 26th of Dec. 1849, on the occasion of the celebration of the 200th anniversary of the settle- ment of the town of East Hampton together with an appendix con- taining a general history of the town. 100p. Sag Harbor 1850. 974.725 Ea72
Families, p. 36-72.

Hedges, H: P. History of the town of East Hampton, N. Y. including
an address delivered at the celebration of the bicentennial anniversary of its settlement in 1849; introduction to the 4 printed volumes
of its records and genealogical notes. **344p.**   Sag Harbor
1897.   974.725 qEa7
Genealogy of Easthampton, p. 244-344.

Huntting, Nathaniel. Records of marriages, baptisms and deaths
in East Hampton, L. I. from 1696 to 1746. (*see* New York genealogical and biographical record)   929.1 qN421

    Oct. 1893, 24:183-94   Jan. 1895, 26:38-44
    Jan. 1894, 25:35-40   Ap. 1897, 28:109-10
    July "   25:139-40   Jan. "   29:18-21
    Oct. "   25:196-97   July "   29:166-70

Jameson, J: F. Montauk and the common lands of Easthampton.
(*see* Magazine of American history, Ap. 1883, 9:225-39)   973 M27

Lamb, *Mrs* M. J. R. (Nash). Manor of Gardiner's island. (*see*
Magazine of American history, Jan. 1885, 13:1-30)   973 M27

Pelletreau, W: S. East Hampton. **42p.** (*in* History of Suffolk
county, New York. 1882)   974.725 qH62

Tooker, W: W. Indian places named in East Hampton town, L. I.
with their probable significations. Sag Harbor 1889. L. I. hist. soc.

—— —— (*see* Easthampton. Records of the town of East Hampton.
1887-89. 4:pref. 1-10)   974.725 Ea71

Huntington

Cooper, J. B. Babylon. **34p.** (*in* History of Suffolk county, N. Y.
1882)   974.725 qH62

Davidson, Robert. Historical discourse on the bicentennial commemoration of the founding of the first christian church in the town
of Huntington, L. I. delivered Nov. 19, 1865. **64p.**   Huntington 1866.   285.1747 H92

Huntington. Huntington town records, including Babylon, Long
Island 1652-1775; with introduction, notes and index by C. R:
Street. v.1-3.   Huntington 1887-89.   974.725 H92
Very largely deeds.
Contents: v. 1 1652-88.   v. 2 1688-1775.   v. 3 1776-1873.

Huntington, St John's church. Annals of St John's church,
Suffolk county, N. Y. also historical and descriptive; ed. by C. W.
Turner. **87p.**   Huntington 1895.   N. Y. hist. soc.

Lockwood, L. C. Historical discourse on the rise and progress of <del>Local hi Smithto</del>
the presbyterian church of Melville, delivered Sep. 10, 1876.   11p.
n.p. n.d.   L. I. hist. soc.
Sketch of presbyterian church in Huntington from its organisation in 1628
down to the separation in 1829.

Platt, H: C. Old times in Huntington, an historical address delivered
4 July 1876.   83p.   Huntington 1876.   974.725   H921

Street, C. R: Huntington.   90p.   (*in* History of Suffolk county,
N. Y.   1882)   974.725   qH62

Turner, C. R. Annals of St John's church, Huntington, Suffolk
county, N. Y. also historical and descriptive notes.   87p.   Huntington 1895.   283.747   H92

Wood, Silas, *anon.* A brief statement of the claim of the trustees of
the freeholders and commonalty of the town of Huntington to
Cap-Tree island, Oak island and Grass island, situate in the South
bay on the south side of Long Island in Suffolk county.   16p.
Brooklyn 1816.   L. I. hist. soc.

—— Sketch of geography of Huntington, L. I. with history, etc.
Wash. 1824.
Entered in *American bibliopolist* 4:540, 010.5   Am3.

—— Sketch of the town of Huntington, L. I. from its first settlement to the end of the American revolution ; ed. with genealogical and historical notes by W: S. Pelletreau.   63p.   N. Y.
1898.   974.725   H922
Edition in 215 copies.

Islip

Town of Islip.   17p.   (*in* History of Suffolk county, N. Y.
1882)   974.725   qH62

Riverhead

Bayles, R: M. Riverhead.   22p.   (*in* History of Suffolk county,
N. Y.   1882)   974.725   qH62

Shelter island

Lamb, *Mrs* **M. J. R. (Nash).** Manor of Shelter island; historic home
of the Sylvesters. (*see* Magazine of American history,   Nov. 1887,
18 : 361–89)   973   M27

Pelletreau, W: S. Shelter island.   14p.   (*in* History of Suffolk
county, N. Y.   1882)   974.725   qH62

Smithtown

Smith, J. L. Smithtown.   42p.   *in* History of Suffolk county,
N. Y.   1882)   974.725   qH62

Southampton

Hedges, H: P. Address delivered before the Suffolk county historical society Oct. 1st, 1889.   14p.   Sag Harbor 1889.   974.725 So93

On the controversy concerning priority of settlement of Southold and Southampton.

———— Centennial and historical address delivered at Bridge-Hampton, L. I. July 4th 1876.   24p.   Sag Harbor 1876.   974.725   B76

Colonial period, p. 1-10.

———— Historical address and appendix.   34p.   Sag Harbor 1886.

285.1747   B76

Bicentennial of the presbyterian church in Bridge-Hampton Nov. 10, 1886.

Herrick, S: E.   Our relation to the past a debt to the future.   (*see* Magazine of American history, July 1890, 24 : 54–61)   973   M27

Address at celebration of 250th anniversary of the settlement of South-ampton, June 12, 1890.

Howell, G: R.   Early history of Southampton, L. I. New York; with genealogies.   318p.   N. Y. 1866.   974.725   So8

Births, marriages and deaths, p. 200-308.

——— ——— Ed. 2.   473p.   Alb. 1887.   974.725   So81

Genealogies, p. 201–444.

———— Long Island early affairs. (*see* New England historical and genealogical register, Ap. 1861, 15 : 129–32)   929.1   N422

———— When Southampton and Southold on Long Island were settled 14p.   Alb. 1882.   974.725   So84

Lamb, *Mrs* M. J. R. (Nash).   Southampton in history. (*see* Magazine of American history, July 1890, 24 : 62–65)   973   M27

List of ye inhabitants of ye towne of Southampton, old and yong, Christians and hethen, ffreemen and servants, white and black, anno 1698. (*see* N. Y. (state)–State, Secretary of.   Documentary history of the state of New York)   1849–51.   1 : 665–69.   974.7   N424

1850–51.   1 : 437–47.   974.7   qN423

Pelletreau. W : S. Centennial celebration at Southampton, Long Is-land, N. Y. July 4, 1876.   26p.   Sag Harbor 1876.   974.725   So83

———— Indian deeds and documents relating to the town of South-ampton, L. I.   8p.   n. t.-p.   Sag Harbor 1863.   L. I. hist. soc.

———— Southampton.   54p. (*in* History of Suffolk county, N. Y. 1882)   974.725   qH62

Southampton. Addresses delivered at the celebration of the 250th anniversary of the village and town of Southampton, June 12, 1890, by H: P. Hedges, G: R. Howell, W: S. Pelletreau, & S: E. Herrick incl. introduction, programme of proceedings and original odes. 104p. Sag Harbor 1890. 974.725 So82

————— Books of record of the town of Southampton, with other ancient documents of historical value. 3v. Sag Harbor 1874–78. 974.725 So85

Contents: v. 1 1639-1660. v. 2 1660-1717. v. 3 1717-1807.

————— Patent of the town of Southampton, published by authority of the town. 12p. Sag Harbor 1835. L. I. hist. soc.

————— Selection from the town records. 59p. n. t.-p. L. I. hist. soc.

Southampton, Presbyterian church. A register and manual for the use of members of the presbyterian church of Southampton, L. I. prepared Feb. 1870. 40p. N. Y. 1870. L. I. hist. soc.

Tooker, W : W. Analysis of the claims of Southold, L. I. for priority of settlement over Southampton, L. I. and how they are disproved by the early records and contemporary mss. (*see* Magazine of New England history, Jan. 1892, 2: 1–16) 929 M27

Southold

For controversy between Southampton and Southold concerning the priority of settlement, see the former town, p. 460.

Case, Albertson. Historical sketch of Southold towns read, July 4, 1876 at the celebration held in Greenport, L. I. 16p. Greenport 1876.

Griffin, Augustus. Griffin's journal; first settlers of Southold: the names of the heads of those families, being only 13 at the time of their landing; first proprietors of Orient, biographical sketches, etc. 312p. Orient 1857. 929.1 G87

Howell, G : R. Settlement of Southold. 4p. Babylon 1894. 974.725 So84

King, Rufus. Inscriptions from the churchyard in Orient, Suffolk county, N. Y. (*see* New York genealogical and biographical record, Ap. 1875, 6: 107-9) 929.1 N421

1699-1766.

Lamb, *Mrs* **M. J. R. (Nash).** Southold and her historic homes and memories, 1640–1890. (*see* Magazine of American history, Oct. 1890, 24: 273-82) 973 M27

Local history Southold **Lambert, E : R.** Southold, L. I. (*see his* History of the colony of New Haven. 1838. p.180–85)   974.67 L17

List of the names of old and young, Christians and heathens, ffremen and servants, white and black, etc. inhabitteinge within the township of Southold. (*see* N. Y. (state)—State, Secretary of. Documentary history of the state of New York)

1849–51.	1 : 669–73.	974.7	N424
1850–51.	1 : 447–56.	974.7	qN423

Moore, C : B. Historical address. (*see* Southold. Celebration of the 250th anniversary. 1890. p. 109–95)   974.725 So92
Contents : Introduction, bibliographic, p. 109–14.
   Address, p. 115–79.
   Notes; deputies from Southold to New Haven and taxes paid there; early inventories; wills and letters of administration; samples of errors in printed records, etc. p. 180–95.

——— *comp.* Town of Southold, Long Island; personal index prior to 1698 and index of 1698.   145p.   N. Y. 1868.   929 3 So9

Pelletreau, W : S. Southold. 56p. (*in* History of Suffolk county, N. Y. 1882)   974.725 qH62

Southold. Celebration of the 250th anniversary of the formation of the town and the church, Aug. 27, 1890.   220p.   Southold 1890.
          974.725 So92
Including addresses by R : S. Storrs and C : B. Moore.

——— Town records copied and explanatory notes added by J. W. Case.   2v.   N. Y. 1882–84.   974.725 So9
To the close of the revolution.

Whitaker, Epher. The early history of Southold, Long Island. (*see* New Haven historical society. Papers. 1877. 2 : 1–29) 974.67 N42
Paper read Sep. 24, 1866.

——— Founders of Southold, L. I. (*see* New York genealogical and biographical record, Ap.–July 1895, 26 : 85–89, 114–18)
          929.1 qN421

——— History of Southold, L. I.; its first century. 354p. Southold 1881.   974.725 So91
1640–1740.

Richmond county, or Staten Island

Bayles, R: M. *comp.* History of Richmond county, Staten Island, New York, from its discovery to the present time. 741p. N. Y. 1887.   974.726 qB34

Brooks, Erastus. Historical records of Staten Island; centennial and
bicentennial for 200 years and more, delivered at Staten Island,
November 1st, 1883. 39p. n.p. n.d. 974.726 B79
Reprinted from *Proceedings of the bicentennial celebration of Richmond county.*
1883. 974.726 R41.

Carteret's claim to Staten Island. (*see* New Jersey (province).
Documents relating to the colonial history of the state of New
Jersey. 1880. 1 : 349–53) 974.9 N42

Clute, J: J. Annals of Staten Island, from its discovery to the present
time. 464p. N. Y. 1877. 974.726 qC62
Old families, p. 335–438.

Davis, W: T. Staten Island names: ye olde names and nicknames
with map by C: W. Leng. p. 20–76. New Brighton 1896.
917.4726 D29
Special no. 21 of the proceedings of the Staten Island natural science association.

Disosway, G. P. Early history of Staten Island, N. Y. (*see* Historical
magazine, May 1862, 6 : 144–46) 973 H62

——— Huguenots of Staten Island. (*see* Continental monthly, June
1862, 1 : 683–88) 051 C76

Indian deed for Staten Island in 1670. (*see* Historical magazine, Dec.
1866, 10 : 375–77) 973 H62

Koenen, H. J. Pavonia. (*see* Nijhoff, J. A. Bijdragen voor Neder-
landsche geschiedenis. 1847. 5 : 114–32)
Entered in Rees. *Geschiedenis.* 1855. p. 136.
Pavonia was the colony founded on Staten Island in 1628.

Leibert, Eugene. Sketch of the history of the congregation on Staten
Island, N. Y. (*see* Moravian historical society. Transactions.
1876. 1 : 57–63, 78) 284.6 M791

Morris, I. K. Old hotels of Staten Island. 7p. n.p. 1893.
974.726 M83
Special no. 14 of the proceedings of the Staten Island natural science association.

Papers relating to Staten Island. (*see* O'Callaghan, E. B. History of
New Netherland. 1846–48. 2 : 575–77) 974.7 Oc11
Contents: Indian sale to Baron van der Capellen, 1657.
Sale by Cornelis Melyn to the directors of Amsterdam, 1659.
Surrender by Baron van der Capellen to the company of his in-
terest, 1660.

Richmond county. Proceedings of the bicentennial celebration, Staten Island, N. Y. Nov. 1, 1883. 23+54p. n.p. 1883. 974.726 R41

Historical records of Staten Island, centennial and bicentennial, by Erastus Brooks, p. 1–39.

Speeches by Perry Belmont, A. S. Sullivan, H. J. Scudder, G: W: Curtis and L. B. Prince, p. 39–54.

Staten Island. (*see* New Jersey Historical society. Proceedings. 1856–59. 8: 109–13) 974.9 N421

Reprinted from *Newark daily advertiser*, Feb. 11, 1858. Staten Island as part of New Jersey.

Staten Island and the New Jersey boundary. (*see* Historical magazine, Oct. 1866, 10: 297–99) 973 H62

Tysen, R. M. Lecture on the history of Staten Island; delivered before the Tompkinsville lyceum, Ap. 12, 1842. 13p. Staten Island 1842. 974.726 T98

Whitehead, W: A. Staten Island and the New Jersey boundary. (*see* New Jersey historical society. Proceedings. 1867–69. ser. 2, 1: 31–36) 974.9 N421 v.11–12

Wilson, W. S. Staten Island. (*see* Wilson, J. G. *ed.* Memorial history of the city of New York. 1892–93. 4: 33–38) 974.71 qW69

Northfield

Northfield. Account of the centennial celebration of the 4th of July, 1876 incl. the oration by G: W: Curtis, and historical sketch by J: J. Clute. 23p. N. Y. 1876. 974.726 N81

Port Richmond, Dutch reformed church. Ancient baptismal record of the early Dutch church. (*see* Bayles, R: M. History of Richmond county. 1887. p.368–94) 974.726 qB34

Westfield

Lossing, B. J: Billopp house. (*see* Potter's American monthly, Ap. 1876, 6: 242–47) 973 qAm3

Whitehead, W: A. Billopp house, Staten Island. (*see* Potter's American monthly, May 1876, 6: 344–45) 973 qAm3

Hudson river counties

For a more complete bibliography of the Hudson river, see

Wheeler, M. T. *comp.* Contribution to the bibliography of the literature relating to the Hudson river, found with a few exceptions in the New York state library. Alb. 1891. (*in* N. Y. (state)-Library school. Bibliographies. 1891) 016.91747

In manuscript.

Cooper, S. F. Hudson river and its early names. (*see* Magazine of American history, June 1880, 4 : 401–19) 973 M27

Grant, B. R. Early Dutch times on the banks of the Hudson. (*see* Potter's American monthly, Feb. 1875, 4 : 104–6) 973 qAm3

Lossing, B. J: The Hudson from the wilderness to the sea. 464p. N. Y. °1866. 917.47 L89

Schoolcraft, H: R. Comments, philological and historical, on the aboriginal names and geographical terminology of the state of New York; pt 1 Valley of the Hudson. (*see* New York historical society. Proceedings. 1844. p. 77–115) 974.7 N421

Sketches of the North river. 119p. N. Y. 1838. 917.47 Sk2

Ver Planck, W: E. Old Dutch houses on the Hudson. (*see* New England magazine, Mar. 1895, ser. 3, 12 : 71–82) 051 B34 v.18

Westchester county

Atkins, T: A. Manor of Philipsburgh; a paper read before the New York historical society, June 5, 1894. 23p. n. p.1894. 974.727 P53
Published by the Yonkers (N. Y.) historical and literary association.
Estate of Van der Donck and the Philipse family forfeited at the time of the revolution.

Baird, C: W. Westchester county, N. Y. marriage records. (*see* New York genealogical and biographical record, Oct. 1877, 8 : 181–82) 929.1 N421

Bolton, *Rev.* Robert. History of the county of Westchester, from its first settlement to the present time. 2v. N. Y. 1848. 974.727 B63

—— History of the protestant episcopal church in the county of Westchester, from its foundation, A. D. 1693 to A. D. 1853. 749p. N. Y. 1855. 283.747 W521

Bolton, *Rev.* **Robert.** History of the several towns, manors and patents of the county of Westchester, from its first settlement to the present time carefully revised by its author. 2v. N. Y. 1881. 974.727 B631
Flora of Westchester county by O. R. Willis in v. 1.

Campbell, C: A. The Philipse family and its connection with the colonial history of New York. (*see* Potter's American monthly, May 1875, 4:332–38) 973 qAm3

Coffey, W: S. Colonial period, 1683–1774. (*see* Scharf, J: T: History of Westchester county. 1886. 1:161–77) 974.727 qSch1

Cumming, W: S. Civil history. (*see* Scharf, J: T: History of Westchester county. 1886. 1:639–57) 974.727 qSch1

De Lancey, E: F. Origin and history of manors in the province of New York and in the county of Westchester. 160p. N. Y. 1886. N. Y. pub. lib.

—— —— (*see* Scharf, J: T: History of Westchester county. 1886. 1:31–160f) 974.727 qSch1

Lamb, *Mrs* **M. J. R. (Nash).** Van Cortlandt manor-house. (*see* Magazine of American history, Mar. 1886, 15:217–36) 973 M27

Mills, Richard. Richard Mills to Connecticut concerning Westchester, 1662–3. (*see* Massachusetts historical society. Collections. 1885. ser. 5, 9:48–50) 974.4 M38 v.49

Papers relating to Westchester county. (*see* N.Y. (state)—State, Secretary of. Documentary history of the state of New York)
1849–51. 3:919–58. 974.7 N424
1850–51. 3:555–79. 974.7 qN423

Pelletreau, W: S. *ed.* Early wills of Westchester county, N. Y. from 1664 to 1784; a careful abstract of all wills (nearly 800) recorded in New York surrogate's office and at White Plains, N. Y. 488p. N. Y. 1898. 929.3 W52

—— Philipse manor in the highlands. (*see* Magazine of American history, Aug. 1889, 22:106–13) 973 M27

Scharf, J: T. History of Westchester county, New York, including Morrisania, Kings Bridge and West Farms which have been annexed to New York city. 2v. Phil. 1886. 974.727 qSch1

Watson, W. C. The Philipse family. (*see* American historical record, Sep. 1873, 2:410–13) 973 qAm3

Wood, James. Discovery and settlement of Westchester county. Local hist. Greenburg (*see* Scharf, J: T: History of Westchester county. 1886. 1 : 20–31)

974.727 qSch1

Bedford

Baird, C: W. Births and marriages, Bedford, N. Y. (*see* New York genealogical and biographical record, Ap. 1882, 13 : 92) 929.1 N42I

—— History of Bedford church; discourse delivered at the 200th anniversary of the founding of the presbyterian church of Bedford, Westchester county, N. Y. Mar. 22, 1881, with an account of the proceedings on that occasion. 149p. N. Y. 1882. 285.1747 B39

Barrett, Joseph. Bedford. (*see* Scharf, J : T : History of Westchester county. 1886. 2 : 574–608) 974.727 qSch1

Heroy, P: B. Brief history of the presbyterian church at Bedford, N. Y. from the year 1680, with an account of the laying of the cornerstone and services at the dedication of the present edifice in the year 1872. 34p. N. Y. 1874. 285.1747 B39I

Luquer, Lea. Centennial address delivered in St Matthew's church, Bedford, N. Y. Aug. 20, 1876. 27p. N. Y. 1876. L. I. hist. soc. Early history of the parish including Rye, Mamaroneck and Bedford from its organization, 1694.

Cortlandt

Cumming, W : J. Cortlandt. (*see* Scharf, J: T: History of Westchester county. 1886. 2 : 365–436) 974.727 qSch1

Rodman, E. M. Historical sketch of St Peter's parish Cortlandt-town, N. Y. delivered, Aug. 9, 1867. 32p. Peekskill 1867. 283.747 P34

Terhune, *Mrs* **M.. V. (Hawes).** The Van Cortlandt manor-house. (*see her* Some colonial homesteads. 1897. p. 171–200) 973.2 T27

Eastchester

Coffey, W : S: Commemorative discourse delivered at the centennial anniversary of the erection and the 60th of the consecration of St Paul's church, East Chester, N. Y. Oct. 24, 1865. 45p. N. Y. 1866. Providence pub. lib.

—— East Chester. (*see* Scharf, J: T: History of Westchester county. 1886. 2 : 720–64) 974.727 qSch1

Greenburg

Bacon, E. M. Chronicles of Tarrytown and Sleepy Hollow. 163p. N. Y. 1897. 917.4727 B13

Local history Harrison **Centennial** souvenir, brief history of Tarrytown from 1680 to 1880, with a map of Tarrytown as it was 100 years ago. 24p. Tarrytown 1880. 974.727 T17

Cole, David. Historical address. (*see* Tarrytown, First reformed church. 200th anniversary. 1898. p. 109–54) 285.7747 T172

Hall, William. Ancient Sleepy Hollow church in Tarrytown, on the Hudson, N. Y. (*see* Potter's American monthly, Oct. 1877, 9: 257–59) 973 qAm3

Mabie, H. W. Tarrytown-on-Hudson; its historic associations and legendary lore. (*see* Powell, L. P. *ed.* Historic towns of the middle states. 1899. p. 137–67) 974.7 P87

Stewart, A. T. Historical discourse delivered at the First reformed protestant Dutch church of Tarrytown, N. Y. May 13, 1866. 49p N. Y. 1866. 285.7747 T17

Tarrytown, First reformed church. 200th anniversary of the old Dutch church of Sleepy Hollow, Oct. 10 and 11, 1897. 170p. N. Y. 1898. 285.7747 T172

Including sermon by J: K. Allen, addresses by J: B. Thompson, J: M. Ferris, D: D. Demarest, C: W. Fritts, A. F. Mabon, H. W. Mabie, Theodore Roosevelt and David Cole; and list of members, 1697–1715.

Todd, J: A. Greenburgh. (*see* Scharf, J: T: History of Westchester county. 1886. 2: 172–283) 974.727 qSch1

Harrison

Baird, C: W. Harrison. (*see* Scharf, J: T: History of Westchester county. 1886. 2: 709–20) 974.727 qSch1

Harrison (N. Y.) Friends society. Marriage records 1742–85. (*see* New York genealogical and biographical record, Jan. 1872, 3: 45–51) 929.1 N421

Lewisboro

Keeler, J. W. Lewisboro. (*see* Scharf, J: T: History of Westchester county. 1886. 2: 535–61) 974.727 qSch1

Mamaroneck

Danforth, Elliot. Address delivered at the 250th celebration of the purchase of Mamaroneck, N. Y. from the Indians, Sep. 21, 1891. 26p Mt Vernon N. Y. n. d. N. Y. pub. lib.

De Lancey, E: F. History of the town of Mamaroneck in the county of Westchester and state of New York. 43p. N. Y. 1886. 974.727 qM31

De Lancey, E: F. History of the town of Mamaroneck in the county ~~Local hi~~ ~~New Rocl~~ of Westchester and state of N. Y. (*see* Scharf, J: T: History of Westchester county. 1886. 1:846–88) 974.727 qSch1

Obadiah Palmer & others, complainants vs Jacobus Van Cortland & Adolph Philipse, defendants. In Cancellaria Novae Eborac. n.p. n.d. F. N. Y. 1727.

Grolier club, p. 28, no. 72.

Suit brought to determine title to the Great Neck at Mamaroneck. But one other perfect copy is known.

Mount Pleasant

Todd, J: A. Mount Pleasant. (*see* Scharf, J: T: History of Westchester county. 1886. 2:283–321) 974.727 qSch1

Newcastle

Barrett, Joseph. New Castle. (*see* Scharf, J: T: History of Westchester county. 1886. 2:608–28) 974 727 qSch1

New Rochelle

Bolton, Rev. Robert, *anon.* Guide to New Rochelle and its vicinity. 67p. N. Y. 1842. 917.4727 B63

Darling, C: W. Antoine L'Espenard, the French Huguenot, of New Rochelle. 20p. n.p. n.d.

Reprinted from the *New York genealogical and biographical record,* July 1893, 24:97–116, 929.1 qN421.

Hague, William. Old Pelham and New Rochelle. (*see* Magazine of American history, Aug. 1882, 8:521–37) 973 M27

—— —— (*see* Scharf, J: T: History of Westchester county. 1886. 1:709–13) 974.727 qSch1

Huguenots of New Rochelle. (*see* Continental monthly, Jan. 1863, 3:1–7) 051 C76

Lindsley, C: E. New Rochelle. (*see* Scharf, J: T: History of Westchester county. 1886. 1:685–701) 974.727 qSch1

List of the towne of New Rochelle, etc. Sep. 9, 1710. (*see* N. Y. (state)—State, Secretary of. Documentary history of the state of New York) 1849–51. 3:946–47. 974.7 N424
1850–51. 3:571–72. 974.7 qN423

New Rochelle, Episcopal church. Petition of the established church of England in New Rochelle. (*see* New York genealogical and biographical record, Oct. 1876, 7:173–74) 929.1 N421

New Rochelle press almanac. 1880. New Rochelle 1880. 974.727 N42
Local history of New Rochelle by L. J. Contant, p. 17–32.

Rupp, I. D. Names of males at New Rochelle in 1710. (*see his* Collection of upwards of 30,000 names. 1876. p. 463–64) 929.3 P38

Smith, H. E. The Huguenots of New Rochelle. (*see* Independent,
Ap. 21, 1899, v. 50, pt 1, p. 503–4)   205 fIn2

North Castle

Barrett, Joseph & Horton, W. H. North Castle. (*see* Scharf, J: T:
History of Westchester county. 1886. 2:629–43) 974.727 qSch1

North Salem

Culver, C: E. North Salem. (*see* Scharf, J: T: History of Westchester county. 1886. 2:499–535)   974 727 qSch1

Ossining

Fisher, G: J. Ossining. (*see* Scharf, J: T. History of Westchester
county. 1886. 2:321–65)   974.727 qSch1

Pelham

Lindsley, C: E. Pelham. (*see* Scharf, J: T: History of Westchester county. 1886. 1:701–8)   974.727 Schq1

Poundridge

Smith, G: T. Poundridge. (*see* Scharf, J: T: History of Westchester county. 1886. 2:561–74)   974.727 qSch1

Rye

Baird, C: W. Chronicles of a border town; history of Rye, Westchester county, New York, 1660–1870; including Harrison and the
White Plains till 1788; illustrated by Abram Hosier. 570p. N. Y.
1871.   974.727 R98
Families, p. 395–500.

———— Rye. (*see* Scharf, J: T: History of Westchester county. 1886.
2:643–709)   974.727 qSch1

Scarsdale

Butler, A. M. Scarsdale. (*see* Scharf, J: T: History of Westchester
county. 1886. 1:657–84)   974.727 qSch1

Somers

Culver, C: E. Somers. (*see* Scharf, J: T: History of Westchester
county. 1886. 2:469–98)   974.727 qSch1

Westchester

Morris, Fordham. Borough town of Westchester; an address deliv- Local hist
Yonkers ered on the 28th day of October 1896 before the Westchester county historical society. 22p. White Plains 1896.   974.727 W52

——— Westchester town. (*see* Scharf, J: T: History of Westchester county. 1886. 1 : 768–822)   974.727 qSch1

O'Neill, D. P. History of St Raymond's church, Westchester, N. Y. 23p. Westchester °1898.   N. Y. state lib.

Trial for witchcraft of Katherine Harrison of Westchester, 1670. (*see* N.Y. (state)—State, Secretary of. Documentary history of the state of New York)   1849–51.   4 : 136–38.   974.7 N424
                      1850–51.   4 : 87–88.   974.7 qN423

White Plains

Mitchell, J. S. White Plains. (*see* Scharf, J: T: History of Westchester county. 1886. 1 : 714–44)   974.727 qSch1

Yonkers

Allison, *Rev.* **C: E.** History of Yonkers from the earliest times to the present. 454p. N. Y. °1896.   974.727 qY8

Atkins, T: A. Indian wars and the uprising of 1655; Yonkers depopulated; a paper read before the Yonkers historical and library association, Mar. 18, 1832. 14p. Yonkers 1892.
Griffin, p. 1047.

Cole, David. Historical address delivered at the 25th anniversary of the reformed church of Yonkers, N. Y. on the 23d of Ap. 1868. 109p. N. Y. 1868.   285.7747 Y8
Early civil and religious history of the region; p. 1–46 introductory.

——— Yonkers. (*see* Scharf, J: T: History of Westchester county. 1886. 2 : 1–172)   974.727 qSch1

Dawson, H: B. Papers concerning the town and village of Yonkers, Westchester county; a fragment. 45p. Yonkers 1866. (Gazette ser. v. 2)   974.727 Y8
26 copies printed.

Edsall, T: H. Kings Bridge. (*see* Scharf, J: T: History of Westchester county. 1886. 1 : 744–68)   974.727 qSch1

Terhune, *Mrs* **M.: V. (Hawes).** The Philipse manor-house. (*see her* Some colonial homesteads. 1897. p. 239–75)   973.2 T27

Yorktown

Cumming, W: J. Yorktown. (*see* Scharf, J: T: History of Westchester county. 1886. 2 : 436-69. 974.727 qSch1

Orange county

Brodhead, Edgar. Picturesque corner of three states; a chapter of
Indian history and tradition. (*see* Magazine of American history,
Oct. 1883, 10 : 267–83) 973 M27

Denniston, Goldsmith. Survey of Orange county. 103p. Alb.
1863. 917.4731 D42
Extracted from transactions of New York state agricultural society, 1862.
Early history and settlement, p. 5–19.

Eager, J: M. An early canal. (*see* Historical magazine, Mar. 1864,
8 : 114–15) 973 H62
Built in Orange county between 1728 and 1760 by Gov. Colden.

Eager, S: W. Outline history of Orange county, with an enumeration of the names of its towns, villages, rivers, creeks. 652p.
Newburgh 1846-47. 974.731 Ea3

Fowler, R. L. Historic houses and revolutionary letters. (*see* Magazine of American history, Aug. 1890, 24 : 81–100) 973 M2'
Ellison house, New Windsor, Orange county.

Howe, J. F. St David's parish, Orange county, N. Y. (*see* American
historical record, May 1874, 3 : 195–98) 973 qAm3

List of the inhabitants in the county of Orange, 1702. (*see* N. Y.
(state)–State, Secretary of. Documentary history of the state of
New York) 1849-51. 1 : 366–67. 974.7 N424
1850-51. 1 : 239. 974.7 qN423

Minisink Valley historical society. Bicentennial celebration of the
200th anniversary of the settlement of the Minisink valley, held
under the auspices of the Minisink Valley historical society July 22,
1890. 28p. Port Jervis n.d. L. I. hist. soc.
Addresses by S. W. Mills, C. E. Cuddeback, T. D. Talmage, Hiram Clark,
A. A. Haines and J. H. Van Etten.

Ruttenber, E: M. History of the county of Orange ; with a history
of the town and city of Newburgh; general, analytical and biographical. 424p. Newburgh 1875. 974.731 R93
Almost the same as his *History of Newburgh*.

Ruttenber, E: M. & Clark, L: H. *comp.* History of Orange county, N. Y. with illustrations and biographical sketches of many of its pioneers and prominent men. 820p. Phil. 1881. 974 731 qR93

Stickney, C: E. History of the Minisink region, which includes the present towns of Minisink, Deerpark, Mount Hope, Greenville and Wawayanda, in Orange co. N. Y. from their organization and first settlement to the present time; also including a general history of the first settlement of the county. 211p. Middletown N Y. 1867. 974.731 St5

Blooming Grove

Riotous proceeding in Blooming Grove, Orange county in 1772. *(see* Historical magazine, June 1862, 6: 189-90) 973 H62

Cornwall

Beach, Lewis. Cornwall. 200p. Newburgh 1873. 974.731 C81

Deerpark

Gumaer, P: E. History of Deerpark in Orange county, N. Y. 204p. Port Jervis 1890. 974.731 D36
Published by the Minisink Valley historical society.

Mills, S : W. 1737-1878, reformed Dutch church of Deerpark, Port Jervis, N. Y. historical discourse read at the opening of the memorial chapel, Oct. 22, 1878. 64p. Port Jervis 1878. 285 7747 P83

Montgomery

Dickson, J. M. The Goodwill memorial; or, The first 150 years of the Goodwill presbyterian church, Montgomery, Orange co. N. Y. 163p. Newburgh 1880. L. I. hist. soc.

Howe, J. F. Dutch church at Montgomery, N. Y. *(see* American historical record, Jan. 1873, 2 : 21-24) 973 qAm3

Maclise, D. M. The former days; a historical discourse regarding the Goodwill presbyterian church, Montgomery, N. Y. delivered on New Years day 1865 in commemoration of the 125th anniversary of the settlement of the first pastor of the church. 31p. N. Y. 1865. Providence pub. lib.

New Windsor

New Windsor, Presbyterian church. Record of baptisms, marriages and births, entered by the Rev. John Close, [1764-96]. *(see* Historical society of Newburgh bay and the Highlands. Papers. 1896. p. 9-31) N. Y. state lib.

Niven, A. C. *ed.* The centennial memorial; a record of the 100th anniversary of the A. R. presbyterian church of Little Britain together with a sketch of the Clinton family.   251p.   N. Y. 1859.   285.1747 L72

Newburgh

For history of the palatines in Newburgh, see Palatines, p. 502.

Emery, Rufus. Church of England in Newburgh and vicinity previous to the revolution. (*see* Historical society of Newburgh bay and the Highlands. Papers. 1896. p.38–46)   N. Y. state lib. Read Jan. 2, 1885.

Papers relating to the palatines and to the first settlement of Newburgh, Orange county. (*see* N. Y. (state)–State, Secretary of. Documentary history of the state of New York)

              1849–51. 3 : 539–607.   974.7 N424
              1850–51. 3 : 325–64.   974.7 qN423

Ruttenber, E: M. Historical sketch. (*see* Carter's centennial city general and business directory of the city of Newburgh, N. Y. for the year 1876. p.9–56)   917.4731 N42

——— History of Newburgh. (*see his* History of the county of Orange. 1875. p.111–420)   974.731 R93

——— History of the town of Newburgh.   322p.   Newburgh 1859.   974.731 qN42
Biographic and genealogic sketches, p.259–322.

Skeel, Adelaide. Newburgh, the palatine parish of Quassaick. (*see* Powell, L. P. *ed.* Historic towns of the middle states. 1899. p.107–35)   974.7 P87

Rockland county

Cole, David, *ed.* History of Rockland county, N. Y. with biographical sketches of its prominent men.   344+75p.   N. Y. 1884.
                                          974.728 qC67

Ferdon, J: W. Indians of Rockland county. (*see* Cole, David, *ed.* History of Rockland county, N. Y. 1884. p.21–26) 974.728 qC67

Green, F. B. History of Rockland county.   444p.   N. Y. 1886.
                                          N. Y. pub. lib.

Clarkstown

Clarkstown, Reformed church. Baptisms at Clarkstown from Aug. 13, 1749 to Dec. 28, 1794. (*see* Cole, David, *ed.* History of Rockland county, N. Y. 1884. apx.p 54–75)   974.728 qC67

Fay, H. P. Town of Clarkstown. (*see* Cole, David, *ed.* History of Local hist Dutchess county Rockland county, N. Y. 1884. p.112-36) 974.728 qC67

Haverstraw

Freeman, A. S. & Pelletreau, W: S. Town of Haverstraw. (*see* Cole, David, *ed.* History of Rockland county, N. Y. 1884. p. 137-96) 974.728 qC67

Orangetown

Ferdon, J: W. Town of Orangetown. (*see* Cole, David, *ed.* History of Rockland county, N. Y. 1884. p.197-253) 974.728 qC67

Tappan, Reformed church. Baptisms at Tappan from Oct. 25, 1694 to Jan. 10, 1816. (*see* Cole, David, *ed.* History of Rockland county, N. Y. 1884. apx. p. 3-50) 974.728 qC67

Tappan, Second reformed church. Baptisms of an irregular congregation at Tappan, existing from 1767 to 1778. (*see* Cole, David, *ed.* History of Rockland county, N. Y. 1884. apx. p. 51-53) 974.728 qC67

Ramapo

Cobb, E. B. Town of Ramapo. (*see* Cole, David, *ed.* History of Rockland county, N. Y. 1884 p. 254-319) 974.728 qC67

Stony Point

Gay, Ebenezer, jr. Town of Stony Point (*see* Cole, David, *ed.* History of Rockland county, N. Y. 1884. p 320-44) 974.728 qC67

Dutchess county

Bailey, H. D. B. Local tables and historical sketches 431p. Fishkill Landing 1874. N. Y. hist. soc.

Huntting, Isaac. History of Little Nine Partners of Northeast precinct and Pine plains, New York, Duchess county. v. 1. Amenia 1897. 974.733 P65
Lineage of some families of Amenia and Pine Plains 1:316-95.

List of inhabitants and slaves in the county of Dutchess, 1714. (*see* N. Y. (state)–State, Secretary of Documentary history of the state of New York) 1849-51. 1: 368-69. 974.7 N424
1850-51. 1: 240 974.7 qN423

List of the freeholders in Dutchess county, 1740. (*see* N. Y. (state)–State, Secretary of. Documentary history of the state of New York) 1849-51. 4:205-8. 974.7 N424
1850-51. 4:134-36 974.7 qN423

Papers relating to Ulster and Dutchess counties. (*see* N. Y. (state)–
State, Secretary of. Documentary history of the state of New
York)   1849–51. 3:959–96.   974.7   N424
1850–51. 3:580–601.   974.7   qN423

Smith, J. H. History of Duchess county, N. Y. with illustrations and
biographical sketches of some of its prominent men and pioneers, by
J. H. Smith, assisted by H. H. Cale & W: E. Roscoe. 562p.
Syracuse 1882.   974.733 qSm5

Smith, P. H: General history of Duchess county, from 1609–1876,
inclusive. 507p. Pawling 1877.   974.733 Sm6

Ver Planck, W: E. Old Dutch houses on the Hudson. (*see* New
England magazine, Mar. 1895, ser. 3, 12: 71–82)   051 B34 v.18

Amenia

Reed, Newton. Early history of Amenia, N. Y.   151p.   Amenia
1875.   974.733 Am3

Fishkill

Brinckerhoff, T. V. Historical sketch of the town of Fishkill, from its
first settlement. p. 50–98. Fishkill Landing 1866.   974.733 F53

Celebration of the 150th anniversary of the church at Fishkill. (*see*
Historical magazine, Oct. 1866, 10: 323–24)   973 H62

Craig, *Mrs* **M.. D.** Life and times of Catharyna Rombout or Madam
Brett. (*see* Historical society of Newburgh bay and the Highlands.
Papers. 1896. p. 51–58)   N. Y. state lib.
Read Sep. 30, 1895. Owner of patent including Fishkill.

Fishkill, First reformed church. Account of the exercises in
connection with the 175th anniversary of the First reformed
Dutch church of Fishkill, Sep. 16, 1891.   47p.   Fishkill
1891.   285.7747 F535
Historical address by A. P. Van Gieson, p. 12–38.

Fishkill inscriptions; from the grave yards. (*see* New York genealogical and biographical record, Oct. 1892, 23:212–16; Jan. 1893,
24: 26–37)   929.1 qN421

Kip, F. M. Discourse delivered on the 12th of September 1866, at
the celebration of the 150th anniversary of the First reformed Dutch
church, Fishkill.   64p.   N. Y. 1866.   285.7747 F536

——— Historical sketch of Fishkill and its ancient church. (*see* New
York genealogical and biographical record, Ap. 1890. 21: 51–58)
929.1 qN421

Van Gieson, A. P.   Historical address.   (*see* Fishkill, First reformed church.   Account of the exercises in connection with the 175th anniversary.   1891.   p. 12–38)   285.7747   F535

Poughkeepsie

Van Gieson, A. P.   Anniversary discourse and history of the First reformed church at Poughkeepsie.   128p.   Poughkeepsie 1893.
285.7747   P86

Red Hook

Lewis, J: N.   Reminiscences of Annandale, N Y.   (*see* American historical register, Mar.–Ap. 1896, 4: 29–35, 151–60)   973   qAm31

Rhinebeck

Drury, J. B.   Reformed Dutch church, Rhinebeck, N. Y. an historical address delivered at the 150th anniversary of its organization. 68p.   Chatham N. Y. 1881.   285.7747   R34

Smith, E: M.   Documentary history of Rhinebeck, in Dutchess county, N. Y. embracing biographical sketches and genealogical records with a history of its churches and other institutions.   239p. Rhinebeck 1881.   974.733   R34

Putnam county

Blake, W: J.   History of Putnam county, N. Y. with an enumeration of its towns, villages, rivers, creeks, lakes, ponds, mountains, hills and geological features; local traditions; and short biographical sketches of early settlers, etc.   368p.   N. Y. 1849.   974.732   B58

Pelletreau, W: S.   History of Putnam county, N. Y. with biographical sketches of its prominent men.   771p.   Phil. 1886.   974.732   qP36

Southeast

Macoubrey, A. R.   Historical sermon delivered in the South-east center presbyterian church, Aug. 20, 1876.   32p.   N. Y. 1877.   285.1747   So8

Ulster county

For history of the palatines in Ulster county, see Palatines, p. 502.

Concerning Ulster county records.   (*see* Ulster county historical society.   Collections.   1860.   1: 241)   974.734   Ul7

Hasbrouck, A. B.   Address.   (*see* Ulster county historical society. Collections.   1860.   1: 25–39)   974.734   Ul7
History of Ulster county.

Local history
Hurley

Lefevre, Ralph. Huguenots of Ulster county. (*see* Historical society of Newburgh bay and the Highlands. Papers. 1894. p.41–55)

N. Y. state lib.

List of colonial statutes referring to the county of Ulster. (*see* Ulster county historical society. Collections. 1860. 1:100–3)   974.734 Ul7

List of documents relating to Ulster county contained in the Clinton papers in the state library at Albany. (*see* Ulster historical society. Collections. 1860. 1:103–5)   974 734 Ul7

List of patents granted from the 5th Dec. 1666 to the 8th Sep. 1709 to sundry persons in the county of Ulster. (*see* New York genealogical and biographical record, July 1871, 2:143–48)   929.1 N421

Names of the male inhabitants of Ulster county, 1689. (*see* N. Y. (state)–State, Secretary of. Documentary history of the state of New York)   1849–51.   1:279–82.   974.7 N424
                                                1850–51.   1:171–75.   974.7 qN423

Papers relating to Ulster and Dutchess counties. (*see* N. Y. (state)–State, Secretary of. Documentary history of the state of New York)
                                                1849–51.   3:959–96.   974.7 N424
                                                1850–51.   3:580–601.   974.7 qN423

Scott, C. Indian forts of 1663. (*see* Ulster county historical society. Collections. 1860. 1:234–40)   974.734 Ul7

———— Origin and meaning of the word Shawangunk. (*see* Ulster county historical society. Collections. 1860. 1:229–33)   974.734 Ul7

Sylvester, N. B. History of Ulster county, N. Y. with illustrations and biographical sketches of its prominent men and pioneers. 2v. in 1. Phil. 1880.   974.734 qSy5

Ulster county sheriffs. (*see* Ulster county historical society. Collections. 1860. 1:98–100)   974.734 Ul7

Hurley

Hasbrouck, J. W. Hurley. (*see* Ulster county historical society. Collections. 1860. 1:71–72)   974.734 Ul7

Kingston

Brief notice of the Rev. Hermannus Meier. (*see* Magazine of the reformed Dutch church, Jan. 1828, 2:296–303)   205 M27

Pastor of the church at Kingston.

Brodhead, J: R. Notes and documents relating to the early history of Kingston, Hurley and Marbletown. (*see* Ulster county historical society. Collections. 1860. 1 : 49–54) 974.734 Ul7

Forsyth, M.. I. Old Kingston; New York's first capital. (*see* New England magazine, Nov. 1893, new ser. 9 : 345–55) 051 B34 v. 15

Holland society of New York. Celebration in Kingston, N. Y. 1886. (*see* Holland society of New York. Year book. 1886–87. p. 11–108) 974.7 qH71

Contents : Exhibition of relics relating to Kingston and the old Dutch settlers, p. 19–34.

Oration of Gen. G: H. Sharpe on old Kingston, p. 35–52.

Tappan homestead, p. 53.

Old Dutch reformed church, p. 53–58.

"Senate house", p. 58–60.

Dederick house, p. 60–61.

Hasbrouck house, p. 61–62.

The part relating to the old Dutch reformed church is by J: C. F. Hoes and seems to be abridged from his account in Sylvester, History of Ulster county, 1880, p. 220–33.

Kingston church. (*see* Magazine of the reformed Dutch church, Sep. 1826, 1 : 190–91) 205 M27

Kingston, Dutch church. Baptismal and marriage registers of the old Dutch church of Kingston, Ulster co. N. Y. (formerly named Wiltwyck and often familiarly called Esopus or 'Sopus), for 150 years from their commencement in 1660, transcribed and edited by R. R. Hoes. 797p. N. Y. 1891. 929.3 qK61

Names of Dutch settlers in Esopus, compiled from the old court records of Wildwyck (Kingston). (*see* Holland society of New York. Year book. 1897. p. 117–32) 974.7 qH71

Reply to the Brief notice of the Rev. Hermannus Meier. (*see* Magazine of the reformed Dutch church, May 1828, 3 : 55–56) 205 M27

Schoonmaker, Marius. History of Kingston, N. Y. from its early settlement to the year 1820. 558p. N. Y. 1888. 974.734 qK61

Westbrook, F: E: 200th anniversary of the erection of the building occupied as the senate house of the state of New York in 1777 at Esopus, now city of Kingston, together with sketches of old prominent citizens of Kingston, etc. 48p. Kingston 1883.

974.734 K611

Newpaltz

Elting, Irving. Dutch village communities on the Hudson river. 68p. Balt. 1886. (Johns Hopkins university studies in historical and political science. 1886. v.4) 305 J62
Newpaltz used as a typical Dutch community.

Eltinge, Edmund. Account of the settlement of New Paltz by the Huguenots. (*see* Ulster county historical society. Collections. 1860. 1:40-48) . 974.734 Ul7

—— Huguenot refugees of New Paltz. (*see* Magazine of American history, Sep. 1893, 30:142-47) 973 M27

Lefevre, Ralph. Huguenots of Ulster county. (*see* Historical society of Newburgh Bay and the Highlands. Papers. 1894. p. 41-55) N. Y. state lib.
Newpaltz.

New Paltz, Reformed church. Records of the reformed Dutch church of New Paltz, containing an account of the organization of the church, and the register of consistories, members, marriages and baptisms. 269p. N. Y. 1896. (Holland society of New York. Collections. v. 3) 285.7747 N422

Stitt, C. H. History of the Huguenot church and settlement at New Paltz. (*see* Ulster county historical society. Collections. 1860. 1:184-209) 974.734 Ul7

Vennema, Ame. History of the reformed church of New Paltz, Ulster county, N. Y. from 1683 to 1883. 40p. Rondout 1884. 285.7747 N42

Rochester

Agreement relative to the working of a lead mine in Rochester township. (*see* New York genealogical and biographical record, July 1871. 2:148-49) . 929.1 N421

Sullivan county

Quinlan, J. E. History of Sullivan county; embracing an account of its geology, climate, aborigines, early settlement, organization; the formation of its towns, with biographical sketches of prominent residents, etc. 700p. Liberty N. Y. 1873. 974.735 Q4

Greene county

History of Greene county, N. Y. with biographical sketches of its Local hist
prominent men.   462p.   N. Y. 1884.   974.737 qH62 Columbia county

Contents: Athens, W: S. Pelletreau, p. 151-95 including baptismal records
of Zion's lutheran church.

Cairo, H: Whittemore, p. 203-28.
Old Catskill, H: Brace, p. 86-118.
Coxsackie, W: S. Pelletreau, p. 229-55.
Durham, J. G. Borthwick, p. 256-88.
Greenville, H. Bogardus, p. 289-317.
Hunter, E. C. Holton, p. 322-44.
Jewett, G: H. Hastings, p. 345-49.
Lexington, E. C. Holton, p. 350-65.
New Baltimore, H. Bogardus, p. 366-79.
Prattsville, G: H. Hastings, p. 380-92.
Windham, O. B. Hitchcock, p. 392-414.

Genealogies of some of the old Dutch families of Greene county
by Henry Brace, p. 418-45.

Rockwell, Charles.   The Catskill mountains and the region around;
their scenery, legends and history, with sketches in prose and verse
by Cooper, Irving, Bryant, Cole and others. 351p. N. Y. 1867.
                                                917.4738 R59

Colonial period, p. 1-51.

Catskill

Pinckney, J. D. & others.   Reminiscences of Catskill; local sketches
by Pinckney, together with interesting articles by Thurlow
Weed, Edwin Croswell, S. S. Day and Joseph Hallock.   79p.
Catskill 1868.   L. I. hist. soc.

Columbia county

For history of the palatines on the Livingston manor, see Palatines, p. 502.

Clarkson, T: S.   Biographical history of Clermont or Livingston
manor before and during the war for independence.   319p.
Clermont 1869.   929.2 L76

Ellis, Franklin, anon. History of Columbia county, N. Y. with
illustrations and biographical sketches of some of its prominent men
and pioneers. 447p.   Phil. 1878.   974.739 qEl5

Glenn, T: A.   Clermont and the Livingstons. (see his Some colonial
mansions and those who lived in them.   1898.   1:295-331)
                                                929.1 G48

Papers relating to the manor of Livingston, including the first settlement of Schoharie, 1680-1795. (*see* N. Y. (state)—State, Secretary of. Documentary history of the state of New York)

1849-51. 3:609-841. 974.7 N424

1850-51. 3:365-501. 974.7 qN423

Sedgwick, Theodore. Sketch of Robert Livingston, first proprietor of Livingston manor. (*see* Sedgwick, Theodore. Memoir of the life of William Livingston. 1833. p. 17-44)   923.27 L761

Terhune, *Mrs* **M.. V. (Hawes).** Oak Hill, upon the Livingston manor. (*see her* Some colonial homesteads. 1897.   p. 201-38)
973.2 T27

Claverack

Zabriskie, F. N. History of the reformed P. D. church of Claverack; a centennial address. 95p. Hudson 1867.   285.7747 C57
Social and civil history of the town by E. S. Porter, p. 35-56.
Addresses in the grove and church, p. 57-75.

Hillsdale

Collin, J: F. History of Hillsdale, Columbia county, N. Y. a memorabilia of persons and things of interest, passed and passing; ed. by H. S. Johnson. 143+195p.   Philmont N. Y. 1883.
974.739 H59
Biographic sketches of early settlers, apx. p. 1-131.

Rensselaer county

The old Van Rensselaer mansion. (*see* Scribner's monthly, Oct. 1873, 6:651-58)
051 Scr31

Sylvester, N. B. History of Rensselaer county, N. Y. with illustrations and biographical sketches of its prominent men and pioneers. 564p.   Phil. 1880.   974.741 qSy5

Weise, A. J. History of the 17 towns of Rensselaer county, from the colonization of the manor of Rensselaerswyck to the present time. 158p.   Troy 1880.   974.741 W43
Published in Troy daily times.

Lansingburg

Weise, A. J. History of Lansingburgh, N. Y. from the year 1670 to 1877.   44p.   Troy 1877.   974.741 L29

Schaghticoke

Viele, E. L. Knickerbockers of New York 2 centuries ago. (*see* Local hist
Harper's Magazine, Dec. 1876, 54 : 33-43)   051   H23 Rensselaer wyck
Knickerbocker estate at Schaghticoke.

Troy

Lamb, *Mrs* **M. J. R. (Nash).** Beginnings of the city of Troy. (*see*
Magazine of American history, July 1892, 28 : 1-19)   973   M27

Weise, A. J. History of the city of Troy, from the expulsion of the
Mohegan Indians to 1876 ; with maps and statistical tables by
A. G. Bardin.   400p.   Troy 1876.   974.741   T75
Colonial period, p. 1-353.

—— Troy's 100 years, 1789-1889.   453p.   Troy 1891.

                         974.741   qT75
Colonial period, p. 1-18.

Rensselaerswyck

Rensselaerswyck, or the manor of the Van Rensselaers, included parts of
the present Columbia, Rensselaer and Albany counties.
For Van Curler, see Van Twiller, p. 336.

Barnard, D. D. Discourse on the life, services and character of
Stephen Van Rensselaer; delivered before the Albany institute,
Ap. 15, 1839.   144p.   Alb. 1839.   923.27   V35
Stephen Van Rensselaer was born in 1764, but this sketch contains material regarding his ancestors, the patroons.
Includes an account of the manor of Rensselaerswyck.

—— —— (*see* Van Rensselaer, *Mrs* Sarah, *anon.* Ancestral sketches.
1882. p. 281-375)   923.27   qV35

—— An historical sketch of the colony and manor of Rensse-
laerswyck ; read before the Albany institute, Ap. 25, 1839. (*see his*
Discourse on the life, services and character of Stephen Van
Rensselaer. 1839. p. 97-144)   923.27   V35
Noticed in *North American review*, Oct. 1839, 49 : 478-83.

Conditions freely assented to and accepted by Killiaen Van Rensselaer in his quality as patroon of his colonie named Rensselaerswyck,
and by Dr Johannes Megapolensis as preacher to administer and
promote divine service in the aforesaid colonie for the term of six
successive years.   (*see* O'Callaghan, E. B. History of New
Netherland. 1846-48. 1 : 448-50)   974.7   Oc11

Curler, Arent van. Letter to the patroon, dated at the Manhattans, 16 June 1643. (*see* O'Callaghan, E. B.   History of New Netherland.   1846–48.   1 : 456–65)   974.7   Oc11

Glenn, T : A. Patroonship of the Van Rensselaers. (*see his* Some colonial mansions and those who lived in them.   1898.   1 : 139–68)   929.1   G48

Insinuation, protest and presentment on behalf of the patroon of the colonie of Rensselaerswyck 1643. (*see* O'Callaghan, E. B.   History of New Netherland.   1846–48.   1 : 466–68)   974.7   Oc11

Lamb, *Mrs* **M. J. R. (Nash).** Van Rensselaer manor. (*see* Magazine of American history, Jan. 1884, 11 : 1–32)   973   M27

Legal custom against the abuse of outstanding accounts in the colonie of Rensselaerswyck. (*see* O'Callaghan, E. B.   History of New Netherland.   1846–48.   1 : 442–47)   974.7   Oc11

List of freeholders in the city of Albany and manor of Rensselaerswyck.   1742. (*see* Munsell, Joel.   Annals of Albany)

1850–59.   2 : 186–90.   974.743   M92
Ed. 2.   1869–71.   2 : 282–83.   974.743   M921

Memorandum for Dominie Johannes Megapolensis, this 3d June, 1642, proceeding to the colonie by the ship De Houttuyn. (*see* O'Callaghan, E. B.   History of New Netherland.   1846–48.   1 : 451–54)   974.7   Oc11

Names of settlers in Rensselaerswyck, 1630 to 1646. (*see* Munsell, Joel.   Annals of Albany)   1850–59.   1 : 15–23.   974.743   M92

Ed. 2.   1869–71.   1 : 64–76.   974.743   M921

——— (*see* O'Callaghan, E. B.   History of New Netherland.   1846–48. 1 : 433–41)   974.7   Oc11

O'Callaghan, E. B. Colony of Rensselaerswyck, 1614 to 1646. (*see* Munsell, Joel.   Annals of Albany)

1850–59.   1 : 183–206.   974.743   M92
Ed. 2.   1869–71.   1 : 9–43.   974.743   M921
From O'Callaghan.   History of New Netherland.

——— Colony of Rensselaerswyck 1646 to 1664. (*see* Munsell, Joel. Annals of Albany)   1850–59.   2 : 13–52.   974.743   M92

Ed. 2.   1869–71.   2 : 9–47.   974.743   M921
From O'Callaghan.   History of New Netherland.

Papers relating to the colonie of Rensselaerswyck. (*see* O' Callaghan
E. B. History of New Netherland. 1846–48. 1 : 466–78)

974.7 Oc11

Payment and expenditure which Kiliaen van Rensselaer has advanced
and paid in his life-time as patroon of the colonie called Rensselaerswyck for the support of said colonie together with what has been
expended and paid after his decease in behalf of said colonie. (*see*
O'Callaghan, E. C. History of New Netherland. 1846–48.
1 : 429–32) . 974.7 Oc11

Pepper, Calvin. Manor of Rensselaerswyck. 34p. Alb. 1846.

974.743 P39

Reynolds, Cuyler. Relics of Rensselaerswyck. (*see* Cosmopolitan,
Dec. 1897, 24 : 136–41) 051 qC82

Roever, N. de. Kiliaen Van Rensselaer en zijne kolonie Rensselaers-
wijck. (*see* Oud–Holland, 1890, 8 : 29–54, 241–59) 059 qOu2

Tenney, Jonathan. The manor and the Van Rensselaers. (*see*
Howell, G: R. & Tenney, Jonathan. Bicentennial history of
Albany. 1886. p. 286–92) 974.742 qH83

Van Rensselaer, Johan. Commission of Gerrit Swart, schout of
Rensselaerswyck; and, Instructions drawn up for Gerrit Swart as
officer of the colonie. (*see* O'Callaghan, E. B. History of New
Netherland. 1846–48. 2 : 564–66) 974.7 Oc11

Van Rensselaer, *Mrs* **M. D. (King).** The Van Rensselaers of the
manor of Rensselaerswyck. 21p. n.p. °1888. 929.2 qV35
Composed largely of portraits.

Albany county

Albany county. Early records of the city and county of Albany and
colony of Rensselaerswyck, 1656–75; tr. from the original Dutch
with notes by Jonathan Pearson. 528p. Alb. 1869.

974 742 qAl1
Translation of two manuscript volumes labelled Deeds, A & B, in county
clerk's office. Reprinted in Munsell. *Collections.*

——— Records, 1654–78. (*see* Munsell, Joel. Collections on the
history of Albany. 1865–71. 3 : 1–224; 4 : 225–510)

974.743 qM92

Translated by Jonathan Pearson.
Body of the text reprinted from Albany county. *Early records.* p. 1–510.

The beaver and the fur trade. (*see* Holland, G: R. & Tenney, Jonathan. Bicentennial history of Albany. 1886. p.296-300)

$\qquad\qquad\qquad\qquad\qquad\qquad\qquad\qquad\qquad$ 974.742 qH83

Colonial military affairs and wars in Albany county. (*see* Howell,
G: R. & Tenney, Jonathan. Bicentennial history of Albany.
1886. p. 382-90)   974.742 qH83

County of Albany. (*see* Munsell, Joel. Annals of Albany)

$\qquad\qquad\qquad\qquad$ 1850-59.   1:142-48.   974.743   M92
$\qquad\qquad\qquad$ Ed. 2. 1869-71.   1:191-95.   974.743   M921

Doig, Robert. History of the township of Berne. (*see* Howell, G: R.
& Tenney, Jonathan. Bicentennial history of Albany. 1886.
p. 800-23)   974.742 qH83

Dutch and Indian names for Albany and vicinity. (*see* Munsell, Joel.
Annals of Albany)   1850-59.   2:226-33.   974.743   M92
$\qquad\qquad\qquad$ Ed. 2.   1869-71.   2:311-19.   974.743   M921

Fernow, Berthold. Genealogical data gathered from Albany county
and New York city records. (*see* New York genealogical and
biographical record, Oct. 1890, 21:170-72)   929.1 qN421

Hall & Patterson, *advertising agents.* History of Albany county,
1683-1867.   50p.   Syracuse 1867.   040 P   v. 2119

Howell, G: R. & Tenney, Jonathan. Bicentennial history of
Albany; history of the county of Albany, N. Y. from 1609 to
1886.   997p.   N. Y. 1886,   974.742 qH83
Includes also their *History of the county of Schenectady, N. Y. from 1662 to
1886.*

Land patents, settlements, leases, titles and boundaries. (*see* Howell,
G. R. & Tenney, Jonathan. Bicentennial history of Albany. 1886.
p. 292-95)   974.742 qH83

List of the freeholders of the city and county of Albany, 1720. (*see*
Munsell, Joel. Annals of Albany)

$\qquad\qquad\qquad$ 1850-59.   1:231-34.   974.743   M92
$\qquad\qquad\qquad$ Ed. 2., 1869-71.   1:263-68.   974.744   M921

——— (*see* N. Y. (state)—State, Secretary of. Documentary history
of the state of New York)

$\qquad\qquad\qquad$ 1849-51.   1:370-73.   974.7   N424
$\qquad\qquad\qquad$ 1850-51.   1:241-46.   974.7   qN423

List of the heads of families and the number of men, women and ~~Local histos~~
~~Albany coun~~
children in each household in the city and county of Albany, 1697.
(*see* Munsell, Joel. Annals of Albany. 1850–59. 9:81–89)

974.743 M92

List of the inhabitants and slaves in the city and county of Albany,
1714. (*see* Munsell, Joel. Annals of Albany)

1850–59.	3:243.	974.743	M92
Ed. 2. 1869–71.	3:334.	974.743	M921

MacMurray, J. W. Houses in ancient Albany county. (*see* Pearson,
Jonathan. History of the Schenectady patent. 1883. p. 441–50)

974.744 qSch2

Markle, J. S. History of Coeyman's township. (*see* Howell, G: R.
& Tenney, Jonathan. Bicentennial history of Albany. 1886.
p. 824–40) 974 742 qH83

—— History of the township of Bethlehem. (*see* Howell, G: R. &
Tenney, Jonathan. Bicentennial history of Albany. 1886.
p. 775–800) 974.742 qH83

Masten, A. H. *anon*. History of Cohoes, N. Y. from its earliest
settlement to the present time. 327p. Alb. 1877.

974.742 C66

Munsell, Frank. Bibliography of Albany; being a catalogue of
books and other publications relating to the city and county of
Albany in the state of New York. 72p. Alb. 1883.

016.974742 M92

Includes also many books published in Albany but not relating to Albany
affairs.

New York colonial manuscripts relating to Albany and vicinity. (*see*
Munsell, Joel. Annals of Albany. 1850–59. 7:257–302; 8:37–74)

974.743 M92

Parker, A. J. *comp*. Landmarks of Albany county, N. Y. 3v.in 1.
Syracuse 1894. 917.4742 P22

Pearson, Jonathan, *comp*. Contributions for the genealogies of the
first settlers of Albany. (*see* Munsell, Joel. Collections on the
history of Albany. 1865–71. 4:92–184) 974.743 qM92

—— Contributions for the genealogies of the first settlers of the ancient
county of Albany from 1630 to 1800. 182p. Alb. 1872.

929.1 P31

Local history
Albany

Pearson, Jonathan. Contributions to the history of the ancient Dutch families of Albany. (*see* New York genealogical and biographical record, Oct. 1871. 2:190-92; Ap. 1872, 3:81-83) 929.1 N421

—————— Introduction to Albany county records. (*see* Munsell, Joel. Collections on the history of Albany. 1865-71. 3: pref. p. 7-8) 974.743 qM92

Proctor, L. B. Bench and bar; or, Legal history of Albany county, (*see* Howell, G: R. & Tenney, Jonathan. Bicentennial history of Albany. 1886. p. 123-203) 974.742 qH83

Tenney, Jonathan. History of population in Albany county. (*see* Howell, G: R. & Tenney, Jonathan. Bicentennial history of Albany. 1886. p.271-76) 974.742 qH83

—————— History of the county of Albany. (*see* Howell, G: R. & Tenney. Jonathan. Bicentennial history of Albany. 1886. p. 12-80) 974.742 qH83

Albany

Albany institute. Proposed erection of local historical monuments; report of special committee an archaeology. p.137-44. Alb. 1881. 974.743 Al1

Extracts from *Transactions of Albany institute*, 1883, 10: 137-44.

—————— —————— (*see* Albany institute. Transactions. 1883. 10:137-44) N. Y. state lib.

Banks, A. B. Albany bicentennial; historical memoirs, 1686-1886. 461p. Alb. 1888. 974.743 B22

Barnes, T. W. *ed.* Souvenir of the Albany bicentennial celebration, July 1886; containing the official programme with the only authorized descriptive and illuminated lithographs of the great historical pageant. 63p. Alb. 1886. 974.743 qAl 11

Colonial history, p. 5-10: chronological record, 1540-1776 p. 10-17.

—————— Settlement and early history of Albany. 25p. Alb. 1851. 974.743 B261

A prize essay delivered before the Albany young men's association, Dec. 26, 1850; covers period 1609-86.

—————— —————— Ed. 2. 100p. Alb. 1864. 974.743 B29

Edition of 300 copies.

Battershall, W. W. Albany. (*see* Powell, L. P. *ed.* Historic towns of the middle states. 1899. p. 1-37) 974.7 P87

Child, E. B. & Schiffer, W. H. Brief history of the city of Albany. Local hist Albany (*see* Albany directory for 1831–32. 1831. pref. p. 29–35)

917.4743 Al1

Gives list of mayors and recorders from 1686–1831.

City of Albany. (*see* Munsell, Joel. Annals of Albany)

1850–59. 1:138–41 974.743 M92
Ed. 2. 1869–71. 1:185–90 974.743 M921

Curtis, F: C. Glimpses of early medicine in Albany. (*see* Albany medical annals, Oct. 1886, 7:289–300) 610.5 Oo

Fernow, Berthold. Albany and its place in the history of the United States, a memorial sketch written for the 200th anniversary of its birthday as a city. 98p. Alb. 1886. 974.743 F39
Chiefly colonial period.
Author was selected as historian by Albany bicentennial committee.

Geschichte der Deutschen in Albany und Troy nebst kurzen biographien von beamten und hervorragenden buergen. 274p. Alb. 1897.

917.4743 G33

A glimpse of an old Dutch town. (*see* Harper's magazine, Mar. 1881, 62:524–39) 051 H23

Hill, D: B. 1686–1886; oration delivered at the bicentennial celebration at Albany, July 22, 1886. 46p. n.p.n.d.

974.743 H55

Colonial period, first 15 pages.
Gov. Hill was selected as orator by the bicentennial committee.

Macauley's account of Albany. (*see* Munsell, Joel. Annals of Albany. 1850–59. 10:172–88) 974.743 M92

Mather, F: G. City of Albany; 200 years of progress. (*see* Magazine of American history, Feb. 1886, 15:105–26) 973 M27

Mayors of Albany. (*see* Howell, G: R. & Tenney, Jonathan. Bicennial history of Albany. 1886. p. 657–66) 974.742 qH83

Mayors of the city of Albany. (*see* Munsell, Joel. Collections on the history of Albany. 1865–71. 4:1842) 974.743 qM92

Municipal history of the city of Albany. (*see* Howell, G: R. & Tenney, Jonathan. Bicentennial history of Albany. 1886. p. 461–85) 974.742 qH83

Murray, David. Industrial and material progress illustrated in the history of Albany. (*see* Albany institute. Transactions. 1883. 10:85–104) N. Y. state lib.

Proctor, L. B. Albany as a historical city. 15p. n. p. 1893.
Read before the Albany institute, Feb. 7, 1893.

Springer, A. O. *comp.* Albany's bicentennial; a chronicle of local events, 1686–1886. 48p. Alb. 1886.   974.743 qAl11
Advertising pamphlet containing many items of interest connected with early history.

Rosendale, S. W. An early ownership of real estate in Albany, N. Y. by a Jewish trader. (*see* American Jewish historical society. Publications. 1894. 3:61–71)   296 Am3

Street, A. B. Glimpses of the early history of Albany. (*see* Fort Orange monthly, May 1886, 1:186–204)   051 F771
17th century.

Watson, J: F. First settlement of Albany. (*see his* Annals and occurrences of New York city and state. 1846. p. 14–35)
974.7 W331

Weise, A. J. History of the city of Albany, New York, from the discovery of the great river in 1524, by Verrazzano, to the present time. 520p. Alb. 1884.   974.743 W43
Colonial period, p. 1–353.

Dutch period

Albany was called Beverwyck till 1623, Fort Orange till 1647, and Williamstadt till 1664.

See also Albany county and Rensselaerswyck.

For Anneke Jans, see New York city, Dutch period, p. 412; and New York city, Religious history, p. 433.

Albany. Albany records, 1639–59. (*see* Munsell, Joel. Annals of Albany)   1850–59.   4:40–97.   974.743 M92
Ed. 2.   1869–71.   4:33–87.   974.743 M921
Selections from records kept at New York by the secretary of the Dutch West India company.

Albany; historical reminiscences. (*see* historical magazine, 1837. 4:83–86)   N. Y. state lib.

English period

Albany. By-laws of the city of Albany, 1686. (*see* Munsell, Joel. Annals of Albany, 1850–59. 7:170–77)   974.743 M92

———— City records. (*see* Munsell, Joel. Annals of Albany. 1850–59)
974.743 M92

Contents: 1686–95, 2:88–145   1713–18, 7:9–85
1695–1700, 3:7–56   1718–26, 8:229–312
1699–1705, 4:98–199   1726–31, 9:9–80
1705–10, 5:114–206   1731–43, 10:9–152
1710–13, 6:242–91

Albany. City records. (*see* Munsell, Joel. Annals of Albany. Ed. 2. Local histor Albany
1869–71)   974.743 M921
Contents: 1688–95, 2 : 82–269
1695–1700, 3 : 1–51
1699–1705, 4 : 88–187

————— City records, 1753–83. (*see* Munsell, Joel. Collections on the
history of Albany.   1865–71.   1 : 81–354)   974.743 qM92

————— Orders regulating the Indian trade, 1686. (*see* Munsell, Joel.
Annals of Albany.   1850–59.   8 : 205–14)   974.743 M92

Capitulation of thé Dutch to the English, 1664. (*see* Munsell, Joel.
Annals of Albany)   1850–59.   4 : 28–31.   974.743   M92
            Ed. 2.   1869–71.   4 : 21–24.   974.743 M921

Dongan, *Gov.* **Thomas.**   Charter of the city of Albany, 1686. (*see*
Munsell, Joel. Annals of Albany)
                1850–59.   2 : 61–87.   974.743   M92
            Ed. 2.   1869–71.   2 : 56–81.   974.743   M921

Hoffman, L. G.   Albany 159 years ago. 23p. (*see* Albany directory
for 1845–6.   1845.   p. 59–91)   917.4743   Al1

Miller, G: W.   A retrospect of two centuries ; a bicentennial discourse,
Albany, N. Y. July 18, 1886. 16p. Alb. 1886.   974.743 V35

Munsell, Joel.   Men and things in Albany two centuries ago. 32p.
Alb. 1876.   040P v. 2119
Also in *Transactions of Albany institute.* 1879. 9 : 28–56.

N. Y. (province) – General assembly.   Synopsis of the principal
acts relating to Albany, passed from 1691 to 1713. (*see* Munsell,
Joel. Annals of Albany) 1850–59. 4 : 203–18. 974.743 M92
            Ed. 2. 1869–71. 4 : 191–205. 974.743 M921

Papers relating to Albany and adjacent places. (*see* N. Y. (state)—
State, Secretary of. Documentary history of the state of New
York)   1849–51. 3 : 869–917 974.7 N424
                          1850–51. 3 : 523–53. 974.7 qN423

Papers relating to the Sons of liberty of Albany ; including constitution,
list of members and correspondence, 1765–66. (*see* American historian and quarterly genealogical record, Ap. 1876, 1 : 145–53)
                                                   973 Am31
Published in Schenectady.

Records of the court of assize relating to Albany and its inhabitants,
1666–72. (*see* Munsell, Joel. Annals of Albany)
                1850–59. 4 : 7–27. 974.743   M92
            Ed. 2.   1869–71. 4 : 1–20. 974.745 M921

Localities, buildings, etc.

Local history Albany **Mather, F: G.** Schuyler house at Albany. (*see* Magazine of American history, July 1884. 12: 1–16)   973 M27

O'Callaghan, E. B. First stone house in Albany. (*see* New York genealogical and biographical record, Jan. 1873, 4: 21–23)
        929.1 N421
Built 1658 as a residence for the vice director, with accommodations for the court of justice.

Proctor, L. B. Historic memories of the old Schuyler mansion; thrilling events within its walls. 7p. n. p. n. d.   974.743 qP94
Written for the Albany historical society.

Terhune, *Mrs* **M. V. (Hawes).** Two Schuyler homesteads, Albany N. Y. (*see her* More colonial homesteads. 1899. p. 187–223)
        973.2 T271

Van Rensselaer, Maunsell. Our ancient landmarks, sermon delivered in St. Paul's church, Albany, on the bicentennial commemoration of the city's charter. 32p. Alb. 1886.   974.743 V35

Lists of residents, church records, etc.

Albany, Reformed Protestant Dutch church. Baptisms, 1683–93. (*see* Munsell, Joel. Annals of Albany. 1850–59. 2: 146–74)
        974.743 M92

———— Baptisms from 1693 to 1707. (*see* Munsell, Joel. Annals of Albany)   1850–59. 3: 61–113. 974.743 M92
        Ed. 2. 1869–71. 3: 284–333. 974.743 M921

Curtis, F: C. Medicine in Albany county. (*see* Howell, G: R. & Tenney, Jonathan. Bicentennial history of Albany. 1886. p. 203–47)   974.742 qH93

Dutch church burials, 1722–57. (*see* Munsell, Joel. Annals of Albany)
        1850–59. 1: 235–49. 974.743 M92
        Ed. 2. 1869–71. 1: 131–47. 974.743 M921

Halenbeek burial ground. (*see* Munsell, Joel. Collections on the history of Albany. 1865–71. 2: 410–16)   974.743 qM92

Pearson, Jonathan. Diagrams of the home lots of the village of Beverwyck. (*see* Munsell, Joel. Collections on the history of Albany. 1865–71. 4: 184–224)   974.743 qM92

Pearson, Jonathan. Key to the names of persons occurring in the early Dutch records of Albany and vicinity. (*see* Munsell, Joel. Collections on the history of Albany. 1865-71. 4:84-91)   974.743   qM92

Tenney, Jonathan. New England in Albany. 126p. Bost. 1883.
L. I. hist. sor
Colonial period, p. 2-12.

Description

Albany 50 years ago. (*see* Munsell, Joel. Collections on the history of Albany. 1865-71. 2:1-31)   974.743   qM92

Chandler, Samuel. Diary, 1755. (*see* Munsell, Joel. Collections on the history of Albany. 1865-71. 2:373-75)   974.743   qM92
Reprint of part relating to Albany.

Dankers, Jasper & Sluyter, Peter. Journal, 1680. (*see* Munsell, Joel. Collections on the history of Albany. 1865-71. 2:358-73)
974.743   qM92
Reprint of part relating to Albany and Schenectady.

Grant, *Mrs* **Anne (Macvicar).** Description of Albany and manners of the inhabitants, 1764. (*see* Munsell, Joel. Annals of Albany)
1850-59.   2:53-60.   974.743   M92
Ed. 2.   1869-71.   2:48-54.   974.743   M921
From her *Memoirs of an American lady.*

Jogues, Isaac. Father Jogues's account of Rensselaerswyck (*see* Munsell, Joel.   Annals of Albany.   1850-59.   9:130-31)
974.743   M92

Kalm, Peter. Visit to Albany, 1749. (*see* Munsell, Joel. Annals of Albany)   1850-59.   1:262-75.   974.743   M92
Ed. 2.   1869-71.   1:43-63.   974.743   M921

Miller, John. Ancient Albany, 1695 with a plan of the city. (*see* Munsell, Joel.   Annals of Albany.   1850-59.   1:136-37)
974.743   M92

Vries, D. P. de. De Vries in Albany. (*see* Munsell, Joel. Annals of Albany.   1850-59.   9:124-29)   974.743   M92

Wadsworth, Benjamin. Journal. (*see* Massachusetts historical society. Collections. 1852. ser. 4, 1:102-10) 974.4 M38 v. 31
Kept while in Albany, Aug. 1694, as a commissioner from Massachusetts to treat with the five nations.

Religious history

Albany, First Lutheran church. Manual, 128p. Alb. 1871.
284.1747 Al1

Albany, Reformed protestant Dutch church. Deacon's account
book, 1665–1715; and, Seatings of the Dutch reformed church,
1730–1770. (*see* Munsell, Joel. Collections on the history of
Albany. 1865–71. 1 : 2–80)   974.743 qM92

Blayney, J. M. History of the First presbyterian church of Albany,
N. Y. list of its officers and a complete catalogue of its members
from its organization. 124p. Alb. 1877. 285.1747 Al11
Organized in 1762 or 1763.

De Lancey, E: F. Memoir of the Rev. Harry Munro, the last rector
of St Peter's church, Albany, under the English crown. (*see* New
York genealogical and biographical record, July 1873, 4 : 113–24)
929.1 N421

Dutch church papers. (*see* Munsell, Joel. Annals of Albany. 1850–
59. 7 : 232–39)   974.743 M92

Dutch reformed church in Albany. (*see* Munsell, Joel. Annals of
Albany. 1850–59. 6 : 67–96)   974.743 M92

Episcopal church in Albany. (*see* Munsell, Joel. Annals of Albany.
1850–59. 6 : 50–66)   974.743 M92

Evangelical Lutheran Ebenezer church, Albany. (*see* Munsell, Joel.
Annals of Albany) 1850–59. 1 : 122–29. 974.743 M92
          Ed. 2. 1869–71. 1 : 148–65. 974.743 M921

First presbyterian church, Albany. (*see* Munsell, Joel. Annals of
Albany) 1850–59. 1 : 130–32. 974.743 M92
          Ed. 2. 1869–71. 1 : 170–76. 974.743 M921

Hooper, *Rev.* **Joseph.** History of Saint Peter's church in the city of
Albany with an introduction and description of the present edifice
and its memorials by the Rev. Walton W. Battershall. 556p.
Alb. 1900.   283.747 Al17

Rectors of St Peter's church, Albany. (*see* N. Y. (state)—State,
Secretary of. Documentary history of the state of New York)
          1849–51. 3 : 1151–55. 974.7 N424
          1850–51. 3 : 697–99. 974.7 qN423

Reformed protestant Dutch church in Albany. (*see* Munsell, Joel.
Annals of Albany) 1850–59. 1 : 86–121. 974.743 M92
          Ed. 2. 1869–71. 1 : 78–147. 974.743 M921
Including list of members, 1683.

Religious institutions. (*see* Howell, G: R. & Tenney, Jonathan.
Bicentennial history of Albany. 1886. p.749–74)   974.742 qH83

Rev. Gideon Schaets. (*see* O'Callaghan, E. B. History of New Netherland. 1846–48. 2: 567–68)   974.7 Oc11
Second pastor of the Dutch church in Albany, 1657–83.

Rogers, E. P. Historical discourse on the reformed protestant Dutch
church of Albany, delivered on Nov. 26, 1857, in the North
Dutch church. 120p. N. Y. 1858.   285.7747 Al11

St Peter's church and other matters. (*see* Munsell, Joel. Collections
on the history of Albany. 1865–71. 1 : 388–91)   974.743 qM92

Stanton, *Rev.* H. C. Origin and growth of presbyterianism in Albany,
historical discourse delivered in the State street presbyterian church,
Albany, July 18, 1886. 27p. Alb. 1886.   974.743 V35
The first presbyterians came to Albany about 1760 and the first church
was built in 1776.

Saratoga county

Bond, L. A. Old and new Saratoga. (*see* National magazine, July
1892, 16:313–36)   973 M271

Bullard, E: F. History of Saratoga; an address delivered at Schuylerville, N.Y. July 4, 1876. 22p. Ballston Spa 1876. 974.748 Sa71
Includes also *Saratoga county* by G: G. Scott, and *Saratoga and Kay-ad-
ros-se-ra* by N. B. Sylvester.

Scott, G: G. Saratoga county; an historical address and a centennial
address by J. S. L'Amoreaux delivered at Ballston Spa, N. Y.
July 4, 1876. 47p. Ballston Spa 1876.   974.748 Sa71

Stone, W: L. Reminiscences of Saratoga and Ballston.   451p.
N. Y. 1875.   974.748 Sa7
Bibliography, p. 441–48.

Sylvester, N. B. History of Saratoga county, N. Y. with illustrations
and biographical sketches of some of its prominent men and pioneers.
514p.   Phil. 1878.   974.748 qSy5

——— Saratoga and Kay-ad-ros-se-ra; an historical address delivered
at Saratoga Springs, N. Y. July 4, 1876.   52p.   Troy 1876.
                                           974.748 Sa71

Walworth, E. H. Saratoga; the struggle for the great waterways.
(*see* Powell, L. P. *ed.* Historic towns of the middle states. 1899.
p.39–70)   974.7 P87

Washington county

Corey, Allen. Gazetteer of the county of Washington, N. Y. comprising a correct statistical and miscellaneous history of the county and several towns from their organization to the present time. 264p. Schuylerville 1849.   917.4749 C81

Fitch, Asa. A historical, topographical and agricultural survey of the county of Washington. (*see* New York state agricultural society. Transactions. 1848. 8:877–975)   630.6 K2
History of the county down to the revolution.

Hall, Hiland. New York Dellius patent. (*see* Historical magazine, Feb. 1868, ser. 2, 3 : 74–76)   973 H62 v. 13

Jermain, G: W. Historical address. (*see* Smart, J. S. & Noble, Henry, *comp.* Proceedings of the centennial anniversary of the old town of Cambridge. 1874. p. 16–42)   974.749 C14

Johnson, Crisfield, *anon.* History of Washington county, N. Y. with illustrations and biographical sketches of some of its prominent men and pioneers. 504p. Phil. 1878.   974.749 qJ62

Kellogg, Lewis. Sketch of the history of Whitehall, civil and religious; a discourse delivered on the 27th of June 1847 by Kellogg, being the 10th anniversary of his ministry in the place. 16p. Whitehall 1847.   974.749 W58

Mackenzie, W. A. Union presbyterian church of Salem, N. Y. historical sermon delivered Oct. 29, 1876. 45p.   Salem 1876.   285.1747 Sa3

Salem, (N. Y.) historical committee. Salem book, records of the past and glimpses of the present. 250p.   Salem 1896.   974.749 Sa3
Genealogy and biography, p. 28–79.

Smart, J. S. & Noble, Henry, *comp.* Proceedings of the centennial anniversary of the old town of Cambridge. 111p.   Camb. 1874.   974.749 C14
Historical address by Hon. G. W: Jermain and other speeches.

Sprague, E: P. Historical sketch of the presbyterian church in Salem, Washington county, N. Y. delivered June 4, 1876. 49p. Salem 1876.   285.1747 Sa3

Thurston, E. P. History of the town of Greenwich, from the earliest settlement to the centennial, also an oration delivered by D. A. Boies, at Greenwich, N. Y. July 4th, 1876. 78p.   Salem 1876.   974.749 G83

Mohawk valley

Earl, Robert. Mohawk river in history; a paper read before the Local histo Schenectady county Herkimer county historical society, Sep. 8, 1896.　4p.　n. p. n. d.

974.761　qEa7

Also in Herkimer county historical society. *Papers.* 1896. p. 62–68, 974.761 H42, and in *American historical register,* Oct.-Nov. 1896, 4 : 571–82, 973 qAm31.

—— Mohawk valley and the palatines.　6p.　n. p. 1898.

974.74　Ea7

Also in Herkimer county historical society. *Papers.* 1898. p. 57–62, 974.761 H42

—— Reminiscences concerning several persons connected with important historical events.　8p.　n. p. 1896.　N.Y. state lib.

Also in Herkimer county historical society. *Papers.* 1896. p. 83–90, 974.761 H42

Kapp, Friedrich. Die Deutschen am Mohawk. (*see his* Geschichte der Deutschen im staate New York. 1869. p. 146–70)

325.243　K14

Mohawk country. (*see* Historical record, Schenectady) 974.7　qH62 Jan.-Ap. 1872, 1 : 20–21, 32–34, 49–51, 65–68

Papers relating to the Oneida country and Mohawk valley 1756–57. (*see* N. Y. (state)—State, Secretary of. Documentary history of the state of New York)　1849–51. 1 : 507–34. 974.7　N424

1850–51. 1 : 327–43.　974.7　qN423

Smith, G : W. The royal grant. (*see* Herkimer county historical society. Papers. 1897. p. 7–24)　974.761　H42

Warren, *Mrs* **M. S.** The first settlers of the Mohawk valley. (*see* Herkimer county historical society. Papers. 1896. p. 36–43)

974.761　H42

Schenectady county

For Van Curler and his journal, see Van Twiller, p. 336.

Backus, J. T. Discourse containing the history of the presbyterian church, Schenectady, during its first century and of a pastorate through a third of a century.　32p. Alb. 1869.　285.1747 Sch2

Brief chronicle of the reformed Dutch church at Schenectady. (*see* Magazine of the reformed Dutch church, Feb. 1828, 2 : 328–30)

205　M27

Burning of Schenectady, 1690. (*see* Munsell, Joel.   Annals of Albany)
      1850–59. 4 : 240–74. 974 743 M92
    Ed. 2. 1869–71. 4 : 226–59. 974.743 M921

Carpenter, G : W. Account of the burning of Schenectady in 1690
 drawn up from manuscript records. (*see* Albany institute. Transactions. 1833–52. 2 : 263–74)   N. Y. state lib.

Darling, T. G. Historical sketch of the 1st presbyterian church. (*see*
 Pearson, Jonathan. History of the Schenectady patent. 1883.
 p.399–408)   974.744 qSch2

The destruction of Schenectady. (*see* New York historical society.
 Collections. Publication fund ser. 1870. 2:165–76) 974.7 N42

Ecclesiastical societies of Schenectady. (*see* Howell, G : R. &
 Tenney, Jonathan. History of the county of Schenectady, N. Y.
 1886. p. 86–113)   974.742 qH83
 Contents : Reformed nether Dutch church.
    St. George's church (episcopal).
    First Presbyterian.

Glenville. (*see* Historical record. Schenectady, Feb. 1872, 1 : 43–48,
 62–64)   974.7 qH62

Griffis, W : E. Historical discourse. (*see* Schenectady, N. Y.
 First reformed church. 200th anniversary. 1880. p.31–53)
    285.7747 Sch2

Holland society of New York. Bicentennial of the burning and
 massacre of Schenectady. (*see their* Year book. 1890–91.
 p. 112–37)   974.7 qH71
 Including lists of persons killed and taken prisoners.

Howell, G : R. & Tenney, Jonathan. History of the county of
 Schenectady, N. Y. from 1662 to 1886. 218p. N. Y. 1886.
 (*in their* Bicentennial history of Albany. 1886) 974.742 qH83 ·

Landon, J. S. Schenectady, the provincial outpost of liberty. (*see*
 Powell, L. P. *ed.* Historic towns of the middle states. 1899. p. 71–
 106)   974.7 P87

MacMurray, J. W. St George's church, episcopal. (*see* Pearson,
 Jonathan. History of the Schenectady patent. 1883. p. 389–98)
    974.744 qSch2

———— Schenectady. (*see* Pearson, Jonathan. History of Schenectady
 patent. 1883. p. 436–40)   974.744 qSch2
 Various forms of the name.

Munsell, J. History of the county of Schenectady, 1662–1885. (*see* Howell, G: R. & Tenney, Jonathan. History of the county of Schenectady, N. Y. p. 1–66) 974.742 qH83

The noche triste. (*see* American historian and quarterly genealogical record, Oct. 1875, 1 : 41–46) 973 Am31

Burning of Schenectady, 1690.

Papers relating to the invasion of New York and burning of Schenectady by the French, 1690. (*see* N. Y. (state)—State, Secretary of. Documentary history of the state of New York)

1849–51. 1:283–312. 974.7 N424
1850–51. 1:177–95. 974.7 qN423

Contents: Receipt of news of burning of Schenectady in Albany.
List of people killed and taken prisoners.

Pearson, Jonathan. Adult freeholders, who settled in Schenectady before 1700, together with a description of their house lots and other possessions. (*see* Pearson, Jonathan. History of the Schenectady patent. 1883. p. 82–230) 974.744 qSch2

———— Borough and city charter 1765 and 1798. (*see his* History of the Schenectady patent. 1883. p. 426–32) 974.744 qSch2

———— Burning of Schenectady. (*see his* History of the Schenectady patent. 1883. p. 244–70) 974.744 qSch2

———— Contributions for the genealogies of the descendants of the first settlers of the patent and city of Schenectady from 1662 to 1800. 324p. Alb. 1873. 929.1 P311

———— Division of lands ; how the lands purchased by Van Curler from the Mohawks in 1661 were divided among the first proprietors. (*see his* History of the Schenectady patent. 1883. p. 58–81) 974.744 qSch2

———— Extract from the doop-boek or baptismal register of the reformed protestant Dutch church of Schenectady, N. Y. (*see* New England historical and genealogical register) 929.1 N422

Ap.—Oct. 1864, 18 : 148–50, 231–37, 357–61
Jan. 1865, 19 : 69–73 July 1866, 20 : 217–20
Oct. 1865, 19 : 315–17 Ap. 1867, 21:128–31

———— History of the church ; some facts for the history of the Reformed protestant Dutch church of Schenectady. (*see* Schenectady (N. Y.) Reformed church. 200th anniversary. 1880. p. 54–264) 285.7747 Sch2

Local history
Schenectady
county
Pearson, Jonathan. Introduction; historical sketch. (*see his* History of the Schenectady patent. 1883. p. 1-57)   974.744 qSch2

—— Notices of the ministers of the reformed protestant Dutch church of Schenectady, N. Y. (*see* New England historical and genealogical record, July 1865, 19:204-6)   929.1 N422

—— Old French war, 1744-48. (*see his* History of the Schenectady patent. 1883. p. 290-97)   974.744 qSch2

—— & MacMurray, J. W. Fortifications and garrisons. (*see* Pearson, Jonathan. History of the Schenectady patent. 1883. p. 304-33)   974.744 qSch2

—— Indian trade. (*see* Pearson, Jonathan. History of the Schenectady patent. 1883. p. 409-25)   974.744 qSch2

—— Reformed nether Dutch church. (*see* Pearson, Jonathan. History of the Schenectady patent. 1883. p. 334-88)   974.744 qSch2

Pearson, Jonathan *& others.* History of the Schenectady patent in the Dutch and English times; being contributions toward a history of the lower Mohawk valley; ed. by J. W. MacMurray. 466p. Alb. 1883.   974.744 qSch2

Political history of Schenectady county. (*see* Historical record Schenectady, Mar.-Ap. 1872, 1:58-59, 68-69)   974.7 qH62

Sanders, John. Centennial address relating to the early history of Schenectady and its first settlers; delivered at Schenectady, July 4, 1876. 346p. Alb. 1879.   974.744 Sa5
Early settlers, p. 21-208.

Schenectady, First reformed church. 200th anniversary of the First reformed protestant Dutch church of Schenectady, June 20th and 21st, 1880. 264p. Schenectady 1880.   285.7747 Sch2
Contents: Proceedings, p. 7-29.
Historical discourse by W: E. Griffis, p. 31-53.
History of the church by Jonathan Pearson, p. 54-261.

Schuyter, P. *& others.* Account of the massacre at Schenectady in a letter dated Albany, 15th Feb. 1689-90. (*see* Whitmore, W: H. *ed.* Andros tracts. 1874. 3:114-20)   974.4 W59

—— Letter from the convention of Albany to the government of Connecticut concerning the destruction of Schenectady, 1690. (*see* Magazine of American history, July 1883, 10:65-68)   973 M27

Terhune, *Mrs* **M.. V. (Hawes).** Scotia, the Glen-Sanders house, Schenectady, N. Y. (*see her* More colonial homesteads. 1899. p. 155–86) 973.2 T271

Toll, D. J. Narrative, embracing the history of two or three of the first settlers and their families of Schenectady, with a description of the winter evening visits, recreations and of the tea-parties of olden times. 57p. Schenectady 1847. 974.744 Sch2

Van Rensselaer, Maunsell. Memoir of the French and Indian expedition against the province of New York which surprised and burned Schenectady, Feb. 9, 1689-90: (*see* New York historical society. Proceedings. 1846. p.101–23) 974.7 N421

Watson, J: F. First settlement of Schenectady. (*see his* Annals and occurrences of New York city and state. 1846. p.26–34) 974.7 W331

—— —— (*see* Munsell, Joel. Annals of Albany. 1850–59 9:116–23) 974.743 M92

From Watson. *Annals.*

Schoharie county

Danforth, G: L. Historical address. (*see* Middleburg (N. Y.) Reformed church. Centennial exercises. 1886. p.9–40) 285.7747 M58

Hawley, Gideon. Letter containing a narrative of his journey to Onohoghgwage in 1753. (*see* N. Y. (state)—State, Secretary of. Documentary history of the state of New York)

1849–51.	3:1031–46.	974.7	N424
1850–51.	3:625–34.	974.7	qN423

Travels through Schoharie county.

Middleburg (N. Y.) Reformed church. Centennial exercises of the reformed Dutch church of Middleburg, N. Y. Aug. 19th, 1886. 40p. Alb. 1886. 285.7747 M58

Church organized before 1732; building erected 1786.
Includes an historical address by G: L. Danforth.

Papers relating to the manor of Livingston, including the 1st settlement of Schoharie, 1680–1795. (*see* N. Y. (state)—State, Secretary of. Documentary history of the state of New York)

1849–51.	3:609–841.	974.7	N424
1850–51.	3:365–501.	974.7	qN423

Local history **Roscoe, W: E.** History of Schoharie county, N. Y. with illustrations
Palatines   and biographical sketches of some of its prominent men and pio-
                 neers, 1713–1882. 470p. Syracuse 1882.   974.745 qR71

* **Simms, J. R.** Frontiersmen of New York; showing customs of the
    Indians, vicissitudes of the pioneer white settlers and border strife in
    two wars, with a great variety of romantic and thrilling stories never
    before published.' 2v. Alb. 1882–83.   974.7 Si4
    Prerevolutionary history, 1: 1–463.
    Really a 2d edition of his *History of Schoharie county.*

————— History of Schoharie county and border wars of New York
    containing also a sketch of the causes which led to the American
    revolution; and interesting memoranda of the Mohawk valley.
    672p.   Alb. 1845.   974.745 Si4
    Colonial period p. 1–212.

Palatines

Account of the families of Germans settled upon Hudson's river in the
    province of New York, 1718. (*see* N. Y. (state)—State, Secretary
    of. Documentary history of the state of New York)

                         1849–51.   1 · 692–93.   974.7   N424
                         1850–51.   1 : 470.   974.7   qN423

Brown, J: M. Brief sketch of the first settlement of the county of
    Schoharie by the Germans. 23p. Schoharie 1823. 974.745 B81

Cobb, S. H. The palatine or German immigration to New York and
    Pennsylvania, a paper read before the Wyoming historical and
    genealogical society. 30p. Wilkes-Barré, Pa. 1897. 325.243 C63

————— Story of the palatines, an episode in colonial history.   319p.
    N. Y. 1897.   N. Y. state lib.

Croll, P. C. Conrad Weiser, the interpreter, (*see* American historical
    register, Nov. 1894, 1 : 221–32)   973 qAm31

Earl, Robert. Mohawk valley and the palatines; an address delivered
    before the Herkimer county historical society, Nov. 12, 1898.
    6p.   n. p. 1898.   974.74 E27
    Also in Herkimer county historical society. *Papers.* 1898. p. 57–62,
    974.761 H42.

Earl, Samuel. The palatines and their settlement in the valley of the
    Mohawk. (*see* Oneida historical society.· Transactions. 1881.
    p. 31–51)   974.762 On2

Edgett, *Mrs* H. R. The palatines. (*see* Fort Orange monthly, June
    1886, 1 : 252–60)   N. Y. state lib.

Ermentrout, Daniel. Our people in American history. (*see* Weiser, Local hist Palatines
C. Z. Life of (John) Conrad Weiser. 1876. p. 408–39)

923.9 W43

Homes, H: A: The palatine emigration to England in 1709. 28p.
Alb. 1871. 908 H75
Includes a sketch of their later history.
From *Transactions of the Albany institute.* 1872. 7: 106–31.

Kalm, Peter. Treatment of the palatines in New York. (*see* Rupp,
I. D. Collection of upwards of 30,000 names. 1876. p. 452)

929.3 P38

Kapp, Friedrich. Die erste Pfälzer niederlassung in Neuburg am
Hudson; massenwuswanderung der Pfälzer im jahre 1709. (*see his*
Geschichte der Deutschen im staate New York. 1869. p. 78–98)

325.243 K14

—— Die Pfälzisch-Schwäbische zwangs-kolonie am obern Hudson;
and, Flucht der Deutschen nach und ansiedlung in Schoharie; die
beiden Weiser, vater und sohn; besiedlung des Schoharie thals.
(*see his* Geschichte der Deutschen im staate New York. 1869.
p. 99–145) 325.243 K14

Lists of palatine emigrants to New York and Pennsylvania. (*see*
Weiser, C. Z. Life of (John) Conrad Weiser. 1876. p. 393–400)

923.9 W43

Contents: Names of early settlers of Berks and Montgomery counties, Pa.
who were naturalized, 1729–30.
Names and ages of the heads of families remaining in the city
of N. Y. 1710.
Names and ages of male children apprenticed by Gov. Hunter,
1710–14.
Names of male palatines, above 21 years old in Livingston
manor, N. Y. in the winter of 1710 and summer 1711.

Lord, E. L. Schemes for employing emigrant labor in the production
of stores. (*see her* Industrial experiments in the British colonies of
North America. 1898. p. 42–55) 338 L88
Includes Governor Hunter's palatine experiments.

Montgomery, M. L. Lecture on the life and times of Conrad
Weiser, the 1st representative man of Berks county. 37p. Reading,
Pa. 1894? 920 W43

—— Weiser monument, under auspices of board of trade of Reading:
Life and times of Conrad Weiser, the 1st representative man of
Berks county. 36p. Reading, Pa. 1894? 920 W43

Local history
Palatines **Papers** relating to the manor of Livingston, including the 1st settlement of Schoharie, 1680–1795. (*see* N. Y. (state)—State, Secretary of. Documentary history of the state of New York)

    1849-51.   3 : 609-841.   974.7 N424
    1850-51.   3 : 365-501.   974.7 qN423

Papers relating to the palatines and to the first settlement of New Burgh, Orange county. (*see* N. Y. (state)—State, Secretary of. Documentary history of the state of New York.)

    1849-51.   3 : 539-607.   974.7 N424
    1850-51.   3 : 325-64.   974.7 qN423

Rupp, I. D. Name, age and occupation of those who accompanied Rev. Joshua Kocherthal who settled on lands on Quassick creek, then Dutchess county, N. Y. in the spring of 1709. (*see* Rupp, I. D. Collection of upwards of 30,000 names. 1876. p.439-42)
                                                929.3 P38

———— Names and ages of male children apprenticed by Gov. Hunter, 1710 to 1714. (*see* Rupp, I. D. Collection of upwards of 30,000 names. 1876. p.445)   929.3 P38

———— Names and ages of the heads of families in the city of New York, 1710. (*see* Rupp, I. D. Collection of upwards of 30,000 names. 1876. p.443-44)   929.3 P38

———— Names of male palatines above 21 years old in Livingston manor, N. Y. in the winter 1710 and summer 1711. (*see* Rupp, I. D. Collection of upwards of 30,000 names. 1876. p. 446-49) 929.3 P38

Ruttenber, E: M. The palatine parish by Quassaig. (*see his* History of the town of Newburgh. 1859. p. 19-35)   974.731 qN42

Thompson, J: B. Palatines in Ulster county, N. Y. (*see* Historical magazine, Jan. 1871, ser. 2, 9 : 15-17)   973 H62 v.19

Todd, C: B. Robert Hunter and the settlement of the palatines, 1710-19. (*see* Wilson, J. G. *ed.* Memorial history of the city of New York. 1892-93. 2 : 121-50)   974.71 qW69
Also in *National magazine*, Feb. 1893, 17 : 287-309, 973 M271.

———— Story of the palatines. (*see* Lippincott's magazine, Mar. 1883, 31 : 242-52)   O51 L31

Walton, J. S. Conrad Weiser and the Indian policy of colonial Pennsylvania. 420p. Phil. °1900.   N. Y. state lib.

Weiser, Conrad. Authentic autobiography. (*see* Weiser, C. Z. Life of (John) Conrad Weiser. 1876. p. 440-49). 923.9 W43

—— Copy of a family register in the handwriting of Conrad Weiser translated from the German by H. H. Muhlenberg. (*see* Pennsylvania historical society. Collections. 1853. 1 : 1-6)
974.8 P385

Weiser, C. Z. Life of (John) Conrad Weiser, the German pioneer, patriot and patron of two races. 449p. Reading Pa. 1876.
923.9 W43

Lists of emigrants to New York and Pennsylvania, p.381-400.

Montgomery county

Frey, S. L. An old Mohawk valley house. (*see* Magazine of American history, May 1882. 8 : 337-45) 973 M27
Built by Henry Frey, 1739 in Montgomery county.

Frothingham, Washington, *ed.* History of Montgomery county. 450+349p. Syracuse 1892. 974.746 qF93
Family sketches, pt 2, p. 1-325.

History of Montgomery and Fulton counties, N. Y. 252p. N. Y. 1878. 974.746 fH62

Patent of Tiononderoga. (*see* Munsell, Joel. Collections on the history of Albany. 1865-71. 1 : 355-69) 974.743 qM92

Queen Anne's chapel, Fort Hunter, N. Y. (*see* Putnam's monthly historical magazine, 1893-94, ser. 2, 2 : 226) 929.1 qSa31 v.4

Reid, W. M. Ye history of St Ann's church in ye city of Amsterdam, N. Y. and its original, Queen Anne's chapel at Fort Hunter, in ye Mohawk country, 1712-1897. 38p. Amsterdam N. Y. 1897.
283.747 Am3

Fulton county

Frothingham, Washington, *ed.* History of Fulton county embracing early discoveries; the advance of civilization; the labors and triumphs of Sir William Johnson; the inception and development of the glove industry; with town and local records. 635+177p. Syracuse 1892. 974.747 qF93

History of Montgomery and Fulton counties, N. Y. 252p. N. Y. 1878. 974.746 fH62
Fulton county, p. 173-241.

Lossing, B. J: Johnson Hall, in the Mohawk valley. (*see* Potter's
American monthly, Jan. 1875, 4 : 1–7)   973 qAm3

Terhune, *Mrs* **M.. V. (Hawes).** Johnson Hall, Johnstown, N. Y.
(*see her* More colonial homesteads. 1899. p.1–64) 973.2 T271

Herkimer county

Benton, N. S. History of Herkimer county, including the upper
Mohawk valley, from the earliest period to the present time.
497p. N. Y. 1856.   974.761 B44
Biographical sketches of the palatine families, p. 129–97.

Cox, H : M. History of the reformed church of Herkimer, N. Y.
from the settlement of Herkimer county in 1723. 77p. Herkimer 1886.   285.7747 H42

Earl, Robert. Fort Herkimer; an address delivered before the
Herkimer county historical society, Oct. 8, 1898. 3p. n. p.
1898.   N. Y. state lib.
Also Herkimer county historical society. *Papers.* 1898. p. 47–49.
                                         974.761 H42

———— John Jost Herkimer; an address delivered before the Herkimer
county historical society, Jan. 11, 1898. 7p. n. p. 1898.
                                         920 H42
Also Herkimer county historical society. *Papers.* 1898. p. 5–8.
                                         974.761 H42

Hardin, G: A. & Willard, F. H. *ed.* History of Herkimer county,
N. Y. illustrated with portraits of many of its citizens. 550+276p.
Syracuse 1893.   974.761 qH21
Family sketches, pt 2, p. 1–253.

Herkimer county historical society. Papers for 1896–98 compiled
by A. T. Smith. Herkimer 1899.   974.761 H42

History of Herkimer county, N. Y. 289p. N. Y. 1879.
                                         974.761 fH62

Oneida county

Durant, S: W. *comp. anon.* History of Oneida co. N. Y. with
illustrations and biographical sketches of some of its prominent
men and pioneers. 678p. Phil. 1878.   974.762 qD93

Hartley, I: S. Fort Schuyler in history. (*see* Oneida historical society.
Transactions. 1881–84. p. 168–89)   974.762 On2

Papers relating to Fort Stanwix. (*see* N.Y. (state)—State, Secretary of. Documentary history of the state of New York)

1849–51.   4 : 521–28.   974.7   N424

1850–51.   4 : 323–26.   974.7   qN423

Wager, D. E. Forts Stanwix and Bull and other forts at Rome. (*see* Oneida historical society. Transactions. 1885–86. p. 65–77)

974.762   On2

Northern New York

Including counties of Franklin, Hamilton, Jefferson, Lewis, St. Lawrence

Curtis, Gates, *ed.* Our country and its people; a memorial record of St Lawrence county, N. Y.   3 pts. in 1.   Syracuse 1894

974.756   C94

Durant, S: W. & Peirce, H: B. *anon.* 1797; history of Jefferson county, N. Y. with illustrations and biographical sketches of some of its prominent men and pioneers.   593p. Phil. 1878.

974.757   qD93

Hough, F. B: History of Jefferson county in the state of New York from the earliest period to the present time. 601p. Alb. 1854.

974.757   H81

—— History of St Lawrence and Franklin counties, N. Y. from the earliest period to the present time.   719p.   Alb. 1853.

974.756   H81

—— Thousand islands of the river St Lawrence; with descriptions of their scenery and historical notices of events with which they are associated. 307p. Syracuse 1880.   974.758   H81
Colonial period, p. 9–51, 97–106.

Hurd, D. H. *anon.* History of Clinton and Franklin counties, N. Y. with illustrations and biographical sketches of its prominent men and pioneers.   508p.   Phil. 1880.   974.754   qH93
Franklin county, p. 375–508.

Sylvester, N. B. Historical sketches of northern New York and the Adirondack wilderness; including traditions of the Indians, early explorers, pioneer settlers, hermit hunters, etc. 316p. Troy 1877.

974.75   Sy5

Watson, W. C. Occupation of the Champlain valley. (*see* American historical record, May 1872, 1 : 200–4)   973   qAm3

Lakes George and Champlain

Including counties of Clinton, Essex, Warren, Washington

Barnes, Melvin, *anon.*   Reminiscences of Lake Champlain.   (*see his*
  Reprint of a short biography of Col. Ebenezer Allen.   1852.   p.20–
  32)   923.57 Al52

Battle of Lake George.   (*see* Atlantic monthly, Oct. 1884, 54 : 444–56)
                                                           051 At6

Bibliography and cartography [of Lake George].   (*see* Society for the
  preservation of scenic and historic places and objects.   Annual
  report.   1900.   p.65–68)   N. Y. state lib.

Butler, B: C.   Lake George and Lake Champlain from their first discovery to 1759.   240p.   Alb. 1868.   974.75 B97
  Devoted mostly to the events of the wars between French and English
  colonists.

Canfield, T: H.   Discovery, navigation and navigators of Lake Champlain.   (*see* Hemmenway, A. M.   Vermont historical gazetteer.
  1867–91.   1 : 656–707)   974.3 H37

Cook, Joseph.   Home sketches of Essex county, first number; Ticonderoga.   139p.   Keeseville 1858.   974.753 T43

Dayne, M. A.   Ticonderogue–Fort Carillon.   (*see* American monthly
  magazine, Oct. 1896, 9 : 319–27)   973.3 Am3

De Costa, B: F.   Lake George; its scenes and characteristics, with
  glimpses of the olden times, to which is added some account of
  Ticonderoga.   181p.   N. Y. 1868.   917.4751 D35
  Colonial period, p. 72–119.

———— Narrative of events at Lake George, from the early colonial
  times to the close of the revolution.   74p.   N. Y. 1868.
                                                      974.751 qD35
  75 copies printed.

———— Notes on the history of Fort George during the colonial and revolutionary periods, with contemporaneous documents.   78p.   N. Y.
  1871.   974.751
  Colonial period, first nine pages.

George 3, *king of Great Britain*.   Patent of the town of Queensbury,
  N. Y. 1762.   (*see* Historical magazine, Oct. 1867, ser. 2, 2 : 237–40)
                                                       973 H62 v. 12

Holden, A. W. History of the town of Queensbury in the state of New York with biographical sketches of many of its distinguished men and some account of the aborigines of northern New York. 519p. Alb. 1874. 974.751 Q3
Includes much about Lake George and Lake Champlain.

Hurd, D. H. *anon.* History of Clinton and Franklin counties, N. Y. with illustrations and biographical sketches of its prominent men and pioneers. 508p. Phil. 1880. 974.754 qH83

Marvin, Henry. Complete history of Lake George; embracing a great variety of information and compiled with an especial reference to meet the wants of the traveling community; intended as a descriptive guide, together with a complete history and present appearance of Ticonderoga. 102p. N. Y. 1853. 917.4751 M36
Guide book, with chapters on historic events connected with the lake in French wars.

N. Y. (state) – Historian. Muster rolls of a century; from 1664 to 1760. (*see his* Annual report. 1897. 2:371-956) 974.7 N415
Includes muster rolls of the battle of Lake George.

Palmer, P: S. History of Lake Champlain from its first exploration by the French in 1609 to close of the year 1814. 223p. Plattsburg 1853. 974.754 P18

———— ———— 276p. Alb. 1866, o'53. 974.754 P181

Papers relating to the French seigniories on Lake Champlain. (*see* N. Y. (state)–State, Secretary of. Documentary history of the state of New York) 1849-51. 1:535-86. 974.7 N424
1850-51. 1:315-76. 974.7 qN443

Parkman, Francis. Historic handbook of the northern tour; Lakes George and Champlain; Niagara; Montreal; Quebec. 180p. Bost. 1885. 973 P23

Smith, H. P. *ed.* History of Essex county, with illustrations and biographical sketches of some of its prominent men and pioneers. 754p. Syracuse 1885. 974.753 qS65

Society of colonial wars–New York state society. Account of the battle of Lake George, Sep. 8, 1755; compiled by the committee on historical documents and Lake George memorial committee of the society. 15p. N. Y. 1897. 973.2 qS74

Thompson, B: F. Battle of Ticonderoga, 1773. (*see* New York historical society. Proceedings. 1847. p. 112-17) 974.7 N425

Torrey, J. Discovery and occupation of Lake Champlain. (*see* Vermont historical society. Proceedings. 1860. p.13)

N. Y. state lib.

Van Rensselaer, Cortlandt. Historical discourse on the occasion of the centennial celebration of the battle of Lake George, 1755, delivered at the court-house, Caldwell, N. Y. Sep. 8, 1855, with notes and a map. 80p.   Phil. 1856. 908 V35

Watson, W. C. General view and agricultural survey of the county of Essex. (*see* New York state agricultural society. Transactions. 1853. 12:649–898)   630.6 K2
Prerevolutionary history, p. 649–92.

——— Military and civil history of the county of Essex, N. Y. and a general survey of its physical geography, its mines and minerals and industrial pursuits. 504p.   Alb. 1869.   974.753 W33

——— Occupation of the Champlain valley. (*see* American historical record, May 1872, 1 : 200–4)   973 qAm3

——— *ed. & comp.* Pioneer history of the Champlain valley being an account of the settlement of the town of Willsborough by William Gilliland together with his journals and other papers and a memoir and historical and illustrative notes. 231p.   Alb. 1863.

974.753 W68

Williams, Thomas. Campaigns against Crown Point in 1755 and 1756; correspondence of Dr Thomas Williams, a surgeon in the army. (*see* Historical magazine, 1857–75, ser. 2, 7 : 209–16)

973 H62 v.17

Central New York

Including counties of Cayuga, Cortland, Madison, Onondaga, Oswego, Tioga, Tompkins

Bartram, John. Observations on the inhabitants, climate, soil, rivers, productions, animals and other matters worthy of notice, made in his travels from Pensilvania to Onondaga, Oswego and the Lake Ontario in Canada, to which is annexed a curious account of the cataracts at Niagara by Mr Peter Kalm.   94p.   Lond. 1751.
917.47 B28

——— ——— Geneva N. Y.   1895.   917.47 B281
300 copies reprinted from the London edition of 1751.

Bruce, D. H. Onondaga's centennial; gleanings of a century.   2v. Bost. 1896.   974.765 qB83
Relations of the English with the Indians, 1:82–134.

Churchill, J: C., Smith, H. P. & Child, W. S. *ed.* Landmarks of
Oswego county, N. Y. 854+72+348p. Syracuse 1895.
974.767 qC47

Clark, G: T. Oswego; an historical address delivered July 15, 1896 at the centennial celebration of the evacuation by the British of Fort Ontario, Oswego, N. Y. and their surrender of the military posts of the northern frontier to the United States. 26p. n. p. 1896. 974.767 C54

Clark, J. V. H. Onondaga; or, Reminiscences of earlier and later times; being a series of historical sketches relative to Onondaga; with notes on the several towns in the county, and Oswego. 2v. Syracuse 1849. 974.765 C54

Geddes, George. Report on the agriculture and industry of the county of Onondaga, state of New York with an introductory account of the aborigines. 140p. Alb. 1860. 917.4765 G26
From the *Transactions of the New York state agricultural society*, 1859. History, p. 5–19.

Goodwin, H. C. Pioneer history; or Cortland county and the border wars of New York from the earliest period to the present time. 456p. N. Y. 1859. N. Y. pub. lib.

Hammond, *Mrs* **L. M.** History of Madison county, state of New York. 774p. Syracuse 1872. 974.764 H18

Harris, G: H. Aboriginal occupation of the lower Genesee country. 96p. Rochester 1844. 974.788 qH24
This work comprises the first 15 chapters of the *Semi-centennial history of Rochester*, ed. by W: F. Peck.

Johnson, Crisfield, *comp. anon.* History of Oswego county, N. Y. with illustrations and biographical sketches of some of its prominent men and pioneers. 449p. Phil. 1877. 974.767 qJ62

Jones, M. M. Lieutenant-colonel James F. Mercer and the fall of Oswego in 1756. (see Potter's American monthly, Sep. 1876, 7: 178–83) 973 qAm3

—— A scrap of early Oswego (New York) history. (*see* Potter's American monthly, Nov. 1875, 5: 832–33) 973 qAm3

Mulford, H: D. Onondaga county centennial; historical address prepared at the request of the Onondaga historical association and delivered in the reformed Dutch church, Syracuse, N. Y. Sunday, May 27, 1894. 28p. Syracuse 1894. 974.765 Sy8

Local history
Southern
central
New York

Papers relating to the first settlement and capture of Fort Oswego, 1727–56. (*see* N. Y. (state)—State, Secretary of. Documentary history of the state of New York)

1849–51. 1:441–506 974.7 N424
1850–51. 1:287–326. 974.7 qN423

First settlement of the English in western New York.

Relation de la prise des forts de Choueguen ou Oswego; et de ce qu s'est passé cette année en Canada. Grenoble. 1756.
Grolier club no. 275, p.91.

Smith, W: H: Pelham papers; loss of Oswego. (*see* American historical association. Papers. 1890. 4:367–79) 973 Am32

Southern central New York

Including counties of Broome, Chenango, Delaware, Otsego, Sullivan

Campbell, D. M. Sketch of the history of Oneonta. 67p. Oneonta 1883. 974 774 On2

Campbell, W: W. & Seward, W: H: Centennial celebration at Cherry Valley, Otsego county, N. Y. July 4, 1840, the addresses of Campbell and Seward with letters, toasts, etc. 59p. N. Y. 1840.
974.774 C42

Gould, Jay. History of Delaware county and border wars of New York containing a sketch of the early settlements in the county. 426p. Roxbury N. Y.? 1856. 974.736 G73

History of Delaware county, N. Y. with illustrations, biographical sketches and portraits of some pioneers and prominent residents. 363p. N. Y. 1880. 974.736 fH62
County was organized 1797, but many of the towns were settled earlier.

Papers relating to the Susquehannah river, 1683–1757. (*see* N. Y. (state)—State, Secretary of. Documentary history of the state of New York) 1849-51. 1:391–420. 974.7 N424
1850–51. 1:257–74. 974.7 qN423
Includes map of the head waters of the Susquehanna and Delaware; embracing early patents on south side of the Mohawk river 1790.

Sawyer, John. History of Cherry Valley from 1740–1898. 156p. Cherry Valley 1898. 974.774 C423

Western New York

Including counties of Allegany, Cattaraugus, Chemung, Genesee, Livingston, Monroe, Ontario, Orleans, Schuyler, Steuben, Wayne, Wyoming,
Yates

Local hist
Western
New York

Barton, J. L. Address on the early reminiscences of Western New York and the lake region of country, delivered before the Young men's association of Buffalo, Feb. 16, 1848. 69p. Buffalo 1848. 974.78 B28

Conover, G: S. *ed.* History of Ontario county, N. Y. with illustrations and family sketches of some of the prominent men and families, comp. by L: C. Aldrich. 518+396p. Syracuse 1893. 974.786 qC76

Doty, L. L. History of Livingston county, N. Y. from its earliest traditions to its part in the war for our union, with an account of the Seneca nation of Indians and biographical sketches of earliest settlers and prominent public men; to which is prefixed a biographical introduction by A. J. H. Duganne. 685p. Geneseo 1876. 974.785 D74

O'Reilly, Henry. Settlement in the west; sketches of Rochester; with incidental notices of western New York. 416p. Rochester 1838. 974.789 Or3

Parker, *Mrs* **P. J. (Marsh).** Rochester; a story historical. 412p. Rochester 1884. 974.789 P22
Early pages give sketch of vicinity of Rochester before its settlement in 1812.

Peck, W: F. Semicentennial history of the city of Rochester; with illustrations and biographical sketches of some of its prominent men and pioneers. 736p. Syracuse 1884. 974.789 qP33

Turner, Orsamus. History of the pioneer settlement of Phelps and Gorham's purchase, and Morris' reserve; embracing the counties of Monroe, Ontario, Livingston, Yates, Steuben, most of Wayne and Alleghany and parts of Orleans, Genesee and Wyoming with a supplement of the pioneer history of Monroe county. 624p. Rochester 1851. 974.78 T851

—— History of the pioneer settlement of Phelps and Gorham's purchase, and Morris' reserve, to which is added a supplement or continuation of the pioneer history of Ontario, Wayne, Livingston, Yates and Allegany. 588p. Rochester 1852. 974.78 T85
Purchase was made in 1788, but the introductory pages contain much pre-revolutionary history.

Local history
Lake Erie
and Niagara

Turner, Orsamus. Pioneer history of the Holland purchase of western New York, embracing some account of the ancient remains. 670p. Buffalo 1850. 　　　　974.79　T85

Contains much early history of western New York.

—— —— 666p. Buffalo 1849. 　　　　974.79　T852

Lake Erie and Niagara
Including counties of Chautauqua, Erie, Niagara

For list of early descriptions of Niagara Falls see

A few words regarding the falls of Niagara. (*see* N. Y. (state)—Niagara reservation. Commissioners, Annual report. 1894. 10:72-107)　711　N421

Briggs, Erasmus. History of the original town of Concord, being the present towns of Concord, Collins, N. Collins and Sardinia, Erie county, N. Y. 977p. Rochester 1883. 　　　974.796　C74

History of Fort Niagara, 1668-1759. (*see* Historical magazine, Nov. 1864, 8:367-72)　　　　　　　973　H62

History of Niagara county, N. Y. 397p. N. Y. 1878.
　　　　　　　　　　　　　　974.798　qH62

Johnson, Crisfield. Centennial history of Erie county, N. Y. being its annals from the earliest recorded events to the 100th year of American independence. 512p. Buffalo 1876. 　　974.796　J63

Journal of the siege of Niagara, 1759, translated from the French. (*see* Historical magazine, 1869, ser. 2, 5:197-99)　　973　H62　v.15

Kalm, Peter. Letter to his friend in Philadelphia, containing a particular account of the great fall of Niagara. (*see* Bartram, John. Observations. 1751. p.79-95)　　　　　　917.47　B28

Dated 1750.

Ketchum, William. Authentic and comprehensive history of Buffalo, comprising historic notices of the six nations or Iroquois Indians, including a sketch of the life of Sir William Johnson. 2v. Buffalo 1864-65. 　　　　　　　　　974.797　K49

Mostly history of Seneca Indians.

Marshall, O. H. The Niagara frontier; embracing sketches of its early history, and Indian, French and English local names; read before the Buffalo historical club, Feb. 27th, 1865. 46p. Buffalo 1865? 　　　　　　　　　　　974.798　M35

Printed for private circulation.

Marshall, O. H. The Niagara frontier. (*see* Buffalo historical society. Local hist Lake Erie Publications. 1880. 2:395–429)   974.797 B86 and Niag

——— —— (*see* Munsell, Joel. Historical series. 1887.   15:275–320) N. Y. state lib.

Mixer, M. E. Fort Erie and the mouth of the Niagara river. (*see* Magazine of Western history, Ap. 1886, 3:711–26)   973 M271

Porter, A. H. *anon.* Historical sketch of Niagara from 1678 to 1876. 51p. n.p. n.d.   974.798 P83

Porter, P: A. Brief history of Old Fort Niagara. 84p. Niagara Falls 1896.   974.798 F77

——— Champlain not Cartier made the first reference to Niagara falls in literature. 15p. Niagara Falls ^c1899.   974.799 qP83

A short history and description of Fort Niagara, with an account of its importance to Great Britain, written by an English prisoner, 1758; ed. by P. L. Ford. 18p. Brooklyn 1890.   974.798

Wiley, S: T. & Garner, W. S. Biographical and portrait cyclopedia of Niagara county, N. Y.   640p.   Phil. 1892. 920.074798 qW64
Sketch of colonial history of the region, p. 17–46.

Young, A. W. History of Chautauqua county, N. Y. from its first settlement to the present time with numerous biographical and family sketches. 672p. Buffalo 1875.   974.795 Y8
Early history of Chautauqua by Obed Edson.

INDEX

The superior figures tell the exact place on the page in ninths; e. g. 362[2] means page 362, beginning in the third ninth of the page, i. e. about one third of the way down.

Brodhead, Edgar. Picturesque corner of three states, 472².

Brodhead, J: R. Address before New York historical society, 1844, 300⁴, 308⁷.

———— Communication from Paris 1842, 300⁵.

———— Communication to governor, 1842, 300⁵.

———— Duke of York's approval of New York bill of rights, 350⁶.

———— Dutch governors of Nieuw Amsterdam, 360⁷.

———— Final report to governor, 1845, 300⁶.

———— Government of Sir Edmund Andros over New England, 351⁵.

———— Impeachment of Lord Cornbury as a forger, 357⁴.

———— Kingston, Hurley, and Marbletown, 479¹.

———— Lord Cornbury, 357³.

———— Memoir on early colonization of New Netherland, 325⁵.

———— Report, 1841, 301³.

———— State of New York, 308⁸-9¹.

Brookhaven, 455⁹-56⁶.

Brooklyn, 305³, 389⁶, 444⁷-47¹.

Brooks, E. S. Jacob Leisler in The Begum's daughter, 352⁷.

———— Selection of books touching general story of state of New York, 297⁷.

———— Story of New York, 304¹.

Brooks, Erastus. Historical records of Staten Island, 463¹.

Brooks, J. W. Court of common pleas of city and county of New York, 380⁶.

Broome county, 512⁴.

Brown, J: M. First settlement of county of Schoharie by the Germans, 502⁶.

Bruce, D. H. Onondaga's centennial, 510⁶.

Bryant, W: C. & Gay, S. H. Popular history of United States, 322², 341¹.

Buckingham, John. Diary of land expedition against Crown Point, 358⁹.

Buddingh, Derk. De hervormde hollandsche kerk in de Vereenigde Staten, 397³.

———— Kerk, school en watenschap, 397⁴.

Buell, Samuel. Faithful narrative of revival of religion in congregation of East-hampton, 456⁶.

———— Import of the Saint's confession that the times of men are in the hand of God, 457⁷.

Buffalo, 514⁷.

Buffalo historical society. Publications, 294⁴.

Bullard, E: F. Saratoga, 495⁶.

Bunker, M.. P. Long Island genealogies, 385⁶, 440².

Burdge, Franklin. Second memorial of Henry Wisner, 370⁶.

Burke, Edmund, 377⁴.

———— European settlements in America, 307².

Burnaby, Andrew. Travels in North America, 369⁸.

Burnett, William, 361⁴, 361⁵.

Burton, R. English empire in America, 347³.

Bushwick, 444⁶-47¹.

Butler, A. M. Scarsdale, 470⁶.

Butler, B: C. Lake George and Lake Champlain, 508³.

Butler, B: F. Anniversary discourse before Albany institute 1830, 304⁹.

———— Outline of constitutional history of New York, 378⁶.

Butler, Frederick. United States, 309¹.

Bibliography bulletins. This series is mostly selected from original bibliographies presented by the library school students as a condition of graduation. The library is glad to receive suggestions of subjects on which bibliographies or reading lists are specially needed, and contributions of available material are invited.

1 Guide to the study of James Abbott McNeill Whistler. 16p. May 1895. *Out of print.*

2-4 Colonial New England; Travel in North America; History of the 17th century. 80p. July 1897. *Price 10 cents.*

5 Selection of reference books for use of cataloguers in finding full names. 22p. Jan. 1898. *New edition in preparation.*

6-8 Japan; Venice; Out-of-door books. 64p. Feb. 1898. *Price 10 cents.*

9-11 Netherlands; Renaissance art of 15th and 16th centuries; History of latter half of 15th century. 128p. Ap. 1898. *Price 15 cents.*

12 Best books of 1897. 28p. June 1898. *Price 5 cents.*

13 Fairy tales for children. 30p. June 1898. *Price 5 cents.*

14 Index to subject bibliographies in library bulletins to Dec. 31, 1897. 62p. Aug. 1898. *Price 10 cents.*

15-17 Russia; Nature study in primary schools; Biography of musicians. 150p. Jan. 1899. *Price 15 cents.*

18 Best books of 1898. 28p. May 1899. *Price 5 cents.*

19 College libraries in the United States. 52p. Dec. 1899. *Price 10 cents.*

20 House decoration and furnishing. 20p. Dec. 1899. *Price 5 cents.*

21 Best books of 1899. 28p. May 1900. *Price 5 cents.*

22 Domestic economy. 144p. Jan. 1901. *Price 20 cents.*

23 Connecticut local history. 114p. Dec. 1900. *Price 15 cents.*

24 New York colonial history. 272p. Feb. 1901. *Price 35 cents.*

25 China and the far east. *In press.*

Manuscript bibliographies. The following bibliographies are available in manuscript for consultation in the library or may be lent under certain conditions. The *Decimal classification* subject number precedes each title.

012 Phillips Brooks. G: W. C. Stockwell, '95

012 Hawthorne. N. E. Browne, '89

012 Ben Jonson. Mrs Mary (Wellman) Loomis, '90

012 Charles Kingsley. E. E.. Burdick, '90

012 Poems on Lincoln, Grant, Sherman and Sheridan. M.. L.. Sutliff, '93

012 John Lothrop Motley. M.. E. Robbins, '92

012 Robert Louis Stevenson. E. S. Wilson, '98

012 Charles Sumner. H. W. Denio, '94

012 Bayard Taylor. W: S. Burns, '91

012 John Wesley. E. L.. Foote, '92

013 Members of the A. L. A. H.. C. Silliman, '95

016.0285 Lists of books for children. J. Y. Middleton, '91

016.2217 Higher criticism of the Old testament: select. Rev. W: R. Eastman, '92

016.246 Christian art: select. M.. L. Davis, '92

016.27 Church history: reading list. Elizabeth Harvey, '90

016.28 Religious denominations of the United States: select. G: F. Bowerman, '95
Published by Cathedral library association. N. Y. 1896. Price 75c.

016.33185 Clubs for boys and working girls. J. D. Fellows, '97

016.33622   Single tax. Ethel Garvin, '98
To be printed as New York state library bibliography bulletin.

016.339   Tramps and vagrants. L. D. Waterman, '97

016.352073   Municipal government. M.. L. Jones, '92; J. A. Rathbone, '93; E. D. Biscoe, '96

016.36   Scientific study of philanthropy. I. E. Lord, '97
Printed in American journal of sociology, Jan. 1898, 3:566–76. Reprint 25c.

016.361   New philanthropy: reading list. H.. G. Sheldon, '93

016.3722   Fröbel and the kindergarten. Aimée Guggenheimer, '99
To be printed as New York state library bibliography bulletin.

016.376   Education of women. M.. E.. Hawley, '93

016.37813   Consolidated index to university extension periodicals. Myrtilla Avery, '95

016.3982   English works on King Arthur and the Round Table. F. R. Curtis, '96

016.7   Art of the 17th century: reading list. N.. M. Pond, '96

016.7266   Some famous cathedrals: reading list. Mrs L. M. (Sutermeister) Delap, '90

016.75   Ten popular paintings: reading list. Ada Bunnell, '91

016.77   Photography, 1880–98. E. A. Brown, '98

016.792   Greek and Latin plays produced by schools, colleges and universities in the United States. G: G. Champlin, '95

016.796   Cycling. Mrs Louise (Langworthy) Gage, '97

016.799   Angling, 1883–93. Henrietta Church, '93

016.811   Minor American poetry, 1860–97: select. B. S. Smith, '97

016.82   English literature of later 18th century: select. M.. C. Swayze, '89

016.823   Fiction for girls: select. A. B. Kroeger, '91

016.907   Study and teaching of history. J. I. Wyer jr, '98
Printed in annual report of American historical association, 1899, 1 : 561–612.

016.91   Graded list of history and travel prepared in the Lincoln (Neb.) public library for the use of the Lincoln public schools. E. D. Bullock, '94

016.914   Books to read before going to Europe: reading list. S.. W. Cattell, '90
Printed in Book news, July 1890, 8: 393–95.

016.916   English and American explorations in Africa since 1824: reading list. H.. W. Rice, '93

016.91747   Literature relating to the Hudson river. M.T.Wheeler,'91

016.9174753 Adirondack mountains. C. A. Sherrill, '98
To be printed by New York state forestry commission.

016.9178   Travels west of the Mississippi prior to 1855; a partial bibliography of printed personal narratives. K. L. Sharp, '92

016.92   200 books in biography for popular library: select. Mabel Temple, '90

016.9207   Josephine and the women of her time. Mary Ellis, '92

016.94144   Edinburgh: reading list. W. G. Forsyth, '93

016.9737478 Missouri in the civil war. B. E. Rombauer, '99

016.9752   Maryland; colonial and revolutionary history. W. I. Bullock, '92

020.5   Consolidated classified index to the *Library journal*, v.1–12 B. R. Macky, '92; J. L. Christman, '93; C. S. Hawes, '94; J. G. Cone, '95

Lightning Source UK Ltd.
Milton Keynes UK
UKOW07f1858230415

250239UK00006B/213/P